APPRENT

This was no ordinary advertisement. But Douglas Brightglade was no ordinary young man. Apprenticed by the Wizard Flarman Firemaster—and indoctrinated into a fantastic world of magical spells and unearthly creatures—Douglas unlocked his natural-born flare for Pyromancy . . .

And just in the nick of time. A Dead Winter has fallen over the valley, chilling the blood of all who live there. Only one Wizard could inflict such cruelty, such dark and powerful magic—Frigeon, the Ice King.

Only fire can warm his frozen soul. Only Flarman Firemaster and his Apprentice can defy him.

Douglas Brightglade had better be a fast learner.

PYROMANCER

"The Sorcerer's animated kitchen is a delight, as is his brassy Bronze Owl. I liked the revelation that the job of a fire-magician is to control fire as well as to make it. That never occurred to me before. I like the notion of a person's good qualities being sealed in a pearl, so that he can be properly evil, and have to guard that pearl from his enemies, who will use it to make him (horrors!) less evil. There are nice original touches here."

—PIERS ANTHONY

"Charming! A fantasy quest with aspects of a fairy tale. A thoroughly engaging first novel."

—CRAIG SHAW GARDNER

Ace Books by Don Callander

PYROMANCER
AQUAMANCER
GEOMANCER

PYROMANCER

DON CALLANDER

ACE BOOKS, NEW YORK

This book is an Ace original edition,
and has never been previously published.

PYROMANCER

An Ace Book / published by arrangement with
the author

PRINTING HISTORY
Ace edition / May 1992

ISBN: 0-441-69222-2

Ace Books are published by The Berkley Publishing Group,
200 Madison Avenue, New York, New York 10016.
The name "ACE" and the "A" logo
are trademarks belonging to Charter Communications, Inc.

PRINTED IN THE UNITED STATES OF AMERICA

10   9   8   7   6   5   4   3

This book is dedicated, with great love and gratitude, to Margaret Millikan Callander, my wife, who saw to it I had ample time, a comfortable place, and the all-important encouragement to write fantasy—of all things!

For me, she suspended her disbelief in fantasy.

Don Callander
August 1990

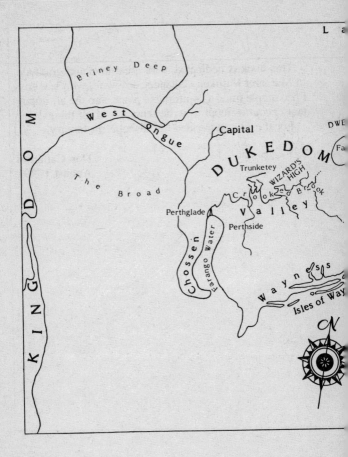

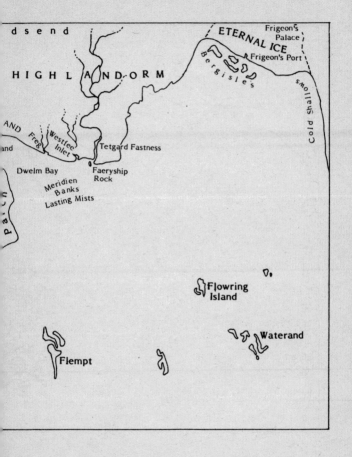

dsend

HIGHLANDORM

ETERNAL ICE

Frigeon's
Palace

Frigeon's Port

Bergisles

Cold Shallows

AND Freg

Westfee
Inlet

Tetgard Fastness

and

Dwelm Bay

Faeryship
Rock

Meridien
Banks

Lasting Mists

Patch

Flowring
Island

Waterand

Flempt

Pyromancer: A Wizard or Magician who has mastered the arts and sciences of drawing upon the elemental powers of Fire to effect his professional mysteries.

—*Chronicles of Flarman Flowerstalk*,
Book One, Chapter 1, Page 2

Chapter One

THE sign nailed to the twisted, rickety gate in the broken-down wall read:

APPRENTICE WANTED

to learn the *MYSTERIES* and *SECRETS* of

WIZARDRY in the Discipline of FIRE

from a MASTER MAGICIAN, SUPREME
SPELLCASTER

WONDERFUL WIZARD
AND PRESTIGIOUS PYROMANCER!

I require a bright, obedient, well-witted lad of at least ten
summers and at most sixteen winters to assist me and
learn the ART and SCIENCE of PYROMANCY.
Must be neat, prompt, well spoken
and have a
LARGE BUMP OF CURIOSITY.
Also should be able to read, to write a fair manuscript,
and not snore except when asleep on his back.

Signed . . .
The Wizard Flarman Flowerstalk

INQUIRE WITHIN

The young boy put down his bundle and read the sign three times carefully, wondering what a "Pyromancer" could be. At last he pushed through the rusted gate. He climbed the stone path to the wide green front door of the cottage under the brow of the rounded hill beside the rushing stream.

He stood on the rough stone stoop about to lift his hand to knock or ring—there was a bronze owl knocker in the middle of the door and a rope bellpull hanging to one side—when the owl spoke:

"Well, will you knock or ring or both?"

The boy started but, deciding that a talking door knocker was only to be expected at a Wizard's door, summoned a portion of courage that was large for his size.

"I was about to ring . . . or knock," he announced stoutly. The owl ruffled brazen wings with a loud clatter, a creak, and a rustle but said no more, so the visitor reached out and pulled the bell rope firmly.

Deep within the house there was the sound of jingling, like sleigh bells in winter across a far field. The lad waited.

And waited.

His name was Douglas Brightglade. He was about fourteen years old, but smallish for that age. He shifted from foot to foot and tried to decide whether it was polite to sit on the stoop while he waited, or to ring again. He was tired and had come a long way since morning.

He was plainly dressed in a pair of stout corduroy trousers of the sort that Seamen wear, and a striped green-and-white cotton jumper, worn but neatly mended at the elbows. His hair was fair, down to his shoulders, and his eyes were a clear sky blue. Between them was a short stub nose, a wide, generous mouth below, and strong chin that made up in determination what the nose lacked in maturity.

"I've rung," he said at last, addressing the bronze owl knocker. "What now?"

The owl looked right, then left, as if seeking anyone who might be eavesdropping—and from the thatched eaves above dropped a tiny green lizard, which scuttled away swiftly before either boy or owl could comment.

"Try knocking," suggested the knocker in a hoarse whisper.

So Douglas—who hesitated to take such a liberty with the

metal bird—instead rapped on the oaken panel of the green door with his knuckles.

With his third rap the door swung abruptly open wide and in it stood a plump, bearded little man whose pink scalp showed through wisps of snowy, uncombed hair. Dressed in a long deep-blue robe that fell to his ankles, dotted with tiny stars and moons, he was half a head taller than the boy. He was frowning in a most unfriendly fashion.

Douglas gulped nervously.

"Well, well!" said the Wizard, puffing out apple-red cheeks, "and what can I do for you, my good man?"

More than a bit flustered yet flattered by being called a "man" when he was used to being addressed as "little boy," Douglas stammered somewhat, saying: "I saw your sign and thought . . ."

"Sign? What sign? What are you talking about?"

"Why, the sign at the gate," gasped Douglas. "The one . . . it says . . . Apprentice Wanted. . . ."

"Oh! Oh, yes! Oh, oh, oh, yes, yes, *that* sign. I thought I took that down ages ago. Not many apprentices pass this way these days. Once upon a time there were dozens, you know."

Douglas's disappointment showed on his face and drooping shoulders and stopped the Wizard Flowerstalk from continuing. "Oh, I see. You were about to apply for the position!"

"Yes, sir," said Douglas. He smiled halfheartedly but went on, "If the position is filled . . . would you consider a second apprentice? I will work very hard and try to learn everything and I can be useful in many other ways, too. I can cook some and sew a little and talk to plants and horses. And I am small—I don't eat overmuch . . ."

"Well, well, young man," said the other, embarrassed. "I really . . . really . . . there was a time when I thought . . . no, I didn't hire anyone at all. No one answered the advertisements, you see, and I had to make other . . . arrangements. . . ."

"Other arrangements, hogwash!"

The metal owl had been listening with evident interest, its brazen eyes swiveling with metallic clicks first to one and then the other speaker.

"Hogwash," he repeated when the two stopped in surprise. "You made a surrogate, didn't you? Tried it out as an apprentice, but it didn't work!"

"That's true, entirely," admitted Flarman Flowerstalk, sheepishly. He paused to smooth the white strands of hair over his pink bald spot.

"It was a sad mistake, of course. When you make clones you can't help but make 'em too much like yourself. I tried my best to get it to apprent but it just wouldn't! Too many of my own bad characteristics. Anyway, he's gone, thank goodness! . . . And I've changed my mind now. Fewer people around the place the better, I say. Hmmph!"

He turned as if the conversation were ended

"And he made those terrible stenches, too. Stinks, I should say. No, no, no, no apprentices need apply. Good day to ye, Sir!"

He appeared so worried and unhappy that Douglas hesitated, looking for assistance to the owl.

The Bronze Owl winked (with a soft clash of eyebrows), as if to say, don't give up yet, laddie.

Douglas took a deep breath and said, calmly enough to surprise even himself, "Well, I am certainly very disappointed. When I saw the sign I said to myself, what a good apprentice magician—Wizard, I mean—I would make! I'm bright. I'm fairly obedient and I suppose I do have a wit or two. I've been making my own way for some months now and I guess that takes some wits."

"Ummm," Flarman said, hesitating in the doorway.

"Sounds like just the boy you'd be wanting, if you wanted one," observed the Bronze Owl.

"I can read very well and I write, although I must admit I need some practice on the writing."

"Hire the boy," urged the Owl, abandoning all pretense at subtlety. "Maybe you could get him to polish me once a week or so. I'm rather dullish these days, you can see."

The Wizard snorted wryly, jumped up and clicked his heels together twice, then bent down and touched his toes, a feat that belied his rather ample tummy, Douglas thought. The Wizard closed his bright, gray eyes and intoned in a low voice:

"Merlin, Oscar Zoroaster Diggs, Mandrake, Harry Houdini, and Gandalph the Gray!"

Then he motioned the boy to follow him and, turning,

went through the green door into the cottage, saying, "Take down the sign, please, before you enter."

Running back to the gate, Douglas pulled the board from its place with a creak of rusty nails, tucked it under his left arm, winked at the owl, and trotted happily after the Wizard. They turned into the first room on the left and the Wizard waved his applicant to a seat.

The room was rather small but sunny and chintzy, a bright parlor full of overstuffed furniture with crocheted doilies on their arms and furred bottoms, as if they had been used by generations of kittens to sharpen claws. A large redbrick fireplace—he later found that every room in the cottage at Wizard's High had a stove or a fireplace—sprang afire as they entered.

"Well, well, we'll have some tea and talk, anyway," said Flarman. "Mind you, I'm not convinced that you can be my Apprentice, or even that I want one these days. But it won't harm to talk and then look at the tea leaves. You can tell a great deal from a man's tea leavings, you see."

He proceeded to pour water from a blue enamel teakettle over a generous pinch of tea leaves in a stoneware pot, making a swirl of pink steam.

"Sugar? Milk?"

"No milk, please, but a bit of sugar would be pleasant," said Douglas, who had learned manners at his mother's knee. He perched on the edge of an overstuffed armchair. The chair said softly, "Lean back and relax, youngster. Make yourself comfortable."

"I'm afraid I'd go right off to sleep," apologized the boy, beginning to get used to this talking-to-things business. "Begging your pardon, chair, and thank you so very much."

" 'S all righ'," murmured Chair, drowsily. "I like everybody to be at ease."

"Now," said the Wizard, frowning mightily at the chair and passing a cup of fragrant pink tea to Douglas. They sipped in silence except for small talk such as all polite people make at tea parties—or used to in those days—until at last the Wizard said, "Now, where were we?"

"You were going to study the tea leavings," prompted the Owl, who could hear everything from his nail in the middle of the open front door.

"Yes, but some talk first. What is your name, sir, for a beginning?"

"Douglas Brightglade. I am the son of Douglas of Perth-side, the famous shipwright, sir. My father and mother and I lived on the edge of Farango Water to the west for as long as I can recall; since I was born, I suppose. Five years ago my father went to Sea in one of his new ships. After two years, when he didn't come home, as the law goes, he was declared missing and presumed drowned."

Said Flarman, grimly: "But to be lost at Sea is never for certain, they say."

"It was five years this last spring. People who depended on my father needed their money. His workers needed to be released to look for work elsewhere. She tried to carry on but two years ago my mother decided to sell all, settle accounts, release her workers. She put herself in the Nunnery of Glothersome.

"As for me, I was placed into apprenticeship of a family friend in the shipyard business some distance from Perth-side. I parted from Mother and home with a heavy heart, but I tried to do it with courage and determination, too.

"All could have been well, except that I soon discovered that the friend who had agreed to take me as apprentice couldn't afford to feed his own sons. All were older than I and more advanced in their craft.

"So I asked to be released from indenture. After much discussion he agreed. He actually had little choice. There just wasn't enough work."

He paused to take a deep drink of the bracing pink tea and Chair said, sympathetically, "There, there, boy, lean back and let me hold you for a moment."

"Sorry," said Douglas, swiping a tear from the corner of his right eye.

"The truth is," said the Owl, "that your lady mother in her nunnery doesn't know you are out on your own in the world?"

"Her order forbids any kind of contact with the world for two years after initiation," Douglas explained, "which is why I hoped to get a place before that time came so that she would have no need at all to worry."

"If you had been able to stay with the wright?" Flarman left the question dangling.

"I already know a great deal about working wood and using tools, and about ships and their ways, too. My father taught me from my earliest years. And he was the best of shipwrights, everyone said."

"Yes, yes," said Flarman, thoughtfully. "Handy thing knowing how to work wood, use tools, saw and all. Handy for an Apprentice Wizard, too . . ."

"Used to hard work and long hours, too, I'll warrant," put in the metal bird from the doorway.

There followed an embarrassing silence during which Douglas finished his tea, the owl remained silent, and the magician stared pensively into the fire.

"Well, I really mustn't take any more of your valuable time," said Douglas. "I've got to be moving on to find a place for the night. How far is it to Trunkety, please? I hear they have a good blacksmith there who might have some work for me. . . ."

He picked up his bundle and started out the door. The owl stopped him with a rattling wing.

"Where are you going?"

"I thought to go on to Capital. There are jobs there. I could become a cook in the Ducal Palace, don't you think? I wouldn't go hungry, at any rate."

The Bronze Owl twirled his head fully around and screeched in his loudest voice, "Tea leaves, you oaf of a Fire Wizard!"

From within came the sounds of a roused Wizard. "What? Where? Eh! Oh, yes!" and the man appeared in the doorway carrying Douglas's teacup. He grasped Douglas's hand with his own left and held the cup to his eyes with his right, studying the leavings intently, muttering, "Hmmm! Very interesting! Yes, yes, yes, most diverting . . ."

This continued for several moments while Douglas stood patiently by, trying not to fidget in the Wizard's surprisingly strong grasp. The owl stared off into space, humming to himself.

"Patience!" said Bronze Owl to the boy at last.

"Oh, I'm being patient," said Douglas, "but my hand is going to sleep!"

Flarman opened his eyes wide, looking shocked. Then he chuckled aloud.

"Here, my boy! Stay, Douglas Brightglade! I've decided

to keep you, to take you on as Apprentice! Bring your things
and shut the door. It's beginning to look like a rainy evening.
Welcome to Wizard's High, your new home!

"I'll have to draw up an indenture for you to sign," he
went on, leading the lad down the central hall. To Douglas's
surprise, the Bronze Owl flopped off his doornail and flew
after them, with great clashings.

"Meanwhile, let's have some supper and get to know
everybody! A party! You've got a lot to learn, Apprentice
Wizard, and a lot to unlearn, relearn, and learn again, and
even to forget to learn!"

Chapter Two

THAT first evening Douglas was introduced to the strange ways of the Wizard's household.

"You came on a good day to begin," said Flarman. "I'm not at work this day, but at leisure. Be my guest this evening and sleep well in your new bed because the work will surely begin tomorrow!

"First, let's see what's cooking for supper, my boy," he said, and he led the way down the center hall of the cottage to a vast kitchen in the rear.

The kitchen was aglow with the light of three large lamps burning sweet-smelling oils . . . did he imagine it, or did they spring alight when the Wizard entered the room?

An enormous stove was the stage for a strange ballet. The big, blue teakettle directed the show from the front of the fender, waving her spout and issuing steamy orders in a hot, whistling tone, which sounded like a shriek, yet comfortable and pleasant to hear.

"Grill, now hop to it, get hot over there! The cakes are mixed and in a trice will be popping into the oven. Where's that peeler? Oh, my, there you are! Done so soon? Fine, old boy, move them spuds into the blue-speckled pot over the fire, will you? That's a boy!

"Here's the Master. Everybody say hello to the new Apprentice. His name's Douglas Brightglade. Then get back to work. Dinner in half an hour, Master Wizard . . ."

The pots, pans, griddles, ladles, spoons, forks, spits, grills, turners, spatulas, knives, and all jumped about and gave a happy "Hello!" to Douglas and the Wizard, who, in return, introduced them all to the boy.

"Do for him as you would for me," he admonished them all.

9

"What a good-looking youngster," spoke a pan from the back of the cupboard.

"Don't be saucy," called out the Blue Teakettle. "Now, all get to work! She's a little saucepan, you see," the Teakettle apologized to Douglas.

"No harm, no harm," said the brand-new Apprentice, laughing. "What's for dinner, ma'am?"

"All the good things; good thick soup of beans flavored with ham and fennel and marjoram and a dash of garlic, the Magician's Friend," the Blue Teakettle said, a serious craftsman discussing her work. "Then a salad of green from the brookside and spring onions topped with a delicate pink dressing. A roast of beef from Farmer Frenstil's herd, done to a turn, pink and brown and juicy just the way Flarman loves it, with white potatoes and gravy. And dessert? What would you like best, young Douglas? I planned a flan, but that would seem too bland for a young tongue and tummy. What do you love most?"

"Green apple pie," answered the boy without pause to consider.

"So it shall be, with clotted cream, too! Slicers! Graters! Get to your work, sirs! There's pastry under the cloth that's short as short can be, I warrant. Oven is hot ... hot green apple pie and clotted cream'll be ready when you have cleaned your plate of roast beef and mashed potatoes."

Shortly they sat down to a feast and were regaled by the antics of the salt and pepper shakers and the serious, droll sayings of the Gravy Boat, who also chanted Sea songs and seamen's ditties for them.

A pair of fire tongs did a clattery clog dance on the hearth, and Blue Teakettle herself acted as ringmistress over it all and kept the good food hot and savory, coming at just the right pace and intervals. Toward the end the entire chorus of pots and pans sang old favorites with the crocks and cutting board humming along in perfect harmony. And never once did Douglas consider how odd this little household was.

When he at last pushed back his plate, having wiped up the last bit of rich, brown beef gravy with a warm stoup of fresh bread, Douglas somehow managed to put two thick slices of green apple pie into the odd corners of his stomach, while Flarman helped himself to a glass of cool, tawny apple cider and a slice of golden, buttery cheese as well.

Then the Wizard sat back and lighted a big, curving clay pipe and puffed clouds of smoke from the aromatic leaf in the bowl. By now Douglas was not surprised that he used neither matches nor a spill from the fireplace to light up—he merely glanced into the bowl as if in curiosity and a glowing eye of fire appeared deep within and a curl of blue smoke rose to tickle Douglas's nose.

"I've eaten many a meal in this kitchen, Blue Teakettle, but none I can recall as jolly or as delicious. My compliments to the chef! We'll need to sit awhile," he said to Douglas, "just to appreciate fully such a marvelously prepared repast."

Douglas heartily agreed and leaning back in his chair, chatted with the Wizard and some of the tableware, especially the Sugar Caster, who was the elder statesman of the table, the majordomo of the place settings.

He was a bit vain of his silver top and a bit patronizing of one so much younger than himself. Even Flarman spoke to Sugar Caster with respect for, as he said, "That Sugar Caster was my great-grandmother's and my grandmother's and my mother's after her. You can see he has been on the premises a long time. A long, long time!"

The dishes cleared themselves away and began to wash up. The Wizard cleared his throat and began to dictate the Articles of Indenture to a magnificent peacock's plume pen, which appeared on the table before him. A footed lamp trotted closer to shed his light on the work in progress.

The dishes pushed each other onto their shelves, and after a period of murmuring and clattering, with remonstrances in a kindly but firm voice from the Sugar Caster, the whole house settled down to a late-evening quiet. Even the mice under the thatch upstairs and the cows in the byre cave muted their evening activity and sounds as the Wizard did his work.

The document, inscribed with appropriate flourishes and curlicues, was four closely written pages long. The Wizard delighted in the full, exact and endless sentences of courtly language.

Articles of Indenture, in the custom of World in those days and in that place were collectively a contract between the Master Craftsman and his Apprentice, setting down as exactly as practical what the duties and obligations of each

Party would be. Failure of either Party to fulfill the agreement could lead to the Articles being dissolved and the relationship broken off between Master and Apprentice. In some very serious cases, Douglas found, failure to follow the guidelines and rules laid out in the Articles could result in prison, a fine, or even more serious punishment.

Douglas was left to imagine what punishment would be meted out by a Fellowship of Wizards to a sinning Apprentice.

When the period of Apprenticeship was completed to the satisfaction of the Master and at least one other Master of the Craft, the articles were to be countersigned to that effect by the two Masters and given to the Apprentice as certification that he had earned the title, pay, and status of Journeyman. The then Journeyman kept the certification until he was adjudged by his peers to have gained the rank of full Master, and then he would be ceremoniously inducted into the Fellowship and would be entitled to burn the Articles to signify his new freedom from his old Master.

(Douglas Brightglade, it must be said, when he reached the rank of full Wizard, did not burn his Articles but preserved them. They became a valued artifact in his family archives.)

On the other hand, the rules applied to the Master, too.

In many beautiful sentences, handsomely illuminated and scrolled by the peacock-plume pen, the Articles set down what Flarman Flowerstalk agreed to provide—shelter, food, and clothing reasonable to the season. He would carefully train and educate the Party of the Second Part in the mysteries, skills, crafts, arcana, and secrets of the Profession of Wizardry in the Field of Pyromancy, the uses of magic through the medium of fire, to the limits of his, Flowerstalk's, ability and knowledge and Douglas's ability to learn them.

In return the youth pledged himself to be obedient, prompt, neat and clean in body and in spirit, thrifty, sober, responsible, respectful of his elders and betters, kind to his inferiors, diligent in his studies, and so on and so on and so on at great length, even to the number of undershirts the Wizard was to provide and the numbers of times a night the Apprentice could legally be called from his bed to do some task or other.

At long last it was done, Flarman roused the sleepy

youngster to read the entire document to him once again, asking him if he had any further questions. Then they both signed. A witness was unnecessary—a man of fourteen was considered capable of keeping his word and knowing his mind. The Wizard then tucked the parchment away into his wide left sleeve and led the way up the broad stair, yawning cavernously.

For a few minutes Douglas lay awake, listening to the distant sounds of the old man moving about his own room and the night sounds of the cottage, the garden, and the hill. Then without warning he drifted smoothly into a deep, dreamless sleep.

Not quite dreamless. Sometime before morning he did dream of himself, arrayed in silver and black robes figured with stars and moons and pentagrams and open eyes, walking by Sea's side, watching Sea churn restlessly.

Offshore a fleet of tall ships caught the setting sun behind them in flares of brilliant oranges and golds. Suddenly between him and the fleet from the roiling waters upreared a monstrous, ice blue Sea Serpent, breathing chill clouds of dense fog.

In his dream, with supreme confidence, Douglas waved his hand in a mystic gesture . . . and the Serpent disappeared in a fabulous flash of intense light and heatless fire.

And then a great black cat jumped on his chest, planted padded paws on his shoulder, and tickled his nose with long black and silver whiskers rumbling a deep, deep purr.

It was Black Flame and the brilliance of a new morning shining through his window saying in no uncertain terms, "Time to get up, sleepyhead Apprentice!"

Douglas Brightglade jumped from his bed, scattering Black Flame and his wives before him in a jubilant parade out the bedroom door, down the hall, down the stair. They trooped to the washstand outside the kitchen door in the courtyard, already filled with steaming water, to wash his face and hands and comb his hair.

From the kitchen he could hear the Blue Teakettle scolding a pancake turner for letting the pancakes get too brown—"You know how Flarman likes them!"—and from across the courtyard came pounding . . . the Pyromancer already at work.

It was time to get started! ■ ■ ■

In those days the Wizard Flarman Flowerstalk lived in a half cottage, half cave built into the side of a freestanding hill called Wizard's High. The hill and the cottage overlooked Crooked Brook, which rushed and rambled by twists and turns down to Sea by way of the long narrow fjord of Farango Water.

There, among the many small waterside villages of Perthside, was one called Brightglade, Douglas's home. The distance from Wizard's High to Brightglade was about forty miles as a bluebird flies, but considerably farther by the road, following the course of the winding Brook.

The cottage under the High was low, as if partially sunken into the grassy lawn before it. Take a second look, however, and one would realize that it was, in many places, two or more stories tall. It was thatched, built most sturdily of yellow, brown, and blue fieldstone. The front faced the stream and the meadows and hills to the south and was filled with bright windows, like so many cheerful eyes.

It had twelve chimneys, if you bothered to count, and therefore must have had at least a dozen rooms, including the sunny front parlor where Douglas and Flarman first talked and drank pink tea. There was the big kitchen at the back—opening onto a wide courtyard—with the huge iron stove and an oven big enough to bake a dozen pies at one time.

In the middle of this kitchen was an acre or so, it seemed, of oak table, its round top scarred, burnt, and dented yet smooth as silk from long use. Along one wall was a vast stone fireplace equipped with black wrought-iron racks and spits, guarded by fierce-looking fire dogs who surveyed the vast room from the ashes with bright shiny eyes.

Opposite, the wall was covered from floor to beamed ceiling with all manner of pots, pans, hooks, cake tins, griddles, gridirons, long-handled forks, and hand-hammered spoons on hooks and shelves.

Slowly, over the first few days, Douglas discovered other rooms in the Wizard's home, although it seemed he would always be finding new rooms, closets, attics and cellars, cupboards, nooks and crannies, and window seats he had never seen before.

At the head of the broad stair winding up from the front hall was the Wizard's own bed-sitting room filled to overflowing with all sorts of splendid things, such as the stuffed head of an antelope, a box filled with pieces of pink and blue coral, or a case with a display of "totemic amulets," according to a hand-lettered card.

One window, overlooking the Brook and the Valley beyond, had been pierced to allow entrance to a hive of bees, whose humming and strumming served as a lullaby when the Wizard suffered from insomnia. They allowed Blue Teakettle to extract honey for her table as their rent. The bees also served as an early warning of the approach of visitors or of inclement weather.

In the Wizard's room was his enormous testor bed, draped in black netting spangled with silvery stars and moons in swirling patterns. A deep down comforter ensured the old man's warmth on chilly nights. An oil lamp on a tall standard lighted his nightly studies. A brass-bound telescope pointed up through a skylight built into the roof.

The southern windows were filled with a profusion of flowers and herbs growing in pots and tubs in the day-long sun, giving the rooms a delicious fragrance as well as lively, bright colors.

Around a corner and down a narrow hall, to the west end of the house under the low eaves, was Douglas's own room. It was small and low ceilinged, with two diamond-paned windows that made rainbows on the walls in an evening sun. The windows' leaves swung wide to admit any westerly breezes that cared to come calling, bringing the smells of ripening timothy in the meadows, wildflowers in the fields, and of distant woodlots in full leaf for summer.

Douglas's bed was almost as big as his room. It was covered with a down pallet on rope springs stretched between stout wooden frames, and was dressed with soft lamb's wool blankets for wintertime—and a daintily quilted coverlet with a pattern of flowers sewn into its blue-and-white background, intermingled with letters and words that made no sense, even to Flarman. The quilt had been given to him years ago in a faraway place where he had tarried not long enough to learn the tongue, let alone the hand.

Between the two bedrooms and connected by wide doors to both was a library so crammed full of books, rolled-up manuscripts, unbound sheaves of closely written text, prints, pictures, paintings, and all other sorts of memorabilia that the boy despaired of knowing ever a tenth of the contents and meanings.

Yet the Wizard had an uncanny ability to know, not only what was there, but exactly where it was, when it was needed. To Douglas it often seemed the objects, especially the books, moved about the big library of their own accord when no one was looking.

The personal items collected by the Fire Wizard were just as fascinating, especially to a young boy with a large bump of curiosity. Hanging from the walls, ceiling, standing in corners, resting in glass-front cabinets, or heaped in disorder in the middle of the floor were beautifully curved daggers with precious gems set in their ornate hilts; large, sharp swords with finely engraved blades, inlaid with gold and silver and ivory in intricate floral designs or scenes from ancient battles.

There were stuffed lizards and live snakes. There were wooden boxes of cut diamonds the size of peas and emeralds the size of peach stones! Shelves of books were held up by heavy, roughly carved, hollow-eyed, squat, and evil-looking godlings of terra cotta or of a dark, oily wood. On tables stood tiny, delicate figurines of beautiful ladies dancing on tiptoes, their graceful, gauzy gowns floating about them like smoke.

"How old *are* you?" Douglas had once asked.

"Not *old*," said Flarman. "Yes, well, I know—every good question deserves a good answer," he said. "Well, yes . . . I have not kept track after the first hundred years or so but I suppose I'm . . . er . . . at least four hundred and eighty, give or take ten years. Or twenty."

The question of answering questions arose that first night at Wizard's High when Flarman had included this clause in the Articles of Indenture: "The Party of the First Part does agree . . . that he will never knowingly refuse or neglect to answer a sensible question by the Party of the Second Part."

It was an important part of their relationship, because, if he had had none of the other attributes required by the Pyromancer—and he did—Douglas *did* have that "large bump of curiosity."

The next most important rooms—actually rooms and caves—were lumped together by the Wizard under the name

Workshop. They were carved into the hill directly opposite the kitchen door across the rear courtyard. Wide sliding doors gave entry. The workrooms ran back into the High for several hundred feet, ending in cool, dark storerooms and vaults. There was more floor space under the hill than under the roof of the cottage.

The workrooms were practical places—forge, tin shop, woodworking shop, chemistry laboratory, aquarium, and potting workbench, places for throwing pottery on a wheel and oasts for firing the shaped clay.

If there was a common theme here, Douglas realized, it was that of fire. Fire being used in so many different ways to accomplish useful things.

The floors of the shops were wood, but deeper in the hillside they became hard-tamped sand and at last solid rock. A spring deep within filled a cistern, which overflowed into a stone channel, which in turn brought cold, clear water to the kitchen well. From there the water chuckled merrily out of the courtyard and down to join Crooked Brook.

One corner of the caves was partitioned into stalls for farm animals. At the time of Douglas's arrival there were no horses in residence but four brown-and-white, sloe-eyed cows with short horns and placid manners. They grazed all day in the brookside pastures and at twilight climbed to the courtyard gate to be admitted, milked, and bedded down for the night. Douglas and his "Ladies" soon became fast friends. In return for his loving care, they gave rich milk, not to mention thick cream, which churned into golden butter tasting of clover.

The Wizard and his Apprentice were not the only inhabitants of this strange household. There were cats—Pert, Party, and Black Flame, the last a male, the first two, his wives. The females dropped litters regularly and didn't mind that their progeny were quietly given to neighborhood farm wives. The ladies of the Valley felt, with justification, that a Wizard's cat's kittens were bound to grow up to become fine mousers as well as affectionate lap pets.

Party was the huntress, keeping field mice in bounds about the cottage storerooms and pantry. Pert was what her name said . . . a bit flighty, fey, play-loving girl, a comfortable cat who liked nothing so well as to curl up on your lap while you read before a fire in the evening time.

Black Flame was a long and vastly lazy tom who preferred to be fed regularly by his new "boy." He managed to be about whenever there was any magic being performed or even discussed or taught. Douglas came to realize soon that Black Flame was, in fact, Flarman's *familiar,* somehow assisting the Fire-Adept in his practice.

All three cats were black, although the girls had white in some mixture somewhere on their bodies. Black Flame was completely without white and, Douglas noticed, all his male offspring, by whichever wife, were all coal black, too.

All of the cats had remarkable emerald green eyes.

Regular tenant of Wizard's High was a large but well-regulated family of house mice. They lived in the thatch above Douglas's bed. He suspected that a quiet war was fought between the hardworking Mama and Papa Mouse and the cats, especially Party. He felt protective of his mice friends and saw to it they got occasional bits of cheese or bread crust from the kitchen, and that his door was closed when he wasn't there, to bar Party's raids.

In return the mice never chewed his boots or left droppings in his bed.

Bronze Owl usually hung from the nail in the center of the big green front door, but he was not always on duty there. Douglas once asked him where he went. The Owl admitted that he often spent the nights gliding over Wizard's High and the surrounding Valley, gathering news of the doings of the Valley folk.

The Apprentice found also, when he was admitted to the Workshop, that the metal bird acted as a sort of consultant to the Wizard. Flarman Flowerstalk listened to him with care and respect, especially if the subject was flying or metalwork of any kind.

Douglas asked the Wizard if the metal bird had a name, and Flarman looked surprised.

"I always just call him Bronze Owl," he said at last.

Douglas asked Owl himself and received the same surprised reply. From the very first full day of his residency at the cottage Douglas's duties included briskly polishing the bird. He was amply repaid by fascinating and often fantastic tales of Elves, Fairies, Witches, Brownies, Dwarfs, and other Little People.

"Did you observe the ring of toadstools down by the Old

Well?'' Bronze Owl asked as the boy wielded his polishing rag on the doorstep in the morning sun.

"Yes, I did!" replied the boy. Little about the High escaped his sharp eyes and fine curiosity.

"Do you know what it means?"

"No, I can't say that I do," answered Douglas as he buffed Owl's left wing. "Someone once told me that Fairies sat upon the toadstools."

"That and much more, really. There was High Court held there last night. The Fairies were trying one of their own, accused of stealing a pail of milk from a Valley farmer. The farmer is in good repute with the Faerie Kingdom and appealed to the Queen of Faerie, Marget. The High Court found the culprit guilty of stealing the milk without cause."

"I should have said"—Douglas paused in his polishing—"that there was no good cause for stealing."

"You don't understand the Faerie Folk," said his bronze tutor. "They consider themselves wardens of human behavior in the lands where we live together. They reward neatness, cleanliness, hard work, and a generous nature—generous to themselves, especially—and they punish meanness and filth and messy keepings.

"You see, Fairies live only where they are believed in by other creatures, especially Man. They find that careless, slovenly people tend not to believe in Fairies. Therefore to harass the slovenly is really a matter of protecting their homes."

"I see," murmured Douglas thoughtfully. "I never gave it any thought, but I *do* believe in Fairies although I have never seen one."

"Oh, you will," said the Owl. "In this case, the farmer keeps a neat, well-run farm, a clean barn. He has a good reputation among the Fairies. His daughter, a comely lass, is his milkmaid. She puts out bread and bowls of fresh milk at least twice a week for the Little Folk."

"So the Court found for the farmer?"

"Oh, yes! The Queen awarded the farmer double production from his cows for a month in repayment. The farmer forgave the thief who stole the milk. And he got his bucket back, too, of course."

"This all took place down by the Old Well? Last night?"

"Right!" said the other, twisting his head all the way

around to the back to inspect the polishing job Douglas had
done on his tail feathers.

"And you were there?"

"Nobody watches a Fairy Court without special invitation, on pain of much bad luck," answered the bird, clashing
his way to the nail in the middle of the front door. "I heard
about it from a friend of mine, an Elf, who heard about it
from a Pixie who lives in the Brook bank near the Old Well.
She heard the proceedings from her cubby. Even this Pixie
didn't dare to watch; just listen."

"I thought Sprites were Fairies," protested Douglas.

"Only in a broad, general sense. They are related, but not
the same. Pixies are much smaller, for one thing. This one is
only about as tall as your middle finger."

Douglas caught up his bottle of polish and his rags. "I'd
like to meet some of your friends. I've never met an Elf or
a Sprite. Or a Fairy, for that matter."

"All in good time," said Bronze Owl, winking merrily at
a passing robin.

The Valley farmers were awed by the presence of a Wizard in their midst. Their fear of his powers was not as strong
as their pride that he chose to live among them. They tended
to leave Flarman undisturbed except for an occasional business call, delivering flour from the Trunkety Mill or a side of
beef in the early winter. The Wizard paid cash—always
welcome to these country folk—in addition to an odd spell
or amulet when someone happened to mention the need.
"Not for myself, mind you . . . but Old Buddling down to
South Field is ailing . . ."

Flarman cheerfully interrupted his work to provide these,
seldom asking even a token price from his neighbors. There
were mutual respect and good opinions between the Valley,
the Trunkety dwellers, and those at the High.

The Apprentice had increasing contact with these country
and town folk as time went on. He had the good sense not to
pretend that he shared in his Master's powers. They refrained from asking Douglas about his studies and were, in
time, friendly enough and honest enough in their dealings
with the Apprentice, despite his youth and inexperience.

Douglas looked, listened, tried to understand events in the
wider world of Dukedom. He reported what news he heard

in the countryside or the village to the Wizard. He was sure Flarman took little notice of Valley events at all, nor the state of the Dukedom around them.

In time he learned better.

Chapter Three

"WIZARDS," said Flarman Flowerstalk, "sorcerers, magicians, pyromancers, aquamancers, witches, warlocks, all that sort, all have one thing in common: they are all ordinary, everyday Men just like Farmer Frenstil. They are not Near-Immortal like the Fairies, the Elves and Dwarfs, and of course are completely different from the true Immortals, the Aspects and the Attributes."

It was the first day of lessons for the new Apprentice, after he had enjoyed several days to settle in.

"All of Mortal magickers practice the same sort of magic, with, I must point out, varying degrees of success. And their degree of success is in direct ratio to how much dedicated, hard, long, brow-sweated study each puts into the learning of the craft and its mysteries. Some Apprentices never do get the hang of it, just don't have the knack. Some are born to it and catch it the first time it goes past their ears.

"Time alone will tell where you are between these two extremes. I have hopes that you are not totally inept!"

He glanced for a long moment at the eager Apprentice. Douglas was remembering his dream that first morning in his bed under the thickly thatched roof at the west end of the cottage . . . himself in flowing robes slaying terrible ice serpents with a confident and practiced wave of his hand.

The Wizard tired of looking serious and suddenly grinned instead, and said: "What I have just said is very true. I admit I said it to deflate your dreams—at least until lunchtime. I just don't want you to believe I can make you even a passing sort of Wizard unless you are willing to pay for the lessons with lots and lots of mental agony.

"Of course," he added, turning to lead the way into the Workshop, "the real questions are these: (a) Are you good at learning this sort of thing? And (b) do you enjoy the process? You just can't make the grade as a Journeyman Wizard, no matter how much desire you have, without the books and the lectures. It just will not work!

"There are so many third-rate magicians running around! A few of them are not just incompetent, they're *evil,* because they don't have the drive to be good at it. Black magic is so much easier. Remember that, m'boy! White magic doesn't erode your soul, as an old friend of mine once said."

He stopped at his vast worktable in the center of the first Workshop room. It was just hip high—to an average man. It came to midstomach for both of them, the largest, longest, strangest table Douglas had ever seen. There had been full-rigged ships on the ways of Perthside with less deck space.

On it were stacked, piled, and massed in bewildering confusion a wild array of bottles, empty or filled with green or clear or brown or murky liquids. Beakers, retorts on iron stands, curled glass condensers, rebuses, graduated cylinders and cones, flasks filled with liquids bubbling over spirit lamps, and yards and yards of glass and rubber tubing.

There were glass rods, glass plates, glass cylinders with open ends, and mirrors of all sizes and shapes, not to mention all shapes and kinds of lenses in the colors of the rainbow.

Scattered among all this paraphernalia in every scant spare space were books, pamphlets, charts, and slips of paper covered with numbers and scribbled words or cabalistic designs and glyphs. On shelves and in drawers around the walls and under the tables were knives, spatulas, spoons, ladles, and microscopes. In jars with lead tops were stored dried roots, leaves, and flowers of a hundred plants. Beneath these on the floor stood thick glass carboys with ground glass stoppers. These were filled with dull gray, pure white, or coal black powders, or multifaceted crystals.

Upside-down bottles had glass and rubber tubing with clamps to stop or regulate the flow of their contents: clear ruby, bright amber, oily green, royal purple, or thick, syrupy orange liquids. Many seemed to roil and boil of their own volition.

All the bottles and jars were tightly stoppered. Each bore a label written in spidery script with rusty brown ink. Some were fresh while others were so old and faded they could hardly be read.

The boy stood, wide-eyed and in awe as the Master Wizard cleared a place in the center of one end of the huge table. He pulled up a tall stool, upon which he perched, legs dangling cheerfully a long way above the floor.

He took off his cap—a tall, black cone with a gold tassel on the top—and placed it carefully to one side. Then he continued his lecture, which had begun at the breakfast table.

"Now, a lot of your success in this profession, and it *is* a profession, *not* just another trade or craft—where was I? Oh, yes! You are lucky because *if* you work hard and *if* you like what you learn and *if* you have a natural aptitude for magic, you've got one other advantage."

He paused to turn toward Douglas standing beside him, and looked him full in the face.

"Because you have one thing no other Wizard's Apprentice has or has ever had—*me!*—your Master, teacher, guide, example, and friend. That sounds very, very"—he turned back to face the table again—"well, *immodest* of me to say, but it is true."

"I . . . er . . . I believe you, sir."

"It *is* true," chimed in Bronze Owl, flying through the doorway with a metallic clatter and rattle. He swooped to a perch on an enormous epitome chained to its own reading desk.

"Great grumbles!" exclaimed the Wizard, quite delighted. "You seldom are so flattering, Owl."

"Only saying what is true," replied the bird. "May I listen to the first lesson?"

"You may, although it is all but finished. For the First Lesson is simply put: hard work, take advantage of your luck, be alert, study long and hard, and above all ask lots of questions. And I will expect you to answer any questions put to you as well as you can, also."

Douglas nodded, having no comment or question at the moment. It seemed to him a very good rule. The Wizard polished his reading glasses with the sleeve of his tunic and went on.

"That was Lesson One. Here is Test One: Will you accept the challenge? Will you promise to work hard and do your very best at all times, even when the times are easy?"

"Yes, sir," Douglas said quickly. "Although I would have said 'times are hard,' not 'easy.' "

"Ah, but it is hardest to work hard and pay attention and all those things when things are going well," Flarman replied. "In easy times it takes special application to do well at lessons. Think about it, m'boy!

"But I say! You have passed Test One! Let's begin Lesson Two. The topic is: what is—or are—Magic?"

Douglas thought carefully about the question while the Wizard and the Owl watched in silence. Finally he said, "I think magic must be . . . anything that accomplishes something . . . for . . . for which . . . for which a person watching can see or find no ready cause nor method."

"Good! Good!" The Wizard clapped his hands in delight, and the Owl chuckled and rattled his tail feathers, a sign of pleasure. "A good answer, or rather a good *first* answer, because it isn't altogether true. A place to begin, however."

He motioned to another stool nearby and the stool walked stiff-legged across to them, settling near Douglas. "Be seated, please," Flarman said. When the boy was settled atop the stool leaning his elbows on the table in front of them, Flarman resumed: "You see dinner being prepared each evening? Well, that is practical magic in action, but separate the magic from the ordinary, *natural* phenomena. Blue Teakettle spoke and gave directions and the other utensils followed her orders. The meals are prepared in due time—and excellent they are, as you know. But it was not the meal that was magical; it was the method. Do you see what I'm getting at?"

"Perhaps, a little."

"Did you see the heat from the stove bring the water to a boil for the tea and to blanch the vegetables and making the gravy?"

"No, but I knew it must be there," Douglas replied.

"By your definition, the heat, the fire, the boiling force, for which you can give no rational explanation, is magic?"

"They could be, yes, although I have a feeling that there is a *natural* explanation for heat and fire and boiling, if I were to look for it."

"There could be, yes, and I know people who *can* explain these things in a way that we could perfectly understand— something to do with air combining with the wood when heated to cause a chemical reaction we call combustion. Again a very sharp reply! And if I were to have my friend explain the phenomena of burning and that of boiling to you, you would eventually see that they are *not* magic, for they have a *natural* explanation. You would agree?

"Yes, sir!"

"It seems to me we have altered your definition to 'magic is any action or reaction for which we can find no logical, *natural* explanation.' "

"I would say so, yes," said Douglas, who was enjoying this method of learning very much.

"At this point you must believe me when I say that there are such a magnitude and variety of natural phenomena on World that to learn to recognize even the most important of them would take years, even for a Wizard. So, we need a different, more workable approach to understanding what is natural and what is magic.

"As the phylum Magicus is relatively tiny compared to the phylum Naturalis, it is wiser to consider what is *included* in magic, rather than what is excluded. Even this path to knowledge is long and hard and filled with pitfalls and fallacies.

"In the end you will realize that there are just a few magic phenomena about which you can be certain. I can name you a few examples—the art of transporting yourself or others or objects instantly from one place to another. By all known tests this is at total variance with natural laws—that is, it is strictly impossible. Yet . . ."

He gestured casually at the handiest loose object, which happened to be Bronze Owl. The bird disappeared with a *poof* of in-rushing air from his perch on the book stand and immediately popped into existence fifty feet away across the vast room. Owl was unruffled by the suddenness of the trip.

"Teleportation," said Flarman quietly. "One kind of magic that is universally recognized as true magic. Magic with a capital *M*. Another is extrasensory perception."

He closed his eyes and put his left hand to his forehead, saying, "I can sense . . . sense . . . sense that an old beggar approaches our front door and is about to ring, there being no knocker on duty" (with a momentary scowl in the direction of Bronze Owl). "He wears rags but good, sound boots and is neither old nor a beggar at all. He is a paid spy for the Duke Eunicet. Our Duke has a great shortcoming. He is convinced that if one is not completely *for* him, one is *against* him, completely.''

He hopped down from his stool.

''I have refused to sell my services to this false Duke on several occasions. He considers me his enemy even though I have never said or done a thing against his person, his rule, or his property . . . yet.''

Flarman waved to his pupil and his knocker. ''Come along. You'll learn more from this than you will watching me shoot Bronze Owl across the room and trade insults with him about the ethics of involuntary Teleportation,'' he said over his shoulder.

And with that he led the way from the Workshop, across the courtyard, through the kitchen, and down the long hallway to the front door.

The door stood ajar, as it usually did on fine days. As they approached there came the sound of the doorbell pealing softly behind them, then an urgent tapping on the doorframe.

Sure enough, standing on the stoop, staff raised to tap again, was a man in the most tattered and forlorn rags Douglas had even seen. His eyes were red, as though from weeping, and his cheeks were wrinkled, gray, and haggard with suffering and troubles. A very poor old man, it seemed. As they appeared at the door he stepped back, but he kept his staff raised as if to protect himself from a blow.

And, Douglas noticed, his boots were whole and sound, as the Wizard had predicted. His oldness was an illusion, he decided, too. Flarman gestured the visitor to move into the hall.

''Crimeye,'' the Wizard said sternly, before the other could speak, ''why do you come to Wizard's High? Your master has my answer. I cannot nor will I help him in this new enterprise of his. Tell His Grace that he should stay to home and encourage the raising of sheep on the uplands. 'Twould profit him and his Dukedom more.''

''I see you recognize me despite my excellent disguise,'' said the false beggar, not in the whining, high, plaintive voice Douglas had expected, but in a youthful, well-modulated tone.

On close inspection, Douglas saw under the gaudy rags and filthy tatters that the man Flarman called Crimeye wore a good jacket and a hauberk of fine steel links. The handle of a long knife in a plain scabbard was half-hidden by his wide leather belt. The wild, greasy hair was actually a wig, and the deep creases and wrinkles on Crimeye's face were ordinary lines emphasized with paint.

"You should know you can't fool even the greenest recruit in magic arts with a disguise," Flarman said.

"Ah, of course, but then I have already learned what I was sent to learn. Who is this lad who spent this week with you, old Firemaster? I hear he is of Brightglade in Perthside, son of Douglas the Shipwright, lost at Sea some years back. Is't not so?"

Douglas gasped in shock that this stranger should know his name and origins.

"I'm not surprised you have found another informer in the neighborhood," said the Wizard sternly. "And he won't do your Ducal Master any good, any more than the last three spies. Throwing good money after bad, I'd say."

"My Lord Duke seldom asks anyone's advice, let alone yours and mine," sighed the spy, mildly. "Who am I to complain when it gives me steady work of great interest and good pay, too? I—"

"Let me give you information that your paid spy couldn't know, Crimeye. The young man is who you say, and he didn't just spend the night at Wizard's High. He will be living here for a long time to come. Last night, as is our right even under your Duke's badly conceived laws, we two signed Articles of Indenture, and this young man, Douglas of Brightglade, is now my Apprentice. You are even now interrupting his lessons in Wizardry. So see to it you treat him carefully, Crimeye. Apprentice Wizards are not to be trifled with!"

The spy drew himself up and squinted a moment at Douglas.

Douglas regarded him in return with a calm, straightforward look, and said, "Here I am and here I stay, Master Spy! Cross me now or ever or I'll try lesson three on you! Now, if you've had your say and seen your eyeful, I think it is time you crawled off."

He leaned forward and gestured quickly, clearing his throat fiercely. The spy turned on his heels and ran from the door yard, through the gate, and off down the path to the

Brook, crossing the bridge quickly to put water between himself and the Apprentice's spells.

He disappeared in the direction of a straggly orchard owned by a man named Priceless.

"Ah, as I suspected," said Bronze Owl. "Poor Priceless has accepted the Duke's pay to report on your doings, Flarman."

"That's just fine with me," said Flarman with a cheerful grin. "I advised Priceless to accept the Duke's pay when he told me of Crimeye's offer. He can use the money, goodness knows, and the Duke would only throw the money away on some other wicked scheme if he didn't pay it to Priceless. Crimeye isn't fooled either. He knows he isn't going to get much of use out of Priceless."

He led them back inside and down the hall on the way back to the Workshop.

"Crimeye is not a fool, nor is he at all a bad sort, strange to say. He will pay Priceless enough to buy a new bed for his wife, Lilac, before winter, and a new bull for his heifers. We all understand—except Eunicet—what we are about."

Back in the Workshop he resumed his perch on the tall stool.

"I must remember to remind Priceless not to make the same mistake his predecessor made, however."

"Which was?" asked Douglas.

"A farm woman living nearby." Flarman shook his head. "Oh, she thought my doings so dull she began making up all sorts of odd goings-on at Wizard's High under dark-o-moons, times like that. Crimeye was so intrigued that he came over himself last dark-o-moon and got nothing for creeping about in the dew and crouching in the laurel bushes for an entire evening . . . except a severe head cold."

"And a terrible pain in the back," added Bronze Owl. "Served him right. You should have seen the look on his dial when Flarman invited him in to midnight supper! Ha!"

"I gave him a specific for the head cold and a poultice for his back. Ground sprouted acorns and pomegranate pods, as I recall, and advice about standing around in the cold and damp of late-spring evenings."

"I see," chuckled Douglas. "So, if Priceless refrains from embroidering his tales . . ."

"Then the money will come in much longer."

"And this man Crimeye, is he harmless?"

"Oh, I should think so, basically. He was once a schoolmaster, underpaid, honest, sincere. Eunicet cut off state funds for education, which put him out of work. He simply plays a part written for him by the Duke. Duke Eunicet is another matter, of course. He is power hungry, petulant, vain, slightly mad, and tyrannical as well as incompetent and just plain foolish when it comes to ruling. In time we'll see him settled with, I think. Meanwhile, what harm if we tolerate the spying of his Crimeye? Back to school, young man! Not time for lunch, yet!"

Lessons, learning, and living proceeded apace as the summer moons rose, waxed and waned, with much to interest the Apprentice and much to consider when he burrowed into his feather bed at the end of each day.

Above him the thatch mice talked quietly. Below stairs the pots and pans rattled sleepily. Frequently one or another of the three cats came to keep him company, to sleep at the foot of his bed. But when the Wizard sat up late in his bed, reading or writing, Black Flame would be there, cozily curled inside his long, fluffy tail yet awake and alert all the while.

"Hagwort is specific for headache and for lady's troubles except where there is an effusion of blood," Flarman would say in the morning. Douglas questioned him about the effusion, knowing nothing about female anatomy or biology. It led to three days of fascinating lectures on the subject.

"Fire is the dominant element most of the time," said Bronze Owl, who in many ways was as good a teacher as the Master. "It can usually overcome the other three—Water, Earth, or Air—except under certain specific circumstances.

"The wise woodsman, for example, knows to build his night's fire in a sheltered spot where Water—rain—will not drown it, nor Air—the wind—will not blow it about. And when he is ready to move on, he snuffs it out with Earth—dirt—so that it will not destroy the forest."

"But Fire boils Water away," said the Apprentice with a nod, "and even burns or melts Earth if it is hot enough. And Fire needs Air to burn, and a middling wind will make a Fire burn more fiercely."

"Good, good," praised the Owl. "There, you see, it isn't difficult at all, because it is logical. Even the hardest magic is logical, once you know the system.

"But think of this: A Pyromancer can make fire burn under Sea. He can strike fire from Earth, or call it down from Air. He can call upon Fire to do things it would not naturally do—this is the goal you'll be striving for in your studies, my boy!"

The Apprentice asked a question about systems of logic and four weeks later felt that he was beginning to understand the simpler systems.

"Salt your meat after it is cooked, not before. It draws out the juices and makes meat stringy and tough, especially beef," tutored Blue Teakettle. "When you spill candle wax on your trousers rinse the spot immediately with very hot water. Don't rub!"

"Master likes his toast almost burnt," she told him, "and soft butter, so we have to keep it near the stove in winter. He likes his coffee very hot, very strong, and very sweet, at any time of the year, so we put Coffeepot to work earliest in the morning, every morning, without fail. Sugar is hard to get these days, harder than coffee for some reason I don't understand. Make a list every week for market and on Market Day, which is Wednesday in Trunkety, you'll know exactly what we will need. Never shop for food on an empty stomach!"

On she rattled, filling the boy's head with a thousand useful things of homemaker's lore. As the Wizard preferred not to shop and as Blue Teakettle couldn't, it fell to Douglas to do the marketing for both food and drink, as well as an occasional item of material or apparel. He learned to make lists.

"When next you go to market," said Flarman Flowerstalk, "buy me a spool of the heaviest red silk thread. You'll have to go to the seamstress to get it, as Old Dicksey doesn't handle silk thread. The red must be the shade of the flowers on the big vase in the sitting room, you understand? While you're there buy me three pairs of woolen stockings. She knits them herself. She'll charge you at least two thalers a pair if you let her, but you tell the good wife that they are for me, the Wizard of the High, and if she charges you more than ten percent over cost, I'll put a blight on her peaches next spring. She knows I am only joshing but we both enjoy the game.''

Douglas jotted ''silk thread—red of Ch. vase'' and ''wool sox—3 prs. for Wizard (peach blight)'' on his growing list and Wednesday morning set off afoot with a large wicker basket on his back to shop at the Trunkety Wednesday Market.

Market was held in the town square of Trunkety, the largest—and only—town in Valley. It boasted two hundred families and a cheerful collection of small cottages built of local stone and trimmed with carved and painted timber from the forests on the north slopes of Valley, beyond the sheep runs and the small holdings in the uplands. Under a spreading walnut at one end of the Square was an ancient, spired church with a yardful of old tombstones carved with family names and dates that went back, some of them, four hundred years.

At the other end of the Square, which was quite large and kept clear and grazed short by the town sheep, a grove of five wide-spreading, very ancient oaks spread their gnarled limbs protectively over a tavern called the Oak 'n' Bucket. Its front doors were flung open wide to the morning sun and evening breezes all summer. A passerby could hear the laughter and singing within and smell the tangy mustiness of good ale.

Along both sides of the Square were neatly aligned cottages belonging to the better-off citizens, the doctor, the town's mayor, and the owner of the mill, to name but three.

On Market Day the farm women in their brightly patterned work dresses and aprons, with red or yellow or blue kerchiefs on their heads, set up stalls under the tavern oaks and industriously sold their eggs and cream, chickens and butter, sweaters or socks hand-knitted from their own lamb's wool.

Their customers were each other and the townsfolk who were not lucky enough to be farmers of the bountiful soil of Valley—and any strangers or travelers who might come along on a Wednesday morning. Bargaining was their pleasure—although the chiefest pleasure was gossip at the top of female voices. The whole cacophony was music to the ear of anyone used to such commercial enterprises in a small town.

The farmers, meanwhile, sat at trestle tables in the shade

of the mighty oaks before the Oak 'n' Bucket and exchanged news and views, swapped harness and seed, occasionally bought or sold a cow or a plowhorse—the Valley was famous for its big, strong, and willing workhorses. Meanwhile they sipped judicious jacks of the Innkeeper's bitter, foamy homemade ale, brown as a chestnut, from an oaken keg rolled out onto the lawn and set on sturdy cross jacks.

Douglas dived right into this melee, happily shooting back comments and jokes with the ladies while he selected the best tomatoes, potatoes, radishes, turnips, and beans. For what he bought he paid in the silver thalers of the Dukedom—they were always scarce and thus doubly welcome to the housewives.

He bought sacks of flour from the miller, and sometimes baked goods from the baker as a special treat. The baker's ovens also produced the tasty haunch of beef that always stood ready to hand at the Oak and Bucket for guests' dinners and snacks. Blue Teakettle, of course, roasted her own.

Farmer Frenstil was there, sitting under the oaks, flagon of ale in one hand, a long-stemmed pipe in the other. The best and most prosperous farmer in Valley, Frenstil was as disliked as his jolly wife was loved. He was a hard-nosed, driving, strict man, honest to a fault but often overbearing and sarcastic of those less energetic and successful. Many of the farmers felt Frenstil was "too good for the likes of us, or so he thinks," with a sniff.

But when they were in serious trouble, or times were hard, they turned to Farmer Frenstil for advice and assistance. Nor did they ask in vain.

He treated Douglas with easy respect and Douglas in turn was respectful to him. Douglas decided he really liked the man despite his growls and sarcasm.

Flarman, for his part, considered Frenstil the most sensible man in Valley and encouraged Douglas to cultivate his friendship and trust.

The walks to Trunkety on Wednesday mornings in summer were welcome changes for the Apprentice from the daily routine of study, chores, lectures, reading, writing, and laboratory work. He strode along, shoulders back and head high, whistling and singing as he hiked beside beautiful

Crooked Brook. He greeted everyone he met with a warm smile and easy courtesy. He was soon aware that he had won the approval of the far-from-simple farm and village folk.

He made special friends about the countryside. He visited hapless Priceless and his wife, Lilac, on his way to Market, making a list of their needs and often bringing them a present or a special purchase on his way home again.

Douglas realized that much of what he said found its way into Priceless's reports to Crimeye. But he had sense enough to not say anything that could be misconstrued. Priceless, for his part, had a keen sense of propriety in this spying business. As Flarman had observed, it was a fine arrangement where everyone benefited in the exchange.

Chapter Four

THE very first visitor arrived two months after lessons began. He came openly to the front door late one August afternoon while Douglas was sweeping grass clippings from the path with a withe broom and chatting with Bronze Owl about illusions. The metal bird was hanging from his favorite nail in the center of the front door.

He said suddenly, "*Hssst!* Someone's coming up from the bridge."

Turning, Douglas saw a well-dressed, handsome young man of about twenty-five years, broad of shoulder, slim of hip, with an air of the Seaman about him, carried with some authority. A Seacaptain, I'll wager, Douglas thought to himself.

Seeing the Apprentice awaiting him, the stranger gave a friendly wave and turned in at the gate.

"You must be the Wizard's Apprentice," he called. "I've heard Flarman had one, at last. Splendid! My name is Thornwood."

Douglas introduced himself. Bronze Owl spoke to the man at once, showing that not only was the newcomer known to him but a trusted and respected friend as well. Bronze Owl usually played dumb door knocker when strangers arrived.

"Delighted to see you again," fluttered the Owl. "It has been years since you've come to Wizard's High, my Lord."

"None of that 'my Lord' business, friend Owl. I'm not that sort these days."

"Uh, what sort is that?" asked Douglas, blushing afterward at his temerity. The habit of asking questions, once ingrained, is hard to break.

"Simply put, the sort I was and the sort my half uncle,

Eunicet, would like very much to be but will never be, if you get my drift.''

"I think so . . . ," replied Douglas.

"Good! Is your Magister at some vital stage of his work where he cannot be interrupted by an old acquaintance?''

"Oh, I suspect not," said Douglas, regaining his composure. "I believe my Master would rather greet an old friend than almost anything else.''

"You are as perceptive as you are courteous, I see.''

"Thank you and come this way, Captain Thornwood. You've been at Wizard's High before?''

"Yes, but I was just about . . . no, even younger than you . . . when first I came here. 'Twas a dark and changeling sort of night then, as they say. I'll have to tell you all about it one evening when we have time and a good fire going in the stone fireplace there. Ah, here is the Wizard Flowerstalk himself, daubed in blue powder. How like a Wizard!''

Flarman brushed blue *flangeuin* from his nose and beard, beaming delightedly as he threw his short arms about the husky newcomer.

"Thornwood, as I wiz and bang! You're twice, no thrice, the size you were last time we met! How good to see you here, safe and sound. You've met my Apprentice, Douglas Brightglade? Yes? Good! How delightful to be called from the depths of driest thaumaturgy to greet you. Blue! Blue!'' he cried toward the kitchen. "Here, Douglas, rouse old Blue Teakettle and let's have some of the western tea from the green jade box. Hurry! In the parlor!''

"No, no,'' protested Thornwood. "We shall have our tea in the kitchen, or in the Workshop. That's how I remember this place. Anyone can have a parlor. Only a Wizard can have a magical Workshop such as Flarman's.''

So in they trooped, boy and man and Wizard, followed by Bronze Owl, Party, Pert, and Black Flame, through the kitchen—pots and pans rattled and Blue Teakettle puffed blue steam in greeting—across the courtyard and into the Workshop.

Flarman swept a corner of the huge table clear of a crazy, tangled mess of tubes, retorts, condensers, beakers, flasks, and petcocks to make room for Silver Tea Service, which scuttled in soon after on its short, silver legs, hopping onto the tabletop without spilling a precious drop of the imported tea or fresh cream and brown sugar.

"Just like it was," sighed Thornwood, contentedly. "And Black Flame, do you remember an old playmate? You didn't have such pretty wives when I was first here."

He scratched the black cat's head, ears, and shoulders while Black Flame purred like a kitten in welcome.

They sat down to tea and fresh-baked muffins, the Wizard to ask questions, Thornwood to answer, and the rest to listen. Finally, bursting with curiosity, Douglas asked for the Sea-captain's story.

"Well," began Thornwood, "you must know that my Lady Mother was selected by the Great Moot to be Duchess-regent until I came of age after my father's untimely death. To make that story, a sad one, shorter, less than a year later, Eunicet, her half brother, came forward and demanded the coronet.

"The Great Moot was confused and divided. Some thought my mother should rule; some felt that the Dukedom needed a man's hand to rule the country and raise me, the next Duke. There were fierce arguments and some blows landed when suddenly—my mother disappeared.

"A few of her close friends and retainers spirited me out of Capital, fearing that Eunicet was responsible. They brought me to Wizard's High to seek the Wizard's help and advice."

"I had the sad duty to tell them that for the moment Eunicet and . . . another person . . . were successful. Your Lady Mother was beyond finding."

"Of course, I was too young to fully understand. I thought you meant she was dead."

"I am not at all sure myself still," said Flarman. "I advised them to hide you."

"I remember. You said my 'time would come' and I believed you."

"It is near," said Flarman quietly.

Thornwood looked at him a long moment, and then went on:

"We were followed from Capital by the Duke's soldiers. After speaking to Flarman, my friends rode off into the mountains to the east, leaving me alone here, seeking to draw off the pursuit. Many years later I learned that they

fought a short and sharp battle there and would have perished had it not been for the Dwarfs of Dwelmland, who
rescued them.

"They dared not return to Dukedom as Eunicet's spite
and memory are long. The survivors eventually were taken
into the service of the friendly Chieftain of Highlandorm, to
the east. I stayed a year and a day at the High with one good
man—old Frenstil. How is my beloved friend, Flarman?"

The Wizard said the former servant was in fine fettle when
last seen. Douglas's estimate of Farmer Frenstil rose sharply,
and he began to understand the farmer's melancholy moods
and short temper.

"Well, Douglas," Thornwood went on, "I was here with
your Master for a year, as I say. It was an absolutely marvelous time of my life, as you can imagine better than anyone else! I had to stay hidden, but Flarman let me watch him
at work and we talked a great deal about the world and life
and chemicals and all. I would have liked to stay here
forever. But I didn't have a talent for Wizardry.

"In the end Flarman sent me southward across Lessen
Hills, by night on foot, to a friend of his named Wroughter.
Michael sends his regards, Flarman."

The Wizard nodded his head in reply.

Thornwood leaned far back on his stool, standing it on
two legs and resting his broad shoulders against the Workshop wall.

"And so I became a Seaman. A very good one, too. I
started as deck hand, then traded on my own and earned
enough profit to buy my first ship from Michael, who had
taken it in payment for some work he had done. I talked three
Waynessmen into crewing for me on shares. They had
learned to tack and reef and kedge and tie knots with their
teeth before they learned to walk.

"Now I've got eleven capital ships and eleven top-rate
crews. We carry iron ingots and brass goods, textiles and
dyes, timber and wheat, wool and apples, beer and potatoes
as far away as the Vale of Ind and Far Reaches. We bring
back silks and spice, copper, tin, sometimes furs and fine
leathers and rare chemicals and ores. We also offer safe
passage to overseas points and return.

"It has been a fine and exciting—and profitable—time.
This spring I decided I could afford to let the business run

itself for a while and come up and see how Uncle Eunicet
was running the Dukedom. I've found it is past time to toss
him out on his ear!

"Until I reached the Oak 'n' Bucket last night I had a full,
bushy beard. I shaved it off this morning and that rascal of
an innkeeper might have recognized me, although I trust he
will keep his flap buttoned, eh?"

"You can be sure that the Innkeeper will be silent," said
Douglas. "And I will remind him when next I go to Market.
You didn't happen to speak to Priceless, did you?"

"No, although I borrowed a few apples from his boughs
as I passed," said the Seaman. "Mine uncle is obviously an
ambitious and downright dangerous man," added Thornwood seriously. "My blood boiled more than once. Men are
being impressed into an Army, a rabble in arms! Farmers are
being forced to sell their crops for half price or less. Children
are having to help their parents meet the new quotas or be set
to work making arrows! Worst of all, womenfolk left when
the men are impressed are likely to starve—unless they
agree to board his soldiers. Their lives are perhaps the least
that is in danger with a houseful of lazy, rascally so-called
soldiers!

"Well," he sighed at last, "I imagine you know it all,
although it hasn't reached Valley as yet, from what I heard
at Oak 'n' Bucket. I think Eunicet is more than a bit afraid
to tackle Valley, what with you here. Thank goodness!"

Flarman Flowerstalk smiled grimly and nodded.

"What did you then?" Douglas asked.

"I was really tempted to reveal myself and raise a revolt
but it seemed to me the usurper already has too much armed
power. I headed south to see what my old adviser, Flarman,
would say about it."

"You partook of wisdom with your mother's milk," said
the Wizard with great seriousness. "Eunicet is about to
make war on Tet of Highlandorm. On the face of it, it's
ridiculous. Each Highlandormer is born and bred a warrior;
man, woman, and child—even dogs! But ... well, I will
stick to what I know to be fact, not rumor or speculation,
Thornwood. More and more soldiers are coming under Eunicet's gray banner, and his generals, a bunch of wool-clad
scoundrels if ever there was one, are arming and training
them.

"Now, Tet of Highlandorm is an old friend of ours, and he knows he can call on me for advice and assistance, at any time. He tells me his borders are alive with spies and scouts. There are already incidents, so he is prepared for war if—when—it comes."

"Hmmm," mused Thornwood, "I've never met Chief Tet. Can you give me a letter of introduction? Perhaps my ships can help him."

"Certainly! I'll write it tonight. But surely you'll stay for a while and rest from your travels?"

"I had hoped you'd invite me for a few days," Thornwood said with a laugh. "To see what you are up to, if nothing else."

"Delighted again! And stay as long as you like and welcome every moment. Have some more tea?"

Talk of war stopped at once, although Douglas had been very interested while it lasted. He had heard the rumors of Eunicet's Army and the impressment terrors up north.

The discussion turned to Flarman's latest experiment. It dealt with capturing a spot of very deep cold in a magic box, creating, as Flarman put it, an "environment of controlled low temperature."

The device was a thick, oaken cabinet lined with galvanized tin sheets, with a thick, metal-clad door. Inside, Douglas knew, for he had helped build and ensorcell it, was a thick rime of frost. A white cloud of cold vapor slipped out when the door was opened, rolling across the tabletop and cascading to the floor.

"It *is* cold!" exclaimed their visitor.

"The inside is chilled to the point where a beaker of water placed inside will all but freeze in a few minutes."

"Steams like a wolf's breath on a winter's morning," observed Bronze Owl, disapprovingly.

"The frost is frozen dampness in the air," explained Douglas eagerly. "The wood and the metal—it is zinced iron, which will not rust—were added to help the spell work longer and better."

"I guess I understand, although the magic is beyond me. I am an Adept only in navigation and Seamanship. Yet, here we have it, Flarman's icebox spewing forth chill at the opening of a little door!"

"Flarman, why didn't we build the box with the door in

the *top*?'' Douglas suddenly asked. ''That way, when you open it up, you wouldn't lose so much cold air.''

''Masterly question, masterfully put,'' crowed Flarman. ''My answer is another question, which is an exception to my rule: Why didn't *I* think of that?''

And he suited action to words, turning the box on its back, so that the door was on top. The flow of white vapor ceased immediately. He closed and latched the door.

''Now only one question remains,'' said Thornwood with a twinkle in his eye. ''If I may ask?''

''Be my guest, as you are already,'' answered Flarman.

''Of what *use* is it, Magister?''

Flarman was surprised but Douglas was not—he had meant to ask the same question himself when the time was right.

''Use your head, sailor! Think! The Old Kings paid handsomely in silver and servant's lives to bring ice down from Tiger's Teeth by runner every day in summer to cool their drinks and their sleeping chambers—*and* to preserve their food in summer's heat. Cold meat spoils slowly, if at all. If frozen solid it will outlast that terrible salted and smoked stuff you feed your sailors at sea when the fresh food is used up. Our great grandsires knew that . . . hence icehouses filled with block ice cut from winter lakes and buried in sawdust.''

''Think of carrying a box or two like this one on your ships sailing into tropical waters,'' put in Bronze Owl.

''Now I can see!'' cried the merchant sailor. ''And fresh fruit, too? It would stave off the dread Sailor's Disease to have fresh oranges and lemons on a long voyage.''

He immediately asked Flarman to build him eleven of the boxes, properly ensorcelled, for his fleet.

''Only larger, if possible, I would need them to hold a ton or two of meat, fruit, and vegetables in each ship.''

''We'll give the manufacturing over to our old friend Michael Wroughter,'' decided Flarman. ''He can make them any size and shape you need. I can easily install the spell, and he can renew it once it runs down. By the time you return from Highlandorm I will have the plans drawn in final form and a manual written for care of the . . . what did you call it? Icebox? We'll call them that. Good enough!''

''What then?'' the late Duke's son asked.

''Then? Well, by then there may be other work for you to

do. If not, continue to make money and build your fortune, but take care! Eunicet may or may not know that you are alive. There are spies even here, watching me.''

"I'm glad I came. My visit has already repaid me many times over in happier and healthier crews, if nothing else. We must agree on a price, Magister.''

There followed a spirited session of haggling that would have been of high interest to the sharp-witted, sharp-tongued farm wives of Trunkety Market, just to hear master bargainers at their work. Douglas went to start Blue Teakettle on supper.

Soon it was ready and they dined with much mirth and great good spirits, the pots and pans jumping in and out of the dishwater quickly, so as not to miss a word.

Somewhere in the middle of the Firemaster's tale of a far-off land where the women fought battles with one another and their husbands stayed at home to tend babies and keep house, the young Apprentice fell fast asleep with his head on a fresh, warm loaf of Stove's best white bread.

''Our tall-tale tellers woke the rooster this morning with their talk,'' Owl reported when Douglas awoke in his bed. ''I don't expect to hear any more from them soon. Shall we go to lessons?''

So they went to school under the eaves of the barn loft, filled just the week before with late summer's sweet-smelling hay, laid up against the coming of winter.

Thornwood stayed a fortnight. It was a happy time, for he was both interested and interesting, not only in the world and work of the Wizard Flarman, but in the studies and ideas of the Apprentice Wizard, too.

When he finally left one crisp, clear morning, Douglas truly regretted his going. Thornwood invited him to come visit him on the Isle of Wayness, far to the south, over the rugged and dangerous Lessen Hills. Flarman promised him that he would go to Sea one day—when his own lessons were more nearly completed.

Several days passed before Douglas found an appropriate time to ask a question that had been on his mind for some time.

''Magister,'' he began, adopting the word from Thornwood, ''I always understood that you did not want to involve yourself in politics. You refused to visit Duke Eunicet when you might have dissuaded him from his warlike ambitions. As I recall, you only advised him to take up sheep raising. Yet you were most helpful to and filled with advice and ideas for Thornwood.''

''Simple, my son. I *like* Thornwood. He would make a very good Duke. I *detest* Eunicet. However, if I were to do the actual unseating of Eunicet, the Men of Dukedom would insist that I take his place. I do not believe in mixing Wizardry and Politics. Magicians of any quality do not make good rulers. They always come to bad ends and, more important, so do their supporters and subjects.

''So, I'll help Thornwood—but I won't lead him or push him. I know my limitations. And you should have figured out that answer for yourself, Douglas Brightglade. As punishment, next question you ask I'll answer with a question of my own.''

''I thought I knew the answer,'' protested Douglas, ''but I did want you to say it in your own words.''

''Get the *Bestiary*, Apprentice. I will quiz you on the flora and fauna of Landsend, now.''

As the boy ran off to fetch the tome, the Wizard seated himself on the bench by the big, stone fireplace and murmured to himself, ''Take easy times as they come, old man. Matters can wait awhile longer yet.''

Not every visitor to Wizard's High came by afternoon's golden light and found joyous feasts and long tale telling.

As fall crept up on the beginning of winter, one clear, chilly midnight Douglas was awakened by a rap-rapping on his bedroom shutters, a tapping like someone feeling with a key for a keyhole.

He jumped quickly from his bed in consternation, looking wildly about for a moment and called out, ''Who is it?''

The scrape-tapping paused, then resumed, sounding more ominous, now, like a skeleton finger on a coffin lid.

''Pert, Party, fetch the Master!'' said the boy, and the two lady cats jumped from the feather bed and slipped through the half-opened door. Douglas approached the shuttered windows, feeling the cold draft that was slipping as silently as the cats around the edges of the sash. The room was filled with a deep darkness and the night outside was moonless, immensely still. There *was* something outside the window. He could tell—he didn't know how.

The tapping became more urgent.

"Is that you, Owl?" he called out.

"No owl," came a wistful, whispery voice from beyond the casement. "Let me in, please. I have an urgent message for Flarman Firemaster. No harm! No harm!"

The Wizard's name even in these eerie tones restored the lad's courage. He stepped forward and threw open the heavy shutters to the night air. A strong gust swept him back from the window. It whipped his nightshirt about his knees until he could fight it down and wrap it about his ankles. When he looked up again the shutters had swung closed.

A very strange sight met his eyes.

Before him floated an apparition of chill, wispy mist, shot with tiny sparkling lights that wove back and forth in spiral patterns, darting here and there like pale, pastel comets in irregular orbits. The light airs drafting about the small bedroom seemed to waft the figure back and forth, as if it were smoke. It had the face of a young girl with long, straight, blue-gray tresses.

The being spoke, still in a whisper, but clearly and without the wavering, fearful tone it had used—she had used—outside the window. It occurred to Douglas that she had sounded uncertain because the sprite had been afraid. Somehow the thought gave him the final bit of confidence to face this strange visitor.

"I seek Flarman Firemaster the Pyromancer. Is it my ill fortune that he is not here? I understood that he lived here alone."

"No, I have sent for him. I . . . uh, please have a seat while we wait for him."

"Ah, thank you. I have little chance to sit or rest," said the stranger. She floated effortlessly to the edge of the bed and sank down with a wan smile of gratitude.

"May I ask your name and who you are," she inquired, breaking the awkward silence that followed. "I must admit the sight of you humans always gives me a turn. Sort of scary, you know. *May* I ask? I mean, is it proper? I'll tell you one of mine, so you can speak of me and to me, if you wish."

"Douglas Brightglade," he answered stoutly, feeling

more and more at ease with this creature who thought *he* was scary. "I am the Wizard's Apprentice."

"That is good! I understand that, Apprentice and all. You can call me Deka, Douglas Brightglade—what an awesome name! Brightglade, I mean. Deka is my short name—my 'name to be given to friends.' In my—place—we never tell anyone except closest friends and lovers our *real,* real names."

Before he could reply, the Wizard appeared in the door, preceded by a lighted candle and three black cats. By candle-light, Douglas noticed, the visitor took on a more substantial appearance. He could at least no longer see completely *through* her to the wardrobe behind.

"I am Flarman Flowerstalk," the Wizard announced without ado. "And who are you? I know what you are, Wraith, Starlight Being. Do you give a name of Authority or Commission?"

The Wraith hesitated shyly, then nodded toward Douglas. "He knows. I told him my name. . . ."

"I'm sorry," stammered Douglas. "Her 'name to be given to friends' is Deka. They don't give their *real,* real names except to—"

"I know, I know," said Flarman, testily. "Well, Deka, did you just happen to drop by to get out of the starfall or do you have a message for me?"

"A message, Flarman Firemaster, if so you are. Yes, I see you are, although you said . . . Flowerstalk? What shuddery names you Men find for yourselves, Douglas Brightglade! My message is, Sir Wizard, *confidential*."

"You may say whatever you wish or have been asked to say, before this company," Flarman said. "But we are really being very rude, Douglas, not offering Wraith Deka rest and sustenance. Can we give you to eat or drink?"

"Oh, er, well, no really . . . well, perhaps we could have some more candlelight. I feel stronger by candle-light. And perhaps a drop of mistywine. It would be most welcome . . ."

They moved—the Wizard, his Apprentice, both still in their night clothes, three cats and Bronze Owl, who had appeared out of nowhere, and the Wraith—down the stairs to the kitchen, where Stove stirred himself to produce a chill-killing glow and Blue Teakettle in her cozy roused three

more candles and a mug of cool lemonade from somewhere.
Blue Teakettle almost always amazed Douglas—and often
the Wizard, too.

"Now, now, that is much better, the firelight and the
candlelight and all. Thank you! I have really come a long
way. My thanks should be couched in poetic stanzas,
but . . ."

"But my message, first, please," requested Flarman. He
accepted a steaming cup of tea from Douglas, who poured
one for himself.

"Of course," said the Wraith. "My message comes from
One who knew you when you were called Firemaster, not
Flowerstalk, and he said that you would know his name
when I mentioned a Gray Pearl."

Flarman nodded. "Of course! I know your patron and it
doesn't surprise me at all that he has chosen you to bring me
word. Shall I speak his name aloud to you so that you may
know that I understand the password?"

"Speak rather the third word of the Spell of the Garnet
Flame. My patron said that you and he alone shared knowledge of it and he told it to me for just this purpose."

"*Tronsetium*," said the Wizard immediately.

"My message, then, is this," the Wraith began without
further hesitation. "Quoting: Trouble in the far northeast of
Dukedom. Flames have been seen in the frontier villages and
smoke dims the sky of Landsend. An old friend sent word
three weeks ago by Sea gull. Will you come now? The study
of the Pearl is still far from ended. Tell this Wraith your
decision but let it be soon, as I am filled with misgivings
about the winter next to come, not for us here but for you.
End quoting, sir."

"Have another mug of lemonade," Flarman said kindly,
although he was obviously preoccupied. "I must think well
of my reply, if you will excuse me for a few minutes. My
Apprentice will see that you are comfortable."

Without another word he left the kitchen and they could
hear him climbing the stairs. Bronze Owl, who could move
silently when he wanted to, followed. Black Flame went up,
also.

They were gone for nearly an hour. Douglas got to know
Deka quite well. As she drank a fourth lemonade—which

she called misctywine—she talked more freely of herself and her kind.

"Wraiths inhabit a slightly offset kind of place, a slightly different plane, if you prefer. We are able to cross its boundaries at will so we have become professional messengers for all sorts of beings on all planes. No one can go from one spot on your World to another as fast.

"I am told that by ship it would take a human messenger as much as two moons to bring this message to the Wizard Flarman from . . . his friend of the Garnet Flame Spell. Barring accidents, of course.

"As it was, I can't tell you exactly how long it took me, but it seems that I left the . . . sending party . . . just a few minutes ago."

"You said we were 'scary' to you," asked Douglas, spooning Blue Teakettle's breakfast porridge. It was almost time to get up anyway.

"Oh, I . . . I suppose we Wraiths seem weird to you, and you look strange, or worse, to us. Actually until I got his call, I hadn't seen a Human up close for many a century. It was something of a shock, but then I'm fairly young in the business; only fourteen."

"Fourteen! Why, it's almost the same as my age," Douglas said, laughing. Deka looked startled.

"Fourteen *hundred* years, I meant. Wraiths are Immortals, didn't you know?"

"I myself find you strange but any fear I had of your sudden appearance in the middle of the night, rapping on a window twelve or fifteen feet off the ground, has gone by now," Douglas told her. "In fact, I find you rather beautiful and certainly fascinating. I hope you don't mind my being so frank about it."

"Not at all, my dear Human, not at all! I am rather flattered and will tell you the truth, also. In my own place I am considered rather plain, yet. As I build merit my beauty will increase. Let me exchange a favor for your compliment, which is our custom. If you ever need a fast messenger, anywhere in your World, or anywhere, simply call on me and I'll come immediately."

Douglas was impressed. "Now *I* am flattered, Deka. But what name do I call? Will you come if I yell 'Deka'?"

"No, no, I must whisper to you another of my names, the

'name for calling.' Still not my *real,* real name, you understand. I like you but . . . well, that just isn't done. Perhaps
after a century or two, who knows?''

She came close to him and, bending to his ear, whispered,
"Fryonhep-clader.''

Douglas struggled with the pronunciation in a whisper,
also, causing them both to laugh. At the peak of their merriment the Master came down the stairs with a scrap of parchment rolled in his hand and a deep frown on his face.

"Can you carry it in writing or must you repeat it by word
of mouth? I ask because it is a difficult and complicated
reply, partly encoded. Perhaps it would be better if you
carried it in writing?''

"Wizard, I will and can memorize words, drawings, numbers, actions, expressions, gestures, even pregnant pauses,
exactly and immediately. But if you wish, I can also carry
the paper. I am honor bound not to look at it, if the contents
are secret even from me.''

"Good, then! Here is the written message, and here is the
same, verbally:

"To my old friend and fellow pearl fancier—not yet, but
soon. He is beginning on the course we expected but we
cannot act against him yet. His diversion, while just a diversion, is a real danger to many innocents. Collect your forces.
Communicate with me by this Wraith. The password is *salamander*. The authenticator is *eel*.''

There followed a string of nonsense words and numbers,
which were obviously the coded part of the message.

The Wraith, when the Wizard finished, repeated the whole
cryptogram perfectly, word for word and number for number, even imitating the Master's voice and intonations. Then
she announced she was about to depart.

"Forget not my name for calling,'' she said to Douglas.
"I will hear and come to bear your words. . . . Farewell,
Wizard Flowerstalk! Farewell, Douglas! Farewell, friends
all!'' She ended by waving at Blue Teakettle, Stove, the
candlesticks, the cats, and Bronze Owl.

Then she stepped into the kitchen fireplace and melted
into the shimmering blue smoke from the Sea-coal embers.

And was gone.

"A most unusual visitor,'' mused Douglas, yawning.

"With a most disturbing message," grunted the Wizard, still evidently preoccupied.

"Which meant what?"

"Should I tell you yet? No, I think not. In time, Douglas, in time! You did," he added, laying his hand on the boy's shoulder a moment, "very well. Very well, indeed. Many another would have been terrified by such a night apparition."

"Owl had mentioned such things as Wraiths. Along with Fairies, Dwarfs, Brownies, Elves, and other Half-worldlings."

"Your education is proceeding at a satisfactory pace, I should say. Now, things you don't know about are going on in World, and in time I will explain them to you, when you can better understand and help do something about them. That is, when you have a good foundation in our profession. Besides, many of these things are secrets that are not mine to share. Not yet. They are grimmer secrets than those we talked of concerning Duke Eunicet—much grimmer, I must say."

Douglas nodded, turned the nod into a yawn, and Flarman threw his arms up and stretched mightily.

"The watchword for good Apprentices is *patience*. Well, well ... it is best we try to get some sleep before dawn. Lessons begin anew this morning and I am going to drill you on those Halfworldlings and Immortals Owl has been telling you nice tales about. Perhaps I can tell you a thing or two even he doesn't know. Up you go!"

And he shooed his Apprentice to his bed again. Yet as he drifted off once more, Douglas was sure the light under the Wizard's chamber door burned even brighter than ever.

A third visitor came yet another way.

A month after Deka the Wraith had appeared and then disappeared up the chimney, winter brought the first snowfall. Wizard's High on that morning was transformed into a wooly white place of soft, even curves, strange shapes that turned out to be familiar old things, such as well housing or Priceless's apple trees across Crooked Brook.

The Brook itself had disappeared under a skin of crystalline ice and a blanket of snow, but you could still hear it murmuring to itself, deep under it all, as if the stream welcomed the restfulness of the cold season.

The morning was bright and clear, cloudless and entirely silent so that Douglas went to tend the cows in the byre, listening to the byre ladies chew their cud fully fifty paces away across the courtyard. As he tossed down fresh bedding from the loft above and began to milk, he spoke softly to them. He heard the first of many dull *shhh-pops* as precariously hanging shoulders of snow detached themselves from the eaves and dropped to the ground. One narrowly missed him as he carried the two pails of fresh milk out of the byre cave. He laughed and blew billowing clouds of steam at the intense blue sky over the High.

"Can ye blow a ring?" a deep, rumbly-sounding voice asked.

Douglas stopped so suddenly that he slipped, almost spilling the milk. In the brilliant white of the sunlit courtyard he could see no one.

"Who's there?"

"Just old Bryarmote, come up Coro Kehd," was the matter-of-fact reply. "He who might also be called Freezing, Snowneck, Bluefinger, and Fallsend Visitor. Can ye blow smoke rings with your breath, I ask?"

"I am Douglas Brightglade, the Wizard Flarman Flowerstalk's Apprentice, and I never tried," Douglas said rapidly. "Can you?"

"Thought you'd never ask!" chuckled the voice. A pile of snow under the kitchen eaves grew a red nose, two bright gray eyes, and a pair of arms clad in slate blue. These were followed right on by the rest of a little man not quite as tall as but much broader than Douglas who stepped out of the snowbank and stomped his knee-high boots free of the soft snow. Pursing his lips, he blew a long series of perfect rings of his steamy breath. They floated toward the boy across the kitchen yard to be suddenly whipped to nothingness by a vagrant breeze that came sneaking around the corner of the cottage.

"Wonderful!" exclaimed the Apprentice Wizard and, putting down his pails, he pursed his lips, too, and tried to imitate the Dwarf's trick. But all he got were puffs and clouds, no rings. The Dwarf laughed heartily and blew three more huge rings, almost within each other.

"You must use your tongue at the back of the mouth," he instructed, "and push the breath out a little at a time. It is much easier with tobacco smoke, of course. Not many Beings can do it with steaming breath. Now, I once taught a great Golden Dragon to do this ring thing, and he must be the world's champion—but dragons have special equipment for breathing smoke, you know."

Douglas was trying for a third or fourth time without success when the Wizard popped out of the kitchen door, squinting into the bright sun outside to see who was talking there, laughing and blowing.

"Well, well," he said, " 'tis a Dwarf come down with the first snow."

Bryarmote spun around, almost slipped in the snow, but roared with pleasure to see the Wizard standing there in his morning costume—a silvery gown and black leather slippers with a red nightcap that flopped over his left shoulder and was tucked neatly into his vest pocket.

"A sight for the eyes of any Deepdweller," the visitor shouted, pumping the Master's hand. "I wish I had a diamond for every year that has passed since we two stood together on this spot!"

"Douglas, this little man is my eldest and oldest friend and adviser," Flarman introduced them. "Bryarmote of Dwelmland. Come inside and sit by the big fireplace of stones you yourself quarried and dragged here from all over the world when I was building this cottage."

As they passed into the warm, busy kitchen the Dwarf turned to Douglas with a wink of one gray eye and said, "Wizard's Apprentice, is it? I could teach you the mining of precious stones, gems, the finding of fiery gold, cool platinum, and hard silver. Wouldn't you be suited to that better?"

Douglas shook his head. "You can't tempt me, Sir Bryarmote. I have set my mind and my heart on being a Wizard and a Pyromancer if it takes me ten lifetimes."

"And it well might," said Flarman, waving Bryarmote to a seat on one of the padded benches by the hearth. "Except that dire events are afoot and it may be that the young will have to learn faster, grow of age sooner, before the chill can spread."

"Ah, ah? As bad as that, eh? I feared as much," the Dwarf

said sadly. "Then it is not too early to say 'I am with ye, Flarman Firemaster!' And ye, Douglas Brightglade." And he bowed deeply to them both in turn. "At yer service."

Both returned the courtesy solemnly, and the Dwarf, only able to be dour for a short moment, turned to the fireplace and spread his arms wide.

"My stones! My stones! So well set and so beautiful!" he cried. He marched from one end of the vast hearth to the other like a general inspecting his troops, even walking around behind the grate and out the other side, for there was plenty of room behind for a full-grown man to move, let alone a Dwarf.

"Time for breakfast now, and Bryarmote never neglects his stomach, not when Blue Teakettle runs the kitchen," said the jolly Dwarf. "But when ye have an hour or so to spare and learn, I'll name each stone for ye and tell its story."

While they ate, Douglas asked Bryarmote about a name he had heard him use, Coro Kehd.

" 'Tis the most ancient Faerie name for your stream. It is one of the Three Powerful Waters of their hidden kind, you see. I'm surprised old Wiz didn't tell ye about 'em and it. Name means 'twisting waters' and the folk hereabouts heard the Little Folk calling it Coro Kehd back in the days when ordinary Men and Fairies were still on regular speaking terms. Thought they were saying 'crooked,' ye see? So it took on their version of the name."

"I had no idea," exclaimed Douglas. "I always assumed it was called Crooked because . . . well, because it *is* crooked, isn't it?"

"Come someday to my caverns, m'boy, and in that beautiful place I'll show ye crookedness in streams. In Dwelmland they run first right, then left, then down, then up!"

And for that time, it was all he would say about his country.

Douglas talked weekly with Priceless while Lilac stuffed him with sweets and cookies, but they never asked nor did he volunteer information about the Wizard's strange visitors.

As Bryarmote stayed longer than any of them, into the deepest center of the wintertime, it was certain Priceless saw him and mayhap even reported his presence to Crimeye. The Wizard and his Dwarf friend made no effort to hide his visit, but then most of that time it was stormy and cold with deep snows every fourth or fifth day.

Few Valley farmers cared to go abroad when they could stay at home and mend harnesses, make new hay rakes, and talk about last year's crops and plan those for the coming season.

Even so, Bryarmote left much too soon, Douglas felt. He loved the Dwarf dearly from the first moment of blowing steam rings in the kitchen courtyard and he felt his affection fully returned. Yet one day Bryarmote was gone without a good-bye and only a short note written on a piece of gray slate:

When the Wizard Flarman chooses, come to my land and learn about mines and gemstones and malleable gold and silver, as well as indestructible, stable iron and ever-sharp steel. I will come for you. 'Til we meet, I remain your faithful Dwarf friend and fellow warrior

Bryarmote,
Prince of Dwelmland

As Douglas finished reading the scrawled farewell message a second time, the gray slate began to crumble in his hands and fell to the hearth as dust and was swept up the chimney by the draft of the lively midwinter fire.

The second year of the Apprenticeship of Douglas Brightglade was a happy, wholesome time filled with study and reading, experiments and explanations, excursions, questions and answers . . . and at times long, stiff, difficult examinations by the Wizard that sometimes went on for days on end until everyone at the High was thoroughly sick and tired of formulae, chants, chemistry, physics, thaumaturgy, pyromancy, and mumbly-jumbo, as Bronze Owl grumpily called it one evening.

But then came a blustery March and Douglas's fifteenth birthday. The Wizard called a halt and declared a five-day holiday!

They had a party—in fact, they had two parties. The first was Open House at the High and the farmers of the Valley and the merchants and mechanics of Trunkety were invited with their wives and children to come up, sip cider, and eat fried chicken and hot, fried potatoes and their choice of one of Blue Teakettle's four different enormous cakes with double frosting.

Those who played instruments—and their talents were not at all slight, Douglas found—played and some sang, and did so beautifully. The children danced and did acrobatics on the lawn, which was just beginning to turn soft and green.

Farmer Frenstil, the one who was as close as the Valley had to a real Squire, told a fast rattle of funny tales that had everybody within earshot rolling on the turf in mirth. Possumtail's little boy, a lad of three, managed to fall into Crooked Brook three times, having discovered the first time that the family of Water Sprites who lived just upstream of the Old Bridge obligingly kept him afloat and warm and set him each time safely ashore. The third time his mother discovered his game. Thanking the Sprites breathlessly, if hastily, she hustled him off to the kitchen to dry off and have another piece of double-frosted chocolate cake.

All in all it was the most fun Douglas had ever had. To top it all off at the height of the festivities, a letter arrived (delivered by Crimeye, who was invited to stay for dinner) from Gloriann, Douglas's mother, in her cloister. He had written to her several times since her seclusion had ended but this was the first answer she had been able to get to him from the shores of Farango Waters. Official mails had long since ceased to operate, victim of Duke Eunicet's penury.

On Douglas's actual birth date, the private party given by the Wizard to his Apprentice topped it by more than the altitude of the High itself.

Blue Teakettle had done yeoman work preparing for the four hundred farm and village people who had come to the open house, but she surpassed herself on Douglas's private dinner. They had a superb standing rib roast of beef, the fluffiest of mashed potatoes, a magic salad of early lettuce and pickled carrots, hot, fresh-baked bread with creamy butter—and more of the great chocolate cake, still moist, rich, and delicious!

To this dinner came, to Douglas's delight, Priceless and Lilac, dressed in their humble but spotless best. Bryarmote appeared out of nowhere, standing by his fireplace, puffing a long clay pipe, blowing triple smoke rings, and grinning from ear to ear.

"Bryarmote Springsong, also known as Freshet," he introduced himself to all who had not yet met him. He presented Douglas with a set of coat buttons of blue sapphires set in gold, and then produced a stoutly made leather short coat to go with them, and it was a perfect fit.

Just before dinner was served, while Flarman fretted and bustled about the cottage, making everyone welcome, there was a knock on the front door, and when Douglas opened it, there stood Thornwood, accompanied by a wizened old man who looked at least two hundred years old, dressed in leather from head to foot, including a long leathern apron spotted with paint and scorched by past encounters with soldering irons.

In his belt he carried an assortment of hammers of a dozen sizes and shapes, and in his hand a long, flexible saw.

"This is our good friend Michael Wroughter," introduced Thornwood.

The ancient artisan squinted in a kindly manner at the boy and handed him the saw: "Here is your present," he said tersely. "Happy birthday! Thornwood here tells me you are studying to be a Wizard."

"That's correct, sir," said Douglas.

"Well, even a Wizard can use a set of good tools. Best by-oak friends a man can have, come storm or calm. Next year"—he handed Douglas his leather cap and apron to hang up—"I'll give you a good all-purpose hammer. The next, a set of chisels, and so on. Then I'll give you an awl. And that will be all."

He chortled over his joke all the way into the kitchen, where he was greeted by the company with great respect, for his reputation was widely known in the Valley.

"And did you make Thornwood the iceboxes?" Flarman asked.

"Simple simplicity itself, my dear Flarman. Delivered each one perfectly and on schedule. Even added a few craftsmanly touches."

After the huge dinner Thornwood described his long trek to the northeast to visit Chief Tet of Highlandorm, at a time when Priceless and his wife were being shown about the cottage and workshops by Bronze Owl.

"Tet's people are strong—fierce might be even better to say," Thornwood began. "But they are scrupulously honest, with each other and with all of World. They wear kilts, you know," he added to Douglas. "Tet and I got along famously. We went off together to visit the old man, Frackett, who watches the frontiers of Landsend in the far northland. There's a strange man, if ever I met one!"

"He has been invaluable to me, many times," put in Flarman, pouring coffee and pushing a decanter of brandy closer to Michael Wroughter so he could refill his own glass.

"So he told me at great length," said Thornwood. "He is obsessed with the wastes of Landsend and says that he serves his fellow men by watching the comings and goings there."

"We'll be thankful for Frackett one of these days," promised Bryarmote the Dwarf. "More brandy, please!"

April came with showers and strong breezes, then May with an unusually fine burst of flowers on the hillside and along the brook, but not much else to disturb the even tenor of work, study, and play.

The problems and the solutions became progressively harder, but the Apprentice mastered them with increasing speed and confidence. He was often filled with a feeling of great accomplishment and anticipation—until the next, tougher problem came along to challenge his newly won skills and knowledge.

By that time he was already kindling fire with a certain mystic gesture and a whispered charm word and quenching it with another wave and word.

One late summer's day he was hiking far up-Valley, sent by the Wizard to gather an herb needed for an experiment they were considering. Bronze Owl had come along to keep him company and show the way, for the young Apprentice had never been in this part before.

The bird disappeared, as he so often did, flying creakily off to investigate something or other or to greet this or that friend too shy to meet the Apprentice. It was very warm and the weather had been very dry for three weeks, so that the grass underfoot was yellow and brittle, crunching as he trod on it. There was a hot, dry wind blowing from the south. Leaves on the trees looked helplessly limp, begging for a shower.

Douglas found the swale he was looking for and spent an hour gathering the tiny leaves of the precious herb, then sat down to rest. He was hot and thirsty and tired of bending over, so it was no surprise that he almost at once closed his eyes and fell asleep, knowing the Owl would soon return and awaken him for the long walk back to the High.

It seemed but a moment later when he was awakened, instead, by smoke in his nose, making him sneeze and cough. Springing to his feet, he spun about to find that the south wind had blown down upon him a dense, gray-black cloud of acrid grass smoke. In a moment he realized it was also tainted with the odor of burning wood, a much more terrifying odor in a World of great forests . . . and wooden buildings.

He moved away from the smoke, across the direction of the wind and in a few steps he was in clear air again.

"Owl! Owl!" he called, but the bronze bird was nowhere to be seen or heard. He debated running back to the cottage to get the Wizard's help but realized that with this strong a wind blowing, the whole upland end of Valley could be aflame before they got back.

He moved next to determine the source of the fire and especially the wood-smoke smell—by moving parallel to the wind toward the source. Topping a slight rise, he saw that not only the entire north-facing slope of the next small valley was aflame but that it had just reached the outbuildings of a shepherd's wattle-and-daub cottage snuggled under the shoulder of the south-facing side opposite.

From within came the sound of a dog barking frantically—and of a baby crying. There was no sign of anyone fighting the swiftly moving blaze.

He ran down the slope toward the house, racking his memory for the proper words and chants. Reaching the wall about the sheepfold—empty; the shepherds were obviously off tending their flocks—he dashed across to the house itself, hoping to find a door on the side away from the fire. There was none, not even a window. Turning the far corner, he was forced back by a searing blast of heat that singed his eyebrows and smoldered his shirt.

Here was his new friend, Fire, gone absolutely insane!

For a second behind the cot he almost panicked. . . .

"Now, my brave Apprentice Wizard," he said aloud to himself, "what use are you? First time you face a really big fire you think of running away to hide! You are so proud you

can put out a candle from ten feet away! Or light a laid fire?
And you want to be a Fire-Adept and control the Great
Fires? Shame!''

With this he stood straight, gathered his wits, and jumped
from behind the building. Throwing his arms high in a gesture of magic power, he cried against the deafening roar the
word he had learned to get Fire's attention. . . .

''Teeeayuuu!'' it sounded like, and to the boy it sounded
strangely like thunder against the blast of the wild fire.

''Teeeayuuu!'' again. Suddenly it *was* thunder and the
tumult of the conflagration began to soften and quiet.

Douglas walked forward, no longer feeling the heat. He
stopped when his boot toes touched the blackening that
marked the fire's advance a few feet from the cottage door.

Beyond, the flames still leaped high, waving red tongues
and demanding fire's rights from this mere mortal who had
interrupted its wild career just short of tragedy. Fire, Flarman had once said, loves to be melodramatic—and it has no
conscience. He would have to be very careful.

In the time these thoughts passed through Douglas's brain
it seemed to the fire that he hesitated and the flames roared
forward again, as it thought it sensed uncertainty.

Douglas raised his right hand and spoke as sternly as he
could. ''Back! Back and down! Go back where you came
from and burn here no more. By Horshoe and Washoe and
the Terrible Tempest that may end all in wetness, I command
and abjure you, fire out of control!''

Very faintly but clearly the voice of the flames answered,
at first sneering: ''Who dares? Who dares? Who *dares* to
pre*sss*ume to *sss*top my path of lovely, lively com-
bu*sss*tion? Who and how dares he? *Ssss* peak before I con*sss*-
*s*ume you. I *sss*hall, *ssss*hall, *sss*hall!''

Douglas stood before it and said firmly, loud enough to be
heard above the roar, ''I am Firemaster! I am apprentice to
Flarman the Fire-Adept. I, Douglas Brightglade, say you
back and down, Unruly Fire. Return to your proper place and
await the summons of Man. This place is in my control. And
so are you!''

He made a wide, sweeping gesture as he had been taught.
He no longer felt foolish as he had when he had been drilled
in the arm sweep for hours at a time by Flarman. Suddenly
there was a brief sprinkling of rain on the blackened soot and

soil at his feet before the shepherd's door. Over the brow of the swale came a wind wet with mist from Sea.

A great hissing and screaming arose from the fire, and clouds of steam rose to meet the rain.

"Dougla*sss*! Dougla*ssss*!" whined the fire, no longer sneering, but in pain and terror, "*Sssss*pare me! I am your *sss*ervant, not your enemy. Firema*sss*ter, *sss*tay the downpour and I will return from whence I came. Dougla*sssss*-s-s-s—s—s——."

In a moment the red glow of fire had disappeared and only the whiter steam remained. Douglas waited until the last hissing of the runaway fire had ceased, then gestured sharply. Rain began to fall again, softly but urgently, as if to wash away the soot, stain, and ash.

The Apprentice watched a moment longer and then turned toward the door of the cottage. Bronze Owl clattered up in great agitation.

"I was on the other side of the Valley when I saw the smoke," he said. "I see you have things under control here."

"It was close—too close!—for a few minutes, though," Douglas said with a shake of his head. His knees could barely support his weight.

He lifted the latch and entered the house. He was immediately engulfed by a tail furiously wagging a large, shaggy black-and-tan sheepdog and drenched by a flying, happy tongue. A pretty little girl of about four years ran forward and threw her arms about his knees, wailing in alarm and relief.

Douglas scooped her up in a soothing hug and smoothed her hair until she stopped crying enough to tell them that her mother was off up-Valley, carrying lunch to her father and brothers with the flocks in the hills.

"I'll fetch them," said Bronze Owl. He flew out the door and headed east.

Douglas took the girl, who called herself Prinscilla, and her dog and showed them where the fire had stopped. When her family arrived running a half hour later he had the sobbing—and the licking—stopped completely.

They found Douglas seated on a log bench at the cottage door, with the dog panting proudly at his feet, as if he personally had saved everybody from harm, and Prinscilla sitting on his lap, listening for the third time to Douglas's description of how he had quelled the terrible fire.

Then, of course, he had to tell it all over again, as modestly as he could manage, and the weeping mother and grateful father insisted on giving him dinner and thanking him over and over again for saving their daughter, dog, and household.

They speculated on the origins of the fire but could reach no conclusion. Douglas spent some of the last few hours of daylight trying to decide just how it had happened, but could find no apparent cause he could understand. It might have been lightning—except that the day had been clear.

"From now on," promised Prinscilla's father, "we will take her with us when we leave the cottage. There are too many things that can happen to a babe in the wolds, even with old Faithful here to guard her."

Prinscilla squealed with glee at the thought of going up into the hills with her mother; it is, after all, no great fun being left alone even when there are no fires. As darkness fell Douglas and Owl left with the promise of a load of carded wool, come shearing time, enough to make good, warm sweaters for both the Wizard and the Apprentice for winter, with enough left over for some woolen socks, according to Prinscilla's mother.

They arrived back at Wizard's High well after bedtime and found Flarman reading by the Dwarf's fireplace. He took one sniff of his Apprentice and said: "I don't know whether to send you to take a bath or sit you down and demand you tell me about your adventures."

"Listen to the adventures, of course," cried Bronze Owl, settling on the mantel.

"Well, it really wasn't much of an adventure," said the boy. "And I do need a bath."

"Here, now, let me judge the adventure, won't you? I love a tale of derring-do!" cried Flarman, pushing him into the overstuffed Chair and waving Blue Teakettle to brew some more tea. "Tell me all about it, blow by blow."

So the story had to be told again, although Douglas claimed he was getting a little tired of repeating himself. In the end his Master nodded for a long moment and said he had done very well.

"There are any number of things that could have been

done under the circumstances. Given your training and skill level, you did the perfect thing. Some might have saved the day another way but you are a Fire-Adept now and you handled that situation properly for a Fire-Adept, turning the fire's power back upon itself and regaining control.''

"You know that I am a man who believes in praise where it is due," he added, "as well as blame when it is deserved. And I say you behaved in a praiseworthy fashion throughout."

"Besides," he added when Douglas blushed a deep crimson with embarrassed pleasure, "we can both use some warm sweaters. A hard, colder winter lies just ahead."

It was only a few short weeks before Douglas learned what he meant.

Chapter Five

THE winter that came was deeply, bitterly cold, constantly stormy, and terrible for Men and their beasts.

Crooked Brook froze to its bottom. Hundreds of trees were winter-killed. Winter crops were frozen in the ground.

Across Dukedom, households went hungry where famine had been unknown in memory of living man. Desperate men left their cottages and farms, wandered the ice-encrusted roads looking for a bit to eat for their families.

Some went to small towns such as Trunkety and Perthside, where some warm shelter was offered. Many went to Capital, and had no choice but to enlist in the Duke Eunicet's Army—except to starve to death, for in Capital there was neither charity nor relief, nor work nor food, except on the wicked Duke's terms.

At least in the Army they were issued a dirty blanket against the horrendous cold and quartered out of the biting wind in jerry-built barracks or in homes of terrorized citizens. They got one meal a day and official blindness to any robbery or pillage they might commit to feed and clothe themselves better.

The senseless and ill-disposed thus lived well by stealing and swindling. The Army swelled, doubling and tripling in size at little cost to the government. It was a babbling, rabbling, drinking, and woman-chasing Army. The soldiers preyed on the people until distrust and disgust were a certainty, as well as hatred of the Duke and all his minions. There were savage, senseless murders in broad daylight.

Times were hard—truly hard! The Valley people fought back with little time to wonder about the doings of the Duke and the other Moots.

Priceless and Lilac were glad of a New Year food basket

brought across the snow-covered Brook by a bundled-up Douglas. Their larder was running low and their winter wheat was dead in the ground.

"I think, just *think,* we can last until spring," Priceless told the Apprentice. "I've been on short rations all my life except for the last four or five years, thanks to our Wizard and, of course, Crimeye and the Duke's spying money, but I've never seen it this bad before."

Lilac shifted her four woolen skirts and three knitted shawls to make room for Douglas before their tiny kitchen fire.

"Three men came to the door yestereven," she said, a note of fear that Douglas had never heard in her fine, old voice before. "Took me some convincing to make them believe there was no food here or anywhere else. I was afeared they might take it into their heads to search for food and take all they found, leaving us nothing at all."

Her husband shook his head sadly, saying, "I thought I knew one of them. It mighta been the second son of an old friend of mine; you don't know him, he lives over to—well, I forget, really. They was probably good boys, but hunger can do strange and terrible things to a man's spirit and heart. Terrible times!"

When he finally could make the walk to Trunkety on a day somewhat calmer with no sign of snowfall for the moment, Douglas went to see Farmer Frenstil.

Frenstil was a prudent man, and had laid by extra stores of grain for flour and for seed, sensing something wrong in the last weeks of summer. He had put up extra forage for his cattle, also, and his wife's three sows had each produced large and healthy litters—as if they too sensed the harshness of the coming season.

He told Douglas to spread the word in town that he would sell pork and beef and some mutton, too, at the same prices as the previous winter. Some said *they* were too high but the quality was without doubt. Douglas knew that by the end of Dead Winter Frenstil would be giving his meat away to all who had real need, not even asking for a promise to repay.

Through weeks of the worst January storms that anyone could imagine, the cottage under Wizard's High, where it never got too cold, housed seven to ten large families. Their homes had been gutted by fire in two cases, others made helpless by sickness or injury. Intense cold froze wells to the bottom, broke down bridges over streams, killed livestock where they stood in the fields or byres, and made it impossible to go farther than a few short miles for help.

But the atmosphere at Wizard's High was surprisingly hopeful and as cheerful as the circumstances could possibly allow. Pert and Party and even lofty Black Flame were petted and cooed over and played with by a dozen children from toddlers to a few years younger than Douglas. When Black Flame tired of the petting and playing he found far-off corners next to warm chimneys in which to hide. Only his wives and the mice knew where he hid.

The Ladies of the byre-cave did yeoman service on a diet of dried meadow grass, cornstalks, and wheat straw. Blue Teakettle kept things lively in the kitchen, and the pots, pans, and plates became totally spoiled by ten housewives who insisted not only on washing them after every meal, but on polishing them until they shone.

"We must keep busy," they explained to Blue Teakettle when she at last complained about the spoiling.

And indeed, the cottage was never so spotless, the beds never so promptly made, the linen never so smoothed and fresh smelling. When drifts blocked the big front door for three full weeks and the courtyard was filled with snow to the height of ten feet, Douglas, flexing his firepower, melted tunnels to the Workshop and the byre and even cut a path through to the brook.

The cottage at the High was an island of warmth and comfort in those times. The Apprentice took charge of keeping everyone, adults and children, busy and productive. He taught the children and organized their work to make it seem more like play.

Often the Wizard relieved him, doing tricks to amuse and delight the youngsters and amaze their elders. He loved an audience in the evenings around the great Dwarf fireplace, ablaze with its everlasting fire.

Yet even in the worst of the storms and the bitterest of the cold spells, the Wizard worked harder and harder in his Workshop and Library. In fact he worked with an intensity that Douglas had never seen in him before; long, hard hours that left him drained and exhausted.

Coming in late one night from helping a farmer get a

wagonload of provisions unstuck from a snowbank, Douglas was just in time to see the old man stalk stiffly up the stairs toward his bedchamber followed by a staggering and bedraggled Black Flame.

The menfolk, in the worst weather, donned heavy sheepskin coats to work outside. They kept the stock watered, fed, and warmly sheltered, and helped their neighbors do the same. Both the Wizard and his Apprentice, and more and more the Apprentice alone, worked hard to make the cottages and the farm homes of the Valley livable for all.

When the Wizard was there, they listened to him with renewed respect as he told them of insulation and building better fireplaces to prevent excessive loss of heat and midwinter roof fires, the worst of winter disasters.

The women cut and sewed, stitched and tailored, guessed the sizes of people they hadn't seen in eight weeks of short rations, dyed cloth with natural dyes their grandmothers had told them about, all using old, spare blankets, curtains, and often cloth sacking.

The menfolk hitched their Valley draft horses to sleighs made by putting wooden runners on farm wagons and delivered the clothing to outlying farms and shepherds' cottages, where help was most desperately needed. Several sleighs left at intervals for the same destination. The first, carrying fodder, firewood, and food, established a base camp partway there; the second sleigh, arriving at the base camp some hours later, would find it finished and snug and, after staying the night, would push on as far as they could and establish another camp, where they would be joined the next day by the first and the third sleighs, the latter loaded with clothing and provisions for the stranded and starving families at the end of the journey.

As the Wizard's cottage became overcrowded, Farmer Frenstil threw open his own farmhouse as a second sanctuary, and some of the worst off were bundled with hot bricks and carried in sleighs to the Oak 'n' Bucket in Trunkety, where they could be treated by Dr. Phrunge. He was too old himself to journey in the cold and ice and snow. Despite all of this, people sickened and died. And still the cold grew worse.

In the wake of the most vicious storm yet, Bronze Owl, to escape the noise and confusion inside, went to perch for a while in the relative peace of his favorite nail. On the doorstep he found a huddled, blue and nearly dead figure.

Owl screeched in surprise and the sound brought people running. They picked up the man and brought him into the parlor, where was laid the nearest fire, broke layers of ice from him, rubbed him with snow where he was frostbitten. They stripped him of his clothes, stiff with ice, and tumbled him into Douglas's own bed with warm bricks wrapped in woolen blankets to thaw him out.

At first he cried out in pain as feeling returned to his hands and feet. Then he fell into a fitful sleep, wracked by nightmares. It was not until they brought him to wakefulness long enough to feed him hot chicken soup and good, fresh bread sopped in milk that any color returned to his pinched, blue face. They suddenly recognized him as the Duke's spy, Crimeye!

Despite his poor reputation, the people at Wizard's High never hesitated for a moment to take him in. Flarman and Douglas had no objection—they knew Crimeye was not as bad as most believed—and to be truthful, everyone, from the eldest farm wife to the tiniest baby, welcomed the newcomer as a distraction from the boring, snowbound existence they were forced to endure while heavy snows continued to fall and the temperatures remained well below freezing.

In fact, they bestowed on the unfortunate young snoop all the attention and care that they would have given an old friend—which, they soon discovered, he actually was.

Crimeye was silent for several days after he regained his wits, then asked to speak to Flarman.

"Priceless is the only man other than you in years and years to say a good word for Crimeye the Spy, and I sincerely want you and him, too, to know how I appreciate it. As for me, I've tried to do my job, paid fair prices and more for the kinds of information—tittle-tattle, really it was—the Duke always insisted he wanted. I'm amazed these good folk don't hold it against me too hard. I know well what I was paid to do and the nature of the man who paid me to do it. Spying is the true name of my occupation.

"When I leave Wizard's High this time, however, I'll resign my position and never spy on my friends—yes, *friends*—and neighbors, anymore. So there, milord Duke!"

He turned his head and spat ceremoniously into the fire.

Crimeye's listeners applauded, clapping the ex-spy on the back and laughing at his words for the hated duke.

"Better if you never see or speak to Duke Eunicet again," suggested the Wizard.

"Someday there will be an uprising, and I believe Eunicet and his like will be overthrown," Crimeye said very seriously. "There's hatred in the air."

"It will be more than a year or two before that can happen," thought Douglas, aloud. "This coming summer the crops will be little or nothing after such a winter. There won't be much food to eat until midseason crops are in, even so."

"Let's face it, Valleymen," said Flarman, "we've got to start thinking of ways to work together now, as soon as we can get word out. Else Eunicet has us in the palm of his hand."

"Valley has goods and products it could export," observed one of the older farmers. "Always has, in a small way."

"Of course," agreed the Wizard. "And we have good connections with a merchant sailor in Wayness. If we get a shipment together, come summer, and carry it south to him, he will handle it for us at a small fee. His name is Thornwood; some of you may have met him."

"All of this will require *safe* roads," said Douglas, who until now had remained silent. "There will be many hungry thiefs out as soon as the ways are clear. We'll need a guide who knows the byways, the shortcuts, the back entrances, and who can move secretly from place to place."

"Who do you suggest?" asked the Wizard. There was a twinkle in his eye.

"Why, Crimeye, of course," said the Apprentice. "Who could be better at it?"

Crimeye exclaimed, "Most willingly! I'll repay your kindness and trust with good deeds, the best I have, my services, even my life, if need be!"

It was the beginning of something important. The men and women of the Valley town and farms began to plan again for themselves, not just for survival but for their future. They spoke with increasing sureness of what would have to be done, and how to do it, come spring.

"If it ever comes," murmured Douglas, tired and more than a little discouraged, standing on the front stoop to look at the hard, frozen stars overhead.

"Spring will spring," recited Bronze Owl, beating his wings loudly. "Even the Ice King can't keep her away forever. When it comes time, spring will overcome. A vast struggle is ahead, and Flarman will be in the thick of it, and you and I, too, young Apprentice Wizard."

"You know better than I do, I suspect," said the other. "Tell me about this Ice King. Flarman says he is the cause of this—"

"Hush, boy! Dead of winter, especially this Dead Winter, is not the time to speak of *him*. Wait until we are before the fire again, at least. Ugh! And the man to answer your question is Flarman Firemaster, not this dull, old bronze bird. Let's go in again. Even I freeze in this wind!"

Douglas followed him inside, closing the heavy oaken door firmly behind him. He had to chip away a rime of ice that had frozen along the sill to block the door from fully closing.

"You see?" asked Owl. "Ice is creeping in on us even here, if we don't take care. It is no accident!"

"When spring comes" thus became the most frequently heard phrase under Wizard's High and, in time, in Trunkety and across Valley.

Chapter Six

DEEP under its icy shroud Crooked Brook suddenly chuckled to itself. Upstream the sun shone on a steep cutbank. Here the snow was less deep than in the fields and thickets where weak cows and weaker sheep stamped holes in the tough crust seeking a mouthful of dried weeds.

The wind had fallen and the cycle of life-giving water struggled to free itself from Dead Winter, sliding down clear, crystal icicles and gathering in tiny pools to run off down narrow channels, merging to form minute rivulets.

Like the bare branches of a birch tree, the rivulets joined and rejoined until they were as wide as a man's thumb, then his arm, then his thigh.

Deep under the still ice, Crooked Brook chuckled and knew it, at least, had defeated Dead Winter.

Downstream, Farmer Frenstil, thinner and grayer than he had been in the fall by many a pound and many a hair, rested on his way across Trunkety Bridge, leaning wearily on the railing, staring down at the ice below.

A train of cracks hurried across the clear surface ice. A block the size and shape of a threshing floor broke in two with a loud snap and rubbed edges, making a grating sound. A black stain of meltwater spread across the white ice as it leaked through the crack in what had been a solid sheet for three months.

The farmer ran off the span and around the abutment, slid down the stream bank. He walked carefully onto the ice itself. Kneeling, he stared into a clear, smooth surface where the wind had blown the snow away. Despite the cold he put his ear right down on the ice and listened. He heard—the chuckling!

From the road a voice hailed him and, rising to his knees,

he saw Master Dicksey approaching from town. Dicksey had been, until his shelves had become empty in midwinter, the village general-store man.

"Hoy, Frenstil, are you *insane*? Has it at last gotten to you, this Dead Winter? Wait! I'll come down to you. Don't move, friend!"

And he rushed down the bank by the bridge and slid across the ice, almost knocking the farmer off his knees.

"What *are* you up to, Frenstil?"

"*Listen!*"

They knelt in the middle of the frozen stream, ears cocked.

"It's running again! Crooked Brook is thawing!"

It was the first true sign of the end of Dead Winter.

Frenstil hurried home to his empty kitchen. His hardworking wife had died during the worst of the storms of February, leaving the old man grief stricken and lonely. Now he felt a resurgence of determination. He *would* rebuild. And help his neighbors rebuild their homes and farms and lives. But first there was one important trip to make and one important alliance to cement.

He ate cold cheese without bread in the big empty kitchen where so many had found safety, warmth, and healing care during the storms. From the barns came the sounds of saws and hammers and even some laughter and singing, for he had told his guests the news.

He struggled into a sheepskin coat that reached to his knees, pulled on his fleece-lined riding boots, and took his best saddle from its rack near the kitchen fire. Once Master of Horse to the old Duke, he was not one to put a freezing saddle on a warm horse, especially one as old and faithful as Clopper, his stallion, long past breeding age.

Frenstil walked stiffly toward the stables, stopping at the barn door to speak to Possumtail. Once they had been anything but friends, so very different in temperament and outlook. But now they were closer than most brothers through shared grief and hardship. Possumtail had lost his own wife that winter . . . and his bright young son, who had played with the Sprites at Douglas's party the March before Dead Winter.

"I'm up to Wizard's High to tell them about the Brook," said Frenstil.

" 'Twill be a while yet before spring," cautioned his friend. "There can still be storms."

"Of course, but this is a sign we can begin to rebuild and get ready to plant. We'll need every favorable moment from now on to make our lives as much as they were as possible, Possumtail. The Wizard's not a farmer and will need some sound advice on what must be done now."

Possumtail characteristically said nothing at first.

"Do you want me to ride along with ye? Two should ride together these days."

Frenstil considered, then nodded. "You are right, as usual, Possumtail. Get a warm saddle from the kitchen for Daisy. I'll wait for you at the stables."

They rode slowly along River Road toward the High, rising white and glistening in the clear sunshine ahead of them. Stragglers and robbers, desperate men driven by hunger, grief, fear, and greed from their own homes had been plaguing Valley roads since early in Dead Winter.

"Their corpses, frozen or dead of starvation—of robbery and murder in many cases—will be found on the roadsides and in melting snowbanks now," said Frenstil, sourly. "Dead men and dead animals fouling the fields and roads . . . one more of thousands of things to be concerned with in the next few weeks. Burials as soon as the ground thaws. Including our own poor wives and your little boy, bless them!"

"We should perhaps consider cremating, at very least the stock and horses. . . ."

"Our own people will have to be buried," decided the other. "Your family, my Emmetta. People will expect it, need it. As for vagrants and strangers? Well, it goes against the grain . . ."

". . . not to give any man a decent burial," finished his companion. "Yes, 'tis so. Maybe the Wizard will have a suggestion, though. He is, after all, a Fire-Adept."

"I suspect," said Frenstil, sitting up straighter in his saddle as they rode across the rickety upper bridge, "that if we cremated their remains with appropriate ceremony . . . their people would understand. It will be a terrible job, any way you go at it."

The two men climbed the bank to Flarman's front door. They were admitted by the Wizard's Apprentice, who ushered them straight into the kitchen and offered them herb tea while he went to fetch his Master. The courtyard, Frenstil noted with farmerly approbation, was swept clear of all snow and ice and had been strewn with fresh hay.

Chickens were pecking among the straws for bits of grain and searching in vain for some leftover bugs that might have lived through the winter in the loft. Three black cats were sunning on the well curbing and Bronze Owl was perched over the door to the Workshop, turning slowly in the light breeze that found its way into the yard. Blue Teakettle produced hot bread but without her famous wild-berry jams and jellies, and shortly the Wizard came tramping across the yard.

They launched into their description of the thawing of Crooked Brook at the Trunkety Bridge, and were gratified when Douglas cheered and Flarman beamed brightly. The cups on their hooks in the sideboard clinked themselves together in applause, and the pots and pans did an impromptu jig on the range. Even placid old Blue Teakettle blew steam and rattled her lid, which, to that staid old lady, was the equivalent of doing handsprings.

"The time has come," declared Frenstil, smiling despite himself, "to begin planning for crops to be planted, how we are to live until some crops can be got in. It may be a harsh spring, no matter how welcome, and a hard summer, too, I am afraid."

Flarman nodded emphatically. "My own guests have already begun going back to their homes," he said. "I have had some other signs that Dead Winter is over, although we can expect some more buffets before it entirely becomes a memory."

"I said as much," agreed Possumtail.

"A number of immediate concerns occur to me," Frenstil said, slowly. "First, as we rode over we talked of the serious problem of disposing of the corpses, both human and animal, what with the melting of the snow and ice. Possumtail has suggested cremation, at least for the animals and perhaps for some of the unknown strangers . . . because there may be just too many of them for our limited manpower."

Douglas sighed and shook his head but hastened to say he was not disagreeing. "It is just so horrible," he added.

"I certainly agree," said Frenstil to the boy, now a young man. "But we have to be practical. A few warm days . . .

well, you can see it must be put in train in advance and done quickly. And that is only *one* problem. The shortage of food is not over, by any means.''

''I have sent messages,'' Flarman told them, ''seeking markets by way of the Isle of Wayness and Thornwood the Mariner. He is undertaking to find us places where we can buy food and seed in exchange for timber, wool, and what gold we have stored away, plus some other things we still can offer to sell. Here is a partial list I have been preparing.''

He handed them a slip of paper, woefully short, which they read carefully.

''We are farmers and small tradesmen, not financiers and manufacturers,'' said Frenstil. ''Yet I see no reason why we cannot produce these goods and ship them fairly quickly. I would say, we must look first to to timber while the ground is still frozen. Later, perhaps, raw wool from the flocks.''

''Further to that,'' the Wizard went on, ''I have arranged for Thornwood to advance us cash or food shipments against later delivery. I know this is frowned upon by frugal men like you, Frenstil, but I think we had better think of doing it at least this spring and early summer, until we get some hard cash in hand from our wool and lumber.''

Frenstil sighed, then nodded. ''I will support that, although you know as well as I do that many in Valley will balk at taking loans against future crops.''

Said Flarman, ''Michael Wroughter has agreed to come north to Valley to set up a manufactory to make a certain device that will be useful aboard ships. He will require several dozen men and older boys. They will receive wages and it will return a nice profit by year's end. We need to discover who can devote his full time to this. They should be men who are fairly skilled with woodworking tools. Some of the shipbuilders of Farango Waters will come to help with the highly skilled parts, and they can train our men and boys.''

''That sounds promising, sir Wizard,'' said both Possumtail and Frenstil.

''Which leads me to insist that, as we are going to work closely, let us forget titles and the nonsense of high and low station. Call me Flarman, please,'' interrupted Flarman.

Possumtail was dumbfounded. ''I've been terrified of you since I was a lad and you must forgive me if I am deferential.''

"Terrified? Of me? How ridiculous!" snorted Flarman. "Am I terrifying, m'boy?" he asked, turning to Douglas. "Are people really afraid of me?"

"It comes with being a Wizard, I am afraid," conceded Douglas with a sigh. "Many Valley folk are still afraid of *me*!"

Flarman threw back his head and enjoyed the longest and heartiest laugh he had known since the first snow of the previous fall.

"At any rate," went on Possumtail, "*someone* must take the lead and show the way. Frenstil is the leader of us farmers but the Trunkety folk will look to their mayor and aldermen before they'll follow a farmer. I mean, in ordinary times. This spring—I think they'd follow the Man in the Moon if he could solve their problems."

"There is a danger there," commented Douglas.

"I am a Wizard," Flarman said slowly, "and I will help, along with my Apprentice and my entire household, in many ways. If my name will bring Valley and Village together for the good of all, by all means, use my name. But I will not be dictator, Duke, Sheriff, or any such thing. I can convince, persuade, cajole—but not use my magic powers to swing a single vote. The Valleymen must see the sense of any proposal, on their own."

"I fully agree," said Frenstil.

"And I," echoed Possumtail.

Long after midnight the two Valleymen rose to leave. Flarman said:

"What I am about to say may sound strange but, trust me, I know whereof I speak. This Dead Winter was no mere fluke of Nature. I know for a fact that Dead Winter came when it did, as it did, because of a certain, malignant will. *This is so!* The troubles are not yet over. Indeed, they have just begun."

He waited until they had seated themselves again.

"Our Enemy is known to Men by many names, but the most common is Frigeon. He styles himself the Ice King."

Flarman let his words sink in, then went on.

"His aim is to rule World . . . or destroy it! He believes he has the power—cold, cruel, evil power—and he may, if Men, Immortals and Near Immortals do not at once oppose him, together. Some of us will be called to fight this Ice

King; some will die terrible deaths in the service of our fellows. Others will work harder than ever they have worked to make it possible for a few to fight. That is possibly the role—I hope it is the only role—of most Men of Valley. We will need your support, good wishes, and of course your products and your skills."

Flarman Firemaster stood up and pointed a stern finger at them.

"I have said you may use my name and prestige to accomplish your tasks, and you certainly may. But don't depend on me to be at hand at all times. I have my own tasks to perform.

"Douglas here is my deputy in all things, with all my authority. You can depend on him."

There was a long, dawn-time silence before Frenstil asked, "When?"

Flarman shook his head, suddenly weary. "I . . . I wish I knew. The future is very, very clouded. There are powerful banes and magics abroad. Most good people are just now beginning to awaken to the menace. Dead Winter was merely part of a diversion. Who knows how long before Frigeon really attacks or what form it will take? Soon and certain is all I know for sure."

The four of them stood and studied the hearthstones at their feet for another long moment and again it was Frenstil who broke the silence.

"That bad? That bad! Well, but we've had bad times before, we Men, long enough agone to make us fat and happy-go-lucky. Yet we are tough, we are! We'll manage. Especially with your guidance, Flarman Flowerstalk. We're lucky in that regard, at any rate."

The Wizard thanked them quietly and walked them to the front door in silence, each busy with his own thoughts. Douglas went to get their horses.

When they had said good-bye and ridden off into the early dawn, looking very tired and dejected, Flarman went back indoors and Douglas followed, watched him stop and stand before the fireplace, looking beyond the flames.

He turned to Douglas and said, "I have tried to give them a start, to help them get started on their own. I tried to tell them not just to depend on us to win their battles. Do you think . . . ?"

"I think it was clear to these two," said Douglas, thought-fully.

"I do also," said Flarman. "My friend, son, and Appren-tice, we've decided some important things this night—er, morning, I see it is!"

He climbed to his chamber door and laid his hand on the young man's shoulder.

"So very much to do! Well, there's always some good to be said. For instance, it will never be boring, will it?"

"I should think not," yawned his Apprentice. "Good night, Magister. Sleep soundly."

Douglas woke with a warming sun high above the hori-zon. He arose, refreshed but stiff, decided it was close to noon, and went to find the Wizard. In the Workshop the Master bent over a crucible he had just removed from the fire. Heat shimmered above it and a strange, silvery light illuminated the old man's face as he gazed down into it.

"You recall the Wraith's message? She spoke of a friend who shared the finding of a great Gray Pearl?"

"Yes, Magister. I remember Deka and her message well."

"That friend is an Aquamancer, a Wizard of the Powers of Water, the Fourth Element. It's a long story, but for now I can tell you that the finding of this Pearl gave us our first real hope that we could halt, not just slow, Frigeon's drive for domination or destruction.

"There is still much study, research, and experimenting that must be undertaken. Our time is getting shorter and shorter, as Dead Winter showed. Losing the Gray Pearl was a major blow to the Ice King's plans, and we must find out how to take advantage of it!"

He carefully, slowly poured the molten contents of the crucible into a series of small, round molds.

"Dead Winter, which affected only Dukedom, was a di-rect result of our possession of the Pearl. The Water-Adept and I agree that we have, by finding the Gray Pearl, caused Frigeon to move before he was completely ready. The Wa-ter-Adept's name is Augurian and he makes his home on an island in Warm Seas called Waterand."

"Owl has mentioned him," said Douglas. "Are you now going to tell me what is behind all your worries and our troubles, Magister? I have hesitated to ask because I knew it was not yet the time, from what you said, especially with the rule about answering questions."

The Wizard took off his tall, pointed cap and wiped his brow with it.

"It is time. Have you had enough sleep?"

"Enough, sir."

"Then let's talk about this business. I probably won't be able to cover it all, but as time goes on you can ask about what I may have skipped. We seem to have a quiet morning, today . . . er, afternoon."

He led the young man out of the cave into the courtyard and seated him on a rustic bench beside the well, where the lingering chill of winter was defeated by the early-spring sun. A parade of dishes, trays, and baskets appeared from the kitchen, led by Blue Teakettle, containing a tasty mixture of breakfast and lunch, a first picnic of spring to eat while they talked.

"Frigeon was once a member of the Fellowship of Wizards, among them myself and Augurian, too. He was, in fact, an Air-Adept.

"This was before the Fall of Kingdom. You've read the history of that, eh? So! Last Battle brought the defeat of the Devilmen and the end of their puppet-king Grummist. The cost was horrendous for our Confederation of Light, too. The Fellowship of Wizards was all but destroyed. Many, including the Wizards, gave their mortal lives to save World." Flarman paused a moment to remember friends long gone.

"A few of us survived—myself and Augurian, mainly—and Frigeon. We were sorely hurt and needed centuries to revive and restore our powers. Even now, none of us has the power we once had."

Douglas asked, "You are actually less powerful now than you once were?"

"Oh, I am, my boy! I am! I have recovered a great deal and am relearning, rediscovering much that I once knew—and so is Augurian. Unfortunately, so is Frigeon. The terrible beating we took in Last Battle twisted and corrupted his heart and mind. Since that time . . . well, his thoughts turned inward, to purely selfish ends, glorifying Frigeon rather than serving World as was originally intended.

"Years ago I began to suspect that he was still alive,

although he had hidden himself for centuries, just as we had. At first I was delighted that another Wizard had come through the holocaust, but I found he was moving in strange, evil ways. I looked more closely. Sure enough. He was growing powerful again and was making his influence felt in perverted ways. He was enslaving and enchanting, using magic to conquer Men and Near Immortals. I could not permit it, but lacked the strength to confront him.

"I moved here, built Wizard's High, and soon learned to love it and the people of Valley and Dukedom. I watched helplessly as Frigeon engineered the death of the old Duke, Thorowood, and the disappearance of his Duchess. You know what happened to their son.

"In the old Duke's place, Frigeon elevated Eunicet for the purpose solely of creating turmoil and diversions for us by encouraging vain, cruel, and rather stupid Eunicet to misrule, alienate . . . and to make war.

"To assist Eunicet, Frigeon sent Dead Winter—for two reasons: first, he knew the privations and tragedies of the terrible cold and deep snow would increase the ease with which Eunicet could recruit and field a huge Army.

"Secondly, he thought I would be totally distracted by the suffering of the people of Dukedom, and unable to give enough time to the problem of the Pearl."

Flarman drank from his goblet and wiped his beard with his napkin. Douglas said nothing.

"Well, we proved him wrong! He didn't anticipate that I would find a top-notch Apprentice. You increased my effectiveness more than twofold! Your work these past seven months has proved it beyond a shade of a doubt! As a result, I have been able to devote the necessary time and attention to the Pearl."

Douglas colored brightly and bowed his head, not knowing what to say.

"Eunicet, with Frigeon busy elsewhere with his hurried schedule, has bitten off much more than he can swallow. A war with Highlandorm is about to begin, has probably already started. With some help Tet, an old and fierce warrior, can defeat Eunicet soundly and quickly. The Duke at his best, without Frigeon's daily guidance, can't beat the Highlandormers, kilts and all. It is Frigeon who is distracted, not us!"

He paused to stretch. "This sun is pure delight, don't you think?" he asked, turning his face to it. The chickens, free at long last from the stuffy henhouse, clucked and chuckled about their feet. In the byre the Ladies chewed their cud noisily, waiting patiently to be let out into the meadow as soon as the snow melted enough to expose the new tender shoots underneath. The pigeons quarreled softly over places on the cobbles, talking of mating and flying to the top of the High to see if the rest of the world was still there.

"Now as to the Pearl," resumed Flarman, "to ensure that his power not be adulterated by any pangs of conscience or remnants of humanity, Frigeon took a calculated risk. He magically gathered together his human foibles and encased them in a Gray Pearl, which he then hid in Sea. Suspecting that he would do something like this, I kept an eye out for his hidden spell. I found the Pearl. He knows we have it, but he doesn't know if and or when we will learn to use it against him. He evidently assumes Augurian has it and that it is hidden at Waterand. He is wrong! It is here."

He reached a hand into his wide left sleeve and drew it out again, holding up a shimmering sphere the size of a large marble, a bit less than an inch in diameter. It was lustrous, perfectly smooth, and perfectly round, without feature other than its color—a medium dark gray, somewhat similar to pewter—and its size.

Yet, looking at it, Douglas thought suddenly of strange mixtures of deep, deep cold arctic waters, surging and swirling endlessly in which unknown things moved restlessly just out of sight. He drew in his breath in awe and some fear, yet put out his hand to touch the jewel. The Wizard let him take it in his hand. It was icy cold at first, but warmed rapidly as he held it and began to glow, ever so slightly. The deep, cold Sea color changed to the gray-green of open ocean waters, moving in purposeful ways, no longer sinister.

"Our task is to find a way to release Frigeon's humanity and sanity, returning them to his heart and mind. The alternative is to destroy him, which would mean destroying much that is good and true and beautiful in our World . . . witness the results of the Last Battle of Kingdom! We are still unrecovered from that terrible catastrophe.

"Once the puzzle of the Pearl is solved, Frigeon becomes

human again; a man, albeit a Wizard, capable of humanity—
and of guilt and remorse—and a yearning to be liked, loved
. . . to make amends.''

"I think," said Douglas, returning the Pearl to the Master,
"that he would rather be destroyed than have that happen,
don't you?"

"My thought exactly. It is what makes our task very
difficult."

"I begin to see that."

"Are you afraid?"

The Apprentice Wizard opened his mouth to deny it, then
shut it again. After a moment's thought he looked into the
Wizard's gray eyes and said, simply: "Yes, I am afraid."

"Well said! Honestly spoken, too. Remember, it is not
cowardice to be afraid of fire or of water when they rage, or
of the frozen breath of winter, the blazing heat of summer,
the landslide, the tornado, or hurricane. It is mere prudence.
Courage lies in doing what you can and must do, despite
fear—as you did during the grass fire up at the top of the
Valley last summer."

He put his hand on the young man's shoulder, amazed at
how high he had to reach to do so.

"You've grown. Time has flown so, these years! Well,
well, Douglas Brightglade, I've given you a few weapons to
defend yourself and even to strike back with when danger
comes. As time permits, I'll give you more."

"I don't feel particularly powerful," said Douglas, flexing his fingers and watching the hens pounce on the first bug
of spring under the straw.

"You already know more than enough to be more than
just a pawn in the game, if I can call it a game. If I let the
world believe you are still just a pawn, it is because I deem
it prudent, you see?"

"I . . . er . . . I think so, sir. You wish me to seem just a boy
who sweeps up and brings breakfast and dons or doffs his
cap as he is told."

"Hmmm, yes, quite so! Seem a pawn for now. Learn what
I still have time to teach and be ready to be knight or bishop
or rook or all of them at once when I call. I have decided to
hide the Gray Pearl here, for now, behind the dwarf's fireplace," Flarman told him, looking about. "Only three living

creatures will know of its place, the two of us and Augurian.''

He entered the kitchen, approached the fireplace, walked around behind the fire. Here he found a certain brick which, when he pulled it out, slipped forward to reveal a hiding place in the wall. In the cavity he placed the Pearl and replaced the brick.

"Oh, fool of a pesky prestidigitator! I've forgotten one other important thing. If you ever carry the Pearl, keep it hidden at all times. Show it to no one! It is covered with a simple but powerful spell that makes its possessor wish to show it off. That's how I got it. A sailor on a ship in Westongue Roads showed it to me, and I recognized it at once for what it was. This is Frigeon's way of keeping track of the Pearl, you see. Anyone looking for it will be shown it by its holder and—good-bye, Pearl! Good-bye, Douglas, too, I would imagine."

Douglas nodded dumbly. The Wizard was thinking out loud: "It is best we become more circumspect in our comings and goings from now. I've seen some suspicious crows hanging around the top of the High lately."

"Yes, I noticed them and told Bronze Owl about them. He said he didn't like the cut of their pinions."

"He's a wise old bird, for all of being hard-headed. He knows a spy when he sees one," Flarman said. "I am afraid it is time both of us were much less trustful and open. Dead Winter has already taught us that, I think. The Cold One has been known to use some of the outcast breeds of birds to gather information. No Crimeyes for him! I'm afraid our lives will change, young Douglas, and not for the merrier."

Douglas nodded in agreement, and went in to stir up the fire and add two logs, for it was growing dark outside. Three lanterns on the hutch glowed brightly. Blue Teakettle hustled out of her pantry and began to rustle up dinner with her usual good humor and efficiency.

"Biscuits and butter, old Kettle?" the Wizard questioned. "Spring must be really near if the Ladies of the byre are giving milk with enough cream to churn. Do you agree that we can work better with happy stomachs, Douglas Brightglade?"

The Apprentice Wizard heartily agreed, happy that some things in his World were pleasant and cheerful still. They pulled their chairs up close to the head of the kitchen table and chatted with the plates, pots, pans, and saucers, the salt and pepper—the salt doing most of the talking as, Flarman explained, she had bigger holes in her top than the pepper.

Chapter Seven

IT was several weeks into spring before Flarman started his journeying. They were weeks of study and long hours in the Workshop, the two of them laboring over a dozen tasks.

New visitors came at night, disturbing the short hours of slumber they managed to get. Deka the wraith came three times with messages from the Water-Adept, Augurian Deepmaster. His watchers had observed the Ice King stirring upon Eternal Ice. Vicious men, evil princes, bloodthirsty warriors, ravening beasts, and horrible beings were being summoned to the Ice Palace—some never came back. Those who returned to their own lands immediately began preparations for war.

Armies were being mustered. Warlike clans of terrifying beings were being whipped into a frenzy of hate by eerie trumpets and hideous drumbeats only they could hear.

Crimeye also brought news to Wizard's High. He had guided a ten-wagon train south, accompanied by seventeen stout young Valleymen armed with bows and pikes. They had delivered the first order of iceboxes to Thornwood at Wayness for sale to other ship owners on the southern coast.

"It seems almost all of the bandits who used to haunt the lonely places in the Lessen Hills have either died of starvation or killed each other off," Crimeye said solemnly. "We had no trouble at all. What few remnants we met were too pitiful to stand against us. They told us that most of their kind fled north as soon as roads were passable to join Eunicet's Army."

"If so, they certainly didn't pass through here," said Douglas. "Possumtail has had Patrols out since the roads opened."

"Now," directed Flarman, "I want you to carry this news

and of everything we are doing here, to Tet of High-landorm.''

"Glad to! It'll put me out of reach if Eunicet wonders what happened to me. Tet'll be interested to know that Eunicet's Army is fat and sassy and practicing being soldiers by collecting food and 'taxes'—which is what they call stealing any gold or silver they can find.

"If they haven't come this way," he added pointedly, "it is because Eunicet fears you, Flarman."

"What if they decide to go south through the Lessen Hills?" Possumtail wondered, with a shudder.

"Thornwood has a trap laid for them at Narrow Way. He'd love a crack at his father's murderers," Crimeye said grimly. "Who can blame him?"

Word came south that the Army was being whipped into shape for war. The ordinary people of the northern provinces, especially the Capital area, breathed heavy sighs of relief, for now the brutish and brutalized soldiers were kept too busy during the day and were too exhausted at night to bother them.

Summer came, and the last chills of winter melted away. Although everybody felt a lift of spirits when the days grew warm, and the skies remained the brightest of blues, with white, fluffy clouds drifting, dreamlike, from west to east each afternoon, it brought a frown to the Wizard's brow.

"Too fast. Too fast!" he said to Frenstil. "I should have expected this. Our enemy is now sending us a very hot and very dry summer after Dead Winter. We must counteract at once!"

"But how?" asked the farmer. "We've always had plenty of rainfall in the Valley."

"Believe me, this Ice King can stop all rain for months and months. He can't however, stop the flow of Crooked Brook, for its life is protected by Faerie spells on their sacred stream. That may be our saving. We must dig ponds to hold what remains of the spring runoff first. And build a system of channels leading to your Valley fields."

"Irrigate?" asked Frenstil musingly.

"Without delay," said Flarman firmly.

Mootcall went out. Property owners were bidden to come to Trunkety on Mayday, and none too soon, for Mayday was as hot as most midsummer days.

Moot approved afterward many of the projects already begun: the patrols, the irrigation, the hiring and housing of strangers. The Corresponding Secretary was directed to prepare a report and send it to all the other Moots about the Dukedom, warning their neighbors of what was coming, and what could be done about it.

As Flarman had predicted, the usual mid-June rains failed to come and temperatures rose higher every day. Unwatered soil baked as hard as rock and tender early-summer grains and grasses dried up and blew away in the first of many days and nights of harsh, dry winds.

"Where to this time?" asked Douglas as Flarman packed his knapsack one hot evening late in June. The old Wizard looked both tired and yet eager to be on his way.

"We are making progress on the matter of the Pearl, Augurian and I. In the meantime, we have a war to fight in Highlandorm. I hope to see Bryarmote in his caverns under Dwelmland. No, I don't really know how long I will be gone this time."

"And if you don't return . . . I am not to go looking for you?"

"That is correct, m'boy. What you have to do here is more important than whether I come home to tea or not. Much more important than going off looking for a broken-down Wizard who can't stand here gossiping all night until dawn discovers him on the road for all his enemies to see. So, good-bye . . ."

"Good-bye again," said Douglas, half smiling, half grimacing. He threw his arms about the stout Wizard and squeezed him tightly. "We will carry on, but . . . who will make us laugh?"

"Who, indeed?" chuckled Flarman Firemaster. "Well, it'll have to be somebody else for a while. Wizard Flarman Flowerstalk Firemaster will *not* be killed or captured. He *will* be back!"

He walked rapidly down the path from the front door, past the well, turned to cross the bridge, and disappeared into the deep purple shadows under the apple trees of Priceless's orchard.

■ ■ ■

In July, Douglas received a ragged, battered letter that made him feel much better on one count, at least. His mother wrote from her nunnery:

My Dear Son,
This second period of silence between us, brought on by the terrible winter just past, was by far the more frightening. . . .

The end of January the Abbess called us all together—those of us who had not perished from the cold and lack of medicines—and announced that, if nothing else, the Dead Winter had shown her that our *Rules of Seclusion* was no longer viable. By that she meant that while we had strength and comfort to offer we would do greater service to Heaven and World if we flung open our gates to our "outside" brethren, and warmed, fed, consoled, and nursed them.

So, we asked the unfortunates on the road that runs by our fields to come inside and get warm, have a frugal meal. We gave them work, if they were able to work, in exchange or we sent them on their ways with the best meal and the best advices we could give them.

It didn't matter if they were rich or poor, whether they had turned beggar or thief. Goodness alone knows where all the food came from. I am sure there never was that much in store before the first snowfall. . . .

I have received your wonderful letters—once I received three in one day!—carried by different travelers.

The last was by a strange young man who asked to be remembered to you. His name was Crimeye. We quite enjoyed his talk, as he has obviously traveled far and wide and knows a great deal of what is going on everywhere in the land.

You and your Master have my undying love and admiration. Bless you both and all the good folk of Valley about whom you have written in your letters.

A week or so later he found a moment to begin a reply—and it took him three more weeks to finish the letter and find someone to carry it to Farango Water.

My Dear Mother:
Your letter was like a gentle rain—and rain is the

greatest blessing I can think of right now. It hasn't fallen in Valley for ten weeks!

Thornwood has asked me to say to you and your order that he would appreciate it if you could direct to him any shipwrights, sailmakers, and chandlers on Farango Water who are in need of work. Thornwood also welcomes men willing to sail his ships.

Flarman Flowerstalk, who nowadays prefers to be called Firemaster, has been gone for several weeks. Of course, we miss him. Bronze Owl flew off one morning and has not returned. Some mission of the Wizard's, I daresay. Also missing, I just realized, is Black Flame, our tom, but Pert and Party are here, busy with new kittens, so there is plenty of fun and activity when I have time to play with them.

If I can, I will send you a pair from this litter. You'll love them, as will your sisters. They will make fine mousers and great lap pets, when you have time to sit down.

Today we opened our first channel and the water is flowing merrily along the north slope of Valley to fields just to the west. None too soon!

The High is so empty and the nights so hot that I have taken to sleeping on the grass under the pecan trees beyond the old well. I was there this morning when I was awakened at dawn by a touch on my cheek like a blade of grass blown by a light breeze, but there was no breeze, and when I opened my eyes I beheld a tiny, graceful figure, light and airy as milkweed seed, a shimmery, silvery white lady with dark, auburn hair. Over her shoulders I saw lacy, iridescent wings, very thin and softly glowing. I knew at once she was a fairy and, because she wore a circlet of gold in her hair, not a common or garden-variety Fairy, either.

"Greetings, Lady," I said, with all courtesy—it pays to be especially courteous to fairies, according to Bronze Owl. "I am Douglas Brightglade, apprentice to the Wizard Flarman Firemaster."

She laughed, like a silver bell tinkling, and said "Good morning, Douglas! I am Flowerdweller, Queen Marivus of the Kingdom of Faerie, also known as Cloudpiercer, Innocent, Diligent. But all those are so formal. You may

call me what men have ever called me, and I like it best:
Marget.''

I bowed as deeply as one could seated on dew-damp
grass and asked her how I could serve her.

''Augurian sent me word some days ago but a wretch of
a personal guard would not admit his messenger to me,
and the messenger would not divulge its content to anyone
else.''

''Deka the Wraith?'' I asked.

''The same.'' She nodded. ''I am on my way to consult
with the Deepmaster now, as a result. Augurian said I
should stop by on the way to speak to Flarman, if he is here.
Now, there's a dear man! But I see he is not at home.''

I was sorry to see her go for I believe she is as good as
she is beautiful. Many people do not trust the fairies,
Bronze Owl says, because of a misunderstanding during
Last Battle. I must say, I was impressed.

Crimeye has found me a lad who is walking to Farango
Water tomorrow who has agreed to carry not only your
letter but your kittens. . . .

My dream nowadays, beyond a bath and a bed, is to get
this business over with so I can myself walk down the
road to Brightglade and sit under a blossoming apple tree
for hours and hours with you and talk about everything
that has happened and everyone we've met and known
since we parted.

I send my love along with the kittens. Write when you
can. I am still your

> Most Loving Son,
> Douglas.

Chapter Eight

THE Wizard Flarman Firemaster, known in time of peace as Flowerstalk, returned to his cottage in late summer, welcome as a cool breeze in the stifling night.

Douglas came to the High late that night from visiting Possumtail. As he approached the door, his feet dragging with weariness, Douglas found Bronze Owl hanging from his nail, as if nothing had ever happened.

"You're back!"

"Obviously," said the Owl cheerfully. "I take it you missed me?"

"Very much! Where did you go? I assumed . . ."

"That we followed Flarman? Well, yes. Actually, Black Flame put it to me that we could be of more assistance to the Master if we sort of hung around him on his travels, now. Without his knowing it, you know? And, besides, Black Flame doesn't believe in interfering with new litters. Actually his ladies told *him* to go away. So we went."

Douglas was delighted enough to forget his weariness for a while.

"And what did the Master say when he found you had followed him?

"Ah, my boy, as far as we know he didn't ever know we were nearby. Fortunately, there were only a couple of scrapes he got himself out of without our help. We came on ahead last night and arrived this afternoon a couple of hours before him."

"Then he is here, too?" cried the Apprentice with relief.

"Yes, yes, went right off to bed. Tired, I daresay. Black Flame was almost exhausted himself. We barely made it with me half carrying him. He was dead to the world when the Wizard rolled up. He asked for you and said you were to awaken him when you returned.''

Douglas climbed the stairs, aware again of how tired he was. The door to the Wizard's room was closed, yet there was a strip of light shining under the door, showing the Master, was, indeed, at home.

When he rapped the Apprentice drew no response. He tried the door and peeked in. On his wide, four-poster bed the Wizard, in a dusty cloak and rumpled slouch hat, lay on his back, snoring loudly. Douglas turned out the lamp and let him sleep.

Even so, the Wizard was up before his Apprentice in the morning. Breakfast was sizzling and steaming on the big stove when Douglas came down a few minutes after dawn, yawning hugely.

''Here, is this how you fight the Enemy? Sleeping all morning and letting your betters scrabble for a mere bite to eat after long journeyings? Shame, Douglas Brightglade!''

Douglas hugged his Master for a long moment before he, too, fell upon Blue Teakettle's famous bran muffins and honey, bacon, and eggs.

''We have survived your absence, somehow,'' he told the Wizard around a mouthful of food. ''The ponds are full and the ditches running in many parts of Valley. Crops will be good considering we've had very little rain, except for hail and thunderstorms this past week. And has it ever been hot! This is the first cool morning I can remember since we said good-bye, Magister.''

''Hmmmph! You don't think this coolness is an accident, do you? I brought it back in my hip pocket from the north. I had an idea how hot it was going to be. It's getting hot in Highlandorm, too.''

''So I heard from Crimeye. He's a better messenger than he was a spy.''

''Messenger *and* warrior. I missed him on the road south, then. But that's not unexpected. Both of us take the hidden ways, I guess. Eunicet's Army is on the march. Those brutes with the leather whips have beaten some discipline into them at last, poor boys! They are acting like fairly good soldiers, although they do show a tendency to obey orders to the letter, without thought or common sense. A bad trait for a long war, to my way of thinking.''

He wiped his beard with his napkin.

"Tet's Highlandormers will come down on them like a rock slide, I'm thinking. What good will orders do them then? But then, I'm not a soldier."

Douglas demanded a full accounting of the Wizard. He had been gone more than two months.

"Of course, it wouldn't have taken that long in peace-time," said Flarman Firemaster, holding out his cup for a refill from Blue Teakettle. "Traveling by night is not my idea of a pleasure trip. Anyway, I first saw Tet. Crimeye had been there and gone again. He was made most welcome. Tet values the information Crimeye gathers.

"He won't take the offensive until he knows Thorn-wood's fleet is nearby to guard his sea flank. When the two of them get together, Eunicet will no doubt get his tail badly bent and his Army will come tumbling home to harass us instead. If I know anything about sniveling Eunicet and that fool, foul brute named Bladder they'll come straight for us when they return, looking for revenge."

"Did you notice the lookout post atop the High?"

"No, I must admit I was almost faint with fatigue last night when I came up the path from the Brook. Crawled in, I really did, but I feel tip-top now after a long sleep in the old four-poster."

He rattled on about his visits to the dwarf Bryarmote and the strange old man, Frackett of Landsend. He had also met briefly with Augurian Deepmaster.

"Augurian believes there will be a Battle of Sea. He is convinced Frigeon plans to bring a vast fleet southward—and his cold with it. It will be a terrible blow to the Sea realms—and the whole World—if Frigeon can control Sea."

"Did you speak of . . . the thing we hid away?"

"You have gained wisdom as well as inches! Yes, we spoke of it. We decided it is best hidden away for the moment. We are close to the answer, however. Very close."

Douglas mentioned that the Faerie Queen had left word she was to be called when Flarman returned. Flarman called Deka to pass a message to Queen Marget. It took but a few minutes, and then Marget appeared.

In the end Flarman said, "We can do little that will help Tet. I have given him some valuable advice and useful information. And a couple of good charms to protect his personal safety in the fighting. He is no rear-echelon leader, is Tet.''

''So,'' mused the tiny Faerie Queen. ''History and fate rest for the moment with Tet and his kilted warriors.''

''And with Thornwood and his sailors,'' added Douglas.

''Aye, and a very worldly, non-magical battle, taken all in all,'' agreed the Wizard. ''We must not interfere, for that is exactly what Frigeon expects and wants us to do, rather than spend the time preparing for his Sea attack—and on the Pearl.''

''And what will our enemy do? For we must be realistic, mustn't we?''

The Wizard smiled at the diminutive Queen before saying, ''Well, in victory or defeat Frigeon will do the same, for what is Eunicet to him? The Highlandorm war is but a diversion, a ruse, a feint.''

''You suggest, then, that we continue our preparations in aid of Augurian rather than send our forces to aid Chief Tet?''

''Exactly, my dear. The Battle of Sea will be our real test against Frigeon.''

''I have anticipated it. My Prince Consort and his Nereids are already on their way to the Deepmaster at Waterand. How long do you think we will have, Magister?''

''I estimate the Highlandorm War will be over by the beginning of October. Frigeon will be in position about the middle of November, I would guess. Will Faerie be ready?''

''Of course! We will be cheek-by-jowl, as the Old King used to say, with Augurian by then, with time to spare and ready to give Frigeon's hosts some surprises. Surprise will be important. . . .''

Flarman said, ''Surprise is always important in battle.''

''I have bespoken each and every Nereid and they have sworn to obey when Men lead them. No repeat of the terrible Last Battle this time, Wizard.''

Her voice was suddenly hard and fiercely determined.

Chapter Nine

THE War Dogs of Tet came out of the dawn halflight, fierce yet unbarking, to sprawl at his feet, eager for approval and attention.

Tet, resplendent in bright silver-and-red half armor and a blue-and-green kilt with a tall-crested war helmet in his arm crook, chuckled at them, patted their broad heads in turn, and scratched their necks, ears, and bellies.

To Crimeye they were fearsome creatures—dark brown and huge with burning eyes and great, long, sharp teeth. He would have cringed back from their presence had he not thought it would only attract their attention and insult their master, the Chief of Highlandorm.

They saw him and came to sniff his boots and make questioning growls, until the chief told them Crimeye's name and said he was "friend." Then the war leader listened to their reports, delivered in sniffs, growls, whines, and half barks, plus much shaking of heads and wagging of tails. They spoke to him, one at a time, starting with their leader, Braggor, the largest and most fearsome of them all.

"Braggor says, and the others agree, that Eunicet is now completely within the Outer Circle," Tet said at last to Crimeye. He had taken a liking to the little ex-spy messenger from the Wizard Flarman. Crimeye was not at all sure the honor was deserved—or safe—but he held his tongue, a practice he had learned was wise in his dealings with great men.

"Once Eunicet is within the Outer Circle he will be more easily cut off from resupply and his line of retreat . . . and we can harass him to death, no matter which way he goes. His only escape would be to the north, which would put him into Iron Hills, where there is no water and no wood to burn with

winter coming on. We depend on Thornwood Duke to cut
him off if he tries to go south to Sea.''

"But, Chief Tet," said Crimeye, "we must fight Eunicet
before we can drive him either north or south."

"Of course, my friend. Of course! And that is why I'm
listening to my War Dogs, here. They can tell me exactly
where Eunicet's van is at this moment, and from that I can
tell you when he will be in position for our attentions.''

He listened again to the Dogs before he sent them off to
be fed and groomed, and to rest before darkness came and
time to send them out among the enemy once more.

Then he gestured to Crimeye to come with him. They
walked beyond the tented encampment of the Foreforces of
Highlandorm and sat upon a stone at the edge of a cliff
overlooking Tetgard, Highlandorm's capital. It lay across a
half mile of dark blue water from where they sat; a squat,
strong, blue-black complex of walls and towers, piers that
reached skinny fingers out into the fjord, clutching huddled
fishing boats and a few larger vessels with the high, ornately
carved dragon stems of the Highlandorm Navy.

It would have been a drab sight except for the multicol-
ored flags and pennants flying from the towers and the bright
flower beds beside the seawalls and beneath the towers.

Beyond, Sea showed through a narrow mouth, heaving
and rolling restlessly and endlessly, as if awaiting a storm.
The far gray-blue horizon was empty except for a single
spire of rock in the middle of the fjord's mouth.

"Has it a name?" asked Crimeye, pointing at the islet.

"Oh, yes," said Tet, spreading his thick, red-and-black
cloak so that he would not have to sit with his bare thighs
against the chill, damp stone. "We call it Faeryship Rock
ourselves, but my ma'am once told me that Royal Faeries
once used to live there in exile at some far distant time, and
they called it Trudys Isle, or sommat like.

"Nae, sit ye," and he slid aside to make room on the rock,
laying aside his heavy-hilted sword and thigh-length dagger,
each gleaming sharp but without jewel or decoration, save a
single line of some unknown—to Crimeye—lettering.

Crimeye sat, still looking out at Faeryship Rock as the
Chief of Highlandorm continued to talk.

"The Dogs say Eunicet will be deep between the Circles
by nightfall, except for an afterguard of a hundred and fifty

men, mostly archers with their purple martin-feathered
shafts. Poor martins! I always did like those homey souls in
their big rookeries. Yon Ice Devil must have slaughtered
thousands to get so many of their feathers for his arrows. Ah,
weel . . . as I was saying, Eunicet will be approaching the
Inner Wall sometime tomorrow, late. And then . . .''

"Aye, and then?''

"We will be awaiting the pretender as he tries to climb the
Gut and drive him back between Circles. With Wayness's
fleet bottling the Seaside, they will have to fight their way
back to Dukedom's borders or take their chances in the
north.''

Crimeye digested this for a moment, then asked, ''You
plan a frontal assault on Eunicet?''

"Hardly, for now. He outnumbers me two to one. I may
be a brave man but I am not entirely foolhardy. Nay! We will
be waiting for him in the Gut. You've seen the Gut, haven't
you? Well, we can cut his army in half if he doesn't show
some discretion there. And hold him for days or weeks or
longer, until our friend Thornwood arrives on the scene.''

He turned and gazed out to Sea.

"Aye, we need that Thornwood man, Duke or merchant
or skipper, whatever he prefers to be these days.''

"Thornwood is as good as his word, and the word of
Flarman Flowerstalk! He will be here. Only wind and tide
can tell when, however.''

"Ever thus! Yet if I could have warning of his approach
and tell him exactly what and where to look for Eunicet's
Sea flank . . . then this battle is as good as won and over for
us. You tell me his plan was to swing wide to the east before
driving straight north to Tetgard Fastness. It is all but impossible to find a ship at Sea, they tell me, and I have too few
ships to go looking for him.''

"Yet, sir, I would send the seven you have, nonethe-
less . . .''

"They even now are preparing to sail. I have forethought
you, Crimeye Farrunner. They will try, at least, to intercept
Thornwood's fleet.''

A breath of chill sprang out of the northeast and whipped
the kilt about the chieftain's bare, scarred knees, ruffling the
fur on his war bonnet's crest.

Crimeye shuddered, yet made bold to say, ''I may presume on our new friendship, I think, good Tet, when I make a suggestion.''

"Od's kneecaps, mon!'' the warrior chief laughed. "Of course not. Anything, to my life!''

"No, your life is more precious to me in your own hands, sir. Let me go with one of the seven ships when they sail to find Thornwood.''

"You would prefer to fight from the deck of a ship?'' Tet said, amazed that anyone would rather stand on a bounding deck than on firm, rockbound land. Shipboard fighting was, to him, the very worst of folly, to be avoided at almost any cost.

"No, no, no,'' said the messenger, shaking his head until his ears flew out sideways. "No, but if I could climb yon Faeryship Rock, I could see Thornwood's ships before they come into sight of land and turn them to Westfee directly. Thornwood taught me certain private signals by flags or fire that I can use to warn him and also tell you of his presence.''

"Ah! There's not a coward's heart! Certain, nor a fool's head. Here, I'll give one of the seven ships of mine to you and the crew and captain are to stay with you at the Rock. Under your command until you sight the fleet and bespeak Thornwood with your flags.''

"I . . . I, in command? Oh, sir! Perhaps I should stay on the Rock by myself? The ship will be of greater value to you in this fight.''

"Not so! Your mission is all-important. In addition, I value you as well. Ship *Clarice* is yours. Here,'' he said, and tore a sheet from his order book and began scribbling on it furiously. "Better go at once, friend. Eunicet draws closer and closer to the Gut, or I miss my guess. As for me, I'll take my chances on foot on land, as I always have in the past, thank you. Now get on your way and signal me when the fleet is in the offing.''

To the west in a camp newly pitched at the foot of the Inner Wall, Eunicet and his chief lieutenants prepared for their assault on Tetgard Fastness. Scouts had reported the Gut unfortified, although not unguarded—they had not actually seen any of the Highlandorm warriors up the steep canyon but there had been movement at the top, too distant to make out from below.

The facts made Bladder, an old freebooter, uneasy but only added to the Duke's growing sense of triumph.

"They'll run from us, my dear Bladder!" Eunicet crowed, beside himself with excitement. "Have another brandy."

Bladder shook his unkempt head of black hair and said, "Let us hope so, Your Grace."

He took up his long sword and resumed sharpening its two gleaming edges. Bladder might forget to shave or bathe, but he never neglected his weapons. Eunicet turned from the brandy flagon with raised eyebrows and a raised cup.

"Here's to our victory on the morrow," he said pompously. "And to all our future victories!"

"Yes, Your Grace. Better to get some sleep now, Your Grace. I must check the guard and get to bed myself within the hour."

"Oh, come, Bladder! A bit of fine brandy will only serve to make you sleep sounder," scoffed the Duke. Bladder stood his ground; he knew Eunicet with a morning hangover was bound to be even more irritable and contentious than usual, questioning every decision.

He breathed a silent sigh of relief when the Duke sulkily stoppered the brandy flagon and threw it to his wine steward. As the General left the tent with a bow, the Duke was already composing himself on a vast feather bed that took six men to carry on the march and half filled the huge tent.

Tet stood on a rocky prominence looking down at the campfire in the deep valley. The fires were burning low now, and Eunicet's scouts had retreated back down the Gut. Tet's men, hidden there against the morning's attack, could relax a bit and eat their cold supper and get some sleep.

"I must get some sleep myself," he said with a yawn.

An hour after midnight, Crimeye awoke. He got up from his hard bed on the flat rock summit of Faeryship Rock, strode to the low parapet, and studied Sea to the south. The sky was ink black. No stars gleamed through the overcast. Sea was a black of another sort, intense indigo, but here and there a submerged rock exploded into a lighter gray, as breakers hurled themselves to destruction. The sound of their continuous thunder reached the lookout.

One low star seemed out of place and much too long in the

wink. He watched as two things happened: the slow blink steadied into a continuous beam—and was joined by a second, then a third and a fourth, all blinking slowly at first, then burning steadily, all clumped together near the watery horizon.

The captain of *Clarice* had lent him a sailor's night glass, which he trained on the mysterious lights. There was little more to see than he could see with his own, unaided eyes. Yet, even knowing so little about Sea, he guessed immediately that these were masthead lights of several ships—a fleet, in fact! The only fleet he knew of in these waters was that of Wayness under Thornwood.

He shook his Seaman assistant's shoulder urgently and together they studied the lights. The sailor agreed—they *were* ships just inside the circle of the horizon, coming slowly out of Lasting Mists.

"When will they come within hail?" asked the ex-spy. "By daylight?"

"Nay, by darkest night before first false dawn, the wind as it is and likely to stay. They'll stand off, as they don't know the approaches, though. Only a madman would seek to thread Tetgard Fastness in dark night."

"Perhaps. Yet we shall not take any chances. You signal *Clarice*. Ask her to come for us. I will follow after I've lighted the signal fire to tell Thornwood to await us. Go, now!"

The sailor darted for the top of the stairway and scrambled down, a dangerous thing to do in the dark. Crimeye gathered his bundle of straw and some cut lengths of wood. He swore mightily at the damp tinder and flint-and-steel until he caught a spark and blew it into a tiny flame, which he touched to the dry straw.

"Now, Thornwood, we'll see if old Crimeye can follow directions taught to him."

He sprinkled the smoldering straw and kindling with a few drops of an oil from a vial he had taken from his inner pocket.

Immediately, without charm spoken, the fire leaped into full life, bright and hot against the chill Sea winds. Its light was much brighter than an ordinary fire's. He added a sprinkle of whitish powder, and the flames turned from yellow to a brilliant red-orange. This continued for a minute before the flames returned to their original color. Repeating the sprinkling twice more, he created what he hoped would appear to the ships as a yellow-red-yellow-red flashing beacon. By the time he had finished the sequence, the fire was beginning to die.

Before that, he saw one of the masthead lights out in the darkness turn from white to red and back again three times. Three red winks. Message heard and understood.

The Wayness fleet had arrived!

Chapter Ten

EVEN in the field Eunicet's day centered on his person and his pleasures. The six-man feather bed was just one feature. A four-course breakfast, hot from the ovens and stoves of a corps of expert cooks who accompanied the Duke everywhere he went, was another. The meal arrived at his bedside at precisely nine o'clock, every day, in all places, all weathers and circumstances, served by seven pretty girls in provocative costumes.

On this battle morn the Duke of Dukedom ate all four courses with relish and gusto—as always, a dedicated trencherman. He ate and grappled playfully with his maids, giggling and choking, spilling food on the gorgeous brocade bedspreads.

Between the third course—honeycomb and delicate, fresh-baked wheaten cakes stuffed with roasted almonds— and the fourth—a small rasher of fine, lean bacon, marinated in brandy and served with delicately shirred eggs and a light fruit glaze—his three generals came to his tent and stood at attention in line before his bedfoot.

Eunicet patted his favorite chambermaid and gobbled bacon from her fingers, ignoring the officers until he had finished breaking fast and sent the dishes and girls away.

"Report," he said gruffly. It was his practice to try to speak in a low, growly voice, although his natural voice was rather high. "Make it short. You all have much to do. I must take my ride and then my bath and then morning tea and . . ."

Bladder cleared his throat and the Duke stopped detailing his morning routine abruptly. Eunicet was a little afraid of this bluff, short-tempered man. Bladder knew this and used it.

"Majesty . . . ," General Smorger began, knowing full well that the proper honorific was "Your Grace."

"Majesty, your Army is now entirely ready. The rear guard holds Outer Ring Pass. The rest of your troops are in position here at the foot of this Gut."

"Continue, General."

"Thank you, Majesty. The rearmost troop of cavalry came up during the night, as I say."

This lanky, dirty-looking man had been a highwayman and a horse thief. Eunicet imagined these qualified him as a General of Cavalry.

"Now, fine, General. Very efficient movement. I commend you. Now, you . . ."

He nodded to the second general. Formerly a livestock and dry-goods dealer, bald, with a pink cherubic face, he was General of Supply. He had become preposterously wealthy since Eunicet had snatched him from the Ducal prison some years before.

"I am pleased to report, Your Grace," he said, "that we have in camp sufficient food, drink, arms, and ammunition to last at least six days, providing no pitched battles are fought. In case of battle—and that's what we're here for, isn't it?—I estimate we have arms to fight for three days and nights if necessary, without stint. And, of course, we can expect a certain amount of attrition—"

"Wait, General, what do you mean, *attrition*?"

"Simply, Highness, that in battle we can always expect to have a certain percentage destroyed, killed, captured . . . and so on—in which case it is no longer necessary to provide those men with sustenance."

"Ah, yes, very well thought out, General! And have arrangements been completed to bring more supplies in by what's-its-name? The little seaport down on the coast?"

"As you yourself ordered, Highness," said the cattle-seller general.

"Excellent! I don't expect we will need extra food. But, of course, it will depend much on the success of General Bladder. Step forward, Bladder!"

Despite his unpleasant name and reputation, Bladder was a well-set-up man with thick, black hair and a good nose and brow, rather handsome in a beefy way. Twenty-four months earlier he had been in the Ducal prison, condemned to die for some unpleasantness with the daughter of a rural judge. Twenty-three months ago he had been among the first to see the advantages of enlisting in the Duke's Army. He also managed to persuade a hundred or so of his fellow inmates to enlist with him.

Three months later he was promoted to a lieutenancy; five months after that he earned promotion to Colonel by informing the Duke of thievery by his own superior officers.

In the depths of Dead Winter he discovered a hidden cache of food and drink hoarded by the father of his former mistress, and hanged him without trial.

In short, the new Colonel proved so useful, so resourceful, so quick to catch the brilliance of Eunicet's leadership, that long before the march to Highlandorm he had been brevetted General. He was younger than the other two general officers, but the most influential voice in the War Council. The other two hated his whole being, from his short-cropped black hair to long-cropped black toenails. But they were very pleased to give him full credit—or blame—for the actual conduct of battle.

Bladder had already learned the most important part of his job; not to put himself close to the shooting, lancing, slicing, stabbing, hacking, burning—and dying—of battle, so as not to endanger his valuable skin. He seldom left the Duke's side once the battle began.

He also was, as Flarman had observed some weeks earlier, a nasty, cruel, sly, mean-spirited liar.

"Your Magnificence," he addressed the Duke, "with all your troops in place, I can report that all is ready for our advance into the Gut and over the Wall to attack the Fastness of Tetgard."

"Do you propose," interjected General Smorger, "to proceed with the attack, even though the rear-guard cavalry troops are just now in camp?"

"Generals, Generals," cried Eunicet, waving his hands to dry them. He had just wiped away traces of his breakfast with a hot, scented towel. "Please let General Bladder speak for himself. But I admit, General, that I also am curious. Do you propose to . . . uh, proceed . . . immediately?"

"Only if Your Grace approves, of course," replied Bladder, humbly. "But, yes, that is the gist of my plan. We believe that the vaunted Highlandormers will, upon being vigorously assaulted, fall back at least as far as their Tetgard defenses. As for the horse troops . . . what use are horses in the climb to the top of the Gut?''

''Very well, General. Let the battle begin! However,'' he added, stopping them all as they turned away, ''I do wish you would hold things up long enough for me to take a short ride and a shorter bath. . . .''

Above the Gut, Tet munched a cold chicken leg and drank from a horn of breakfast ale. He saw the first of Eunicet's troops falling into line before their camp in the valley below.

''Well, they'll not wait longer,'' he said to his officers, seated among the rocks, some dozing in the morning sun. ''They are on their way up!''

In a moment everyone was up, scrabbling for weapons and parts of armor laid aside during the night.

''No haste, no need,'' their chieftain said. '' 'Twill take them at least an hour to muster and start the march, at the rate they're going. Finish your meal and then we'll ride over to see if all is ready for them. Have a stoup of this good ale. It was a hard winter for men but a good one for ale, it seems.''

The soldiers themselves expected some to die, more to be maimed, but that, as the balding commissary general had bravely said from his position in the rear, was part of war. It gave the troops something to think about other than poor food, forced marches, and the leather whips of their petty officers.

In fact, Dukedom's Army was in good spirits, singing marching songs as they swung around past the Duke's reviewing stand and into the Gut itself. Their officers saluted smartly and called for rounds of cheers from their men as they marched past.

An Army, thought Bladder, travels on its stomach—and wondered why no one had ever noticed that before. This Army had been better fed, and better housed withal, since the beginning of the campaign than they had ever been in training during the months of Dead Winter.

So they went cheerfully, glad if for no other reason than that the days of long marches and cold nights sleeping on the ground were at last nearing an end.

The vanguard began the climb. As Tet had predicted, they

took an hour to reach a level stretch near the top of the pass. Those who were not deafened by their own hoarse breathing and gasping—for the last third was a steep, hand-over-hand climb indeed—caught a curious, new sound.

"Thunder this time of the year?" they asked their companions, half laughing. "It cannot be! The sun still shines bright before us."

Down on the flat Bladder cocked an ear, too.

"Do you hear anything?" he asked the other generals.

"Sounds like wagon wheels on cobbles," observed the supply general, sleepily. He had been up late the night before sampling new wine that had been sent forward at the last moment. "Like teamsters rushing to try a new vintage . . ."

"You're daydreaming of old times," snarled the cavalry general, who had also excused himself from leading his troops in person. "It sounds like nothing but thunder to me, or . . ."

Far above, the first tight bunch of soldiers stared up in horror. Roaring down on them were half a dozen enormous boulders. They bounded down the steep slope between the Gut's walls, leaping higher and higher with each bound, ringing like bells against the hard ground. They smashed and split, baring razor-sharp edges, blades of glistening raw stone as long as a man is tall.

Eunicet's vanguard froze in horror, then turned as one to flee. They literally flew, almost not touching the ground at all so steep was the way. Some thought to dash to the sides of the Gut only to be flattened against the walls. A lucky few wriggled into cracks or huddled under overhanging rocks, only to be buried alive as the sides collapsed.

Others, not as quick, pitched head over heels down the hill, screaming in fear and pain. They crashed into the horrified lines of pikemen below them.

More great stones smashed into the second line, carrying whole companies before them. Hundreds of crushed bodies were flung down the mountainside.

Many of the third line of soldiers, seeing death crashing and screaming from above, leaped into empty space to either side rather than face the terrible juggernaut of stone and bloody bodies. By then the big stones were joined by rocks torn from the sides of the Gut. Some were the size of houses, some merely the size of marbles that flew at terrifying speed to smashing impacts.

A great cloud of dust arose, choking and blinding both the climbers and the watchers below. Shrill orders were shouted by officers from the safety of the flat. Louder and more profane orders from sergeants in the Gut itself conflicted with them. Even unengaged troops were driven into wild confusion.

This rear guard poured like a flood of waters from the bottom of the Gut, around the camp and onto the rocky flat beyond, gibbering in terror. When a few braver officers attempted to whip them back into ranks the soldiers turned on them, slaughtering them almost to a man.

Finally the rocks stopped falling and the beaten soldiers lay down where they were, panting and sobbing, ranting and raving. Slowly those who survived slinked back to camp, beginning to brag about their courage.

From beginning to end the Battle of the Gut lasted fewer than fifty minutes.

That was as far as Eunicet's Army ever got in their march on Highlandorm. Bladder, recognizing the futility of the situation, if not the downright danger of its mood, ordered the Army that remained to hold the camp in a state of siege.

"They can't get at us. I propose to keep them occupied for a day or two, showing enough strength so they are convinced we mean to try again," he said to Eunicet and the other generals in the evening.

"And then?" sneered the Duke coldly. He could not abide failure . . . in anyone but himself.

"And then we'll call up the supply ships that are waiting down the coast . . ."

"Of course, we must do that or we will be out of arrows and food," said the Supply General. "Do you realize how many arrows were lost in that damnable Gut? Not fired, but just lost! Outrageous!"

"Be silent, you old goat, or better yet, go and signal for the fleet to come up from whatever that place is down the coast," shouted the Duke. "Go! Now!"

As the Supply General slunk away, secretly pleased to be out of range of the Duke's frightened fury, Eunicet turned once more, dangerously sweet, to Bladder.

"Go on, dear Bladder. What do you propose?"

Thinking furiously, Bladder drew himself up on his stool, saying, "I thank Your Grace for your confidence in my abilities. It was hardly my fault that the attack today went badly. Who could have foreseen an attack by stones? Only savages would have thought of it!"

"Who, indeed?" murmured Eunicet dangerously. "Your plan?"

"Ah, yes, my plan," said the petty thief and philanderer, stalling for time and an inspiration. Then his face cleared and he smiled, brightly.

"Here it is, Sir Duke! We won't need the supplies in those ships down the coast, but I propose to use the ships themselves. Perhaps we cannot get up the Gut, but the plateau is not really our goal, is it? I mean, our goal is to take Tetgard Fastness, isn't it? Tell me if I am wrong."

"No, you are right," agreed the Cavalry General, smiling sarcastically. "But how do you propose to take the Fastness without taking the plateau first?

"You're a fool, also, General," said Eunicet suddenly. "Of course, I see! I'll attack the Fastness from the Sea!"

"Perfect, perfect!" cried Bladder, who had the ideal attribute of a flunky—making his own ideas seem like his master's. The Duke would think of them as his own, not recalling that, in the end, the responsibility would be his own, also.

"We will load the cargo ships with the best of our troops . . ."

"At night," added the Duke.

"At night, of course; brilliant idea, Your Grace! Can you do that, Cavalry?"

"Of course; simple!" barked the horse thief, who had not the faintest idea how you loaded a thousand men and horses on a dozen ships, in darkness.

"Then we'll slip around the end of this Inner Wall, attack Tetgard Fastness at dawn from the Sea. When they see we are at their backs, Tet will send troops from the top of the Wall to the Fastness. The balance of our soldiers, left here, will see them withdraw, and will attack up the Gut once again, this time taking it all."

"Brilliant! Purely brilliant," shouted the remaining General and Eunicet, who hopped off his traveling throne and did a jig around it.

"I'll lead the Sea attack in person, Sir," declared Bladder, who fancied the idea of riding to battle on a stately ship. "You must wait for our signal here when the fortress falls, and ride up the Gut and over the plateau to enter in triumph."

Otherwise, he thought to himself, you will just be in my way.

The messenger from Seatower reached the walls of the Fastness. He found the Chief at breakfast eating crisply fried mush and delicious, sweet little whitefish, freshly caught in the Fastness fjord.

"Sir, we have seen twelve boats filled with soldiers leaving Westfee and heading east."

He described what he and his mates had seen and heard. The burly Chieftain chewed his breakfast fish without comment until the report was fully made. Then he turned to Thornwood, who had come ashore to share breakfast with him.

"Now, that's news we've been waiting for, True Duke. Eunicet intends to sail around and attack the Fastness by water."

"As you expected," agreed Thornwood, swallowing his last bite of whitefish. "With your permission, I'll ask Captain Pelance to carry me out to my fleet, immediately. . . ."

Tet bid him good hunting and watched him trot toward the docks.

"Where will my *Donation* be?" Thornwood asked Pelance.

"Standing off and on in the Lasting Mists, toward Meridian Banks, my Lord," answered the Captain. "We'll reach her in an hour or a wink more, with this wind. Sooner if it shifts easterly as it usually does after the sun is up," he added.

"We'll be ready for them in their fat-sided wallowers," said Thornwood grimly.

The crew and officers of *Clarice* were in fine spirits. To set out on a cool, beautiful fall morning, having had ample breaking of fast and before that a sound night's sleep tied to a bollard under the safe loom of the Fastness, was their idea of high adventure . . . especially when they carried an important person to his seaborne fleet. Good humor seemed to lend wings to the pert little ship.

Thornwood stood with Crimeye as they approached *Donation*, smiling grimly. "Crimeye, go back as swiftly as you can and keep a watch from the top of Faeryship Rock. Keep us aware of Eunicet's progress by signal flags. But take care, for you are a friend worth safekeeping."

The ex-spy saluted grandly, grinned in excited anticipation, and as soon as the Wayness commodore had swung himself aboard his flagship he ordered *Clarice*'s crew to make for Faeryship Rock once again, with a freshening east wind abeam, as Pelance had predicted.

Donation swung on her heel and disappeared in the mist.

Chapter Eleven

IT was night, a few days after the Battle of the Gut, although they did not yet know of it in Valley. Bronze Owl was perched on the cantle of a saddle filled by the once-well-rounded rump of farmer Possumtail, now captain of the Valley Patrol. The Man and the Owl chatted amiably as the Patrol rode the eastern end of Valley.

"How far are we from Sea?" a young rider asked. "I've never seen the ocean meself."

One of the patrolmen had gone to Wayness with Crimeye in the spring, and tried to describe Sea to the landlubber. He ventured that the nearest Seashore was perhaps twenty miles from where they now rode.

"A long enough way, yet just then I would take oath that I smelled Sea," said another patrolman. "There! I catch it again on that breeze. Smell it?"

All six horsemen reined in their mounts and raised their noses to sniff the light breeze blowing, sure enough, from the east.

"I think," said Possumtail a moment later, "I think . . . I smell something strange. Is that Sea I smell?"

"Be warned, Captain," laughed a young soldier. "They have a saying on the Farango Waters: Just to smell Sea is to become a sailor."

"Bosh and rot!" scoffed the farmer. They all chuckled at the idea of Possumtail aboard a ship. "I am a man of the soil and barnyard. No Sea for me!"

"Yet it is Sea I smell, too," claimed Bronze Owl. "And that is rather unusual, believe me, for I know the winds and we seldom get even a hint of Sea breeze over High Ridges. Something is happening over there to the east."

A few minutes later the horsemen turned homeward at the

end of their eastward patrol. Sea was still in the air when
Bronze Owl spread his wings and silently lifted himself
toward the crescent moon.

"What's he after, with all that talk of Sea smell?" asked
Possumtail in wonder. They all accepted the metal magic
bird as a companion, respected for his wisdom and night
vision. But the bird, they pointed out, was not "born of the
egg," like all the fowl they had ever known. Despite their
trust in Flarman, there were mysteries they did not care to
fathom too deeply.

Bronze Owl climbed high and higher until the Ridges
separating Sea from the Valley spread beneath him in the
faint light of the narrow moon. He glided silently back and
forth in wide, easy loops, testing the updrafts of the ocean
wind against the rising ridges, looking ever downward and
out to Sea.

He saw three glimmering, white dots racing down the
wind toward the broken land in swift, straight-line, purposeful flight. Bronze Owl waited patiently until the three turned
to beat long, graceful white wings for altitude to clear the
ridges, and then he slid down a slope of air toward them.
Could be messengers, could be spies.

"Sea Gulls," he said to himself. "A night flight of Gulls
from the northeast. Well, we'll soon see. . . ."

He made a quick, noiseless circle almost over the birds,
now topping the highest of the Ridges. A swoop, a fearsome
hooting call, and he was upon them. They had either to turn
back against the breeze or drop down to the rocks below. The
largest gull, pure white except for a black diamond on his
breast and a black tip on each wing, hardly hesitated. Safety
lay in the open water where Seabirds could alight and the
land bird could not. Yet he chose to dive for the rocks,
hoping to reach the solid earth in time to organize his trio for
defense.

The Owl circled without a sound as the leader Gull ordered his two companions to stand back to back with him,
facing outward, sharp beaks agape and thrust forward to
meet an attack. With a strong backsweep of metal wings and
a bell-like clatter, Bronze Owl came to an almost complete
stop, hovering over the three. He cried in a commanding
voice: "Who are you and why do you fly this way by night,

Seabirds? Answer truly, for I am set to guard this coast and the Valley beyond the Ridges.''

"Alight so we can talk more easily," said the leader Gull, craftily. "Tell us your authority and we'll tell you our mission."

Owl was suddenly on the ground facing them.

"Fool of a land lover," screamed the White Gull. "Now we have you!"

And he leaped forward, his beak outthrust for the first blow to his enemy's breast.

"Ho, ho, wait now," cried Bronze Owl, placating. "Now, stop . . ."

The Gull's hard beak struck his breast and rang Owl like a bell. The force of the stab against unyielding bronze hurled the gull to the ground, dazing him and leaving him at the mercy of an attacker.

"Now, now, I'm not going to hurt you," soothed the Owl. "You can't . . ."

The other two birds rushed at him, hoping to save their leader, and they too were sent reeling.

" . . . hurt me."

The three gazed in such awe at him that it struck Owl as funny, and he began to laugh.

"Now for goodness' sake," he said between chuckles, putting out a claw, "settle down and let's not get hurt. Come back here and talk!" This last to the third Gull who had launched himself downwind.

"Tell your boy to come back," Owl added to the leader Gull, now almost recovered from his shock. "I'm not going to hurt anybody. If you were sent by our Enemy, I'll send you back—or give you a decent burial at Sea, if you choose to fight. If you are from friends . . . well, perhaps I can help you on your way."

Seeing that fight or flight were going to get him nowhere, the leader recalled the fleeing member of his party. He turned to Bronze Owl and said, "Just who *is* your Enemy? I am not sure if he is *my* Enemy. And if he isn't, we'll just have to try to get you, metal monster. Or die trying!"

Said Owl, "I serve our Valley folk, the Wizard Flarman Firemaster, and the rightful Duke, Thornwood of Wayness."

"You have said two names we revere," said the White Gull. "We serve Thornwood Duke and bring a war message

from him to the same Flarman Firemaster. We have flown
from Tetgard this day and night with no rest at all. Were we
fully fed and strengthened, we might have been able to best
you, bird of night.''

Bronze Owl laughed. ''No, you could not daunt me, for I
am of pure bronze and magic source.''

''I have no way to prove my good offices,'' said the Gull,
slowly. ''I was told a certain word to say to the Firemaster
when I found him. If you can lead us to the Wizard, then I
can show my trustworthiness.''

'' 'Tis foolhardy, these days, to trust any without proof.
Fly after me westward and seven trees high. We'll reach
Wizard's High in an hour and you'll meet Flarman by midnight. But stay in line behind me,'' he warned as they rose
from the ridge top. ''I can and will strike down any of you
who does not follow strictly my lead.''

They had noted his sharp talons and cruel-looking spurs,
and were duly impressed.

Owl swooped down only to speak a word of explanation
to Possumtail, then led the three Gulls toward the High.

''You spoke of Thornwood as 'Duke,' '' the owl asked,
flying easily. ''Has he then decided to assume the Ducal
coronet?''

''Since you ask, no. Thornwood still styles himself 'merchant' and 'Seacaptain,' '' the Gull said flatly. ''Men, however, address him ever more often as 'Duke' and 'Grace.' ''

''And where is he now? I know he was sailing north and
east to Tetgard Fastness. What happened? Was there battle?''

''In time. In time,'' answered the first Gull. ''Right now
I am in a hurry to bring messages and news to the wizard and
must use all my breath for flying.''

''I understand,'' said the metal bird and he stepped up his
speed until all three gulls *had* to use all their breath to remain
closely behind.

Douglas Brightglade dozed by the Dwarf's fireplace.
Nearby Blue Teakettle whistled him soft lullabies. The
dishes washed themselves quietly and put themselves away.
It had been a very long, hard day and the young apprentice
had not even made it from the supper table, where he had
eaten a late meal. Kittenish Pert leaped onto his lap and

curled herself contentedly, watching the utensils move about, and then fell into a light catnap.

But she heard the coming of the Bronze Owl and realized he was accompanied by other birds, smelling of fish and ship's tar in a strange new way. She dug a warning claw into Douglas's thigh, dropped to the hearth with a loud *plumpity*, then stood staring at the kitchen door expectantly.

Douglas came awake in an instant, feeling for his belt knife as he jumped to his feet. Following the cat's gaze he saw the kitchen door swing open to Owl's push.

"Why, Pert, 'tis only Bronze Owl," he said, yawning, and then stopped when he spied the trio of White Gulls, waddling in awkward single file behind his old friend. "Guests?"

"Messengers, they say," answered the Owl cautiously. "Looking for Flarman. Is he here?"

"As far as I know," said Douglas, sheathing his knife. "Come in, friends. Can we offer you food? You have obviously come a long way to see us."

"Met them beyond the Ridges above the shore," Bronze Owl explained, settling himself on the back of the settle. "Here, Seabirds, roost yourselves."

"Be hospitable!" admonished the Apprentice. "What can I offer you for dinner, Gulls?"

"Fish . . . er, if you have any," said the first Gull. "Or bread, or any meat, or whatever you have. We have flown for a night and a day to reach the home of Flarman Firemaster, as this bronze bird says it is."

"Oh, it is, it is!" said Douglas. "I am Douglas Brightglade, the Wizard Flarman's apprentice. The master is sleeping, I judge, but the lady cat has gone to wake him. Blue, can we give these good Seabirds something to drink and eat? Ah, I thought you'd have something. . . ."

Scraps of fish from Crooked Brook were produced—there were times Blue Teakettle seemed a magician herself—and the gulls were soon dining on the first freshwater fish they had ever tasted.

"A little lacking in salt, if I may make a polite observation," said their leader. Douglas showed him how to use Salt Shaker.

The wizard himself arrived in a swirl of night robe, and the very sight of him immediately set the Gulls' fears to rest.

There could be no mistaking the Wizard, they said. And they had messages for his ears.

"You can speak freely in this house to anyone in it," said Flarman. "We are all friends here and soldiers of one sort or another in the fight against the Ice King. What messages and what news?"

The first Gull strode importantly to the edge of the kitchen table, carefully avoiding Blue Teakettle, who was offering more fish to his companions. He settled down, showing weariness in his ruffled feathers.

"My name is Cerfew," he began. "I am lead flight in the Flock known as Brittleshell Whites, of whom you may have heard, even this far inland. I've never been this far from Sea myself.

"My companions are my wife, Trotta, and my eldest son, Tratto. We come from a long line of far, fast, and high-flying clan leaders. When messages are to be carried we are usually selected to deliver them. We have good memories, which is important because common gulls are chuckleheads and can hardly remember their own names.

"Several years ago we were on the Isles of Wayness, as you call them. We call them Brightshore," he added, aside to Douglas, "because the sand there is so white. We were in Wayness and made friends with a Seacaptain named Thornwood."

"We know Thornwood well, and are his friends, too," said Flarman, nodding.

"So the Bronze Owl said," agreed Cerfew. "Since then we have often carried orders and messages between his ships and between the ships and the shore. The good captain insists on paying us in fresh bread crumbs. We love 'em, although it tends to make us fat. When he set sail for Highlandorm some weeks ago he asked me to guide his fleet—seven tall ships in all—as the year was getting old and the storms and mists of Meridian Banks are increasing."

The Gull paused to sip a bit of warm tea from a cup Blue Teakettle had placed beside him, raising his head to let the liquid slide down his throat.

"We arrived off Meridian Banks right on the dot and on schedule—perfect navigation, if I do say so myself. We were met by signals from atop Faeryship Rock. A small fishing boat came out to meet us in the mist and a man you know, one Crimeye ...''

"We all know old Crimeye," said Douglas, surprised. "He is still with Tet in Highlandorm?"

"Apparently," said the Gull, dryly, "for he brought messages from the Chief to the Duke, then took Thornwood back to shore.

"And they came back, telling all that boats were coming eastward with Eunicet's army to attack the Fastness by way of the fjord. The Army had been beaten at the Gut the day before. To attempt to circle by water and attack Tetgard Fastness from Sea! A foolhardy thing to try at the best of times by the very best of sailors!

"To make the story shorter, the boats had come up to Westfee Inlet and loaded horses, soldiers, war machines, and weapons. They then sailed—wallowed would be a better word—around Seatower Point and right up to Faeryship Rock, which they reached just as the wind changed.

"'Twas a fine, bright cool morning and Sea was as smooth as an egg. All the gulls, terns, bitterns, kestrels, frigates, eiders, and every kind of Seabird came from miles around, including some Highlandorm vultures who don't usually come more than a wingspan to Sea. We sat on the cliffs to watch the show.

"Just as the first of these twelve Army tubs pushed into the shadow of Faeryship Rock the wind took them aback and they stopped. Out from the mist came Thornwood's *Donation, Tolbrand, Fareacher, Brightwing*, and all the other Wayness ships. From the mouth of the Fastness Fjord sailed the five vessels of Tet's navy, too, led by Captain Pelance in his swift *Clarice*. I was above it all and saw Thornwood, on the quarterdeck of *Donation*, sword in hand. And on *Clarice*—young Crimeye with a claymore almost as long as he is tall.

"They had the wind, our ships. Bladder had to put out oars and drive his foot soldiers to pull them. Wasn't that a sight! We figure that even without the opposing fleets, Bladder would have lost half his boats on the rocks, just trying to make Fastness's entrance.

"Ah, as it was the Waynessmen and Tet's doughty fisherfolk came down like sharks on them and in the first clash sank or disabled two freighters. The others turned tail and sailed downwind without even stopping at Westfee Inlet. The ten remaining boats put up a short, sharp fight. Some blood was spilled, most of it on Eunicet's side.

"Pelance's *Clarice* closed on the flagship and boarded her first. Pelance was cut and Crimeye stood over him with his claymore until he could be carried back aboard *Clarice*. It was touch and go, as sailors say, but the bold attack gave *Donation* time to come down on the other quarter and board her in force.

"Five minutes of slash, stab, and hack was enough to make Eunicet's crew and land soldiers throw down their arms and strike their flag. The false Duke wasn't even there! I saw his commodore, one Bladder, escape in a whaleboat at the very last moment, deserting his crew. I tried to warn Thornwood, but by the time I got through to him, Bladder had disappeared toward Westfee Inlet.

"With the flagship struck, all the others surrendered, too. Close to five hundred men were captured alive. Three times that many went to feed the sharks. Sea will be fouled for days!

"Tet told us when word of Bladder's defeat came, Eunicet ordered the rest of his Army to pack up his tent and retreat to Freg, hoping to meet the boats there, I suppose. But just then, Highlandormers charged out of the Gut and cut the rest of the Army to pieces.

"By nightfall it was all over. The next morning Tet, who thought he had captured the usurping Duke, found that the man they had snared in Eunicet's pavilion and in Eunicet's clothes was not the Duke at all, but one of his Generals. Last I heard Tet had put him to work in the Fastness middens."

"And what of the false Duke?" asked Flarman.

"Oh, Eunicet escaped north, into the Wastelands. He might have fared better if he had let himself be taken. Wastelands are barren, waterless, rough as shagreen, and death to travelers."

"I suspect," the Wizard said, shaking his head, "that Eunicet knew what he was about. With a little help from his wicked master he can make it through the badlands north by east to Perpetual Ice."

The Gull leader nodded in turn and sipped more tea.

"There isn't much more to tell. Most of the Army was taken prisoner or killed. Those few who did manage to escape through the Outer Ring into Landsend are being pursued by Highlandormers, and those who fled to Dwelmland are being hunted by Dust Devils. They will be lucky to be captured by Dwarfs! For the others, there is no food left between Highlandorm and Capital, I hear. Eunicet's soldiers ate it all on their march east.''

''Send word to Frenstil and Possumtail,'' Flarman interrupted to say to Douglas. ''As soon as it is light. The militia must be alerted to handle the stragglers who get through to Valley.''

Flarman turned to Cerfew. ''What of our friends? Was Thornwood hurt, or Crimeye? Tet would have enjoyed the whole thing on land, I am sure.''

''All hale and hearty! Thornwood is now hailed as Duke,'' said Cerfew, ''although he is overmodest about it, I think.''

''I suspect he'll agree, now that Eunicet has been driven away or been killed, whatever,'' sighed the Wizard.

Douglas looked at the Firemaster closely, seeing a mixture of triumph and anxiety in his deeply lined face. ''We have at least won a battle and I know that it is only the first and least of our battles. Yet we *did* win. There is some advantage in that, sir.''

Flarman Firemaster grinned suddenly and it was like sunshine after a black storm. He smiled, sat for a long minute, stroking his beard and looking into space. At last he smiled at his own abstraction and thanked the Gull with a pat on the wing. With a last sip of tea, the three seabirds slipped out the door to find roosting spots.

''I must be getting ready to leave . . . ,'' Flarman began.

''Leave?'' cried Douglas. ''Leave? I had thought—''

''Sorry to disappoint you, my boy. Frigeon is about to move. Into Warm Seas, you understand, where he can do the utmost harm to World. I have a mission to perform. So I must go pack.''

He got to his feet, and despite the seriousness of his look, there was a look of excitement, a glow of anticipation in his eyes.

''And it is time for you to go, too. I need you to journey to Dwelmland and Bryarmote's caverns.''

''Which,'' he went on, walking toward the hall and the stairs, ''is only fitting. You are no longer my Apprentice!''

Douglas stared up at him on the stairs in complete dismay and shocked disbelief as Flarman Flowerstalk leaned over from the first landing and smiled down at him.

"Journeying requires a Journeyman, you see."

"A . . . a . . . a Journeyman? Me! But . . . but," Douglas sputtered in confusion. "But I know hardly any magic at all! How can I be Journeyman? I have too much, too much to learn, Magister!"

"No," said Flarman firmly. "No, you are graduated. Matriculated. Whatever. As for magic, you know more than you realize. More than you believe."

Douglas looked after him, stunned. Then he walked slowly back into the kitchen and stopped in front of the Dwarf's fireplace. A fire was laid for dinner, Blue Teakettle had seen to that. Owl perched himself on a chair back, grooming his feathers quietly.

"Journeyman," he said aloud to himself at last. He raised his right hand and pointed at the logs in the grate.

Immediately a thin tendril of blue smoke spiraled upward from a bright spark under the foremost log. Then a yellow flame licked at the wood merrily. Kindling caught and the chimney began to draw. Thick smoke, fragrant and white from the hot burning pine wood, rose straight up and disappeared as the heat increased.

"Journeyman!" sang the former Apprentice. "Blue, put out the good dishes and let's celebrate at dinner tonight! Just you and me and our Master, the cats and Bronze Owl, and I think I'll call Deka the Wraith, and Lilac and Priceless . . . to say good-bye to childhood and student days . . . and to Flarman, once again."

Chapter Twelve

A painfully thin man shuffled painfully along an ice blue corridor lit by a cold, blue emanation from all directions and no direction at all. He turned an abrupt corner and met a tall, bulky man coming the other way. They stopped to look suspiciously at one another.

The very thin man shivered in the everlasting cold. He wore the faded, ragged remnants of silk brocade pantaloons and a thin blue cloak over a velvet doublet, which was open to his waist. His fingers were wrapped in scraps of an old blanket and his feet were showing unhealthy blue-gray toes through his boots.

The younger man was warmly dressed in leather and wool. He had a wool-lined steel helmet on his head with an ermine tail for a plume. His thick-soled boots gleamed with waterproofing oils.

"Bladder?" whined Eunicet, his voice as thin and cold as his body. "Bladder, get me some warm clothing. Better yet, get out of those things you have on. I've been so cold since I came here. . . ."

Bladder, late General of the Dukedom Army, threw back his shaggy head and laughed cruelly.

"Eunie," he gasped between amused chuckles, "Eunie . . ."

"I am your Duke!" shrieked the other, waving his bandaged hands. "Obey me on pain of death!"

"You thin, little piece of weasel castings," said the other, turning angry and mean eyed. "You are no longer Duke of anything and dare not presume to give orders or act so high and mighty. You've lost your Dukedom and your powers and your wealth, don't you understand? You are nothing! Mere garbage! Offal!"

119

Eunicet's face crumpled and his shivering increased piteously, so that even the coarse ex-General was moved. This quaking wreck had, after all, raised Bladder to high command.

"Now, then, it isn't really that bad, is it, old man? Here, put this on." And he gave the weeping man his fur-lined cloak. "What do you say? Come and have a hot drink and warm up . . . as much as you can in this place."

"I went to see Frigeon," Eunicet told Bladder when they sat on either side of a tiny charcoal brazier in Bladder's quarters. "He kept me waiting! Always before it was 'Eunicet, my friend' or 'Your Grace, have a sip of warming liquor.' This time he kept me waiting for a full three days!"

"But you got to see him, in the end. He *is* a very busy King, after all."

"Aye, for about two minutes. No, even less than that. He didn't even thank me for what we had done for him. He simply looked at me with those terrible, chill eyes of his and never once smiled. He growled at me, 'Eunicet, you stupid fool! What am I to do with you, now?'

"I thought he meant to put me to death right then and there. I tried to explain—"

"You mean," interrupted Bladder with a grin, "you tried to beg his forgiveness. You groveled."

"Well . . . yes, I admit that. Why not? I—we—tried our best. He said that, really."

"What? That we had done our best?"

"Yes. Yes, he said, 'You did just about as well as I expected, no more, no less.' That means we did as he had wished, doesn't it?"

"Let it pass. He didn't have you tossed out on the Floes, naked, which is his favorite way of dealing out death. Then he and his people watch you freeze to death through those big ice windows behind his throne."

Eunicet turned even bluer, if that was possible. "No, he simply dismissed me. No food has been given. No fire, not even a place like this to sleep in."

Bladder nodded indulgently and changed the subject. Frigeon had not indicated what he would do with his former ally? There was no task assigned?

"None. I will die here! I can't find the stairs to climb to the warmer levels. I've wandered about for days!"

There was a mad gleam in his eyes that startled and frightened his former officer. Bladder found and gave him a pair of cast-off boots and a piece of half-stale, frozen bread to eat.

"Well, sir, I guess as Frigeon doesn't have any job for you, I could use you. . . ."

"Use me? *Use me! I am a Duke!* Noble blood flows in my veins. People serve me, not I, people. How dare . . . ?"

Suddenly he calmed down. Even his half-crazed brain realized that he would have to eat and earn warm clothing to survive another day. And Bladder was obviously in better favor with the Ice King than he. Once fed and clothed and housed, he could bide his time, couldn't he?

"What will you ask of me, good old Bladder?"

"Get yourself a place to sit and write. I need a man who can read and write, to be my secretary. You're it! I know your strong points, Eunicet, and your bad ones, too, so watch yourself. Any treachery and I'll do what Frigeon did not: turn you out on the Floes!"

He stood and began pacing.

"Behave yourself. Do your work well. Be respectful," he said. "In return you'll be fed—not the best, but good enough—and almost warm. Now get out of here and find a room nearby in which to work. Tell anyone asking that you act in my name, Bladder. You'll learn how respected that name is here and now! Move, now! We will shortly have work to do."

With that he shoved the former duke, dressed in a cast-off cloak and boots, out into the blue-lighted corridor and strode off himself to a meeting with the Ice King.

"Bladder, isn't it?" asked the Ice King, indifferently.

"Y-y-y-yes-s-s-s, Sire. Er . . . at your sublime service . . ."

"There is absolutely no doubt about that," said Frigeon, as warm and brittle as icicles. "What if you were to return to the Dukedom today?"

"Sire, Your Majesty, why . . . why, they'd probably tear me limb from limb, burn me at the stake, scatter my ashes in Sea. . . ."

"Perhaps . . . but perhaps not, for these common Men are unpredictable. They can be as soft as clouds—or cruel as serpents!"

"What do you mean, Sire?" asked a thin, hideously scarred man standing nearby. He wore a silver crown with diamond points that sparkled in the stark light of the chamber.

Frigeon turned a freezing smile on the questioner. The overdecorated flunky flinched.

"Palestro, my dear undead Baronet, the good people of the Dukedom might tear this cringing pilferer apart if they found him, but given a moment or two to consider, they would do something much worse."

"What could be more cruel than d-d-death?" stuttered Bladder.

"How little you understand your fellow Men," Frigeon drawled, running his fingers along the arm of his icy throne.

"You don't think they would hang him out of hand?" asked the courtier named Palestro.

"Much worse than that," laughed the Ice King. "They would give him a fair trial, condemn him, and send him to prison for life. At hard labor!"

Bladder shuddered—as did many of the creatures present.

"And that is still not the worst! After a while, some of them would begin to feel sorry for him. And eventually they would . . . *forgive him!*"

There was a horrified murmur all over the room. Bladder blanched and shook with a terror he had never known.

"And then, when he is a drudging, terrified, stupid serf, bound to the land like a beastly, basest slave, they would heap on his head one more dire punishment: the greatest, the hardest to bear, the most invidious and the most debasing of them all . . .

"They would forget him!"

It may have been the words he said, or the way in which he said them, but Bladder seemed to plunge into a sudden dark pit that cleared only when some hideous minion with cold, cruel talons raised his head and shoved a vial of nasty, head-clearing ammonia salts under his nose.

Frigeon, he was surprised to see, still sat on his throne, watching and smiling disdainfully. Bladder wished fervently that he was being ignored but the Ice King was not finished with him.

"H-h-how can I s-s-serve you, S-s-s-sire?" he blurted out, not waiting to be asked.

"Good, good! Bladder, you will be glad to learn that I have use for you. You will return to Dukedom."

Bladder came within a snowflake of fainting again but the servant thrust the smelling salts to his nose again and he jerked his head back, unwillingly meeting the King's gaze once more.

"You'll arrange it so you won't be caught, won't you, dear Bladder?"

"Oh, yes, of course, S-s-s-sire!"

"I will certainly reward you if you succeed. How does a Dukedom of your own sound to you?"

Greed exploded inside Bladder's thick skull. "Yes! Oh, yes, Sire!"

"There'll be a Dukedom vacant, if you succeed, my boy." Frigeon seemed almost friendly now. "All you have to do is bring me Flarman Firemaster, alive."

Bladder, still dazed, merely nodded and stammered, "Of course, Sire."

"As simple as that," added Frigeon flatly. "Go now and bring me Flarman. Have you no questions?"

"No, none ... but, er, what about ... ?" He had been about to ask what he should do with Eunicet, but thought better of it. The Ice King turned away to resume his council meeting.

Bladder fled to Eunicet, who, after all, had managed to survive for years as Duke, getting his own way almost always.

"Ho, find out where I can find the Royal Steward," ordered Bladder by way of greeting. "What have you been doing?"

"Seeking Clangeon, the Royal Steward," said Eunicet, testily, "as he is the only one who can authorize the issuing of furniture, writing paper, pens, ink, food, charcoal, and clothing."

"Well, forget everything except the food and clothing. We've got a mission. Find this Clangeon and draw from him warm clothes for us both, and a fast ship and a crew. We are to return to the Dukedom."

"Bloodsucking Hecuba! You realize what they will do?"

"Of course I do! We're ordered on a mission, I tell you. We're to capture the Wizard of Wizard's High. Be quick about it! And careful. Get the directions down and right, and get back here within the hour.''

Eunicet fled down the corridors of ice, searching a second time for the Chief Steward. Bladder sat on the stool and adjusted the brazier so it warmed him without melting a hole in the floor to the apartment below. No telling what kind of fright lived there.

"Back to Dukedom," he muttered, and shuddered in turn. "At least we'll be warm again."

Bronze Owl unrolled a large chart in the Wizard's library.

"Here is Wizard's High," said the bird, pointing with one wingtip to the middle of the map. "Here to the west is the Old Kingdom and here . . ."

"Really, Owl, I can read a chart. There is Perthside and here is Trunkety Town."

"Impertinent boy!" scolded the Owl, "I wish to point out what you evidently do not see. There is no road, no possible way directly from here to Dwelmland, going straight northeast."

Douglas leaned over to study the area in debate, tracing Crooked Brook to its source in the first of the High Ridges, then the falling ground to Seashore.

"If I go up the Brook and over the ridges to the Sea, and then follow the shore north, I don't see how I can miss Bryarmote's country."

"That land between is completely empty, deserted. Parch, it is called, and there are no villages, no seaports, no castles, no rivers or lakes, no Men nor even birds or animals, for all I know."

Flarman entered the library, his arms filled with books, which he dropped on the already overloaded table. "What is this all about?"

"The best way for the Journeyman to reach Dwelmland," answered the Owl. "I say he must go north to Capital, then east, following the Old East Highroad, to Bryarmote's domain. His only difficulty is to cross the Uplands."

"Hmmm. That's bad enough, Dwarf's Uplands . . . why, even Eunicet's Army went around Dwelmland to avoid crossing any part of the Uplands. There's some very strong magic there. Blackest and terrible magic."

"Surely not more than a Journeyman Firemaster could

handle?'' Douglas asked, confidently. "I know something of Black Magic. You taught me.''

"I remember you nearly split my skull when I tried to teach you levitation,'' growled the Master. "And what you did with the little dust devil was a scandal. You, my boy, need some cautious study and practice before you are ready to combat Black Magic. Besides, there will be stragglers from the battle at Highlandorm to avoid. No, I don't recommend the northern route to Dwelmland.''

"How, then?''

"They will be expecting you and your burden to go by Sea. Augurian must concentrate on the coming battle. To have the Pearl moving on Sea would only distract him. He would feel that he had to send forces to guard your passage and that might only call attention to you and your burden. We can ill afford that.

"So, Journeyman, a Sea voyage is out of the question.''

Douglas bit his right knuckle. "That leaves the way I was first thinking, sir.''

"Correct, despite what Owl says.''

"There are dangers of all sorts . . . ,'' Owl began to argue.

"There are deadly dangers of all sorts no matter which way the lad goes,'' snapped the Wizard. "I see him better handling Parch coast than the Uplands or open Sea. Besides, you will be with him.''

"I was planning to follow you,'' admitted Bronze Owl.

"Oh, indeed! Yet the last time you accompanied me—you and Black Flame—oh, I knew about it—you were of little assistance.''

"But we were near, if you *had* needed help.''

"Oh, I am not complaining, old friend. I appreciated your thoughtfulness many times on that trip. Douglas's journey is more important than mine. I will have the Gulls to guide me.''

So it was decided.

For the first four days they traveled together east toward Sea, with Bronze Owl and the Gulls flapping and soaring above, keeping watch. The days were pleasantly cool with fall. The trees in the upper part of Valley swooping to the High Ridges were beginning to take on autumn gold, crimson, and purple, except where dark stands of secretive pines grouped about rocky outcrops and sheltered tumbling, tiny streams that fell swiftly to join Crooked Brook.

When dusk came upon them they chose a pine grove on the banks of such a clear, cold trickle. Douglas took from his pocket a large white handkerchief and spread it on a level spot of ground. A word, a magic pass, and the cloth grew twenty times in size and became a dazzling white tent, fully furnished and ready to occupy. Douglas marveled to himself how easily such spells came to him now, almost without thinking.

Flarman gathered wood and built a small, cheery, and fragrant fire. Douglas conjured a hearty, savory dinner following Blue Teakettle's favorite recipes. They sat and ate under the stars, talked and taught for a brief hour before rolling into blankets grown by magic from autumn leaves.

Just before dawn, they ate breakfast, repacked their few real utensils, restored the tent to handkerchief size, and the sleeping bags to their original leafy state before they continued climbing the Ridges.

The afternoon of the third day they had topped First Ridge when they sighted a troop of two dozen armed Men afoot, moving in ragged formation southwestward between the two ridges.

"They are, without a doubt, stragglers from Eunicet's Army," said Owl to Flarman, "but they are too far off to intercept us. We should warn the Valley Patrol, however. They are headed either for the Valley or for Wayness."

"I would have thought they'd go back to Capital," said Douglas.

"I hardly think so. They must know that Thornwood will soon return to Dukedom. They are coming southward, unpaid and unwanted, and hungry. Can you warn Possumtail, Owl?"

Bronze Owl was back in less than two hours and the Wizard's party by then had dropped down into the shallow vale between Middle Ridge and Shore Ridge. They stopped for the third night in the shelter of a towering rock pinnacle overhanging a crystal stream that slid smoothly along a cleft, plunging happily from pool to pool.

The next day the travelers climbed Shore Ridge and the fourth night camped just over the summit, overlooking Sea.

It was Douglas's first glimpse of open Sea. He found it vastly different from the gleaming, smoothly rippled Farango Water upon which he had been born. This water was deepest blue, unmarked here by offshore islands or reefs, deepening to dark purple in the middle distance and making a sharp, clear, black line at the horizon. Parallel curves of white rolled up to the sand beach. Towering clouds moved westward across the sky, trailing black shadows behind them in the water. Their dark underbellies spoke an end to the clear, dry weather they had been enjoying.

"Well, you'll learn how to march in the rain now," said Flarman, gazing at the racing clouds. "And I'll have to remember my specific against seasickness."

"Pinch of aloe, burnt with an inch of sweetsmell, and drink a thimbleful of Seawater," recited Douglas, automatically. "And breathe deeply."

"Fine, fine, now I remember. How did you know? I don't think I ever taught you that."

"I taught him, of course," said Bronze Owl, returning from a sweep northward and westward.

The Wizard nodded sleepily as Bronze Owl described his scout. Not much of interest. By the time they set up camp, storm winds were blowing and rain began to fall heavily. The tent sides billowed and boomed in the gusts and hard-driven rain drummed against the linen. Douglas fell asleep with thunder in his ears.

Morning, fifth day, dawned—hardly at all. The clouds were low enough to touch and sheets of lightning rent the Seaward skies. Winds blew with insane intensity at the tent walls and rain sought, in vain, to enter. For the first time, Douglas heard the stirring sound of Seasurf, breaking on the strand below them, a sound felt through the solid rock on which he made his bed.

"I am afraid I'll have to wait out the storm here," said Flarman, "but my ship will be here by dusk tomorrow. Much as I wish you could stay here until then, Douglas, my son, I am afraid I must urge you to start on your way. Owl says the storm is lessening to the north. I suspect that it was sent by Frigeon to cut any communications with Dukedom. If so, he is five days late. The Gulls came to fetch us in time."

After he had repacked their belongings, Douglas manufactured a dark brown rain slicker from a limp leaf of Sea grape. It covered him from head to toes, and made him look, according to Owl, like a walking rock. It was the color of the Ridge itself.

"That's the whole idea. Camouflage," Douglas said with a shrug.

Turning to Flarman Flowerstalk, he stepped forward and hugged the old man lovingly. "Take care, Magister. Fire can be drowned by water if the water is deep enough."

"I recall that lesson," said Flarman. "Much has happened to test my teaching since then. Have you still confidence in it?"

"Your teachings . . . and in you, Magister."

"Sea is basically friendly, thanks to Augurian," said the Wizard, covering his emotion at the boy's warm remark by blowing raindrops off his little round nose. "I'll take care, nevertheless, m'boy, and do you the same. Your lessons will serve you well, on your own. Give my regards to Bryarmote and his kindred."

"When and where will we meet again, Magister?"

"Fool of an underaged, overrated Journeyman Wizard! On Augurian's island, of course. Bring Bryarmote with you."

"I shall, Magister, friend, second father. It is time I went," Douglas said, a catch in his voice.

"Go on, now. There are a thousand warnings I could give you, but I hate long good-byes. Farewell!"

He went back into the tent, both to escape the renewed rain and to hide his fears and tears. They were at least fifty percent tears of pride.

Douglas slipped down the smooth, stony slope, aware of Bronze Owl overhead. Even that strong bird struggled to stay upright and aloft in the face of the wind. When they reached the narrow strand between the wet rocks and the roaring surf, they turned to look back briefly. They could just spot the tiny square of white linen on the hillside and heard the scawing of the Gulls above the storm, rather enjoying the turbulent airs and salt spray after too many days "inland."

The beaches were strewn with storm wrack and debris, pieces of cloth, broken arrows, pieces of spear shafts, even an unstrung bow, which Douglas retrieved as a staff to aid in walking. He saw a gleam of metal and, digging at it with his toe, he found it was a breastplate buckle, entangled with a timber from a ship's hull. Had all this been blown and drifted from the coast of Highlandorm, after the Battle of Faeryship Rock?

He tossed the buckle into Sea and went on his way. Bronze Owl came often to perch on his shoulder, reporting before noon that the storm was abating, as predicted.

Chapter Thirteen

THREE nights later found Douglas still following the ragged, storm-beaten coast. He pitched his handkerchief in a shallow cave—just a rock overhang, really—halfway up a headland that cut across his path and sheltered on the south face from the worst of the wet wind.

He was tired of the diet of wayfarer's bread and water, although the magic Faerie bread was tasty and sustaining. He dug in his pack; at the bottom he found his fishing gear. He went down to the water in the hope of catching something for supper despite the rain, which still fell but lightly.

The lure plopped into the smooth swell beyond the breaking waves and disappeared. He began to wind in his line, hand over hand.

By the time he had cast his bait ten times the rain was falling in driving sheets again, hissing like a wetted salamander as it struck the freckled waves, beating the wild surf into submission, Douglas, completely soaked and convinced that Sea fish did not bite in stormy weather, made one last cast.

As so often happens with fishing, the last cast hooked a large, pink-and-silver salmon, which the young man played skillfully and hauled into the shallows. Already as wet as he could get, he cleaned the fish, strung it on a piece of fishing line for carrying, and squished happily toward his cave.

He was startled to see a fire burning brightly and cheerily before his tent.

"Owl?" he called, for who else could have laid the campfire? There was no answer and he laid the salmon beside the fire. He stood a moment enjoying the warmth, probing the shadows with eyes and wizardly arts.

"Have you brought us supper?" asked a voice from the

back of the shallow cave. Douglas spun about, hand to his knife.

"Oh, now, don't be hasty, laddy," said the voice. "I mean ye no harm. I be but a Seaman thrown up on an unfriendly strand, I be, and wet and hungry as are ye."

The speaker came out from behind the tent and approached the fire with his hands held before him in a peaceful gesture. He was of middle height and age, well set up with thick, muscular arms, a shock of sandy hair cropped close, and pale blue eyes. He wore Seaman's trousers and a peacoat.

"Although how I do know ye're friendly yerself," the stranger continued, stopping across the fire, "I dinna know. Who ye be and whence, though, I'll not ask, unless ye care to tell."

The Journeyman studied the stranger for a long moment, reaching out with his talents to try to feel the shape and color of the other's intentions.

"I've no objection. My name's Douglas of Brightglade."

"A Perthsider, no less! I've been to that fjord many a time. Best shipwrights in World, I say."

"What did you there?" asked Douglas, not sure of the stranger's leanings as yet.

"I sailed in and sailed out mostly," said the other.

"Be that as it may," said Douglas, "your own name and place would be nice to know."

"Where I sailed from, many a year ago, when I first set out to Sea," began the sailor, "it were no *particoolar* problem to say yer name to strangers, but those were simpler times and friendlier. Would that I could see them again! I've long since learned not to bandy names to strangers in lonely places, sight unseen and tale unheard, as the old salts used to say."

He stood silent for a long moment as if listening to the wind and rain just beyond the cave mouth, a hissing roar that filled the rest of their world as night fell.

"But, then, ye've said yer name and place so I will say mine, and my real monicker I'll give ye, although I've used some false ones, too, having been in such trades as it is wiser not to be called by yer real, true label. I be one Caspar Marlin, and I hail from Westongue in Dukedom."

"Pleased to meet you, Master Marlin. Let's share my salmon over your fire," said the Journeyman, courteously.

The sailor came around the hearth and the two shook hands, both glad to have someone for company.

"I have served me time in many a galley," said Caspar, reaching for the fish. "And, though fish is not me favorite— give me a cut of beef any time for first choice—I knows how to fix it so it hain't half-bad. Here . . ."

And as quickly as anyone could he finished cleaning and filleting the salmon, and set it to broiling between split green twigs held over the coals. Almost at once a delicious smell came to their nostrils as they sat facing the fire side by side and began to talk.

"You were shipwrecked?"

"Not so much become shipwrecked as forced ashore."

"Deserted some ship, then? Was it a Wayness vessel under Thornwood?"

"Not a'tall! Not a'tall. I have sailed in Wayness ships and they be happy ships, alway. No, I had—it's a long tale, really."

"We've time," observed Douglas, turning the fish on the fire.

"Start at the beginning, Caspar," said he. "Eight year ago, maybe nine, I shipped on a barkentine headed for Choin, down there to the far southeast. Never been there. Never met a man who sailed there, so I had this itch to see where and what it was, ye understand. I could tell ye some fancy tales about *that* far empire! Choin is . . . well, I'll keep that for later. . . .

"It took us nigh onto two months to reach, the winds were that contrary. Are ye as amazed as this old Seaman, my boy, to see how big World is, after all?"

Douglas nodded emphatically, realizing he had seen so little of it.

"Well, our skipper, he were a good man, out of West-ongue, me own home port, but when we reached Choin he was taken sick and a Choinese mystic took him into his care, cured his agues and introduced him to the Choinese's strange ways, too, so that in the end he decided to sell his share of *Sally* brigantine (that were her name) and stay the rest of his life in that place.

"Which was fine with us, because by then we had gathered a capital cargo of ivory, silks, incenses and the finest writing paper you ever did see. They'd bring a pretty price back home.

"We made a pact, all of us, to share and share alike. The first mate—man named Quirkle and may the Sea Ghoolies friddle with his skull bone, the foul-breathed mud slinker!—put up the most cash and we elected him captain. We all put up what we could, down to one share just for working the ship on the way home. I'd saved a sockful of coin and bought twelve shares. The First Mate had a hundred, but he were greedy for more. Sea demon Grindle knows, he were greedy!

"The wind was ever fair on the return voyage. We never wanted for food or water—Choin beef got sweeter each day instead of rotting, like ours. We'd set sails and not touch a sheet for eight, nine, ten, twelve days. *Days,* mind ye! Such luck we had."

Douglas fetched his saltbox and they settled down to eat.

"Why, the cook even found a great, lustrous pearl in an oyster that he fished up from deepest Sea. Ha!"

He paused to toss some bones into the fire, then continued, chewing and talking at the same time.

"Pearl as big as . . . what can I say? Well, it was as big across as this." And here he held up his hand and separated his thumb and index finger by a good inch. "Pearl of that size was as good as gold, even though it was off color."

Douglas's ears pricked at this but he hid his surprise.

"That big! And of what color was it, do you say?"

"Silver, sort of, or gray, mostly. Like Sea of a stormy day. Smooth as a maiden's be——a maiden's cheek, it were. None of us ever seen the like; never!"

They soon finished eating and renewed the fire against the chill of the wet wind.

"We were within very sight of Cape Swerm on the southeast coast, y'know. Quirkle—never did get to calling him Captain, none of us—declared 'make and mend'—that's a holiday aboard ship. 'Make and mend,' he says and we lay about and told stories, talked about home, danced a hornpipe or two, I remember. Someone broached a barrel of the Choinese brandy they call *fungwah.* I'm ashamed to say every man jack of us got rip-snortin' drunk and silly, laughing ourselves to sleep before the midnight watch came on.

"Well, I'm even sorrier to say that it wasn't *every* man

jack got falling-down pickled that night. Four of our scurvy shipmates laid off the *fungwah,* and when morning stabbed us in the eyes we was all tied and coiled up so tight we couldn't move a finger. And gagged, too, to boot!''

"No," gasped Douglas. "The first mate?''

"Aye, lad, and three of his special cronies, green Sea slime eat their livers! . . . For they be dead now, I deem. That Quirkle turned *Sally* stem for stern and sailed her southeast by south for three weeks to the Warm Seas. As for us, some of us died in the broiling tropical sun. Others agreed to work the ship in exchange for bad water and worse food. Swill, it were!''

The memory made him spit into the darkness beyond the cave mouth.

"Them pirates run poor *Sally* on a sharp-toothed reef off a deserted island. I still don't know if it were poor seamanship on the part of old Quirkle or if one of us slaves cut the tiller ropes at a crucial moment.

"Well, sir, 'twas a fearful crash in the night and a grinding and a screaming from the ship like she was truly alive. I woke up with me mouth full of salt water, five fathoms down beside the reef. How I swam! Never knew I could swim until then but I did, and just as I thought me lungs would bust for sure, me head pops above water.

"I'd gone down with *Sally,* gotten somehow under or through that reef—and come up *inside* the lagoon! I was the only one to see the inside, too. Every other man, good and bad, perished in the wreck.

"Well, let me say I had a hard time then! I got to shore on that island and it was palm trees, sand dunes, and smoking volcanoes, right up there on the top of the island, rumbling and grumbling all the time, and spitting fire, belching stinking smoke! At first I thought I'd just put off dying and might as well hurry it along. But that's not my way, no sir!

"I found fresh water, and oh how good it tasted, better than any *fungwah,* I tell ye. I managed to kill one of the wild hogs there and didn't coconut-fed pork, roasted over a fire on the sand, taste heavenly!

"I made meself a raft of sorts out of palm logs that had been knocked down by a storm, and went out to look for what were left of *Sally.* She were there, all right, strewn all over the top of the reef, which was almost dry at ebb. I pulled off barrels of *fungwah* . . . but dumped 'em in the lagoon and made a tub boat of the barrels like we used to when I was a lad.

"I loaded her with all kinds of stuff. Damn little food, but some fancy Choinese stuff. I found the best of all wedged between two heads of coral . . . can you believe it? The Carpenter's Chest, filled with the finest Westongue tools, hammers, saws, adzes and axes, and chisels and spokeshaves, and awls. I floated ashore as many of the ship's timbers as were whole and small enough for me to move alone. . . .

"In the end I built meself a neat little sloop, or at least that's what I called her. She was single-masted, gaff-rigged in the Westongue style, and she had a mains'l, a tops'l, and a jib. Tight as a banker's vault, she was. After six months I loaded her with coconuts, salt pork, and smoked hams. I sailed north by west by the stars. . . ."

Douglas couldn't help asking, "And the Pearl?"

"H-How did ye guess?" sputtered Caspar Marlin. "Almost the last day—it were grisly, I don't mind saying, finding that Pearl! I went out looking for a last piece of cordage to complete me sloop's rigging. I saw a mess of it caught on the reef in about twelve, fifteen feet of water. The water there were like blue air, 'twere so clear.

"I needed that cordage for the main lift, the longest single piece of line if ye don't count the anchor chain. I needed it, and there it was just out of dry reach and me with no boat hook or anything. Nothing for it but to dive, so I did. I was that eager to get away from that lonely place. Times since I've almost wished I'd stayed!"

He paused to shake his head and light his stub of a pipe.

"I catched a hold of a bight and dragged it to the surface. Began to reel it in. Most of a half dozen fathoms or more; more than enough, but I went on pulling as ye can never have too much line on a ship, lad. Hand over hand. The sun was on the water; 'twas late in the day. So I wasn't looking down into the dazzle when I reached the end of the line. Talk of bitter ends!

"Me hand reached down—like this, ye see—and suddenly instead of good hemp line me fingers closed on slippery, slimy bone!

"I looked and nearly fell into the water in terror. I've seen dead men aplenty before but this turned me stomach! I had a hold of the wrist bone of a skeleton, all the flesh eaten away from it by the fishes. 'Twere tangled in the line.

"I steeled meself, saying, here, this may be a shipmate and he deserves better of ye than letting him go back into the deep without a look. There were bits and pieces of clothing on him still and I tried to see if I could tell who he had been, in case I got home to Westongue and could tell his widow.

"I found a leathern pouch around his bony neck and it had sommat in it, I could feel, for sure. Then it was I recognized the corpse and flung it back to the fishes with a curse I'm ashamed to recall. 'Twere that homicide Quirkle! He'd stolen the Pearl from the dead cook! Oh, I saved the cursed jewel but I threw Quirkle's bones back into Sea."

He was silent, huddled near the fire, his eyes shining in an eerie fashion as he recalled his last trip to the reef.

"Now, can you tell me what happened then?"

"Oh, aye, matey. I put the Pearl in me housewife—luckily it had come through the wreck in me pocket, needles and thread and all. After that I lost no time but sailed me gay sloop before kindly winds that took me toward home. As I say, sometimes I regret it."

"Why?"

"When I sailed into the harbor of Westongue, the Duke's rogues were laying in wait for all good sailors—and I was pressed into the ducal service! Never got to set foot on land! A disgrace it was, too. Eunicet paid us little or forget it. That's why I came to sell the Pearl."

"To?"

"To an old man with a black cat. He appeared abroad one night, asking questions. We was hove-to off Knightstower Heath in the north. I don't know how he got aboard. . . ."

"I can imagine," Douglas said with a grin.

"Can ye now? He whispered to me and asked had I seen a pearl. I was flabbergasted. That old man . . ."

"Was a Wizard, of course. His name is Flarman Flowerstalk."

"Yes, by the Blazing Beard of Beliol!" cried Caspar. "That was the name he gave!"

"I left him just three days ago on this very coast, awaiting a ship and a change in the weather."

"Ye don't tell me! Here? 'Tis a tiny world, after all."

"What happened to you then?"

"Flarman took the Pearl, paid me well for it, and disappeared as quickly as he'd come. He told me to wait for five days and a chance would come to escape from that hell ship. I did it off Wayness Isle and was picked out of Sea by a Wayness ship.

"Been with that ship and Captain since. Rose to be First Officer—hawsehole promotion, as they say. Five days ago we were carrying supplies to Thornwood's fleet off Highlandorm when we was attacked by a square-rigger flying no flag. The pirates, if that be what they were, hooked onto our chains and boarded. They hunted us down all over the ship. All were pressed into service or killed. As for me, someone left a dory a-towing and I slipped aboard her before they could catch me and lost meself in Lasting Mists. I rowed and sailed four days and landed on this coast in the storm yestereve.

"I left me dory above the surf. Made up me mind to leg it home. Until today I was too sick from drinking Seawater but this morning I started out to find me way home or at least closer than Eunicet ever let me get. I walked along the beach and near nightfall spied yer tent up in the cliff here. I needed news and a direction or two. I'm not much at land travel and I'm afraid to take to Sea, what with bloodthirsty pirates maybe still nearby.

"So I decided to chance it and made this fire to be friendly-like, then hid behind the tent until you came. When I saw you I bespoke ye. Ye know the rest. . . ."

"I'm glad you did!"

"Now, laddy, ye've heard me story from beginning to end. What about yours? I may be way off course, but I'm not entirely green in some things. A youngster like you—this heavy tent?—this out-of-the-way place? And your fancy robe, too, and you being a friend of a Wizard?"

"You're guessing aright," said Douglas. "I am a Journeyman Wizard myself. A pupil of the Firemaster."

"So I had been thinking, or somewhat like." Caspar Marlin grinned. "I be lucky, for once!"

In the morning Bronze Owl returned and had to hear the sailor's story over again. In briefer form, Douglas ensured, or they'd have been there all day. It had dawned cool and dry, a good day for making headway past the Wastelands of Parch just ahead.

"Where will you go?" Owl asked Caspar as Douglas finished cleaning up and shrinking the bedclothes and the tent.

"Uh, well, I intend to head for home, if there is still a home to head to. Westongue is me goal, good Owl."

"Hmmm. That poses some problems," said the bird. "If you go north you'll undoubtedly run into Army stragglers or Dwarfs hunting them. And if you go due west, which is surely the shortest way home for you, you'll end up having to go right through Capital, where the food shortages are the worst and wanderers are still unwelcome. In some places, I hear, they are jailed on sight, or run off to be the problem of the next landholder.

"South is a good way, but the swamps between Wayness and Cape Swerm are filled now with stragglers and outlaws, too. You'd not want to tangle with them alone. Wayness would welcome you as they always do skilled seamen, but Thornwood has all his ships with him to the east."

"No news to me! When we were on that merchantman they told us such."

"You should try to reach Valley. Follow the coast for two days, turn inland over the Ridges and into Valley. The Valley people will take you on your way and give you the latest news of Westongue, I should think."

Douglas looked up from closing his backpack and came over to them.

"And where will ye be going, young Wizard?" asked Caspar.

"I have an errand to run for Flarman," Douglas said, "then I shall join my Master in Warm Seas, if I can."

"Ah, I should go along to help ye, for ye've been most hospitable to me."

"We must travel alone, however," said the Journeyman, firmly. "Owl and I."

"Through Valley, then, it is," said Caspar.

They parted, Douglas to the north and the old sailor to the south.

Caspar walked steadily the whole day, and the next day, too, making very good time on the smooth beach. By noontide of the second day he spotted the Wizard's white tent on the ledge above the shore and climbed toward it.

No one seemed about. He called Flarman's name as he approached, with no result.

"Must've been picked up," he said aloud to himself, "or he'd have come out by now. Wouldn't have left his tent up, would he?"

He hailed, "Ahoy!" several times; lifted the tent flap and looked inside. No one was there. Overhead three large Sea Gulls screamed at him, but aside from the sound of the surf, there was empty silence.

Caspar found blankets tossed all on the floor and one tent pole pulled askew.

"Oh, ho! Been a struggle here! I bet me life it was no friend of the Wizard that came to him. Caught him asleep and carried him off! Question is, where to?"

Being a Seaman, he knew the only way the Wizard-nappers could come and go undetected was by water, so he returned to the beach and cast up and down looking for signs.

His sharp, blue eyes quickly found thin lines and foot-prints in the fine sand at water's edge, the mark where a line had been fastened to a rock and chafed a bit. The signs were fresh, not yet washed away by the incoming tide.

"Now, bucko, I see they come after the last high tide and before the next. Less than twelve hours ago, but probably by night to catch the Wizard asleep."

He retraced his steps to the Wizard's tent and sat down to think it out.

"Caspar, me lad, this Wizard, ye owe him a favor. Meeting his young man saved yer life, maybe, ye were that hungry when ye saw his tent back there, and he's given ye to eat for yer voyaging ahead, too. Caspar Marlin never forgets to repay a favor, ye can bet!

"Besides, didn't ye get a strong feeling, back there, that matters are afoot important enough to call out a Fire Wizard to help. Ye must take what hand ye can, Caspar, now that yer on the lee side of trouble, once again."

He dismantled the tent, rolling the blankets inside, and slung the bundle over his shoulder.

"Caspar, ye've got to find a boat and follow. Maybe you can do sommat for the good Wizard."

He stopped to fill a canteen Douglas had given him, and eat a bite of waybread, too.

High overhead three Gulls were still screaming angrily at him.

"Wonder what's got into *them*?" he asked himself, and headed once more toward the shore.

"You foul old man! You slimy bird's nest! You terrible ... terrible ... you troll! You ... you ... you ... !"

Eunicet's shrill voice reached its highest pitch and broke. He stamped his feet in incoherent rage and, picking up an empty wine flask, threw it as far and as hard as he could into Sea.

Flarman, seated in the bottom of a whaleboat facing aft, his hands tied behind him and resting his back uncomfortably against a thwart, merely watched the former Duke, neither smiling nor frowning. This made the man even more furious.

"You've never, never taken me seriously," Eunicet shouted, shaking his fists at the Wizard. "When I called you to Capital you simply refused to come and sent me back sniveling, impertinent messages. 'Too busy,' you said, or 'Just returned from a long journey and must rest for a while before traveling again!' And worst of all, 'Suggest you encourage the raising of sheep in the Uplands!' Me ... *me*! Eunicet the Great. Father of his people! The grandest Duke the Dukedom ever had! Glorious in battle; generous in peace! Me, pander to a bunch of smelly shepherds! *Arghhh!*"

He ran out of breath and sank down heavily on the center thwart. The sailing whaleboat skimmed placidly across open Sea. A two-man crew tended sheets and tiller. Bladder, green with Seasickness, lolled listlessly on a pile of damp blankets just forward of the mast. He did not join the former Duke's tirade, nor did he move to still it.

Flarman made no comment. The sailors watched out of the corners of their eyes expectantly, for in their world such vile, abusive language led inevitably to violence ... even death.

"Ten snorks on the old Wiz," one whispered, hoarsely. "He won't take it much longer, matey!"

"What can *he* do?" sneered the other, giving the tiller a

shove to starboard, then centering it again. "He's tied hand and foot with good sailor's knots and hasn't said a word since you conked him on that peaked hat and shoved him into the bilge. I'd take your bet, mate, if we could trust either of them two to hold the stakes."

"Aye, but don't underestimate that there Fire Wizard. I hear old King Frigeon turns purple himself at the mention of *his* name. Fair keels over with the jitters, some say."

"Don't let *them* near ye say it, even if 'tis true," warned his companion. "Don't pay to know too much about the doings of your betters, me old pappy once said. *I* know when to keep me hatch battened. You should learn, too, Bigbelly, m'boy."

They had spoken in whispers, almost inaudible under Eunicet's ravings and Bladder's moaning, but at this moment Flarman twisted as far as his bonds would allow him and grinned at the two sailors.

"Good advice," he said, "to keep your hatches battened and you'll both live to see land again."

There was no menace in his voice, but the Seamen looked startled and sheepish at the same time that he had overheard their whispers.

"So, you *can* speak!" shouted Eunicet, thrusting his fat, pocked face close to Flarman's. "Answer me, by retchin' Remmit, or I'll hack off your ears!"

"Oh, were you expecting an answer?" said Flarman, mildly. "I thought you were just enjoying the sound of your own wrath. I really think, old boy, that you should be careful. I've known choleric types like you to drop like a stone, dead, letting their ire get the better of them. . . ."

"Outrageous meddler! Malodorous malingerer! How dare you speak to me, your Duke, in such a tone of voice. Why . . . why . . . !"

"Oh come off it, Eunie," moaned Bladder, struggling to sit up. "You're no longer Duke. Face up to it, man!"

"Oh . . . go eat some rancid bacon fat!" screamed Eunicet, and Bladder, turning several shades darker green, squirmed around to face forward and made no further comment. The crew, under Eunicet's baleful glare, studied their sails and Sea around them in silence.

"If you had come to my service," Eunicet shouted at Flarman, "I *would* still be Duke and not in this miserable boat running errands for Frigeon that might—and might not—get me fair reward. If you had been a help instead of a hindrance, Flarman Flowerstalk . . . !''

"I gave you very good advice. You simply would not take it, Eunicet. Now admit it."

"What sneaking, bloodless advice was that?"

"If I told you once I told you a dozen times; the rearing of sheep for wool and mutton . . ."

Eunicet threw his hands toward the deep blue sky above and screamed in surpassing frustration. He turned from the Wizard and sat down hard upon the center thwart, facing aft. Bladder ignored his master but the sailors watched in horrified fascination.

"Blow me to flinders," gasped Bigbelly. "He's crying like a baby!"

"More like a madman," observed his mate. The sight of Eunicet's tears didn't interest him.

Bigbelly had been looking aft for several minutes. "Say, mate, do us a favor and go aloft. I thought I saw a boat behind us."

Grumbling out of habit, the other Seaman shinnied up the mast and gazed back along the whaleboat's wake. After a few moments he slid down again, glancing at Eunicet, who had finally fallen asleep on the hard, wet thwart, and at Bladder, who was mumbling in his unkempt beard about slimy, green Sea monsters in his stomach.

"Well, mate?"

"A little dory, quite a way back. On the same heading as us but that don't mean he's following us—the wind's set this way, 'tis all, probably."

Bigbelly nodded. "Could be a messenger, or a fisherman trying his luck on Meridian Banks. 'Tis not our duty to inquire, but to get these . . . *gentlemen* . . . to *Icicle Princess*, eh? Well, we'll keep an eye peeled but not mention it to our passengers, at least not yet."

"Aye. Oh, wind's shifted. Lend us a hand, now . . ."

They were busy for several minutes trimming sails and laying on a new course for their rendezvous with *Icicle Princess*, one of Frigeon's vessels. She had been standing on and off for several days while Eunicet and his party had gone ashore to find Flarman, capture him, and bring him back to the ship.

One of the sailors had tapped him on the cap with a belaying pin but the conical Wizard's hat had spells to protect its wearer from far worse blows, and he pretended to be unconscious. It suited him to be carried down the rough path to the shore.

After Eunicet and Bladder fell asleep, he burned the ropes from his wrists and retied his ankles more comfortably. When he heard the sailors discussing the following boat he was surprised and then thoughtful.

No telling who it can be, he mused to himself. But 'tis as likely to be a friend as one of theirs.

He pursed his lips and whistled softly, so high pitched that even the wakeful helmsman didn't hear. A few minutes later a bright eye and white wings appeared just over the side; Cerfew answering his call.

They spoke quietly until the helmsman noticed the bird and shooed him away. Cerfew called him several choice, filthy names and departed on Flarman's errand.

In a short while he returned. " 'Tis an old sailor alone in a dory that's seen some rough knocks, but he's got her sailing smartly. He's staying just out of clear sight but following as closely as he dares. No, I've never seen him before.''

"Go speak to him, please.''

"Oh, I already did. He's met the young Wizard, the Journeyman Douglas.''

"Wonderful!''

"Douglas sent him to Valley after he was shipwrecked on Parch shore, he says, heading to his home beyond Valley. He's a Westonguer, you see, and has been at Sea, impressed against his will. Many were, as you know.

"He arrived just after you were carried off by this scum. He decided he was needed and elected to follow you, to help if he could. Seems a decent sort, I'd say, and I've met a bundle of Seamen in my time.''

Flarman thought about his words for a while. In the moonless dark the Gull was invisible to the crewman at the tiller.

"What's his name?''

"Caspar Marlin, he said.''

"Oh, now, there's a coincidence! I've met him before. He's alone and a long way out to Sea,'' Flarman murmured.

"I'm worried he might get in too deep, if you'll pardon the pun."

"He can take care of himself, I vow," said Cerfew. "He's a canny old salt, sir Wizard. It might be handy to have 'nother pair of hands to side us, later."

"Perhaps, but I think you and I can handle what is coming. No, go back and ask Caspar Marlin to turn northwest to Dwelmland. Tell him to use my name and to ask to be taken to Prince Bryarmote there. Douglas will be with him, or soon will be. He's to tell them what has befallen me. Tell them that I plan to go with Eunicet to see Frigeon, to learn what I can of Eternal Ice."

"You're a brave man, Wizard," whistled the Gull softly. "Not many would willingly face Frigeon alone with little hope of escaping."

"Brave? Perhaps. More likely foolish. Be that as it may, Cerfew, it is a good place to begin and, after all, I'm not entirely helpless when it comes to Wizardry. I have at least one big advantage over Frigeon."

"That is?"

"Unlike Frigeon, I can trust my friends."

And with that he bid the bird good night and settled himself to go to sleep. Cerfew dropped back to give Casper Marlin the Wizard's message and instructions. He and his family continued to track Flarman's captors.

As dawn broke, the helmsman aboard *Icicle Princess*'s whaleboat stretched, yawned, and glanced aft. The strange boat had disappeared. And in all the circle of horizon about him only four objects broke the watery monotony.

Three were large, white gulls bobbing peacefully on the glassy morning swell. The fourth was a tall, black three-master hove-to under short sail. It showed no flag. With a very Seamanly feeling of relief, the helmsman roused his mate and prepared to hail her and put his vessel alongside.

Curious faces lined the rail until the Captain, named Fribby, drove them back to their morning duties. A great mound of a man with the look of many bad days and nights both ashore and afloat, he met Eunicet and Bladder as they climbed up the side.

"Have the prisoner hoisted aboard and put in the brig,"

ordered Bladder. "Take care not to damage him too much. He's to be guest to King Frigeon. Set a triple guard on him."

"Aye, aye," said Fribby, hardly hiding his distaste for Bladder.

"Aye, aye, *sir*!" shouted Bladder. "I will be respected! Do I have to cut off your ear as a lesson? Hop to it, scumbag!"

"Aye, aye, sir!" echoed the Captain. It didn't pay, he thought, to cross a man who might, just might, be in Frigeon's graces.

As *Icicle Princess* came about gracefully and her sails caught the freshening morning breeze, no one paid any attention to three big Gulls screaming insults and threats at them from off her counter. When the ship's cook dumped breakfast scraps overboard later in the morning, they inspected the food with some distaste but selected bits and pieces for a meal.

It was still a long voyage to Eternal Ice and they would need their strength.

Three days after parting from Caspar Marlin, Douglas and the Owl came upon a tiny fishing village sheltered in a deep cove under a lofty Sea cliff.

"Well, at least we are out of Parch," exclaimed Owl.

"The Sea is close by and I imagine the fishing is good. The mountain breaks the back of northerly winds and provides a harbor for their craft."

"True, but what I wonder is, where do they sell their catch? Unless they live solely on fish and Seaweed."

On the outskirts they met a very old woman, sitting on an overturned skiff in the warm sun, mending a net with a huge wooden bodkin. At first Douglas thought she might be deaf or blind, for she gave no hint she was aware of their approach. As they stopped in front of her she suddenly looked up, smiled brightly, showing a full set of very white teeth.

"Good afternoon, travelers! Welcome to Fairstrand."

"Thank you, Grammer," answered the young Wizard, politely. "What a delightful name for a Seaside town! Are all its inhabitants as pleasant to strangers as you, may I ask?"

"Oh . . . more or less," the lady replied with a chuckle. "Fishermen are often a rough lot and might give you a mouthful of knuckles instead of a pleasant greeting. But not too often.''

''As you can see, we are travelers and hoping for a bed for the night ahead,'' said Douglas. ''Would we be welcomed at Fairstrand?''

''No doubt about it! But best you ask our Mayor. I'll take ye to him.''

She put away her mending kit and let Douglas help her drape the net over a drying rack, then led them briskly into the village by its only street, paralleling the shore. Seeing them with her, smiling ladies, girls, and many children came from their neat, whitewashed stone cottages to call hello and follow them into the village center.

This place was half beach, half cobbled pavement, surrounded on three sides by the most substantial houses in the town, a small place of worship with a square tower which doubled as a watchtower, and an impressive stone building that proved to be a combination town hall and warehouse. Here their guide introduced them to a middle-aged gentleman dressed in a leather apron, carrying a heavy, short-handled, ornate gilt mallet.

''This here's our Mayor,'' she said, bobbing to him, then to Douglas and the Owl, a quaint curtsy. ''He's a good mayor but a terrible Seaman, which is why he is not at Sea but here in the warehouse.''

''Now, Mother,'' protested the man, grinning broadly.

''And he's my own son, and I am proud of him, anyway,'' added the old lady. ''His name is Charlie Beckett, and I am Maryam Beckett.''

With which she curtsied again and stepped back, smiling and folding her hands demurely. Charlie Beckett laughed aloud, throwing his head back and wiping tears of merriment from his eyes. Everyone joined in, including the two travelers.

''Welcome! Welcome!'' cried the Mayor when he was able to gasp. ''You must forgive my laughing but my dear mother is my pet and my joy. And she is right, too. I am Lord Mayor of Fairstrand because I never was able to get over Seasickness! So the good folk here made me Mayor and Counter of the Casks.''

Douglas hastened to introduce himself and Bronze Owl

before he would be off laughing again. He asked, "Casks? Casks of what?"

"Bless the boy," said Maryam, who could not keep from any conversation for long, "casks of salt fish, of course. The menfolk catch them in nets. We women tend the salt pans to get fine, savory Sea salt to preserve them, and my son, the Mayor, packs the fish with the salt in casks."

"Then we put the barrels on wains or in our boats, and take them to our customers, as far away as Wayness, but mostly to Dwelmland. Many a tun is bought in trade by the Wayness captains. 'Tis said Fairstrand salt fish lasts longer and tastes better than any others," added His Honor, proudly.

"You deal with Bryarmote of Dwelmland, then?" asked Douglas.

"Our very best customer," Grammer Maryam put in. "But we shouldn't be standing in the chill winds gabbing, Mr. Mayor. Let's go home and put hearty ale and tasty vittles in these good travelers. They've walked a long way and are no doubt hungry. Where're your manners I taught ye?"

With such good-natured banter she hustled them all to the largest house on the square and sat them down before a cheery Sea-coal fire while she and her daughters-in-law and their maids and cook bustled to provide dinner for their guests.

Many of the townspeople who had followed them into the square also followed them into the Mayor's house and all made themselves useful or at home. One gaffer tapped a keg of golden Dwarf ale and filled jacks all around, then kept them filled. An elder with a square-trimmed Seaman's beard of black flecked with white sat in the seat of a bow window and struck up a lively series of airs, sailor's laments, jigs, and rollicking reels on his guitar. He'd but one leg, having a sturdy wooden peg in the place of the lost limb. The guests joined in the choruses and appeared to enjoy themselves immensely.

All but a few who had followed them in from the open square proved to be relatives, and they, almost all female from elderly to early teens. Below that age were boys and girls, very well behaved. The older folk were as sprightly and happy as Grammer Maryam.

Every able-bodied male in the village, except the Mayor and a few youthful helpers who would obviously rather have

been at Sea, worked the fishing boats, as nets were first set
and later taken in, the fisherfolk explained.

"And the Lord Mayor does business for us all," exclaimed that worthy. "Now, come to dinner and I hope you
like fish, for that's all we've got until the casks are delivered
and wains return with supplies."

Douglas, who had eaten fish for five out of the last six
suppertimes, did not look forward to more Sea fare but to his
surprise, when he took a bite of the first dish to be placed
before him, it tasted exactly like the finest veal in a spicy
sauce. He commented upon it to Grammer Maryam, who sat
at his right hand.

"You should know, young Douglas, most sailors and fishermen detest eating fish! At Fairstrand our great-grandmoth-
ers invented recipes to make the fish we have taste like, well,
almost anything we don't have. Keeps things from getting
too monotonous, laddie."

So Douglas dined on fish that tasted like tender roast
beef—very good, medium rare—and fish that tasted like
barbecued chicken—quite spicy, but delicious—and even
fish that tasted like fish, the very finest white tuna.

At dawn he awakened to sounds of men shouting, machin-
ery rumbling, sheaves squealing, bare feet on wooden decks,
sounds he hadn't heard since Perthside's docks and ship-
ways. These and the smell of fresh Sea breezes through his
window brought flooding memories of his childhood, his
mother, and his father.

It was such a nostalgic moment that he lay abed for a long
time, just listening and breathing the air, letting it take him
back.

Then Bronze Owl arrived with a clatter at the window.
Grammer Maryam knocked at the door at the same moment.

"Fleet's in! Get up and see a sight you've maybe never
seen before!"

He dressed quickly, finding his travel-worn and grimy
clothing now freshly laundered and neatly mended. When he
tried to thank Maryam she shoved him through the front door
and took him to see the fishing fleet being off-loaded.

"Breakfast when work's done," she sang. "Here's my
son, Captain Holmes Beckett."

"A record haul," the burly, white-bearded individual in

high boots and a red bandanna was saying to the Mayor. ''Hope you've got the casks for 'em.''

''When have I ever failed you, brother?'' cried the Mayor. ''Here, take a moment to greet our guests.''

After introductions, the work continued and men and boys shoveled a great cascade of silvery fish from the boats into waiting carts that had been trundled onto the cobbled hard. The Mayor's helpers began at once packing the catch into huge wooden casks, layer upon layer—first salt, then fish, then salt again until the cooper declared each well filled. Another layer of salt was added to top them off, and the cooper and his helpers banged home the barrel tops, sealed them all with wax, into which the Mayor ceremoniously pressed the town seal, which he wore on a chain around his neck.

''Later this evening there'll be a big party,'' the Mayor said. ''Dancing and singing, and the young girls have prepared an entertainment for us at the Town Hall. Tomorrow everybody'll turn out to load the wains. We'll draw lots to see who drives the oxen.''

''We celebrate each catch—it's our way of saying thanks to our maker,'' said Maryam. ''We believe He likes to see us working hard, happy, content, and bravely facing whatever accidents come our way. The bad weather of last week made this a particularly good catch, you see.''

''And will some of these fish go to Bryarmote's caverns?''

''I can tell you exactly,'' the Mayor said, leading them into his office, where he opened a huge, canvas-bound ledger.

''Dwelmland, Dwelmland . . .'' He thumbed through the pages. ''Yes, here it is. Fortoot, Bryarmote's Chief Steward, has a standing order for fifteen casks a month, and so far we've delivered twelve. We'll send him three and two more for good measure, as a compliment to good customers.''

Holmes laughed. ''The Dwarfs are especially fond of salt fish. They don't fish for themselves, of course, being miners and engineers. They buy everything from people like us.''

''And if I wished to go to Dwelmland? I have an errand to Prince Bryarmote, you see.''

''Delighted! Delighted! Of course! We have a bit of worry

about our shipments being waylaid, with so many deserters in the mountains, people from Duke Eunicet's Army . . .''

"Yes, I've seen some of them myself," Douglas agreed.

" . . . it would be a blessing to have a friendly Wizard along to help protect the cargo. If that's all right with you, of course. I think it a grand idea."

Douglas was more than willing and the next morning he climbed onto the hard seat of a stout, high-wheeled wagon loaded with two vast casks of salt fish. Beside him, holding the reins that guided six huge, placid, yellow oxen, sat a youth named George. His grandmother, Maryam Beckett, came to say good-bye.

"George, you're my favorite grandson, hear? Take good care of Master Douglas and Bronze Owl, now. Stay away from them brigands, but if they do waylay you, stay out of the Wizard's way. My, I bet he can give bad folks whatever-for in fire, if what Bronze Owl says is true, and I, for one, reckon 'tis!"

"Yes, Grammer," the boy said, and grinned from ear to ear at the lively old lady who was mother, sister, aunt, or grandmother of over half Fairstrand, Douglas had found. "I'd like to see some of them fireworks!"

"Take good care and say my courtesies to Prince Bryarmote," said Maryam to the Journeyman Wizard. "He'll recall me! We've danced a few Fleet Landings, the two of us, in good times past. Good-bye and what are ye waiting for, young 'un? Shove off!"

She waved them off, and Douglas, beside the young giant of a Beckett, watched the six oxen strain up the steep hill behind the village of Fairstrand. Bronze Owl circled over the three wains in the bright morning sunlight, giving off flashes of golden light like semaphore signals to the fishing boats lying at anchor now off the beach.

"We'll be entering Dwelmland by the kitchen door, so to speak, and speak first to the Chief Steward, instead of the Prince, if you get my meaning," George told Douglas as they rolled along.

"I understand. I'm not above going into Bryarmote's house by the back door. I'm sure of our welcome there."

They came to the foot of a broad, shallow ledge in late morning and stopped in a grove of tall, graceful rowans growing close to the cliff wall. At no evident signal, the rock face in front of them split down the center and swung inward silently, revealing a deep, black, square portico behind which a tunnel drove straight into the mountain.

In the doorway stood a Dwarf, small even for his small race. As they approached he greeted George Beckett with a warm smile and, turning, said to Douglas: "Welcome to Dwelmland, Journeyman Wizard, and to you, Master Bronze Owl. You are most welcome and expected, and the Master asks that you be sent on through by the shortest route so that he may see you soonest."

He bowed deeply to Douglas and shook his hand.

"We had foreknowledge of your coming and many of us recognized you both from afar. Also, last evening a stranger came to this door asking for the Prince in the name of Flarman Firemaster, and your own name, too.

"Now, George, it is interesting to listen to folk talk at the doorway but I would prefer you got them casks of mine out of the hot sun, first. Here, Drongle," he said, turning back to the tunnel and clapping his hands, "help the Fairstranders with their cargo."

A dozen burly Dwarfs in leather aprons and tall leather caps came running from the darkness within and began to roll the casks down wide planks and into the mouth of the cave, where they made short work of placing the heavy hogsheads on carts drawn by large green lizards. They would return shortly, Fortoot said, with empty casks from previous deliveries.

The fisherman saluted and reported that his entire load had been carried within. Fortoot took a vast wallet from his belt and paid for the fish.

"I must head for port now, sirs, though I do not relish the trip back alone after your fine company. A million thanks, Wizard!"

George climbed back aboard his wagon seat and bid the travelers and the Dwarf farewell.

"How many Dwarfs live in Dwelmland?" Douglas asked the Steward as they walked into the cavern. A number of oaken doorways opened off the anteroom, most of them closed. The largest one, straight ahead of them, stood open.

"Sixty thousand, counting the House Guard. Can't forget the House Guard," Fortoot laughed. "They eat twice as much when they're here as any bunch of miners the same size. They've already been sent off to Warm Seas, though.''

They strolled on and Fortoot blew a silver whistle, calling a young Dwarf to his side. Douglas could tell he was young by the fact that he had only a short fringe of beard about his chin from ear to ear. The longer the beard, the older the Dwarf.

"Doodle here will show you the short and fast route to the Hall," Fortoot told them. "I'd love to escort you myself but I have this fish and several other shipments to see to. I greet you again, Wizard and Owl! Welcome to my Master's house, and I believe we will meet again. I am much about these caverns on my business."

"Lead the way, Master Doddle," said Bronze Owl, and the Dwarf turned and trotted into the most twisted, mystifying labyrinth imaginable. They turned left three times, then right twice, passing up an incline after the second turn and then crossing a bridge that leaped an abyss from which they could hear the sound of rushing waters. The bridge had no handrail, and Douglas stayed near the center as he crossed.

The turns and twists quickly became too many to recall, and Douglas contented himself with following the young Dwarf along this "shortest" way. Before they reached the Hall, Bryarmote's under-mountain home itself, they had walked for better than two hours.

They came to a section of tunnel more carefully carved from the solid rock than what had come before, and most luxuriously appointed.

"This is the entrance to the Hall of Bryarmote," announced Doddle, proudly and rather formally. "I must here ring for the Chief Butler."

He pulled on a golden cord, which was attached to a silver chain, which in turn disappeared into a tiny hole in the ceiling far above. Deep within, a bell sounded and before its sound had echoed and faded, a dignified Dwarf in morning coat and striped trousers—a sight that made Douglas want to laugh, irreverently—appeared, shoulders squared, back ramrod straight, chins pulled in, beard aquiver, and stomach—usually a source of great pride to male Dwarfs who believed in girth of middle as well as length of beard—pulled as close to his backbone as he could and still breathe.

"Sirs!" he cried—bellowed, almost, and echoes started

from all the passages that opened into this entryway. "Sirs?" a bit more softly. "Pray follow me to Prince Bry-armote, who awaits you."

He turned precisely on his heel and strode away. Douglas ignored his retreating back and took time to thank Doddle.

They shook hands and parted, the Dwarf returning to duty on the other side of the mountain, Douglas and Bronze Owl hurrying to catch up with the impatient Head Butler.

They were led into a bright, airy cavern thickly carpeted with green wool and hung with a dozen fine portraits and mountainscapes. The place was carved from granite Sea cliffs and lay not as deep in the mountains as Douglas thought they might be. The entire wall opposite the door was a window open to a narrow arm of Sea a thousand feet below and beyond. The sun, now in the west, lit a beautiful scene of rugged tumbled mountains and deep blue water patterned with slowly moving lines of breakers approaching the shore. Great white clouds sailed left to right in parade and a good ten miles away a dozen sails stretched to catch an evening on-shore breeze.

After a quick glance at these beauties, Douglas brushed past the Head Butler, who was taking a deep breath to announce them, flung his arms about the stout, grinning Bry-armote, and gave and got a hearty Dwarf hug.

"Well, made it at last!" said the Dwarf Prince. "Well, welcome to Dwelmland. And to you, Bronze Owl."

Douglas caught sight of a second person leaning against the window parapet, smoking a stone pipe filled with fragrant Dwarf tobacco.

" 'Tis Caspar Marlin!" Douglas cried in delight, and he shook the old sailor by the hand and clapped him on the back. "How did you get here? I thought you were heading for Westongue!"

"A long and interesting tale, but soon told," said the sailor. "With Prince Bryarmote's permission, of course."

"Of course, but let's sit on the terrace and have a cool drink before supper, friends. Caspar here has, as he said, a most fascinating story and one a bit disturbing, too, I must add."

"You are making a mystery of this," Douglas accused him. "Let's hear the whole story."

"Not," said Bryarmote, "before I congratulate you on

your advancement to Journeyman Wizard. Well done! And in record time, I think, from what I've heard of such things."

They sat in comfortably overstuffed chairs on the open balcony from which they could watch Sea change colors as the sun set behind them.

"I don't really know if advancement was quick because of ability—or because of the times in which we find ourselves," Douglas said.

"Nonsense," interrupted the Dwarf. "Flarman would not have allowed you to progress to Journeyman if he were uncertain you had earned every bit of it!"

"Let's hear Caspar's story," said the Journeyman Wizard, embarrassed.

When it was told and supper was served—Douglas was never to recall what was served that evening in Bryarmote's mountain fastness—he looked thoughtfully at the Dwarf and said: "What, then, are we to do?"

"My dear young Wizard," said the Dwarf, earnestly, "I was about to ask you the same thing. A Wizard, even a Journeyman Wiz, outweighs a mere Prince, no matter how wise and handsome."

"Wizards aren't automatically wise," said Douglas, slowly. "As witness Frigeon. Flarman's exact words were . . . ?"

"Simply that he and the Gulls would go on to Eternal Ice and see what they could find out there. And that I was to come here in his name and report his words to you," repeated Caspar.

"He had no advice, orders, or requests?"

"Well, if he did the big Gull forgot to tell me of them."

"I don't think the Gull would forget," said Bryarmote.

"Gulls are admittedly short of memory and scattered of brains," put in Bronze Owl, who had been sitting nearby, listening to everything but saying little. "However, in this case, I don't think Flarman's messenger would leave anything out."

"Nor do I," agreed Douglas. "Which leaves us with the original question: What are we to do?"

The Dwarf and the sailor lighted pipes and sat back to think.

"What were your intentions?" asked Bryarmote.

Douglas said, "I was to deliver to you for safekeeping a

certain item of great importance. After that, sail with you to join Flarman at Waterand.''

''Then I submit that is what you had better do,'' said Bryarmote.

''Wonderful! Of course I want you, too, Caspar, if you will come. . . .''

''Westongue can wait,'' said the salt, relighting his pipe. ''Troubles at Sea are a specialty of mine.''

''But the situation has changed. Flarman is a prisoner and nowhere near Warm Seas. Should that change our plans?''

''Only if you say so,'' said Bryarmote. ''I don't mean to abdicate responsibility just because you outrank me, Wizard,'' he added, leaning forward to stress his point with the stem of his pipe. ''But in matters of magic there is wisdom in placing more reliance on the decisions of a Journeyman Wizard than in the notions of a Dwarf. It is yours to decide what must be done and yours to lead once the plan is set. What *will* we do?''

Douglas looked at him for a long, hard moment, then turned his eyes to Bronze Owl, who nodded somberly in agreement. Douglas got up from his chair and stood at the balustrade looking out toward the southeast, his back to the company.

The Journeyman reviewed in his mind's eye the entire magic history of their conflict with the Ice King and the grave responsibility he had of carrying the Pearl on which the ultimate outcome might well solely rest.

''Have I the knowledge? The strength? I must believe so, since Flarman believes so. His decisions will be based on his beliefs about me. Mine must be based on my beliefs about him. Plus, he gave me my instructions, *knowing* he was about to go to Eternal Ice, I feel. Come, young Douglas, you must do what he asked you to do . . . but for one thing!''

At last he turned back to the waiting friends with decision in his face and manner. He had the look of a man, rather than boy.

''We will leave as soon as you can depart, Bryarmote. Just the four of us. I need to move as swiftly as I can to Augurian's isle.''

''I can leave almost at once. I've already sent most of my House Guard to Waterand by Thornwood's ships. It will take me the morning, no longer, to put the running of affairs here in my mother's capable hands. You must meet her, although she sees few outside the family these days. Flarman is a favorite of hers, and she would never forgive me if we left without introducing you.''

''I will be honored,'' replied Douglas. ''We will need a fast ship . . . and you to sail her, Caspar.''

''Dee-lighted,'' said the sailor, knocking out his pipe doddle in the fireplace.

There was one more thing to settle before they could go to bed, Douglas decided. He followed the Dwarf into his office, where the prince began shooting rapid-fire orders to subordinates and a battery of Dwarf secretaries.

He finished at last and sent them away. ''Time to quit for the night,'' he said to Douglas. ''Some things will just have to wait until morning.''

''No trouble, I hope?''

''No trouble! Not a bit! I have been preparing for this since Flarman's visit at the end of Dead Winter. What did you want me for, lad?''

Douglas sat down on a sofa and removed his left boot, from which he took the stuffing in the toe and shook out of it the Gray Pearl.

''You've heard from Caspar how he came by this?''

''Yes, he told me. I recognized the Pearl from his description. I said nothing to him.''

''That's just as well, I think. I trust Caspar Marlin but the fewer know the whereabouts of the Pearl . . . you agree?''

''Of course! What now?''

''Flarman's original plan was to hide the Pearl in the bottom of your deepest mine until he needed it. I think you knew that?''

''Yes, we discussed it.''

''Well, I've decided not to hide it. I'll carry it with me to Augurian. He is the only person other than the Master who understands anything about the Pearl and how it relates to Frigeon. With Flarman in Frigeon's hands I have a strong feeling that the Pearl is better off in the hands of one who next best knows how to use it.''

''I see,'' was the Dwarf's reply.

''Without exact knowledge of the Pearl's whereabouts, Frigeon always will worry about it. It may cause him to make mistakes; Flarman thinks it already has. A moving target is harder to hit, I'm told. So, it will go with us.''

He dropped the Pearl back into the toe of his left boot and replaced the stuffing, firmly.

Flarman settled down to enjoy his own Sea voyage. He was locked in a tiny cabin that was, however, warm and fairly dry—at least as dry and warm as all other cabins and spaces aboard, he knew.

He was served the same food as everyone aboard, but while the crew grumbled and swore about it, the Wizard said a few well-chosen words and made a few discreet passes with his fingers, and the slumgullion and hardtack became hearty roasts or tasty ragouts.

Captain Fribby was an unbad man—that is, he was as good as most men, did his job, and asked no embarrassing questions when authority spoke. He was experienced enough to sail a three-masted square-rigged ship, and smart enough to know not to cross the Ice King and minions like Eunicet and Bladder.

Once they were miles from the coast Fribby ordered the captive Wizard to be released and given the freedom of the deck. Surprisingly, a friendship grew between them: Fribby saw to it that Eunicet and Bladder never knew that Flarman was on deck.

Their course was northeastward for the port that served Frigeon's palace at the southern edge of Eternal Ice, a vast shield of solid ice stretching hundreds upon hundreds of cold miles to World's north pole. The port had no name, he told Flarman as the weather grew colder and colder day by day. *Icicle Princess* was under orders to avoid all land, he added.

"This Duke person don't want to take any chances on you jumping ship," the Captain explained, apologetically.

In time they sighted land, or at least dozens of tiny islets capped with gray-blue ice and white snow, laying offshore from the ice river. Fribby took the helm and gingerly threaded his way through these barrier isles into an almost icebound anchorage. On its shore was a good-sized village, where several hundred ships of all descriptions tossed restlessly at anchor in the harbor. Frigeon's fleet had not yet sailed, Flarman observed.

The crew sullenly hacked frozen spray from halyards and

sheets to work the lines, and shouted insults to the long-shoremen who waited to tie the ship to the wharf.

"Not at all a pleasant place, I'd say," Flarman commented to himself, aloud. "Come in, Captain Bribby! This is your brig, after all. No need to knock on the door."

To have the Wizard know so precisely what he was doing on the other side of the thick, iron-bound oak door rattled Fribby and gave him a thrill of fright.

"By Thoin's groin!" he swore as he entered. "If ye are so good a magicker, why didn't you fly yourself away a week agone and save us the trouble of coming to this cold and nasty place?"

"And you have a message for me from Eunicet?"

"Those two, they told me—"

"That I would stay here aboard your ship until they can get an armed escort to take me to the Palace?"

Fribby ran his hands over his stubbled chin and through his tumbled hair.

"Yes, yes, stay aboard. Escort in the morning. Day's of about equal length as night, now. Did you know that in midwinter the sun hardly rises before it sets?"

"Yes, I knew that, having been in the Far North on several occasions. Anyway, I wish to thank you for the pleasant voyage hither. As you yourself pointed out, I could have escaped whenever I wanted to, but does it occur to you, Frisby—"

"Fribby!"

" . . . Fribby, that I am here because I want to be here? I want to talk with Frigeon—"

"Please, not that name!" cried the Captain with real fear in his eyes. " 'Tis an evil name and one to conjure with!"

"You poor, benighted swab jockey," said Flarman Flowerstalk, sadly. "I'll give you some excellent advice and pray that you have sense enough left to take it."

Flarman gestured with one hand, and a yellow flame sprang to life in the center of the cabin's table. Fribby quailed at the three-foot flame licking hungrily at the low overhead. It gave plenty of light and some heat, but didn't even scorch the wood.

"You are basically a decent man," said Flarman, earnestly. "My advice is to clear out of here, sail south, and join Augurian at Waterand for the fight ahead. After all this is over, you can go back to being a simple, sturdy Seacaptain and your own master, as you once were.''

''What if Augurian and you . . . you know . . . don't win? What then, sir Wizard?''

''In my heart I know we'll win,'' said Flarman, seriously. ''Do you not agree, when you really think of it?''

''Perhaps because I don't really want Fr——that King there to win. What kind of a world would he rule? I ask myself.''

''Well, then?''

The Captain glanced dramatically over each shoulder in turn, squinting in the bright light of the flame. ''No-o-o-o, if I thought about it at all, I thought the war would go along for years, generations, and I'd collect me pay and retire at an old age to some sunny island.''

''You are not any kind of a fool, Fribby! You should know Frigeon better by now. He will not fight unless he can fight dirty. He means to conquer the whole World, then enjoy his depravity and unearned wealth. And fast! Let me tell you, in this Battle in Warm Seas there will be a clear-cut outcome, one victor. And I tell you it must be the Confederation of Light, rather than this crippling, pain-wracked, dark cold— Frigeon's cold.''

''I would make me pay on one side as well as the other,'' said Fribby, but he didn't sound as though he meant it.

''We can never entirely destroy evil. The best we can do is expect it, face it squarely, and fight it. To do otherwise is to let the Dark and Frigeon win, don't you see? Well, *we* will win!''

The flame seemed to flutter and weave at his words like a candle held too close to lips that spoke. Fribby stood entranced, fixed, hypnotized for a long moment, then spoke no more but turned and opened the brig door.

''Captain Tribby,'' called Flarman.

''Fribby,'' the seaman said weakly. ''What can I do for you, Wizard? You say you don't want to be rescued or turned loose, that it is your wish to face King Fr . . . Fr . . . Frigeon,'' the other finally gasped out, trembling. ''You say you wish to be in Frigeon's power. What can *I* do to help?''

His eyes widened in shocked surprise.

''There, did you see? Did you hear? I said his name almost without stammering!''

" 'Tis a pity. 'Tis true," quoted Flarman, seating himself on a sea chest under his porthole.

"You won't even let me take you away from here, tonight?"

"No, I must see and talk to Frigeon. You, however, will stay here until I return and we will sail to Waterand together, friend. If you will. Fribby, now do something smart and right and hard, for its own sake. Stay here tonight and tomorrow night awaiting my return. If I am not back the following day, flee to Augurian and tell him what has happened and that you wish to serve."

"And if Frigeon should order me to sail before you return?"

"Sail and head for Waterand as fast as you can. I will find other means."

Fribby shrugged like a man who has just laid down an intolerable burden, one he hadn't even known he carried.

"I shall await you, Flarman Firemaster. As you order!"

"No, not order. Of your own free will. That's the first requirement to break the Ice King's frozen grip on your soul. Good night, Captain Fribby."

As he strolled back onto the poop, the Captain of the *Icicle Princess* suddenly realized that his name had no longer been mangled. Nor his heart, mind, nor soul, he decided, and he began to whistle softly to himself.

Chapter Fourteen

A few minutes with Bryarmote's mother convinced Douglas that what set her apart from all others were her dignity—which allowed her to don a gardening smock and water her flowers while they chatted—and her serene confidence. Confidence of many years, and of love, the Journeyman Wizard decided. He liked her tremendously from the very first, and it was obvious she liked him, too.

"It is so unfortunate," Finesgold said, tilting her long-necked copper watering can over a pot of red geraniums, "that these disturbances will take you fast away, just when we have met. I wanted to talk to you about gardening and fire magic and how the valley people are faring now. I'm afraid we here in Dwelmland fall behind the news, you see."

She put down the can and turned to him. "Now, Douglas, my young man, let me look at you in the daylight! Flarman's own choice as Apprentice and Journeyman, are you? I trust Flarman's common sense and foresight in all things. He has been known to make mistakes but not this time, I believe. Bless him, for all that!"

And she stood on tiptoe and gave him a kiss on the cheek and laughed when he blushed with pleasure and surprise.

"Does our Flarman still keep Blue Teakettle?" she asked, a sudden change in subject.

"Oh, yes! Blue is still there, although I suppose she doesn't have too much to do with the both of us gone," said Douglas. He was pleased to talk of home with this wonderful lady.

"You know," Finesgold said, "I gave Blue Teakettle to Flarman myself, years and years ago. I taught her cooking and housekeeping because I thought a bachelor Wizard

should have regular hot meals and a freshly made bed to
sleep in.''

"I didn't know that, ma'am.''

"If you don't believe me, just ask Blue Teakettle," said
she, tartly.

"I believe you," Douglas said. "Something about you
reminds me of Blue Teakettle. I suspect Bronze Owl knows
it, though. Bronze Owl knows a great deal about Flarman
Flowerstalk.''

"Ah, here is the door knocker now!" cried Finesgold,
pointing out the window.

Bronze Owl flew in at the wide casement and alighted on
the back of one of the small, ladylike armchairs. He nodded
good morning to them both.

"I was just told that Princess Finesgold was the one who
presented Blue Teakettle to the Wizard," Douglas told him.

"Ah, certainly, I remember that," said Bronze Owl, nodding creakily. "And did she tell you what Flarman gave her
in return?''

"No, I didn't.''

"He gave her a door knocker . . .''

"Not you!" exclaimed Douglas.

"No, no! Another! It's upon her door, out there." And
he indicated the door through which Douglas had entered.
Douglas recalled noting it in passing—a large, bronze
hand.

"It has enchantment on it," explained Finesgold, proudly.
"It will reach out and hold any who attempt to enter without
permission, and raise a terrible alarm if a miscreant tries to
break in.''

"For friends and family it knocks beautifully," said Owl.
"I've always admired its tone.''

Finesgold took Douglas by the hand and showed him her
flowers.

"I have something to ask you," she said, suddenly. "Is
Flarman well?''

"I wish I could say for sure"—Douglas shook his head—
"for he has allowed himself to be captured by Frigeon's
people, and the Gulls told our friend Caspar Marlin that they
were talking him to Eternal Ice.''

"Oh, dear, goodness!" exclaimed Finesgold, although
she didn't seem nearly as upset by the news as Douglas had

expected. "I do hope he thought to take galoshes and a warm cloak. Frigeon always was careless about cold water and drafts, you know. One of the reasons I never liked him, even in the Old Days."

"You know Frigeon!" asked Douglas, surprised.

"Of course! We were all rather neighbors, years gone by. Frigeon was and still is an impatient sort, bossy and wanting to run things *his* way, not let things take care of themselves, as they usually do very nicely, you know.

"Ah, Bryarmote," she said as her son entered, "have tea brought out here, please. I know you are in a hurry but I'm enjoying this young Wizard so much I'm loath to let him go off to battle.

"Oh, yes, I know about Frigeon's plans and all," she continued when they were settled on the balcony. "But what with my son, and my Wizards, I'm not really much worried about the outcome."

"Mother, you're optimistic about this struggle?" asked Bryarmote, respectfully. "It is going to be quite sticky, you know. Many will die, and many could—worse—be enchanted or enslaved, before 'tis over."

"I know," sighed the Lady Dwarf. Then she smiled. "But I do believe we will triumph over Frigeon, no matter what Powers he has gathered to himself. I know all of them on both sides and, you see, I would place a wager on Flowerstalk and Company, any time!"

As she kissed Douglas good-bye she said, "You can carry a message to Flarman for me, Douglas. Don't worry about him, by the by; he can take care of himself. As long as he remembers to wear his galoshes and stays out of drafts. Tell Flarman I still love him best after my son and the memory of my husband. He is to come and see me for a whole month after this business is over."

She waved them out and when Douglas turned back one last time she blew him a kiss.

In the first blue-gray of evening they boarded *Diamondpoint,* Bryarmote's schooner, and cast off, catching not only the ebb tide on that coast but soon an offshore breeze, which grew stronger as they sailed southeastward.

Caspar, now Sailing Master, was as proud as a new papa. Bryarmote, as Captain, was admittedly no Seaman. Within minutes of putting to Sea, Caspar proved he *was*. *Diamond-point* cleaved the waves toward Waterand and Warm Seas, under full ordinary sail.

Chapter Fifteen

FLARMAN stumbled once on the march across the glacier to the Ice Palace and suffered in silence as the soldiers yanked him up by his coat collar. Sensing they intended to repeat the indignity as often as possible, he muttered a spell under his breath.

Thereafter he glided along like a sled without even moving his feet beneath his flowing robe. As he would not oblige them by falling, the Dreads marched faster and faster, trying to spill him onto the sharp ice again.

By the time they reached the gates of the Palace, the normally unflappable Dreads were stumbling and rasping great, white gasps of beer-flavored steam.

Flarman remained quiet and composed.

The gate screeched open unoiled hinges and his escort marched within, the Wizard in their midst. A smaller guard—ten of the largest and ugliest Men Flarman had ever had the misfortune to meet—led him within the vast, black-ice pile, down ruler-straight corridors between empty walls, and past closed doors eleven feet tall; blank sentinels of empty rooms behind.

Most of the rooms stood unused, their doors rimmed with ancient hoarfrost. The dust upon the floor was thick and undisturbed.

"Gloomy, chilly place," he remarked cheerfully to the Captain of Dreads. The officer gave him a grim look. The squad double-timed around a corner and ran down a new corridor. Here there were some signs of life: bits of trash scattered about, frozen remnants of food.

They passed kitchens from which came stale smells of poorly prepared food. The very air had the rancid, thin feel of cold grease. Flarman wrinkled his nose, clucked to himself, and cast a spell that wafted to each soldier's nostrils the most delicious smells buried in their memories.

They squirmed, licked their lips, swallowed—and swore. Flarman imagined just what smells each detected. Was the officer tormented by the memory of his mother's blueberry pie? Was that scarred killer being flooded with the aroma of succulent, tender roast beef? One ruffian, the one with a patch over an eye, was actually drooling!

The Wizard chuckled silently.

The door of his prison closed with a hollow roar and all was suddenly silent. The walls were of ice blocks. It was impossible to tell whether his prison was above ground or a dungeon, as there were no windows, save a thin slit high on one wall through which guards could spy on their prisoner.

Flarman was definitely not impressed with the accommodations. The room was bare, with no light except a single tiny lamp hoisted far out of reach. The least sound boomed and echoed annoyingly. The furniture was a simple pallet covered with dirty straw and a rag of a blanket, a ewer on a rickety stand, and a three-legged metal stool.

Within a half hour the place was much cozier. In rapid fire, with splendid economy of magic phrases and flowing gestures, the Fire Wizard created a large fireplace in the middle of one wall and in it a blazing coal fire throwing cheerful flickers of pleasant red and yellow and blue flame out over a thick, shaggy hearth rug.

"It calls for a cat," Flarman said aloud, and reaching into an inner fold of his traveling cloak, he brought out Black Flame, placing him in the center of the rug. Black Flame meowed once, walked around in a circle twice, lay down, and began to drowse contentedly.

Flarman clapped his hands sharply and the pallet became a sturdy four-poster bed with becoming linens and a firm mattress suitable for a Wizard's old back. Against the chill he wainscoted the walls and created arras to hang above the chair rail. He gave a curious sort of whistle and the stool became an easy chair pulled up to the fire.

He went on with his redecoration, creating a large bay window in one wall with diamond panes and gathered curtains. The view beyond was of sleet-swept darkness but that only enhanced the coziness of the bright interior. He added a table laden with good things to eat and a set of long, high shelves of shiny, leather-bound volumes stamped with gold titles.

Selecting a book of humorous anecdotes, the Wizard seated himself at the laden table; served himself generous helpings of hot, rich stew with lots of meat, potatoes, onions, and carrots; chose a tossed green salad; and poured himself a cup of fragrant, black coffee. Spreading the book open before him, he began to eat and read with every sign of enjoyment, laughing aloud every so often.

Laying aside his book, he moved his hands toward the slit window. The slit became a floor-to-ceiling picture window through which the Dread guards who had been peering at him could easily see every part of the room, especially the sumptuous meal and the warm fire.

As he finished his pudding there came the faint sound of footsteps outside the door. A key rattled. The door did not open.

He ignored it and adjourned to read in the easy chair by the fire. For a long while there was no further disturbance.

A quarter hour later there were louder noises at the door, followed at once by hollow booming knocks.

Most annoying, thought Flarman.

He went to the door, opened a wicket (which hadn't been there before), and peered out. Two dozen Dreads held a foot-thick icicle, fifteen feet long. They were battering at the heavy door—to no avail, it was obvious, for they were cursing and perspiring in the heat of unaccustomed labor. Many had even departed from the *Rules and Regulations Under Pain of Death,* written for them by Frigeon, enough to remove their black leather tunics and baldrics.

"I say, what in the world is all this noise about?" demanded Flarman, pleasantly. "Why are you knocking with a chunk of ice? A knuckle would have done as well. Try knocking in a gentlemanly way, sirrah!" he added, looking at the Dread Captain. He closed the wicket gently.

Within five minutes there came a more decorous rap on the door, knuckles on wood.

Rising from the easy chair, Flarman went to the wicket again.

"What can I do for you, Captain?" He smiled.

"The prisoner will open his door!" shouted the Captain.

"I beg your pardon?"

"Open this door, prisoner!"

"No," said Flarman, firmly, "I have had a hard journey on that old tub of a ship of yours and a long hard walk from the Seashore. I am not a young man, Captain. I intend to stay in my room this evening and tonight, read this excellent book—which I recommend to you, sir—and retire early so as to be at my best when I talk to Frigeon tomorrow morning. Or are you telling me that Frigeon has already asked to see me?"

The Dread Captain was ready to boil right out of his cuirass.

"No, by Toth, *His Majesty* has *not* sent for you. *I* want to take you to another cell. This is a disgrace! Who has ever heard of a prisoner in a comfortable cell, eating better than a Captain of Dreads? Open this door, Wizard! Open it now, or—"

"Now, now, Captain. You'll only make yourself ill by shouting and ranting so. Let me tell you something, Captain. You can batter-ram this door until noon Wednesday next and it won't do you a bit of good. The more you bang, the tougher it's going to get and it won't make a bit of difference if I'm sleeping, either.

"So, go away and don't bother me until you have word that Frigeon is ready to see me. Then knock in a civilized manner, and the door will be opened. Do you understand?"

"I'll batter and batter until the whole damned palace shakes," roared the soldier.

"Suit yourself," said Flarman, and he shut the wicket firmly in the Captain's red face once more.

There came a faint, anguished shout, then silence. There was no more battering, so he returned to the easy chair and resumed his reading. At the end of the chapter he rose, banked the fire, turned out the lights (with a snap of his fingers), undressed, put on a red flannel nightgown with matching nightcap, and went to his warm, comfortable bed, Black Flame curled at his feet. They slept like babes until morning.

He was breakfasting on bacon and scrambled eggs with a touch of chive, drinking hot tea and dunking chocolate-frosted doughnuts in it. There was a polite knock on his prison door.

"Come in," he called, wiping his lips with a damask napkin and turning to the door, which opened at a slight touch, revealing a disheveled Dread Captain of pale face and tousled hair.

"Oh, Captain, good morning! How nice of you to call. Do come in. Have a seat. . . ." A chair appeared across the table and a place setting with gold spoon, knife, and fork.

"Have some tea, or would you prefer coffee? The eggs are delicious. Do you get good common here? No? Sit down, man, sit down!"

Despite himself the Dread seated himself gingerly in the proffered chair and even accepted a heaping plate of eggs and bacon and a cup of tea. He had been up all night and had neither dined nor breakfasted. Flarman's food was heavenly to smell, and even more heavenly to taste . . . which the Captain did quickly, with a regrettable lack of table manners.

"Sir Wizard, my Master, His Majesty Frigeon the First, *Ultimum Horrendum*, bids you wait upon him this morning. Please."

"Fine, fine! All very well, although the hour is a bit late," agreed Flarman, genially. "Frigie used to be an early riser but I guess he's getting old, like me. I love to lie abed when there isn't much to do nowadays, but I only get to do it when I'm a guest somewhere. Is he waiting now?"

"Yes, Magister. Will you come with me and make no further trouble?"

"I? . . . Make trouble? My dear Captain, surely you cannot say that I am a troublemaker!"

The officer growled softly to himself as he rose.

"Yes, well, the less said, the better, then. Shall we go to Frigeon? I suppose he will receive me in his High Hall?"

"Yes, Wizard, that is where I am ordered to escort you."

"Well, I suppose I'm honored, although from a practical standpoint it surely isn't necessary. . . . But if you insist, I will not spoil the boys' fun."

"Boys?" asked the Captain, leading him to the door, which swung open before he touched it. Flarman paused only to sweep Black Flame into his coat pocket.

"Your fellows, the Dreads. Well-trained bunch, I have heard. They have a pretty tough reputation. A soldier must be rough, tough, and relentless, they say. But he has to have a heart, too, don't you think? Otherwise he becomes a machine and reacts unthinkingly rather than acts with loyalty, wisdom, and common sense. Think about that, Captain.''

Up a broad crystal staircase the squad marched.

"When you think about it," said Flarman to no one in particular, "there is nothing funnier than soldiers trying to stay in step climbing a stair, especially one that curves.''

The picture planted in their minds' eyes caused several of the twenty-four ramrod-straight, grim soldiers to stifle laughs and try to control involuntary grins. It also made the harassed Captain want to howl with rage.

They marched down an aisle between ranks of courtiers bundled in the most luxurious furs and woolens. But their eyes were frozen cold and their faces had the blue-white look of frostbite.

The High Throne Room was so large that it took the Dreads a full minute to cross. They came to a spit-and-polish halt exactly sixteen paces from the lowest step of the Ice King's throne, carved from a single massive crystal bathed in a light that made it glimmer and glitter like a magnificent blue diamond. Flarman noted that it was really only a huge rock crystal, after all, albeit impressive in size and clarity.

Flarman kept right on, stepping between two front-rank guardsmen. Before anyone could stop him he marched up the steps of the dais, stopping only when he was looking directly into the chill, cramped, crabbed, cruel, evil, twisted features of Frigeon, further distorted by anger and surprise . . . and a bit of fear, too.

"Ho, Frigeon, old man!" Flarman greeted him. "Long time since we were nose to nose, isn't it? You've changed! For the worse, I fear. Didn't your mother say, when you were a child, 'Don't make such faces, Frigie! It will freeze that way!' It seems yours did!''

He chuckled—a strangely disturbing sound in that vast, cold, and horrid room. Somewhere in the far reaches someone snickered. Frigeon's eyes flashed at once with anger, seeking the laugher. There was no way to tell who had giggled.

When Frigeon turned back to speak to his prisoner, he found Flarman had turned his own back and was thanking the Dreads for their kind escort.

"If you'll take some well-meant advice, Captain," he was saying, loud enough for the whole room to hear, "you'll take your men off and give them a good breakfast. Nothing like a hearty breakfast, especially in a cold place like this. Frigie . . ."

He spun on his heel now to the Ice King, smiling.

"Frigie . . ."

"Guards!" roared the Ice King so loud that half a dozen decorative icicles hanging from the throne's canopy crashed to the floor. "*Guards!*"

The Captain stepped forward, opened his mouth to speak, but Flarman silenced him with a gesture.

"Now, Snowman, you know there is nothing this poor soldier can do about me. Starve me? He tried that last night and ended up hungrier than I. Freeze me? I am a Fire-Adept. You should know as well as anyone that you can't chill me off if I don't want to be chilled.

"I am here because I want to be here," he stated, flatly. "Do you really think I'd have allowed that pipsqueak little ex-General and the sniveling false Duke to capture me if I hadn't *wanted* to come? I can't harm you. You are in your element. You can't hurt me, either, or you would have, centuries ago. Let's face facts and get this unpleasant business over so I can return to my friends, waiting for me in a warmer clime. Send this crowd away," Flarman snapped. "You'll want to talk privately with me."

Frigeon glared furiously back at him but, in the end, ordered the guards and the courtiers to leave.

"Don't think I can't see through you, Frigeon. You have to keep up appearances in front of your tag-tails and your Dreads—what a foul name for a bunch of poor country lads! Can't let 'em see we're on an equal footing, eh?"

Frigeon slumped back into his cushions, growling incoherently. He had not expected to make Flarman grovel—at least not yet, nor here—but he had expected to keep the upper hand in his own Palace.

Meanwhile, Flarman calmly took out his pipe and lit it, knowing his very calmness infuriated the other. He blew smoke rings that rose to the dim reaches of the high ceiling, forming the letters of his name. They changed to the letters of certain pet names that Frigeon once had, and which he hated.

"Stop this nonsense!" Frigeon roared, trying to say it in steely, chill tones, but failing entirely. "What is it you came to ask of me?"

"You brought *me* here," Flarman Flowerstalk pointed out. "Why did you go to so much trouble? Just to give what's-his-name, the ex-General, something to do?"

Frigeon had trouble remembering names. It bothered him as much as anything about himself. He felt his anger getting the best of him once again. He breathed deeply several times . . . but what was the good when Flarman sat there, blowing blue smoke rings?

"I'm going to put you in ice," the King ground out, still seething. "I'm going to put you so deep in Eternal Ice that it will take you a dozen centuries to melt your way out, Fire Wizard! I may not be able to destroy you but I can put you out of circulation so long you won't even be remembered by the Fairies. Or that snot of an Apprentice you've come up with."

"You wouldn't like Douglas Brightglade," said Flarman, for a sentence suddenly dangerously quiet. "He's a warm, honest youth. Besides, he's already passed to Journeyman. A natural Wizard, believe me! How long did it take you to make Journeyman, Frigie? A hundred and eight years, as I recall."

Frigeon made a supreme effort to cool his anger. "Flarman, you blemish on the backside of World, you will *be* in my power, you know. I'll make you prisoner once I've destroyed the poor, helpless, thoughtless ninnies you champion. You can't help them one whit! You'll be out of circulation for five centuries, believe me."

Flarman hitched his chair closer and smiled at his Enemy, saying:

"No, Frigeon, old hat, you are wrong. Ordinarily, I realize, you could do just as you have boasted. But there is one thing, a small but powerful thing, that prevents you now and always will."

"And that is?" asked Frigeon, smugly, reseating himself on his cushioned throne.

"The Gray Pearl, of course! It's out of your reach, hidden from you. And as long as *you* don't know where it is . . . you dare not hinder me! Because," he stabbed his finger at the man on the throne, emphatically, "if you try to put me out of the way, you'll never recover the Gray Pearl."

Frigeon leaped to his feet and snatched a dagger of ice from the belt beneath his blue-and-black robe of state. Darting forward, he sought to plunge it into the Fire-Adept's breast.

But the dagger melted away before its needle point could touch Flarman's jerkin, turning to water, then steam. It burned the Ice King's fingers.

For a long minute the two stood watching each other, unmoving. At last Frigeon sat down wearily on his throne.

"It makes no difference," he lied, and Flarman knew he was lying. "Having the Pearl, and knowing how to use it against me, are different things. Before you can unlock its secret, I will be master of World."

"But wasting time and energy looking for it, at the very least," said Flarman.

"I *will* find it! You'll have to take it from hiding, to study it, to work over it, to discuss it with others, to handle it by the light of day and while you're doing that, not only is it vulnerable to my ten thousand spies, but I will be killing and conquering and laying waste your precious World, turning it to a big ball of ice. Am I not right?"

"Of course you're right, old fellow. And I know it, better than anyone else except perhaps . . . well, let him be nameless. Yes, finding the secret of the Gray Pearl is a hard job."

"When I get it back—and I *shall* get it, for I am nothing if not persistent—that day my rule over World will be complete and you will find yourself in that tomb of Eternal Ice I promised you. And your friend of Warm Seas. And your Apprentice or Journeyman, Douglas Whatever. Even your familiar and your Bronze Owl. I'll remember the important names then, you can believe me!"

"Very interesting," mused Flarman. "Well, I must be going. Some friends are waiting for me. I really think you'll have a much more difficult time subduing us than you think. I was not impressed, for one thing, with your Dreads. They didn't frighten me at all. They have a lot of trouble thinking for themselves, for some reason. I wouldn't put too much confidence in them, if I were you. But then, you probably don't put any trust in anyone, do you, Frigeon?''

''Good-bye, old man,'' snarled Frigeon, his hot temper rising once more. ''I hate you more than words can tell. I will beat you and find a way to destroy you, too. Don't ever forget that.''

''I doubt you will ever have the power to do that, Old Enemy. Depend on it, we'll meet again, however.''

Giving his chair a pat that made it disappear in a puff of smoke, Flarman Flowerstalk started down the steps as Frigeon beat furiously on a great brazen gong beside his throne.

The Dread escort reentered, recovered from their unseemly disarray. They formed a square around the Wizard as he reached the great doors, squeezing through as he passed into the anteroom beyond and started down the crystal stair. A hundred courtiers watched in puzzlement and concern. A few giggled behind their hands, trying to look fierce at the same time, and failing.

Flarman walked straight through the maze of corridors and out through the main gate into the teeth of a howling snowstorm. He never hesitated, gliding over the uneven and slippery road as if skating on the Brook at Wizard's High. A little over an hour later, not even breathing hard, he arrived, serene and smiling, at the docks, surrounded by twenty-five completely winded, snow-covered, frostbitten and once more disheveled Dreads.

''Ahoy, *Icicle Princess*!'' Flarman hailed when he came abreast of the square-rigger. ''Permission to come aboard?''

He strode up the gangplank and hopped down to the deck.

''No, no, Captain,'' he called to the Captain of Dreads, ''you'd better stay here. You'll just get yourself and your men into trouble if you follow me further. Go home and get warm, boys. Remember what I said about a decent breakfast. And thank you again for the escort, Captain.''

He nodded pleasantly to Fribby, who was standing by, flabbergasted at the sight of the Wizard returned and the Dreads gasping in the snow on the dock. The soldiers straggled away into the storm looking very much like whipped dogs.

''Can you get under way in this storm, Captain Fribby?'' Flarman asked.

''Oh, yes, sure, Sir Wizard. Wind's right and the snow

won't keep me from finding passage out of here. Full tide isn't an hour away, so we can weigh at once. Better to put some distance between us and F-Frigeon, I reckon.''

"Good man! You said his name with hardly a stammer that time. Cast off, if that's the right phrase. Who's this at the helm? Bigbelly, isn't it?''

"Yes, sir. Sailing Master Bigbelly, that is, sir. Welcome aboard! A gent what can walk away from Frigeon is worth following, I'd say, Captain Fribby.''

Huddled in a drafty, deserted tavern of very low repute on the docks were two shivering figures wrapped in new, woolen cloaks against the deep, biting cold of the storm.

"Well, I'll be . . . ,'' chattered Bladder. "Did you see that?''

"I would have sworn the old Wizard would be frozen meat by now,'' agreed Eunicet.

"Aye,'' said the other, shivering uncontrollably. "He's a man to watch out for, I'm thinking. He's stolen *Princess* to sail south to join Thornwood and Augurian!''

"I'm sure of it. A battle is shaping up down there. And we must steer clear of it, General. Which is our ship?''

Bladder pointed to a dingy yet rakish brigantine rolling wildly at anchor in the roadstead, barely visible through the heavy snow.

"There she be, and we best be getting aboard, Seasickness and all. The tide has turned and I, for one, don't relish facing either that sour Steward or the King over our requisitioning.''

They stole a small boat tied to the dock and rowed inexpertly and laboriously through the harbor chop to the sloop *Ponderous*. Her skipper gave them no trouble when he saw the Seal of Frigeon on the documents Eunicet had forged. He at once set about getting the ship under way.

"I'm for me bunk,'' said Bladder to Eunicet. "Don't waken me until it gets warmer!''

His companion followed him below, out of the snow and salt spray.

In the night Eunicet's skipper heard faint sounds of a vessel ahead of them, but as they sailed south on *Ponderous's* best course, the sounds were soon heard no more.

"We've overtaken and passed *Icicle Princess*," observed the Captain to his First Officer. "I only hope that our new masters were not planning to follow her. We'd get the blame, you can wager."

"Nothing we could do about it," agreed the other. "We had no orders."

And he continued to hold the ship's head to the south through the night.

Outside *Princess*'s cabin portholes the wind blew steadily and the curling mist that had replaced the snow combined with night to put her in a seamless black sack, with no stars, no moons, and no sight of Sea except for an occasional gray wave top.

"And how long before we sail out of this fog?" asked Flarman at supper. "Too long would put us in Warm Seas, and I understand its waters are filled with sharp rocks and shallows and small, steep islets and such. Am I right?"

"I have never sailed as far south as Waterand, of course," admitted Fribby, "but it is my understanding that you are quite correct, Sir Wizard. However, at this time of the year it is fair in Warm Sea, I'm told. I suspect that's why Frigeon picked this time to attack."

"Yes," put in Bigbelly, "in the summer there are sudden storms called typhoons. In winter the seas between Eternal Ice and the South are often less rough. Earlier or later would make it hard for Frigeon to maneuver and resupply his fleet."

Flarman nodded his understanding.

"How long will we be enfogged, Captain?" he repeated.

"Hard to say," answered Fribby. He glanced at Bigbelly for confirmation. "Could be any minute now, or could be a day or two. We've a way to go, yet. At least, this way we can't be seen by any enemy."

The two officers took their leave, thanking the Fire-Adept for the best meal they had ever had afloat. On deck Bigbelly looked aloft and said, "I can almost see the crosstree, Captain. Fog might just be lifting."

Aboard *Ponderous* the mist had already lifted. The nameless Captain walked to the main cabin door and pressed his ear to the panel.

"Still sound asleep, and no orders yet! Good! We'll maintain our course, helmsman."

And he went to his own bunk knowing he would be called if the wind shifted and a new tack was called for.

Douglas and Caspar were taking a turn around the deck when, like a curtain pulled aside, *Diamondpoint* emerged from Lasting Mists and plunged into the full glory of a perfectly clear night with a million stars bright overhead.

"We'll change course now," decided Caspar.

"Let me help, Caspar. I really would like to learn Seamanship," said the Journeyman Wizard. "What's to do first?"

"Roust out the hands, first," said the new Master of *Diamondpoint*. "Be my bo'sun. Just stick your head down the fo'castle hatch and bawl 'All hands on deck!' at the top of your voice. That'll get 'em up in a rush and we'll go on from there."

Douglas rather self-consciously performed this duty and within ten minutes the brigantine was ready to swing southward along the wall of mist. By dawn the mists were no longer visible. The air was sensibly warmer to the helmsman, a muscular young Dwarf named Pickkol.

He sighed contentedly. Better than ice and snow, he thought to himself. He kept *Diamondpoint* carefully heading across the westerly wind, cruising for Warm Seas.

Eunicet awoke with a bad taste in his mouth, an empty feeling in his gut, grit in his eyes, and a curse on his lips.

"Blast and damnation! Foul slime and sulfurous pits! Where am I? Where's my breakfast? Send in my girls! I want a bath and a change of clothes and . . ."

He went on at some length before he realized that Bladder, lying in the bunk opposite, was grinning from ear to ear, thoroughly enjoying the tirade.

"I'll have your head for this, Bladder! What do you mean laughing at your Duke? I demand respect or I'll have these scurvy sailormen toss you overboard, rotting garbage for the sharks."

Bladder howled with mirth until he could hardly speak.

Eunicet was one of the foulest awakeners he had ever met.

"No more of your fancy ways, Eunicet! Maybe once again you'll have servants and serfs to scream at and order about, but I am Bladder, not your common slave, understand? I serve by my own free will. Get that through your headful of belly-button fluff! We go on together or you go nowhere at all. There will always be a need for Bladder in your life. You are particularly incompetent, so there!''

He thumbed his red-veined nose at the ex-ruler of Dukedom and glared back at him for a full half minute before the other looked down and away.

"Unfortunately you are a hundred-percent right," admitted Eunicet. "I just don't see why you can't at least be civil. Would it hurt? I am, after all, a full-fledged nobleman."

"I'll grant you that, insofar as we are in the company of lesser men," Bladder relented as his anger cooled. "In going about our plans, perhaps—yes, I believe so—we should keep up the appearances of Master and Man. You have the name, the style, and the habit of command as most Men understand it. They believe you when you say you are a Duke, now, don't they? So . . ."

"So?"

"An agreement between us? Master and Man in public. And you will do what I say in matters of planning and action. We did well that way until Highlandorm. Both were satisfied with that arrangement, no?"

"I suppose I agree, yes," said Eunicet, sulkily. "We do make an evil pair. Yes, yes; no more ranting and insulting, except as might be expected from a noble of my high birth."

"We need a plan," observed the ex-General, picking his teeth with a dirty thumbnail. "What do you have in mind, Duke? Take some island kingdom for your own?"

"Not just *any* island kingdom. A *rich* island kingdom where the men have all gone off to fight Frigeon. Easy and rich with lots of women to wait upon me and children to put to hard work. What do you know about this Warm Sea and its blasted isles?"

"Very little, really," admitted the other, regretfully. "Until latterly I was never given much to oceans and islands and such. I am a landsman in me heart."

"I would have said you had no heart at all," observed Eunicet with a sour grimace. "Who would know?"

"Oh, I suppose this Captain or his Sailing Master," said Bladder. Just then the Captain appeared at their door, tying a black cravat about his scrawny neck and settling a short sword at his hip.

"My Lords," he said, bowing. "I await your orders."

"As you know, there is about to be a great Sea battle, probably near Waterand," said Eunicet. "In the next few days, a week at the most, as soon as our liege lord is ready to attack."

"Aye, m'lord. I am aware of the rumors of war," admitted the captain.

"Many of the Seamen Augurian has called up to Waterand are from the island kingdoms to the south, and they have left their home islands virtually unguarded."

The Captain nodded. This is just what might happen, he thought.

"To divert the attention of Augurian's allies at Waterand, we . . . along with a number of others . . . are being sent southward to harry, loot, and . . . well, you know what I mean. It will distract the Water-Adept and the Fire Wizard just when they should be concentrating on battle."

"A most inspired plan, if I may say so," said the Captain.

"Ah . . . our Master of Ice bade us go, but didn't give us specific orders. We were to consult with you, sirrah, and arrive at the best point of attack. We were told you knew these waters well."

"Yes, I suppose I do," said the other, doubtfully, not wishing to contradict Frigeon. "But it has been some years . . . perhaps if we were to look at the charts?"

"A truly inspired idea," cried Eunicet, clapping him on the back. "Let us look at the charts!"

They followed the little Captain into the main cabin, where he rummaged about in a locker and hauled out a half dozen ragged, tattered, much-thumbed charts.

"Yes, yes, yes, here we are, sirs. Chart of Southern Sea, and Islands of Warm Sea. Yes, these are just what we need."

Bladder put on his most pompous look and said, "Show us where we are now, Captain."

After much consulting with the ship's log and the wizened Master, a mouse of a man with a bald head and a dirty red bandanna for a belt, the Captain put his finger on a spot on the blue Sea near an ornamental Sea-Serpent.

"Here we be, sir, exactly, isn't that right, Bullon?"

"Yes, yes, I do see," said Eunicet, who had not the least, most rudimentary knowledge of maps. "Er . . . General?"

Bladder studied the surrounding waters and a hundred small islands shown on the chart. At least he knew something about maps.

"One of this group, I should think? Bad luck to raid an island that didn't send all its able-bodied to the wars, eh? But the Captain here can arrange a scouting shore party. He'd lead it himself, of course . . ."

The Captain nodded, suddenly fearful.

"I'll go myself," added Bladder, who lacked honesty, decency, and moral fiber, but not personal courage.

"How far?" asked Eunicet.

"It'll take us three more days to reach them if this wind holds, and it should, Your Grace."

"Fine! Three days will give us time to prepare. Set the course for this Isle of Flowring, Captain. And thank you for your help. You may tell the crew they will be rewarded. Ten percent of the loot we take, after the island surrenders. Another ten for you two."

Pleased with this promise, the officers retired to study the reefs and shoals shown between them and the island selected.

"Three days to get warm again," laughed Eunicet.

He rose to go on deck and as he stepped to the door he paused, looking back at his partner in crime.

"That Captain, Bladder . . . I don't think he'll be much use to us after we take Flowring, do you? Perhaps you'd better arrange an 'accident' to him."

Bladder nodded emphatically.

Douglas had found his Sea legs almost at once. Bryarmote claimed he'd never lost his. Caspar Marlin merely chuckled and kept a weather eye on a new bank of clouds that was piling up on the northeast horizon, between them and the Far Coast.

Douglas dived eagerly into everything about sailing. The Dwarf Seamen happily stayed their duties to explain lines and halyards, yards, and deadeyes, ratlines, sheets, and tackle—which they pronounced "tay-kell." He was introduced to that most useful and reliable of all sailor's tools, the square knot.

Douglas lost three games of chess to Bryarmote before the watch changed just before midnight. The Dwarf yawned, as he always did at that time of night when he was winning, and bade the youngster a good night.

Still too much awake to retire to his bunk, Douglas walked about the deck enjoying the warm, moist air. They were already far enough south to have overtaken summer.

Musing on this and that, he went forward to the very eyes of the ship where the sides came together at the stem and the bowsprit. Above him white jibs'ls and stays'ls were taut and humming, pulling *Diamondpoint* swiftly along.

Below, the bow wave glowed with an inner light. Douglas Brightglade wistfully remembered his Master's long and earnest lecture on Cold Fires. It seemed like centuries agone, yet must have been less than three years, since they had sat together on the doorstep of Wizard's High on a dark summer's evening, no moon above, and seen a will-o'-the-wisp flicker among the reeds beside Crooked Brook.

"That is Cold Fire," said Flarman, drowsily. "An Aspect, cold, yet fire—so of importance to you as a Pyromancer. You find it in special places, like graveyards or in swamps. Aboard a ship it plays about mastheads on stormy nights, like silent lightning. It ranges alongside when the ship cleaves the waves.

"When you see the glow of it," Douglas could almost hear the Wizard's voice now, "you have but to call. It will come to hand and do as you wish. Cold Fire will always obey a Fire-Adept. Remember that, m'boy. Always obey a Fire-Adept!"

Now, a thousand miles from Wizard's High, he leaned over the bow to examine the darting, shifting lances of phosphorescence beside the ship's cutwater. After a bit he tried commanding it, asking it to spread out in a wide circle, then in straight rays striking from the spot where the cutwater pushed up the bow wave.

As he grew more assured of his commanding he became more and more engrossed in the beauty and mobility of the Sea Fire, not noticing the sudden chill in the air and the first sting of wind-driven rain on his back.

There was a roar, a rocking, and rolling as the storm that had been following them struck *Diamondpoint*'s stern quarter, hard and fast.

In his cabin Caspar shot from his bunk, shouting orders. The helmsman and the deck officer seized the wheel with both hands and struggled to keep the ship on course, not allowing her to broach sideways to the wind.

The crewmen tumbled out of their hammocks to man halyards and sheets to down sails and bare the yards. A sharp crack signaled that one of the topsails had shredded and blown away. Yards of inch-thick line fell to the deck in stinging coils.

It was as sudden to cease as it had been to start, not unusual for these latitudes, Caspar Marlin told Bryarmote. It took an hour of hard work to get things back to safe and normal. By that time the storm was far away.

No one noticed the Journeyman Wizard was not on deck.

Douglas was uncomfortable, but unafraid. *Diamondpoint* had ducked her bow under the water at the storm's sudden surge from behind. Douglas was spilled over the bow into the foaming water alongside before he could grab a hold of rail or sheet.

As he flew into Sea he cried one word: "*Heeeeelp!*"

Missing the ship's keel by mere inches, he sank into the depth like a lead weight.

He thought he ought to struggle to the surface, where he could hail *Diamondpoint* for rescue before she passed beyond hearing.

He found himself settling to the bottom on a sandy stretch between huge, globular coral heads of pink, gray, and bright blue. Startled fish of rainbow hues swirled dizzyingly about him, then disappeared into the dark seaweed forest as swiftly as they had appeared.

He was struck with panic. Holding his breath, he tried to swim to the distant surface—he was at least fifty feet down! He could not rise, nor could he hold his breath any longer. He let his pent-up lungful escape and involuntarily gasped, expecting an inrush of cold salt water—and quick death.

He got, instead, a lungful of salt-tangy air!

Amazed, he forced himself to do as Flarman had always taught—think first.

It was a puzzle for, looking around at the coral, he remembered that above it was full night and very dark, yet here he had plenty of light. The shimmering, darting nature of this light reminded him of . . . the Sea Light in the bow wave! What next?

Best to surface, see if he could hail the ship, he decided calmly. It was too long a walk to Waterand and he preferred to breathe topside air when possible. Not that he was un- grateful to the Sea Light. He wondered . . .

"Take me to the nearest island," he said aloud. He ex- pected at least that the entity might indicate the direction he should walk along the Sea bottom.

He had said, "Take me . . ." however, and Sea Light took him at his word. Douglas was at once lifted off his feet and carried swiftly through the water, accompanied by haloes and shafts of light beside, ahead, and behind him.

Douglas quickly forgot any fear as he became fascinated by his surroundings. The Sea Light illuminated the Seascape through which it traveled, a forest of towering, green Sea- weed, waving in gentle, hypnotic unison.

They were not plants after all, but slender, green, translu- cent fish floating head down to the sandy bottom, gauzy fins and tails pointed upward and moving slowly to keep each fish in exact position. Their bright yellow eyes watched Douglas pass, unblinking. His curiosity piqued, he said, aloud, "I wish I could talk to one of those fish."

Sea Fire, taking him again at his word, slowed, stopped, and set him facing one of the long, green fish. Its jaws were set firmly around a heavy stone as an anchor.

"Can you hear me?" he asked the fish.

"Of course, sir, yes," mumbled the green fish around its rock. It showed a mixture of respect, fear, and irritation. "What can I do for you, please?"

"I'm terribly sorry to be a bother, but you see, I was washed overboard from a ship . . ."

"Congratulations!" said the fish with the first real show of interest and enthusiasm. "You're much better off, safer in our home waters."

"I only wish to ask a few, very quick questions, if you please."

"Squirt away! As long as I am being interrupted, I might as well make conversation. In the next election for School- master it will be remembered that I actually held converse with a creature from the Air. It should be worth quite a few votes."

The thought made the green fish, who was normally quite cold, rather genial to the strange visitor instead.

"This Sea Light is obligingly taking me to the nearest island. Can you tell me anything about this place?"

"Oh, dear," replied the green fish, squirming a bit in embarrassment. "I don't seem to be much help to you, after all. I've never been there myself, although some of my wife's relatives go up one of the island's streams to . . . well, you know, spawn. I believe its name is Flowring. Yes, that's as I recall it. Flowring Isle."

"A very pretty name," mused Douglas. "I suppose it won't take long to get there?"

"Not at the rate you were just moving," answered the green fish. "No more than an hour or two, I should guess. You should ask the Sea Light, of course. It could tell you exactly."

Douglas laughed at himself. "You know, I never thought of that. Of course! Thank you, sir fish."

"Well, well," replied the other. "We get on, you know, no matter what Air creatures do."

Douglas waved farewell and asked the Sea Light to get moving again, leaving the green fish and his schoolmates muttering into their pebbles.

They crossed a series of sharp, rocky ridges running at right angles to their course, with deep, dark crevasses between. Douglas, looking down, gasped to see, lying in the cracks, great, long, smooth-skinned Sea Snakes. They were fully four feet thick and at least fifty feet long, with stubby horns marking their front ends. Douglas thought they looked like snails, but unlike snails, their colors were brilliant hues of green, blue, yellow and pink.

"What are those creatures? Are they dangerous?"

The Sea Light formed words out of light itself against the darker water ahead.

"They are Horniads, or Sea Worms," the Light spelled out in graceful cursive. "They sleep months at a time, then feed for days before sleeping again. They are near their awakening time now . . . perhaps in the next four or five days. They are no danger to Man. They are a danger only to shrimp and oysters and such."

"Tell me more," asked Douglas.

"Men think Horniads eat all the oysters upon which pearl fishers depend for their livelihood. They do not realize that the Sea Worms also plant the pearl seeds that grow to full pearls in the oysters they do not eat. They are, therefore, an important factor in the fisher's weal.

"I have always wondered why these fishermen and the Worms do not cooperate. The Worms could tell them where the pearls are, and the men could feed the Worms, who do not enjoy moving about from place to place looking for their food."

The Journeyman was still digesting this lecture when the Light carried him over the last of the parallel ridges and they began to cross a broad, sandy submarine plain abundantly populated with an amazing variety of colorful fish of all sizes and shapes.

Corals and sea urchins and whelks and oysters grew all over the bottom, most of them attached in groups to rocks, leaving wide stretches of empty, rippling sand.

Glancing up, Douglas saw that the surface was rapidly coming closer. They were not more than twenty feet beneath when he saw a curious sight. It was the bottom of a boat, seen from beneath.

"And who is that?" he asked the Light.

"A fisherman," printed out the Light at once. "Shortly he will dive to the bottom looking for the rare blue coral or pearl oysters, the most valuable things to Man in these waters. Now, Douglas Brightglade, it is beginning to grow light above and I must soon leave you."

"Perhaps if you raise me near the fisherman's boat he'll take me ashore. I'll need someone to introduce me to the islanders."

Without flashing a further word, the Sea Light rose almost to the surface and released the Wizard so that he popped up with a gasp within a yard of the boat.

The bright morning sun dazzled him. He blew the water from his mouth and nose with a combined cough and sneeze, an explosion that brought a startled cry of alarm from the boat.

Douglas, clearing his eyes of salt water, stopped swimming in surprise. He sank and got another mouthful of water.

Standing on the gun'l of the skiff was a beautiful girl of seventeen summers, slim and trim, tanned by the sun, midnight black hair flying in the light wind. She was poised to dive into Sea . . . and she seemed at first to be totally without clothing!

Chapter Sixteen

"HAVE you never seen a girl swimming before?" the fishergirl said, exasperated at being startled.

"Er . . . actually, now that you . . . no, I don't think so," stammered Douglas Brightglade. He quickly regained his composure.

"In fact, now that I think of it, I haven't seen nor bespoken anyone my age in months. Been busy, you see, traveling . . ."

"Well, I do envy your being able to travel," said the girl, seriously. She reached down to help him clamber over the side into her boat. The young man tried not to show his embarrassment. Her clothing consisted of two small pieces of cloth around her slim body where they did the utmost good—and looked the utmost best, Douglas thought.

"My name is Myrn Manstar. I was about to dive for blue coral," she explained.

"Dive for coral?" asked Douglas.

"Certainly! My father usually does this, assisted by my brothers. I have two brothers. They are all off island at the moment."

"Answering Augurian's call?" guessed Douglas.

"Why, yes, so they are. Most of our men and the older boys of Flowring Island have gone to war. What do you think? Is this bed pretty well picked over?"

Douglas grinned. "I didn't see any blue coral. Back there some miles there seemed to be a lot of it."

The young lady was immediately interested but perplexed.

"You've swum all that distance, and underwater?"

"It is a long and somewhat strange story, which I don't

mind telling but I'm cold and hungry. If you could spare a cloak and perhaps a sandwich? I'll pay for it—''

"No, you won't," Myrn spluttered indignantly. "We Flowringers pride ourselves on our hospitality, especially to shipwrecked Seamen."

And she would hear no more talk until she had found him an old cloak and given him a towel and a handful of dried fruit and nuts to eat. Douglas fell to with gusto while Myrn excused herself and dived over the side into the clear water. He had finished and was drying himself in the morning sun when she splashed up out of the depths minutes later.

"You're right," she gasped. "There are no blue corals here at all!"

Douglas introduced himself and mentioned his destination. Myrn listened with great interest once she was convinced that he was an ally of the Water-Adept of Waterand.

"Wanting to help them fight, I suppose," Myrn said.

"Well, I hope I can be a help," Douglas said, blushing.

"Well, I would think so! All Seamen are most welcome in a Sea war against the Ice King."

"Well . . . I'm not a Seaman, really. I'm a Journeyman Fire Wizard. My Master, who taught me everything I know about the magic of fire," said Douglas, who saw no reason to hide his profession, "will be there, too. I hope," he added.

Myrn politely refrained from scoffing at this, but Douglas touched off a small blaze in the sloop's fire box to demonstrate his Wizardry. No longer skeptical, Myrn brewed a pot of tea.

Douglas said, "I am sure I saw lots of blue coral back there a ways, maybe a mile or two. I'm not sure about oysters."

"Of oysters there are aplenty, but they are not necessarily *pearl* oysters. Every year or so for some reason, the oysters stop making pearls. Fortunately for us, blue coral is a valuable substitute. But blue coral is very hard to find."

"Distances are awfully hard to judge when you are scooting along the bottom. If Sea Light were still here I could ask it, but it has gone its way, I'm afraid."

"Of course," said Myrn, "Sea Light always fades as soon as the sun rises. Can you tell me anything else about this blue coral bed? I'm sorry to be so insistent but it is really most important. We need the coral to put cash in our pockets. Not much grows in our soil and we have to buy most of our food and tools.''

Douglas thought hard, then said, ''Well, well, and well . . . I recall it was to the north of here. In maybe fifty feet of water. Just this side of where we saw the Horniads . . .''

Myrn put her hands to her face in horror. ''How terrible! Ugh! Weren't they frightening?''

''Actually Sea Light says they're harmless except that they eat oysters, and it said Flowringers don't like Horniads because of that. But only every few months . . .''

''I was brought up to loathe them,'' said Myrn with a shudder. ''I've seen them sleeping in the water.''

''I thought they were fairly attractive, as those things go. They were pink and blue and a lovely green,'' he said, teasing.

''Ugh!'' She shuddered again. Thinking hard, she added, ''Well, so we'd have to go near the Horniads to get this blue coral?''

''Not too close, I guess.''

''I'll ask Captain Josiah. He's been sailing these waters for almost a hundred years and knows almost everything about Sea there is to know.''

''Better ask him, then,'' agreed Douglas, who, to tell the truth, was eager to get ashore. No matter how attractive this girl might be—and she was extremely attractive, he suddenly realized—it disturbed him to be out of touch with World events.

Myrn slipped on sailor's trousers and a striped shirt and asked him to hoist the anchor while she set the sails.

Douglas admired the sure expertise of Myrn doing the things he had struggled to learn aboard *Diamondpoint*. She moved as if the whole matter of sailing was second nature to her—which it was, of course—and talked as she worked.

''I don't know what I'd ever do if I met a Horniad awake,'' she was saying, taking the helm from him as they got under way. ''I just have a feeling that I couldn't stand them!''

Douglas told her the Sea Light's suggestion about cooperating with the Horniads. She didn't relish the idea, but agreed that anything that helped the islanders harvest pearls was worth exploiting, even Sea Worms.

"Sea Fire says you don't know that the Horniads are responsible for planting pearl seeds, in the first place."

"You're fooling me! Nobody ever told me that! Plant the seed pearls?"

"It explains why pearls are scarce now. Sea Light said these worms have been asleep for almost ten months and haven't been awake to plant any seeds. So, of course, no pearls."

Cried the coral fisher's daughter, "We'd better get busy and wake the old Worms up!"

They sailed around the island to its southwestern coast, where there was a small harbor for the pearl-fishing fleet. As they scraped dockside an elderly, white-bearded gentleman came limping out on the pier. He took the bowline Myrn tossed him and tied it to a bollard with a neat half hitch.

"Ahoy, lass!" he called. "Good fishing?"

"No, and yes, Captain Josiah," Myrn sang back. "No coral, but I've pulled a young Wizard out of the water."

"A Wizard, eh?" said the old seaman, squinting at the couple climbing onto the dock. "Well, they come younger these days, I do say. Yet I suppose a Wizard must start young, just like a sailor, and a young Wizard should be no surprise."

"You are far from wrong, sir," Douglas told him, shaking his hand. "I'm Douglas Brightglade, a Journeyman Pyromancer. My master is—"

"Ah, Flarman Flowerstalk, I'll be bound!" interrupted the old man with a twinkle and a chuckle. "Old Flarman Firemaster! Haven't thought of him in twenty years, I vow. How is old Torch-Finger? 'Tis a tiny, tiny world for all its wastelands and empty waters," Josiah said. "Come on up to Town Hall, laddy, and meet the Ladies of the Flowring Council, taking their menfolk's places, as they are."

Douglas grinned at Myrn and followed the retired Sea-captain through the neat, white-painted village overlooking the tiny harbor.

"Here's Mrs. Parker," said Josiah. "Douglas Brightglade o' Perthside, meet Her Honor the *pro tem* mayor o' Flowring. Her husband, Mayor Thomas Parker, is away fighting for Augurian, ye know."

Douglas bowed to the pleasant, buxom lady of middle years and shook her hand, then those of the whole City

Council, six ladies, who arrived shortly. They were very interested in what he had to say about the struggle with the Ice King and cheered to a woman when he told them that Flarman Flowerstalk, about whom they had heard from Captain Josiah, had taken a personal hand in the struggle.

When Douglas told them what the Sea Light had said about the Horniads, they showed revulsion at first, but they were very interested in what the beasts could do for them in the matter of pearls. They voted on the spot to send a delegation to waken the sleeping beasts to at least get them started planting seed pearls.

"No need to wait for the menfolk," said Mayor Parker, smoothing her robe of office. "I could have gone down it in the old days. Our lasses can do it."

Douglas found time at last to call for Deka the Wraith, to whom he dictated the following:

To Augurian Watermaster of Waterand:
 Flarman Flowerstalk, Firemaster, and I left Wizard's High a month past but our ways parted when we reached the shore of Sea. I went north to Dwelmland; my Magister allowed himself to be captured and taken to Eternal Ice, according to the gull Cerfew, whom you may know. I was with Bryarmote on his ship Diamondpoint *sailing for the Warm Seas when I was swept overboard by a storm and reached this island, Flowring, with the help of Sea Light and a fishergirl named Myrn.* Diamondpoint *should reach you soon if not already. Please tell my friends that I am well, and if possible arrange to retrieve*

> *Your Obedient Servant,*
> *Douglas Brightglade of Perthside,*
> *Journeyman Pyromancer*

"Breakfast," called Tomasina Manstar jovially the next morning. She was capable and hearty, yet firmly feminine, reminding Douglas at times of his own mother—"is served! How do you like your eggs?"

"Scrambled," Douglas decided. He found Tomasina's kitchen bright, sunny, and cheerful, comparing favorably with Blue Teakettle's kitchen at the High.

"My daughter is already down at the docks. She's a hard worker and an early riser, that girl. Rerigging something or other, I guess. She keeps that smack spick and span, better'n her Papa."

The lady kept up a running commentary, a mixture of motherly observations—"Here, let me mend that rip for you. Not fitting for a young Wizard to go abroad with a hole in his pants"—and good-natured gossip about the people of the island.

"Old Captain Josiah gave us fits when the Mayor told him he had to stay behind. He smelled gunpowder, you can bet! But we need him. He knows Sea, ships, sails and anchors, and the weather, top and bottom, better'n anybody. He's a might old, I say, to be firing cannon and swinging a cutlass and such."

Douglas ate his fill, drank fresh milk for the first time in weeks, and nodded his understanding. When he finished, Myrn's mother shooed him off to find her daughter.

Down on the dock Myrn wielded a tar brush on the standing rigging of her father's fishing boat.

"I was going to take you out for a sail," she said in greeting, "but Mayor Parker wants to speak with you. I imagine she wants some help in the Horniad business. Ugh! Not many want to go see the Worms, I daresay. Go on, now, and I'll come shortly to hear what she has to say."

She turned back to her work, humming happily to herself.

After the storm at Sea, the caverns of Dwelmland before that, and walking through the desolation of Parch for days, the bright, warm sun and light airs of Flowring were welcome. Douglas strolled slowly across the grassy common to Mrs. Parker's house, looking about with interest and appreciation.

Captain Josiah appeared from the direction of the shore, carrying a fishing pole, a creel on his hip. Douglas, in no hurry, stopped to await him.

"Ahoy!" called the old sailor. "Have a good sleep?"

Douglas admitted that he'd slept like a log and he and the Captain fell into step.

"Goin' to Mayor Parker's?" guessed Josiah. "Well, she's a good sort and takes her ree-sponsibilities serious-like, ye know. She's been after me already about waking the Sea Snakes and I said, no hesitation on my part, but she should plan to take a few of the Council along to make it official. She said she was goin' to ask you to come along, too, being a Wizard and all. Besides, you an' me are pretty near the only two who aren't scared to death of them Horniads.''

"Why is that? The Sea Light told me the Horniads were harmless.''

"Laddy, everyone has bogeymen, chimeras, monsters, you see. On Flowring 'tis the Horniads the mothers scare their babes with, to get them to bed betimes.''

"And the fact that the worms plant the seed pearls in the oysters?''

"I never suspected 'twas so,'' confided the old sailor with a nod. " 'Twill make a large difference, I think. Well, here is Mayor Parker seeing us a-coming.''

They were still talking at the Parkers' front gate when Myrn arrived from the waterfront with tar bucket and tar brush and a dab of black on her cheek.

"Lassy, let me get that tar off'n you!'' cried the Mayor. She produced a rag and a bottle of turpentine and scrubbed Myrn's left cheek industriously, talking all the while.

"We were talking about them Horniads,'' she said. "Come along with us, Myrn. Most of the Ladies of the Council found more important things to do this morning, ye see. Not that I blame them much.''

"I can . . . can understand that,'' Myrn hesitated. "But if Douglas says the Worms are harmless, I believe him.''

She turned to Douglas and shook her finger at him, "If you are wrong, I will expect you to fry the Worms with Wizard's fire, young sir!''

Douglas said, solemnly, "It is not . . . Certainly I can try and perhaps make it uncomfortable, if they get nasty.''

At four bells of the fore-noon watch, the party, including two ladies of the Town Council, filed down to the dock and boarded *Dove*, Myrn's father's trim and handy fishing craft. Captain Josiah took the helm while Douglas and Myrn worked the sails. A stiff breeze had come up and they made good time out to where Douglas had seen the Horniads asleep.

Once there, Josiah ordered a Sea anchor thrown out. The bottom was five fathoms below the keel. When she was ready to dive, Josiah handed Myrn a heavy iron ring, to help her sink to the bottom quickly.

Nodding to Douglas, the Captain, and the ladies, she leaped feetfirst into the water and sank—but not from view, as they all crowded the rails to watch her through glass-bottomed buckets.

Myrn found a Horniad almost at once, not more than twenty feet from the sloop's anchor. The beast was stretched along the crevice between two ridges, a thing of awe and some beauty, its colors, muted but varied, constantly shifting in the watery light.

Myrn put out a hand and touched its near-side horn, gingerly.

The Worm stirred, rolled its head slowly, and opened an eye, which was startlingly blue and somehow mild and friendly. The eye looked at her for a moment in surprise, then closed again. The beast went back to sleep!

"Drat!" swore Douglas when the girl returned to surface. "Can you try again?"

"O-o-okay," said Myrn. "It's scary, touching it that way."

"You were wonderfully brave," everyone said.

She swam more slowly this time, taking time to look around. The first Horniad was only one of several wedged in the crevice and she decided to try the second in the row this time.

This Horniad stirred at once and turned its head to gaze sleepily at the intruder. Having done that, it fell back asleep.

Myrn returned to the boat, shaking her head.

But her third try was no more successful, and she rose to the surface, where she clung, exhausted, to the side of *Dove*.

"Horniads are not light sleepers," Myrn told them. "I can't even get one to keep its eyes open."

Mayor Parker shook her head with doubt. "Perhaps they just won't waken. It's too bad. I was hoping to present the Mayor with a signed treaty when he returned. . . ."

They hoisted main and jib and tacked back to the harbor, keeping a wary eye on approaching storm clouds—the same storm that the Sea Light had outrun carrying Douglas to Flowring Isle.

"How fast Sea Light carried me!" he exclaimed to Myrn

as she dried herself with a rough, warm towel. "Perhaps it could have taken me straight to Waterand."

"And never met me—I mean us," said the girl, blushing.

"Well, there's that," admitted Douglas. "I have an idea, however. If I call the Sea Light tonight, I am sure it can advise us on how to awaken the Horniads."

"Not tonight," said Mrs. Parker, firmly. " 'Tis going to storm and right soon, too."

"The first calm night, then," agreed the Journeyman.

They whiled away the stormy evening playing checkers by the Sea-coal fire in the Manstar cottage, listening to the rain beating on the windows, the wind rattling the roof shingles.

"Pity the poor Seaman on a night like this," quoted Mrs. Manstar with a huge yawn. "Put out the candles and let the cat come inside, lassy. I'm for bed and you should be too, shortly."

"Yes, Mother," said Myrn, but after she left they sat side by side in front of the small fire, talking in soft tones of their lives before they'd met.

"And ye've no lass waiting for you at home in Valley?" she asked, glancing at him sideways. He had risen to bank the coals for the night. The storm had settled down to a continuous rampage and they could feel waves breaking on the shore through the very rock and soil of Flowring.

"No, none," he responded. "Oh, I knew many nice girls in Valley, but . . . they were all somewhat afraid of me—of the Wizard, rather."

She stood before him, her head cocked to one side.

"I see nothing to fear in you, Douglas Brightglade."

"Perhaps when you know me better . . . ," he began, but the words made them both laugh. "I mean. . . ."

"We'll see," she said. "But I can't believe anyone could fear you."

"Not you, at any rate." Douglas took her hand in his and looked at it. They stood very still and seemed to stop breathing for a long time.

Then Douglas sighed and touched her cheek, highlighted by the glow of the lowering fire. The warmth of her smile was a new kind of fire to the Journeyman Fire Wizard.

■ ■ ■

The next day they walked in the rain to the top of the island, to the north, where the land tipped steeply over cliffs into roaring surf breaking on jumbled rocks. They stood watching and talking for a long time, holding hands as the wind buffeted them from side to side.

In the afternoon, when the sun came out once more, they worked at recaulking *Dove*'s seams, laughing and singing, happy together in a way neither had ever been happy before.

"Should ye let your lass walk and work with a stranger like that?" one of the ladies asked Tomasina Manstar when they met at the creek to draw water for dinner.

"Faith, Regina! Do ye forget your own Bulworth and the walks and caulkings you two used to share. If you do, I do not, for ye stole him from me, for sure!"

"Bosh! Every Flowring lass had her cap set for my Bully, and all he ever talked about on those walks was a new set o'sails and the old keel on his smack."

"Ah, I believe ye about that!" said Tomasina Manstar with a hearty laugh. "Anyway, the lad's a good sort for all of being a Wizard. Did I tell you how he lit the fire under the bath water last night? With a flip of his little finger, is all!"

"Handy to have on a chilly night!" said Regina, hoisting her heavy bucket. "Never get cold with Wizard about, will she?"

"My advice to mothers with daughters is, don't rush things. They'll find their ways fast enough without pushing," another woman said, laughing.

Douglas and Myrn saw Captain Josiah walking toward them.

"Come with us tonight," said Myrn. "Sea has calmed and Douglas has a plan for awakening the Worms."

Josiah, for all his hundred and some years, was nobody's fool.

"Oh, ha! No, I'm much too old to putter around Sea of a night, calm or not. I'll get some sleep. You won't need an old sailor like me along."

"Old Josiah is showing his age," observed the girl after the Captain went his way. "Time was, they say, when he'd jump at the chance to take a midnight sail."

"What time shall we leave?" Douglas asked. "After sup-

per, I hope. I've become addicted to your mother's cooking.''

"It'll be dark by eight bells or so. After supper there will
be plenty of time. Should we invite Mrs. Parker to go
along?''

"If you wish," said Douglas, coolly.

"Of course not!" laughed Myrn Manstar. "Douglas . . . ?''

"Yes, Myrn."

"When you go—and I know you must leave soon—"

"Yes, I must. I will miss you so very much!"

"If I stay here," she said, flatly.

There was a short silence before Douglas nodded. "If it
won't work a hardship for your mother, of course."

"Lots of girls are sailoring, these days. And my mother
can take good care of herself. I want to go and help you and
Flarman and Augurian. It is my island, too, and my Sea. And
I want to be with you."

"I love you, Myrn."

"There's that, too, of course. I do love you, Douglas!"

They stood looking at each other for a moment, then
Douglas said, excitement growing in his voice, "We'll see
Flarman and Bronze Owl and meet Augurian together!
You'll love Flarman Flowerstalk, lass, as I do."

"No need to persuade me, laddy! Even if I didn't love ye,
sir, I'd still go to see the Great People of the Age gathered
to do battle. Maybe do something meself to set the wrongs
to rights, as me father said."

Douglas stood looking at her, feeling rather foolish and
extremely happy, holding her hands and grinning at her grinning back at him. They had come to her mother's front gate
and remained still until the lady called out from the cottage
door, "Hey, ahoy! Stop that mooning for a minute and come
and set the table for supper. Ye're due for a long night ahead
and hard work, too, maybe."

At seven bells they were already miles out to Sea, anchored, waiting for the first sign of the Sea Light. They lay
on their stomachs on the foredeck, gazing into the darkening
water and at each other as well.

When the sun had finally set, Douglas reached down to

touch the water's surface, saying, "Douglas Brightglade calls you, Sea Fire."

Blue light letters formed in the water, spelling out its words.

"I remember you, Douglas Brightglade. We traveled far and fast some days past. What does the Firemaster require of me?"

"Carry us into these depths to the sleeping Horniads. The fisherfolk of Flowring wish us to speak with them of oysters, pearls, and blue coral."

"Wise people!" signed Sea Fire. "Come over the side, both of you, Fire Wizard and Daughter of the coral fisher."

And so they did and were at once able to talk and breathe underwater, truly a marvel to Myrn the pearl diver, as the Sea Light drew them down to where the Horniads slept.

Observed Sea Fire, "But it is not easy to awaken them."

"I did find it so," sighed Myrn.

"The Porpoises will know how," said Sea Fire, spreading its light so that the entire submarine scene was as bright as day around the sleeping Horniads.

"Where do we find a Porpoise?" asked Douglas.

"Coming," signed the Fire simply, and they waited, floating over the Horniads' resting place. Before long, out of the blackness beyond, shot three dark, streamlined shapes, heading for them at tremendous speed.

As the sleek, swift Porpoises drew close they abruptly swirled off to right and left, circling about. One came to face them, grinning and bobbing his head.

"I am Skimmer," he announced in a rather squeaky voice.

"Pleased to meet you, Skimmer! I am Douglas Brightglade and this is Myrn Manstar of Flowring Island."

"I know the Manstar *Dove* well," said the Porpoise, nodding even more vigorously at the girl. Myrn smiled and patted his head in greeting. Porpoises were ever a fisherman's friend. Many a time they had accompanied her on her dives.

"I didn't know your name but I remember your grace and glee," she said. It was just the right thing to say, for the other two came up to greet the young people, nodding and smiling and saying how much they always enjoyed the grace and beauty of *Dove* as she cleaved the waters above them.

"And we have a mutual friend, too," said Skimmer to Douglas. "We have met and loved Caspar Marlin, you see. . . ."

"Old Caspar!" cried the young Wizard. "Have you seen him lately?"

Said the second Porpoise, Leaper, "We knew him long years back when he was shipwrecked on the Isle of Flempt."

"Yes, he has told me the story of that adventure."

"And we saw him two days ago at Sea. We were carrying information from Augurian. Caspar now masters the schooner *Diamondpoint*."

"And *Diamondpoint* is the flagship of the Dwarf Prince Bryarmote of Dwelmland," Douglas explained to Myrn. "I am delighted they are safe."

"Augurian will be pleased to have them arrive, but they were distressed by your disappearance . . . until a Wraith brought your message. Augurian asked us to find you and tell you that he is sending a ship to fetch you."

"Now that we have found you looking for us, instead of us looking for you," added the third Porpoise, Spinner, "what may we do for you?"

Douglas explained. Skimmer, the speaker of the trio, chuckled gleefully.

"It's not hard to awaken a Horniad. You simply swim near their ear holes and whisper 'oysters.' 'Oyster stew' works twice as fast."

Spinner, the youngest of the three, raced eagerly over to the nearest, largest Sea snake and swam close to its horned end for a few moments.

At once the beast stirred. With agonizing slowness it rolled over and raised its head, swiveled it about until it pointed at the Porpoises and the People.

"Come closer," Spinner squeaked. "He will speak with you."

The worm stretched toward them as they approached, still anchored by its nether end to the rocks—"No telling *how* long it really is," Myrn whispered to Douglas with a shudder she couldn't help—until its huge blue eyes were close to them, gleaming softly with interest, not coldly, as Myrn had expected.

"I am pleased . . . to meet you, as we all will be . . . when we are all awake," it hummed slowly, speaking to their minds, not their ears. "It seems to me . . . I have seen you before, however. I know I have seen the lady swimming in the oyster beds and over the corals . . . or it may have been someone just like her."

"You have probably seen me," said Myrn, introducing herself and then Douglas. "If I had known you were watching I would have been terrified. But now we have met, somehow I no longer fear you at all."

"I am very delighted . . . to hear this," said the beast, even more slowly. "But . . . I forget my manners. My name is . . . [an unpronounceable, swishing sound]."

"Oh, my goodness," breathed Myrn. "I'll never be able to say your name, I'm afraid."

The Horniad shook its horned end sorrowfully but said, "Call me any convenient Man name you prefer. I will understand."

After some discussion they decided its name should be Horatio, which fit somehow, and even seemed to please the Sea Snake.

The Porpoises were gleefully awakening all the other Sea Snakes now and a long time was taken with introductions and explanations. The worms first excused themselves courteously to dine delicately in a nearby oyster bed. Once finished, Douglas and Myrn watched and listened while Horatio solemnly showed how Horniads planted seed pearls in the best of the oysters remaining.

The Horniads were most receptive to the Flowringers' proposal and graciously proclaimed that a meeting with the island's officials would be a mere formality, although one they would welcome.

"We see the advantages to us and for you," Horatio told Myrn. A date was set some days hence. Meanwhile Douglas was talking to other Worms, seeking to recruit them for the Battle of Sea.

"We are related to the Sea Dragons . . . although much more peaceful and well behaved. Much slower to anger," they told him. They would consider his invitation to join the fight. Augurian was known to them and admired for the good he had done, but . . . it required slow deliberation.

In fact, Douglas found, the Horniads were slow at everything except hospitality, intelligence, and friendliness. His

saying so pleased their whole clan immensely, if ponder-
ously.

They surfaced at *Dove*'s side and lifted their arms to grasp
the gun'ls. Rough hands grabbed their wrists and yanked
them onto deck. They were pushed none too gently into the
bottom.

"Who are you?" demanded Douglas, recovering his
breath and wits. He quelled the tendency to shiver in the cool
night air.

"We be pirates," said a smooth, oily voice from one of
the five dark figures gathered around them. The starlight slid
wickedly off the edges of drawn blades.

"I am the Pirate King," announced the voice. There was
the sound of a sword being sheathed and someone opened a
bull's-eye lantern to shine on the face of the speaker.

"Eunicet!" exclaimed Douglas, before he could think. He
swallowed his next words. It would be best if the usurper
didn't know he had captured Flarman's Journeyman.

"Do you know me?" asked Eunicet, surprised and flattered.

" 'Tis not important, now," interrupted a second, gruffer
voice. "Truss 'em up and gag 'em tight. We've got scouting
to do afore dawn."

Myrn cried out in anger more than fear as one of the pirate
crew seized her wrists and tied them together. Douglas began a spell under his breath but someone behind him shoved
a gag in his mouth while two other pirates quickly tied him,
also, before he could free a hand to make a magic pass.

"Well, fisherboy," said the gruff voice, "we're for your
pretty little island. We intend to loot, burn, and pillage it and
steal its pearls and coral, then go elsewhere to do the same."

"Toss 'em over the side," cried one of the pirates. "Although the lassy is mighty comely. Toss the boy over and
save the girl, I say!"

"Shut your puling mouths," snapped Eunicet. "Who's
the Captain here? We'll interrogate them first and then we'll
decide what to do with them. Pay no attention to the rough
talk, little lady," he said aside to Myrn. "You will be my
handmaiden and serve me breakfast in beddy-bye each
morning."

Myrn stared back at him wordlessly.

"Cooperate and you may live the day out," Bladder threatened the Journeyman Wizard. "Tell us everything about the Island of Flowring. Who lives where? How many armed men are there?"

"And where," asked Eunicet, thrusting his red-eyed, beard-stubbled face close to Douglas's, "are the pearls?"

He rapped Douglas cruelly on the temple. The Journeyman slumped to the bottom of the boat, unconscious.

Chapter Seventeen

"WHAT shall we do? What *shall* we do!" moaned Mrs. Parker, straining against her bonds. She, Captain Josiah, and Douglas were bound fast to the porch rail of Flowring's Town Hall.

A line of Flowring women and children, prodded and harassed by the pirates, trudged by carrying baskets of food down to *Pinechip*. Eunicet's men had already emptied the island storehouse of a fortune in pearls and coral.

"They've taken all six young marriageable maidens aboard! Myrn is among them!" cried Tomasina Manstar as a pirate with a scimitar rushed past.

Douglas, just regaining consciousness, shook his aching head. "There are too many of them. If I do anything, someone may be hurt before I can stop them. Later, perhaps I can do something, but for now we must wait."

"'Tis nigh impossible," sighed Mrs. Mayor Parker. "But I'll not let these vermin see me cry or despair! I have faith in you, Douglas Brightglade, though ye're no older than those poor lasses. You're our only help."

"If I try Wizardry now," explained Douglas, "they will know who and what I am . . . and may kill us all."

"That wicked Duke—or whatever he is—has them locked in the after hold," another mother cried, near hysteria. A burly Seaman snarled and drove her to her knees with a blow to her back.

"As long as they're under lock and key, nothing untoward will happen to them," said Josiah. "I hope."

The three sat, unable to move legs, arms, or even hands, in the full broiling sun all day. The pirates looted Flowring and loaded *Pinechip*. Still recovering from the head blow, Douglas tried furiously to think, to plan. He tried a dozen or

203

more spells before he had to give up. The pain, exhaustion, and heat destroyed his concentration.

In late afternoon *Pinechip* weighed anchor and slipped southeastward into the twilight. Mrs. Manstar was beside them in a trice with a seaman's knife to slash their bonds. The Journeyman went directly to the town dock and attempted to call Sea Fire but it was still too light.

"What we'll do is wait 'til dark," said Douglas to the Flowringers, with a confidence he really didn't feel. "Augurian has sent a ship, and it will be here at any time. The pirates took all your food and stove in your fishing boats, Mrs. Parker. You must abandon Flowring for the moment and sail to Waterand, where you'll be safe."

"I've no desire to leave my home," wailed one of the ladies. Douglas pointed out that, not only were their husbands and sons there, but that was where he would take their daughters, once he had rescued them from Eunicet.

They all went off to pack some clothes and try to find any food the pirates had missed.

"I'm just thankful that Eunicet and Bladder were not as bloody minded as they have been at times in the past," Douglas said to Captain Josiah.

"Ye done the best anyone could," the old Seaman insisted. "How's the head, laddy?"

Douglas felt better after sloshing his face and head in the cool water of the town stream. The ladies shortly returned, each bearing a sailor's canvas ditty bag stuffed with belongings.

"Now, ladies, stay and watch for Augurian's ship. I must go off alone for a few minutes," said Douglas. He walked slowly inland, head down, mind working clearly at last.

Finding a quiet glade, he lifted his head and called: "*Fryonhep-clander*, Douglas Brightglade needs you! I have great need of a fast messenger . . . ."

The huge disk of setting sun dropped below the horizon, and darkness seemed to leap from the ground. A chill wind stirred the grass at Douglas's feet and rattled the palm fronds above.

A faint, bluish light appeared before him and took shape, a female form in flowing, translucent robes. There was a sound like a caught breath. Deka the Wraith had arrived.

"Hello, Douglas," she said cheerily, belying her somber appearance. "I came as soon as I could."

"Deka! I need a message carried to Augurian at Waterand, at once. It isn't too far, for a wraith?"

"I can be at Augurian's side in moments."

"Tell the Water-Adept that I am on Flowring Island still. The former Duke Eunicet has come with a crew of pirates, stealing all the islanders' wealth and food, and kidnapping six young maidens as hostages . . . or perhaps worse! They sailed southeast from here an hour since in Frigeon's sloop *Pinechip*.

"Say that I will not await his ship but will go to the rescue of the maids. At the very least I plan to keep the pirates so busy running they will have no time to harm the young ladies. End message."

Deka went out like a blown candle in a swirl of chill wind.

Douglas sought out Mayor Parker and Myrn's mother. They huddled glumly together in the town common with Josiah and all the ladies and children of the island, stoically waiting.

"Now, my friends, I have sent a very fast messenger to the Water-Adept. You can rest assured that Augurian will immediately take steps to help us rescue Myrn and her friends. And your treasure, too. In addition, Augurian's ship should be arriving tonight. Go and wait for us on Waterand. When we've gotten the girls away from the pirates, we will meet you there. Will you do this?"

"We will," they all cried. With sensible orders to follow, they were feeling more optimistic.

"My friend the Phosphorescence, the Sea Fire, brought me to Flowring in the first place. It can move through Sea faster than anything. We'll find *Pinechip* in a few hours."

They gave him a packet of crackers and some hard cheese someone had found.

"You haven't eaten, either, since supper last night," Douglas objected, but they insisted. He munched the stale crackers as he made his way to the shore. He hadn't realized just how hungry he was.

He had but to call once and the blue-light words appeared in the gentle swell.

"What does the Wizard Brightglade require of me?"

Douglas slipped into the warm water, waving good-bye to Myrn's mother, saying to her, "Don't worry about Myrn. I'll find her and take her away before anything can happen."

"These are dangerous men, Douglas. Beware!"

"I will," he said, planting a kiss on her plump cheek.

Without further words he ducked beneath the waves, into the bright, warm waters, without a splash or ripple. Sea Fire enveloped him and Douglas felt himself being whisked down and outward, surrounded by the glow of Phosphorescence.

Aboard *Pinechip* the crew was arguing heatedly with Eunicet.

"We're hungry and thirsty," they yelled. "We've plenty of good food from that pearl island. Why not eat? There's plenty—"

"Mongrels! Scoundrels! Bilge rats! You'll eat when and if I say, I—Eunicet! Get back on watch. No food, but a watery grave to the man who doesn't jump to orders. Now!"

The Sea lawyer who had appointed himself spokesman for the crew opened his mouth to demand again but got not a word out before he was seized from behind by the huge and hairy hands of Bladder, lifted high over the former General's head, and hurled over the side, screaming that he could not swim.

"Now, when the Captain-king says 'tis time to dine, we'll dine!" thundered Bladder. "For now, get as much Sea as possible between us and that damn island."

Cowed by the sudden and violent turn of events, the crew slunk back to their duties, grumbling only very quietly. They understood this kind of discipline well. Keep your place, work your trick. Be silent and don't get within reach of the First Mate's strong arm or the Bo'sun's knotted rope.

Eunicet, watching them hurry off, nodded to Bladder and ordered the Master to set all possible sail.

"I've got some sort of premonition," Eunicet told his second in command gruffly. "We had better put that distance between us and Flowring, as you said. Where will we head? Not too close to Waterand, I say."

"But not too far off course, either, Sire. The best place to hide a flea is behind the dog's ear, they say."

"Eh? Flea? Oh, I get your meaning, Bladder. Augurian

will be looking for us sooner or later and most likely not close to his own island, eh?"

"Exactly!" Bladder looked about the quiet deck. "Will ye take a look or two at the captives? I can have them brought up to us at supper."

Eunicet's little eyes gleamed wickedly. The maids of Flowring were the fairest and freshest he had seen in a long string of months. But then wisdom of a sort prevailed.

"No," he sighed with regret. "There'll be time for play when we find a larger, better-endowed island to king it over. 'Twould make the crew even more mutinous, and they might do something dangerous if we disport ourselves too soon."

"Wise, Your Grace! Here're just the two of us and we must sleep sometime, of course. Better feed the crew. That'll keep 'em quiet for tonight," agreed Bladder. "Issue some beer, for that matter. Help them relax. Then keep 'em so busy putting on and taking off sail and changing course all night that they'll drop in their tracks."

"Good thinking, Bladder. I wish we could have some soft companionship, but . . ."

The thought of food and drink crowded ideas of other diversions from Bladder's one-track mind and he followed Eunicet below to their cabin just as the moon showed above the edge of Sea.

Augurian was a tall, rather thin man, fully four inches over two fathoms in height. He had a great flying head of Sea foam–colored hair, like waves breaking in moonlight. His warm blue eyes could laugh as easily as flash with anger, sparkle in good spirits or cut like a rapier.

His familiar was a great white-and-black Stormy Petrel whose beak ended in a wicked hook. The bird was seldom far from the Water-Adept's side, although each morning and evening he could be seen circling the mountains, lakes, sheer cliffs, and smoothly curved sand beaches of the Wizard's island.

The bird's sharp eyes took in every activity, every work afoot, every new arrival or departure. These things he reported to the Water-Adept in his Seaside palace.

"My friend Flarman doesn't approve of the luxury in which I live," Augurian said to newly arrived Bryarmote

one evening as they sat on the broad terrace off his aqua-
marine Great Hall, watching the Petrel flying about the island. The sun was setting behind a dark bar of cloud to the
west.

"But he's never said as much," guessed the Dwarf with
a faint grin.

"True. No, Flarman Flowerstalk never says he disap-
proves luxury. I notice he enjoys it!"

Bryarmote laughed aloud, making the palace walls ring
with his mirth. The Stormy Petrel swooped down to the
balcony rail and simply nodded with approval of what he had
seen. He spoke not a word but, tucking his head under one
long wing, went to sleep.

"When will Flarman arrive?"

"Tomorrow," said Augurian. "The Porpoises Skimmer,
Spinner, and Leaper haven't returned, so they have found the
Fire Wizard and are guiding his ship in."

"And Douglas's message?"

"I have ordered my fastest ship to sail north at once. She
should find Eunicet. We will take him and this Bladder
prisoner and put them where they won't bother anyone ever
again."

"And the girls?"

"Douglas Brightglade has a personal interest in saving the
young ladies, I understand," Augurian said with a smile.

"Good boy, that Journeyman! He will not fail, I know."

Sea Fire moved Douglas swiftly through Sea under the
almost-full moon, past marvels the Journeyman Wizard
would, in less urgent circumstances, have dearly loved to
explore: sunken ships; caves from whose depths came eerie
lights; shifting, changing colors; great drifting cities of seaweed inhabited by millions of tiny, silvery fish who sang
together vast, organlike music and, at an unseen signal,
darted away into hiding.

Tracking *Pinechip* proved to be not as easy as Douglas
had thought. The sloop had not taken a straight course, although the wind was fair for the south. For some reason,
Eunicet was zigzagging wildly—and Sea Fire had its work
cut out for it, making wide sweeps to the east and west in an
effort to find the vessel's path.

Toward dawn, although at the depth they traveled it was

impossible to judge the time accurately, Sea Light flashed a sentence to Douglas, saying: "My powers wane with the rise of the Great Star, Wizard, as you know. I have found the fleeing ship's trace but I fear we will not reach her in time. What is to be done when the daylight grows too strong?"

"Take me as close as you can, Sea Fire. At the last possible moment put me on the surface. I will wait until darkness for you. A piece of flotsam should hold me up until that time. The weather seems calm."

"Yet I feel you would be in great danger," said the script against the blackness. "I have a companion in mind for you and will use my last strength to find her in the deep. Meanwhile, you must swim."

"I can stay afloat for hours with a piece of driftwood," Douglas murmured, almost to himself. He hadn't slept for two nights except in snatches. "I've got to reach Eunicet's ship."

Sleep was driven from his mind when he found himself alone on the surface with the sunrise painting the horizon. Sea Fire was gone, but he saw a bulk of timber floating nearby and grasped it. He could see, some distance away, *Pinechip*'s gray sails. Pushing the wood before him, he began to swim toward the pirate ship, believing it not too distant.

After two hours he stopped to rest. Even with the unhurried strokes he forced himself to use he was fast reaching the limits of his strength, and he could think of no magical way to help himself. He raised up a bit to look around, figuring he had gone less than three miles since Sea Fire had left him. *Pinechip*'s sails were no longer visible, hidden by rising rollers as the wind freshened.

"Fire won't help you here, young Wizard," he said to himself, aloud. "What's that?"

He thought he had seen a flash of movement below him in the water. The Porpoises, perhaps. A V-shaped wake showed a moment on the surface and then was gone.

"Some Sea creature, I guess," he told himself, and turned over on his back to float, squinting into the midmorning sun.

"Harmless, I hope," he added.

Were there sharks here? he wondered, fuzzily. Caspar Marlin had spoken of the great sharks of Warm Seas, who would devour avidly anything they could catch swimming there.

Perhaps they are all with Frigeon, Douglas thought. That's the kind of creature the Ice King likes.

Glancing behind himself once again, he saw the V-shaped ripple. He swam once more, not knowing which way *Pinechip* lay but unwilling to give up. It was becoming exhausting labor just to kick his heels.

He worked to draw the warm air into his lungs, to keep his mouth above salt water. Once more . . . once more . . .

"Well, it's a strange way for a Fire Wizard to die," he thought, again out loud.

He *had* to rest. The sun was fierce and would burn his fair skin in a few minutes, but he remembered a simple sun-block spell in time. His shirt and breeches weighed heavily, but he dared not shed them. He kicked off his boots and they sank into the depths.

It is quite beautiful, he thought, looking about him. But I do not wish to drown! I have to help Myrn.

He gulped several lungfuls of hot, moist air and turned over on his back to float, counting slowly to a hundred. He splashed salt water on his face to cool his exposed skin, and cried out when salt water stung the cracks in his lips.

He tried floating facedown, which was easier, except for the impossibility of holding his breath more than a minute or so. Once, deep beneath him, he saw movement again, a vast, mottled green oval, pacing him directly beneath.

Douglas forced himself to swim another ten strokes, then rested on his back for fifty counts, then on his face while breath lasted, and then tried to swim another ten strokes. Somehow he lost his hold on the timber and it floated away. He watched it go.

He was agonizingly thirsty. His eyes were almost sealed by salt and stung as if there were sand under the lids. He couldn't feel his feet and hands. Turn over and float on your stomach. This was the pleasantest way to go, he decided. The water seemed cool, and it washed the salt crust from his eyes and lips. If he could just breathe.

He watched with calm interest as the shape under him came closer and closer.

Shark? he wondered to himself again.

It didn't have the shape of a shark. He closed his eyes,

thinking that he might be hallucinating. He should turn over and take a breath but his will was almost gone. Somehow he gathered the strength to roll over.

"I really think it's time to take you to an island," said a sad, concerned, deep voice. "You seem to need rest in the shade of a great coco palm and to drink some coconut milk."

The words came from just above his tightly closed eyes, now shaded from the sun. He considered opening them but decided against it for the moment, and against speaking, either. To show he had heard, he nodded his head.

"However," continued the rumbling voice, "Phosphorescence said to help you overtake a certain sloop. It is important, is all he could say about it before he faded. Augurian's friend, he said, and I am always at the Water-Adept's service, you can be sure. Still, some coconut milk and shade seem best, don't you think?"

Douglas was no longer in the water but sprawled on a slightly curved, hot, wet surface of great, regular grayish green tiles. They had the strong smell of Sea salt and a faint odor of fish.

With some pain and much trouble he pried open his eyes and saw that he was being borne along on the back of an enormous turtle, a hundred times bigger than those who lived happily catching dragonflies in Crooked Brook.

"Am I imagining this?" he croaked.

The toothless mouth opened and a laugh came out, long and deep.

"No, no, no, ho, ho! No, sir, please! I am a Great Sea Tortoise and my name is Oval. Sea Fire sent me to carry you on in pursuit of a sloop, somewhere over that way, which I am willing to do. It didn't say why, though. Why, I wonder? Can you tell me?"

Douglas made two attempts to sit up and finally succeeded, balancing without dificulty on the tortoise's broad back. He was surprised to see how low the sun had sunk. He must have swum and floated most of the day.

"How long since daybreak?" he asked, painfully and hoarsely.

"It's about three hours after high noon. I came upon you at high noon, I think. Or an hour or so earlier."

"I thought I saw you moving below me. What made you wait so long?"

"Well, um, you see . . . I'm not at all that familiar with
Men. In fact, I have never seen one this close before. At first
I was uncertain if you were the Man I was sent to aid. Sea
Fire couldn't tell me much about you. He was just about
faded out, poor fellow."

"I understand," answered Douglas, his strength returning
now that he needed no longer swim. He felt much better.

"You seemed to be doing quite well. Um, I was bemused
because you acted just like a young Tortoise enjoying the
sun on the surface. At last I realized that you were spending
too much time resting and less and less time swimming. You
seemed to be growing weak."

"Oh, you were right! I'm extremely glad that you decided
to come up just then, Oval."

He shivered despite the heat. He pulled the material of his
shirt away from his skin as the drying salt began to itch. He
wished he knew some easy water spells. He felt unbearably
thirsty.

"What is your pleasure?" asked the tortoise. "Coconut
milk and shade, or go on after the sloop? I can do either,
equally well."

"I really think I had better have something to eat and
drink and get out of the sun for a while," said the young
Wizard.

The huge animal plowed swiftly through the blue-green
waves, and in almost no time they arrived at a tiny, palm-
covered islet. The Tortoise helped the young Wizard through
gentle surf to walk unsteadily across the wide, white sand
beach to the trees.

"How do I get one down?" Douglas asked, looking up at
the coconuts dangling thirty feet above his head. "I suppose
I can manage a spell of some sort."

"No need. They drop to the sand all the time."

Oval found a large coconut half buried in the sand. It was
bigger than Douglas's head and hard as a rock. With one snip
of her powerful beak Oval cut off the top of the nut, through
the fibrous outer layers and the hard inner shell.

The inner nut was coated with a half inch of white, rich
nutmeat, surrounding a pint or more of milky liquid. Douglas drank thirstily at first, then more slowly, as the milk
slaked his terrible thirst.

Oval broke the emptied shell apart for him and Douglas hungrily dug out the meat in big, fragrant chunks.

"Better'n Blue Teakettle's lemon meringue pie!" he said, bestowing the ultimate accolade. After finishing off a second nut with scarcely reduced relish—and while Oval herself opened and devoured a half dozen—Douglas began to feel himself again.

Then a horrible thought came to him.

"By O'Leary's lantern! I kicked off my boots!"

"Wisely done," observed the tortoise, once she learned what boots were. "No need for them when swimming, although I can see their utility when walking on hot sand."

"You don't understand! There was a . . . something very precious and dangerous in the toe of one of the boots. They must be recovered! Can you search for them? It is a trust, you see, given to me by a great Wizard to carry all the way to Augurian Watermaster."

"They shouldn't be too hard to find," mused Oval. "I'll just backtrack to the spot where Sea Fire left you. It couldn't be very far from there that you shed your boots. Straight down a hundred fathoms, of course. As soon as you are ready to go, then . . ."

Douglas began pacing back and forth to think and to work kinks out of his muscles. The sun was dropping swiftly to the horizon. They had perhaps two hours of light left before the usual sudden nightfall of the tropics. What to do?

"No, the boots must wait," he decided. "Myrn and her companions can't. We'll go back for the boots later, can't we?"

"No reason why not," agreed Oval, and a few minutes later, carrying some spare coconuts tied together with a green vine, they set to Sea once more.

"What, now?" asked Oval as she swam at flank speed just beneath the surface, so that Douglas could keep his head above water.

"Well, let's see," Douglas said, now almost completely recovered from his ordeal. "Sea Fire can retrace our steps and find the boots. I wouldn't want to take time explaining to such a creature the difference between a right and a left boot."

"Sea Fire is a lot more at home in night-dark waters than

even I am," agreed Oval. "But perhaps you'd rather it carried you. It is much faster."

"If it comes to a fight with pirates I'd rather have your size and strength with me. You would be very helpful."

Oval turned her head and grinned at her passenger, pleased.

"Most helpful, if you'll just tell me what you want me to do. I'm not much of a fighter. Ram her amidship? Shiver her timbers? Lift the whole sloop out of the water and drop her a couple of times?"

Two hours after that, such was the Tortoise's speed, they caught a glimpse of a moon-lit topsail ahead of them. A half hour after that they were close enough to see the hull over the horizon. An hour later they heard shouting and cursing as the sailors' evening meal was served.

"Move slowly now, my friend," cautioned Douglas.

Chapter Eighteen

THE Great Sea Tortoise dropped even lower in the water, moving slowly to minimize their wake. Douglas reached out and touched the rough, salt-encrusted timbers of *Pinechip*'s tumble-home.

Just above their heads Eunicet called to Bladder, and there was the sound of footsteps. The ex-Duke and his henchman leaned on the rail not more than ten feet from the Tortoise and her passenger in the shadow of the hull.

"Where is that devil of a Ship's Master taking us, do ye know?" asked the ex-Duke, irritably. "I can make neither head nor tail of those pestiferous charts. I think we're too close to Waterand."

"It gives me the feeling of being watched," agreed the ex-General, gruffly.

Eunicet grunted and called to someone to bring him a cup of wine. He cursed viciously when the cook came with a mug of warm, sour ale. No wine had been found on Flowring. The pearl island had no grapes.

"We're going to have to find a hiding place, soon; one with proper drink," said Eunicet, taking a sip of the ale.

"There's Flempt," suggested Bladder. "It sounds like the place to lay up during the battle, at least. No inhabitants, but fresh water and a protecting reef. Then we can sally forth when everybody is dead, hurt, or looking elsewhere, snap up some prizes. Like old, old times, sir!"

"Ah, egad, yes!" cried Eunicet. "And speaking of spoils, what of our young . . . er . . . lady guests? They've stopped yelling and crying a long time since. Are they still alive?"

"When the cook went in to slop them with the leftovers from dinner they hit him over the head and tried to escape."

Eunicet and Bladder (and Douglas) laughed at the

215

thought. Bladder continued. ''They're still full of fight. Take
'em one at a time, I say. One each, for you and for me?''

''No time for that yet, much as I'd like. I value my skin too
much to dally when the enemy is perhaps just over the
horizon.''

Douglas whispered in Oval's ear to draw away from the
ship a few dozen yards.

Once out of earshot, he said, ''Good, they're safe. But,
what to do? We could hope they are all brought on deck,
create a diversion, and lead them over the side. How is
that?''

''Not too good,'' said the Tortoise. ''Even if they were all
allowed above deck at once, there'd be no room on my back
for six people. Four at the most, I'd judge, if everyone sat as
close as possible.''

''We may have to do it, anyway,'' Douglas said, thoughtfully. ''Some could sit and others could hang on to your
sides and be towed.''

''We're only a few hours' swim from Waterand, right
now. Problem is, I'd be too slow with such a load and dragging more along behind. The island is downwind of the ship
as well as us. They would just clap on sail and catch us up.''

''The longer we wait, the closer we are to Waterand?''

''But you heard, Eunicet is already leery of going any
closer to Waterand than he already is. They might turn away
at any moment.''

The young Wizard had been mulling over a plan ever since
they had left the coconut island. Now he made his decision.

''What if the ship were to catch fire?''

''Sailors fear fire more than anything, including Sea monsters, I have heard. But wouldn't that endanger our captives
too?''

''Not if the fire is my magic! If I can't use my training
now, of what use is it other than starting a campfire on a cold
morning?''

Wondering what a campfire was, the tortoise nodded her
head.

''I have all confidence in you, Douglas. We'd better do
something about it now.''

Douglas nodded and after a moment's thought, gestured
in a certain way and whispered a certain word.

A bright yellow flame sprang up *Pinechip*'s foremast,

licking hungrily at the fore sail. A cry from the lookout and the flickering light alerted the crew. All hands rushed to rig pumps and man buckets.

They took more than an hour to quench the false blaze. Douglas and Oval stood some way off, low in the water, watching the excitement. None aboard *Pinechip* had time or desire to cast a glance over the side. The Master wanted to order the ship hove to. Eunicet, fearing pursuit more than fire, ordered him to sail on, although the wind whipped the flames into greater frenzy.

Eunicet and Bladder came on deck in the midst of the fire fighting and managed to slow matters down even more by shouting conflicting orders. As he built the fire to its highest point, Douglas saw them edging toward the nearest whale-boat.

Douglas allowed the fire to die out before anyone noticed that it wasn't really burning anything. The Sailing Master and Eunicet then began a shrill argument over who was to blame. Douglas and Oval moved closer to listen.

Everyone blamed the cook, except the cook, and that worthy claimed, loudly and profanely, that he *had* carefully covered his fire after the evening meal.

"Hain't never had a batch of females aboard before, either," cried the Bo'sun, realizing that if the fire wasn't the cook's fault it was probably his own.

"Careless any man can get when there is woman flesh to see," put in the Master with a laugh and a leer.

"Then blame the one brought them aboard in the first place," yelled Cookie, treading dangerously close to the edge of Eunicet's quick temper. Marooning—or even worse, hanging—was the fate of a crewman who carelessly allowed a fire to start on a ship.

"Now you blame *me*!" screamed Eunicet, who had plenty of practice at shouting down opposition. "You scurvy, senseless, half-rotten, bloated jellyfish of a cook!"

Bladder drew his master aside quickly. "They'll toss him over the side, sire!"

"Toss him to the fishes, I say!"

"But, sire, he's the only cook we've got . . . ."

One could never say that Eunicet was slow to see the point of a good argument when it hit home. Spinning on his heel, he roared for silence. The Bo'sun added his shrill whistle and the crew quieted to listen to their strange Captain-king.

"Now, men, really," began Eunicet, softly. "Hear me! What's to be gained by all this? What's done is done! And after all, it really is as much my fault as anyone's."

"But, sir," said the Master, "they—we just feel that having females on any ship, begging your pardon, sir, is foulest luck. Always is in a ship, except as they be passengers."

The discussion got raucous again and went on for close to an hour but in the end the cook was let off with a scathing reprimand. It was time to relieve morning watch. Eunicet, exhausted by the set-to, ordered the crew and prisoners fed.

"We'll bathe them and—entertain them—later," he promised Bladder. "I imagine they're getting pretty ripe by now."

"Need a bath meself," snarled the villainous ex-General. "Got a face full of smoke, and pitch in me hair to boot."

"Later, later," rasped the other, petulantly. "I'm for bed, soot or not. Send me a tankard of that ghastly ale. My mouth tastes like last night's bed."

And he stumped off to his cabin.

Douglas clapped his hands silently and patted Oval on the broad, green head. "Well, we did it, old friend! The girls are going to be safe for a while. The crew's too tired, even if they dared to poach Eunicet's property. I think we can arrange to keep them awake all day, too, and really get them tired."

Oval smiled and moved closer to *Pinechip* once more. She bit into a protruding timber at the ship's stern, firmly locked her powerful jaws on it.

"Every minute on this course takes us closer to Waterand," she mumbled around the mouthful of oak.

"True," agreed Douglas.

A second ship had appeared, just within sight to the southwest, on a converging course, but the crew was too busy to notice.

Douglas allowed the off-watch time to settle in their hammocks and fall sound asleep before he launched a spark of fire into the ship's foreward crow's nest. In a few seconds it was burning bright enough to catch the eye of the watch.

Alarms were sounded and the entire crew again turned out to douse the flames. Again no one noticed that these fires did not consume.

It was an hour before Douglas allowed the new fire to die down and disappear. The men flopped down right on the wet deck to catch a few minutes of sleep before dawn.

As the pirate crew ate their first meal of the day another fire was reported in the crew's quarters, and everyone fell to once more, half-asleep, to fight the new blaze.

This time Douglas allowed the flames to destroy some of the hammocks, carelessly rolled and stowed against a bulkhead in the forepeak. A great deal of foul-smelling smoke hung about the ship and made it impossible for anyone to see either the Journeyman Wizard on the Tortoise or the slowly approaching ship. *Pinechip,* virtually untended, continued downwind ever closer to Waterand.

After noon, however, Douglas saw the Master go to the cabin door and call out to Bladder, who came, looking tired and surly, to see what was wanted. Bladder turned and shouted down the companionway to Eunicet: "This blighter says we're within a cat's whisker of raising Waterand and wants to alter course to miss it."

Eunicet appeared in the hatch and shouted at the Master to "turn at once, you stupid, timber-legged, bad-smelling son of a rotting, beached sea urchin!"

Which, Douglas said, proved that Eunicet had learned the fouler sides of seamanship, such as swearing, very quickly.

Pinechip heeled handily to the breeze and laid over on her starboard quarter, on a course to give Waterand a wider miss.

"Time to act, young Wizard," said Oval to her passenger. "She will never be closer to Waterand than she is now."

"Is that ship over there friend or foe? At any rate, we are close enough to Waterand now to take all the ladies under tow to Waterand in a few minutes, and it will be against the wind for either ship, if they choose to pursue."

"Make enough smoke," advised Oval placidly, "and we're bound to attract some attention on the island."

The Journeyman Wizard now sent wicked-looking red flames spouting from the forepeak and the mizzen yards, while thick billows of black smoke, smelling of sulfur and brimstone, belched from the forward hold. The pirates scrambled about in panic, as often as not paying no attention to the orders of their officers.

The Master lost his temper and punched Bladder down an accommodation ladder, but that great hulk caught himself by a dangling shroud. Swinging himself back up to the quarter-deck, he aimed a roundhouse blow at the Master from behind and dropped him senseless to the deck.

"You fool!" screamed Eunicet. "Who will give orders now and set course? Who knows better how to put out a fire, your blithering, bloated, backstabbing idiot!"

And he hit his ex-General smartly over the head with the pommel of his cutlass, sending Bladder staggering over a loosely coiled line. Eunicet took a startled and fearsome look at Douglas's latest effort, flame springing from the main hatch, fifteen feet in the air and licking hungrily at the mains'l clews.

"Man the boats!" he yelled at the top of his voice. "Abandon ship! Women and children be damned! Officers first!"

In an amazingly few seconds the entire crew was in the whaleboats, lowered, and cast off. Eunicet made a panic-stricken, tearful effort to force his way aboard each boat as it was lowered, but the pirate crewmen pushed him away and at last the Bo'sun drove a fist into his face. The blow laid Eunicet out cold beside the unconscious Bladder.

The ship's cook, missing the last boat, threw himself bodily into the Sea, foolishly trusting that his shipmates would appreciate his cooking enough to take him into one of the half-filled boats.

No one gave a thought to the six maids in the orlop.

"Away, away!" screamed the Bo'sun at the men manning the sweeps, swiping at the cook with his heavy leather starter. The oarsmen pulled with all their might and main, heading instinctively for the tip of an island on the horizon, or the other ship now standing in toward them. *Any port in a storm!*

"Or, in this case," shouted Douglas to Oval over the din, "any port in a fire. Take me close aboard. I can handle any who remain."

Douglas kept the fires and smokes going as an encouragement to the fleeing boats. When the Tortoise reached the sloop's waist, there was a commotion alongside and, looking down, Douglas saw two sleek, black shapes surfacing.

"It's the Porpoises!" he cried in surprise. "Here's Leaper and Skimmer! What are you two doing here?"

"We've been carrying messages between Augurian and Flarman, who is on yonder ship," explained Skimmer.

"Flarman's over there? Wonderful!" said Douglas, waving enthusiastically at the approaching square-rigger. Figures on the deck waved back.

"Take care of the ship, young wizard," advised Skimmer. "We'll watch the crew and see to it they come into safe port, if just to hang."

"I doubt Augurian hangs anyone," said Oval, "but I'll come along to help you boys. I may be slower but I've got size and power going for me."

Douglas boarded *Pinechip* alone, fearing what Eunicet would do when he realized that his last bargaining chip was the safety of the six Flowring girls.

He vaulted over the rail, tripped on a loose coil of rope, the same one that had felled Bladder earlier, and went to his knees. A whistle and a thud above his head startled him. He looked up at a foot-long dagger quivering in the rail just inches away.

Terrified, bloodied and disheveled, Eunicet charged him with a sword raised in both hands.

Douglas rolled quickly out of the way and sent a bolt of pink lightning sizzling at the madman's steel. Dazzled by the intense light and stunned by the powerful electric bolt, Eunicet dropped his sword to cover his eyes, screaming.

The Journeyman Wizard stood and, stepping forward, seized the villainous ex-lord by the sword belt and, with a furious tug, slung him over the rail into Sea. Eunicet gave a most satisfying howl of extreme fear and made a great splash.

"Look out for sharks," Douglas couldn't help but call down to him. Oval appeared under the thrashing Eunicet, who, at the sight of the Great Tortoise's huge head beside him in the water, saved everyone a lot of trouble by fainting dead away. He would have drowned, had not gentle Oval taken a mouthful of his doublet.

Douglas leaped to his feet, briefly eyed the unconscious Master and Bladder, ran to the orlop hatch, plunged down a steep companion ladder, and blasted with a furious bolt of blue lightning the big iron padlock that closed the door.

The five young maidens from Flowring were bunched against the far wall, fists raised in defiance. In front of them stood Myrn, smudged, torn, and uncombed, hefting a two-foot wood bar she had found somewhere, clutched in both hands, poised to strike.

"For goodness' sake, Myrn, put that thing down, or some-one—me, for example—might get hurt!"

" 'Tis the Wizard!'' shouted several of the maidens at once. Myrn looked at Douglas, smiled wearily, dropped the heavy billet—and slumped to the deck. Douglas ran forward to catch her as she wilted and held her close, calling her name.

"I was just about to kill you," Myrn whispered, weakly.

"No need, now," gasped Douglas. "Come up on deck. The pirates are gone and the only two remaining out cold. But they should be tied before they come to."

"I know a few sailor's knots I'd like to try on them," cried one of the rescued, and with joyous shouts and relieved laughter they rushed up on deck in time to see a longboat from *Icicle Princess* come alongside and hook into the chains.

They saw Bronze Owl fluttering noisily up to a yardarm, followed quickly over the taffrail by a sleek Black Flame.

"And where Black Flame is, Flarman Flowerstalk is never far behind," Douglas shouted to Myrn.

"Oh, my goodness, Flarman Firemaster and I haven't combed my hair or washed my face in three days," exclaimed the lass.

"Time for that in a few minutes," said Flarman's voice from over the side. "Give us a hand up, so that we may take this ship in the name of the Confederation of Light."

By now all six of the brave Flowring lasses were in full tear, crying with relief and joy at their rescue. They crowded around Flarman when he set foot on deck and accepted the Wizard's handkerchief—which multiplied until each girl had one to wipe away at the tears and dirt on her cheeks and blow her nose.

Except Myrn, who would only accept Douglas's handker-chief, salt stained and damp though it was from hours of immersion in Sea.

"Well, Journeyman," said Flarman in mock severity. "In your haste to join the ladies below you left a loose end or two here on deck. The man holding his head is the infamous General Bladder, once a low pub crawler in Capital, and a ne'er-do-well if ever there was one. The other I don't recognize but he looks like a pirate to me."

Bladder, wincing at the pain in his pate, whined, "Who hit me? You, youngster?"

"Eunicet had something to do with it," shrugged Douglas.

"His Grace!" snarled Bladder, drawing himself up but writhing in pain as he tried. "To you he is 'Your Grace.' "

"No longer," said Flarman, stepping forward and gesturing to the crew of the longboat to take charge of the prisoners. "Thornwood has taken his rightful place and his father's title, now. And Eunicet is safely in our hands and will shortly go on trial."

"Death's the punishment for Eunicet," observed Bronze Owl, having greeted Douglas with relief and affection and been introduced to Myrn.

"Even worse! Augurian, whose writ holds here, means to banish them together, Eunicet and Bladder, somewhere completely isolated," said Flarman, chuckling. "Who would want to be anywhere near either of them for years and years to come?"

Douglas and Myrn stood on the quarterdeck of *Pinechip* sloop as she was warped into dock in Waterand harbor. Oval, Skimmer, and Leaper swam beside her as a crowd of people and other beings on the mole cheered and three big Sea Gulls, the Stormy Petrel and Bronze Owl cried, mewed, and hooted their congratulations from above.

"A fit way to end a voyage," observed Flarman, who had stayed aboard as passenger. "But, youngsters, remember that it is only the end of one part of the adventure. It goes on tonight and tomorrow, and far beyond."

"Maybe I can get one good night's sleep," said Douglas, slumping over the taffrail.

"That's the way wars always are," said Flarman as they watched the prize crew rig a gangplank to the dock. "Hurry up and wait! A few minutes of excitement and days of boredom and frustration."

"Remind me not to complain about the next bit of boredom I meet," said Myrn, seriously. "There are worse things, I vow. Look! Douglas, there's my father and my brothers!"

And she rushed forward to the mole, pulling the young Wizard after her by the hand.

Flarman followed, pacing beside Black Flame, with Bronze Owl now on his shoulder calling friendly bird insults at the Sea Gulls.

Chapter Nineteen

EUNICET and Bladder awaited sentencing on a tiny underground island in a grotto beneath the palace, guarded by a school of foot-long orange-and-black tigerfish armed with flashing sharp teeth. Flarman and Douglas accompanied Augurian when he went down to interview them.

"What's to become of us?" whined Eunicet, faced with his longtime bitter enemies. "Flarman, you've always been a generous man! You won't let those fish get at me, will you? They have nasty teeth and mean eyes."

"You should have gone to sheep raising," answered Flarman, sternly. Douglas saw no twinkle in his eye now. "I have spoken with Augurian about you and Bladder. We agree that you are no good at all, least of all dead. Considering the numbers of good—and bad—men you have sent to their deaths, many think you deserve some particularly painful end yourselves."

"No! No!" cried both prisoners, cowering on the wet rocks.

"*He* made me do it," cried Bladder, pointing at Eunicet with both manacled hands.

"Flunky! Lickspittle! Craven!" howled the ex-Duke, trying to strike his companion.

"If Bryarmote had his way," continued Augurian, "you would spend the rest of eternity in the deepest mines under Dwelmland, never to see the sun again."

"Good old Bryarmote! Better than death!" cried Eunicet.

"Yes, yes, send us to the mines," begged Bladder.

"No, no," mimicked Flarman, "that is not to be your fate. Augurian proposes to maroon you on a sun-blasted, deserted atoll far away to the south, well out of the usual ship lanes, where you will be left alone—just the two of you."

"Just the wicked two of you," Augurian emphasized. "*Unless and until* you sincerely repent, and mend your lives to everyone's satisfaction. Become common men in a world of commoners, farmers, shepherds, craftsmen."

The prisoners were too stunned for words. The thought of spending even a few more hours *alone* with his former master set Bladder to blubbering and wailing for mercy. As the Wizards left the grotto the prisoners were still swearing and screaming at each other.

"It will be a long time before they learn their lessons." Douglas was thoughtful. Flarman nodded his head.

"That's fine," answered Augurian, grimly. "They will have a long time."

"Frigeon's Fleet is drawing nigh," Augurian told them later that day. "My scouts report he has left Eternal Ice. Depending on the wind, he will soon be just where we want to meet him. Then there will be a great Sea battle. And we will all be warriors."

"And worriers, too, I imagine," said Myrn. She looked at Douglas wistfully. A fleeting but curiously contented smile passed between them, and the older men, noting it, exchanged amazed but pleased glances.

"What will be our parts?" asked Douglas of the Water Wizard, tall and very dignified in his shimmering, Sea blue robe.

"In the morning I've called a meeting of my captains and the leaders of the hosts. We will discuss strategy and tactics and assign positions in the line. Thornwood is here with his captains. . . ."

"It was wonderful to see Thornwood again," exclaimed Douglas. "I'd like to fight by his side."

Augurian glanced at Flarman, and now they exchanged smiles at Douglas's eagerness.

"We shall see, Journeyman Wizard, in what post you will be needed. Tomorrow morning at nine in the great reception hall. Be there!"

Douglas nodded agreement.

"But this eventide, Mistress Myrn, perhaps you'd care to climb to the top of Watch Cliffs and compare them with the North End Cliffs of Flowring?"

"Oh, yes, sir, as long as we are home in time for supper.

My mother has arrived, you know, and she doesn't approve of young men and young ladies strolling cliffs alone after sunset.''

The older Wizards watched them walk away. Augurian pursed his lips, somewhat disapprovingly.

"It rarely hits Wizards, you know," said Flarman with a helpless shrug. "But when it does, it hits them hard! And it *can* greatly increase their powers.''

"Conference tomorrow," said Augurian, sighing. "And shipboard probably the next day. Are they ready, old friend?''

"They will be just fine. *I'm* ready. We have accomplished a lot in a year or two, Augurian. A year since, even a month ago, it would have been a much closer thing. Now, I think we have every good chance of winning this battle.''

"Frigeon has been told—I arranged it—that the Pearl is lost once again. He will be both overanxious and distracted because of it.''

"But you know where the Gray Pearl is?'' asked Bryarmote, just then joining them.

"True, my short, ugly friend,'' chuckled Flarman. "It has been recovered by Sea Fire from where it sank in Douglas's boot.''

"We would not do well to underestimate the power and cunning, the genius for evil of this Ice King,'' the Water-Adept said, solemnly.

"I do not,'' answered Flarman. "And neither does Snowlover here. If we seem to jest, it is only to make ourselves more comfortable with our fears.''

"I understand, then,'' the Water-Adept said, nodding. "I wish I were that way. I feel very troubled about what is coming. We could one or all die before many hours slip over the horizon.''

"I think of those we deeply love, going from us into death,'' said Flarman. "I could hardly bear losing the boy. He is truly the son I never had. But risk him I must.''

Flarman laid his hand on the Water Wizard's shoulder.

"Augurian, you must choose an Apprentice for your service soon. Really you must! Wizards do not live forever and your lore and skills should be passed on or they, too, will die.''

"I will tell you, then,'' said the other, "I have already

chosen an Apprentice, and the choice will perhaps surprise you. And delight you, I think. I knew at once when I met her that the pearl fisher's daughter was an ideal candidate.''

''Wonderful news! Have you asked her?'' asked Bryar-mote, who was beginning to think about supper instead of Apprentice Wizards.

''We spoke at length of it this morning and, tomorrow before the War Council ends, I will announce it to all. Now, let us to dinner.''

''A very just and proper proposal,'' said the Dwarf, hitching up his broad belt. ''Sea air, you know, gives ugly little people tremendous appetites.''

''And Wizards, too,'' agreed Flarman.

''Who did ye think I was referring to?'' grunted the Dwarf.

The Great Reception Hall was full, with Men, Fairies, Dwarfs, Elves, Pixies, Nixies, Brownies in chairs placed in rows facing a raised platform. . . . Mortals and Near Immortals of all sorts, sizes, shapes, and colors, from the farmer Militia of Dukedom and the pearl fishermen of Flowring to the Nereids of Faerie, under Prince Aedh, and the Dwarf Home Guard of Dwelmland, all were present.

Not all there were of human shape. These tended to lie on their bellies in the space before the lectern or grasp the balcony railing above with sharp talons or webbed toes: the Great White Gulls, Bitterns, Erns, and Terns.

One side of the Great Hall was a huge tank opening to Sea. Here swam the leaders of the Seafolk: Orcas, Porpoises, Tortoises as well as Mermen and Sea Sprites, all longtime supporters of Augurian.

Douglas, Myrn, and Flarman were ushered to seats to the right of Augurian on the platform, and a moment later the Water-Adept rapped sharply on the lectern. The assemblage fell silent at once.

''Now,'' said the Water Wizard, beginning briskly, ''we have no time for formalities. Most of you know each other and if you don't, just tell each other who you are.''

There was a sudden roar as strangers seated next to strangers leaned over and exchanged names, titles, races, and places.

''I will begin,'' said Augurian when they quieted again,

"with as brief an overview of the situation as I can give. Let me take a few minutes to review, as some of you may never have heard the full story before.

"After the fall of Kingdom, in the Days of Chaos, a tiny remnant of the once-numerous Fellowship of Wizards agreed to keep in touch, to preserve what they could of their fellowship. Each then went his own way, seeking a place where he could rebuild, renew, and recruit apprentices to keep the ideals of the Confederation of Light alive.

"Fortunately, those Forces of Darkness that we had failed to destroy in Last Battle were also in headlong retreat, or we would all be in thrall to them today."

Augurian paused to see if everyone understood, for many there did not speak Old Tongue.

"I returned to the islands and waters of Warm Seas, where I could study and help in difficult times those dearest to me. Flarman Firemaster built Wizard's High in Dukedom's Valley, choosing it, I believe, because it most closely resembled his own homeland, utterly destroyed by our Enemies.

"There were then nine surviving Wizards, including one, an Air-Adept, who some suspected of surviving that dreadful war through cowardice and treachery rather than skill and bravery.

"This Aeromancer had become terribly embittered, insanely determined to let nothing stand between him and his personal survival. He set out to find an empty land in which to prepare his solution to chaos—to conquer World and rule it himself—the ultimate defensive strategy!

"He passed through Dukedom long ago, and Flarman Flowerstalk recognized him and what he had become. Flarman warned me and I joined him in watching.

"This was Frigeon, who now styles himself Ice King. He stayed awhile with the great-great-grandfather of Chief Tet of Highlandorm, accepting the Chieftain's hospitality for a season, returning nothing but trouble to his host. When he demanded the empty land in the north and east of Highlandorm, Tet's ancestor gladly deeded it to him, hoping to rid himself of an unwelcome guest.

"The deeded area seemed worthless—the terminus of a great hundred-mile-wide glacier hundreds of feet thick that had for millions of years crept from the Polar Mountains into Sea.

"It suited Frigeon to live in such a place. He began to gather sycophants, and taught them well the ways of greed and fear. They all had his manic fear of personal freedom and individual responsibility on the part of those they considered their inferiors.

"Frigeon built there a stronghold of ice so cold and hard it is really metal. Men and most other Beings could enter only with the protection of strong spells, which worked only so long as they obeyed the Ice King. Only Flarman Firemaster has ever managed to defy Frigeon in his own fortress and live to tell the tale."

Douglas leaned forward to see the Fire Wizard's reaction to this. Flarman was evidently dozing.

"To make himself invulnerable, Frigeon magically locked the vestigial, pitiful remnants of his own humanity within a great Gray Pearl. This talisman he dropped into deepest Sea, to be forever hidden from his enemies, who might seek to use his own humanity against him. The Gray Pearl remained hidden for more than three hundred years.

"His plans took shape." Augurian told them. "He would move against his old comrades of the Fellowship and against all fair Beings, against Men, Dwarfs, Fairies and any Being else who displayed warmth, kindness, justice, mercy, love, the weaknesses he considered the cause of our downfall in Last Battle. He would destroy them or make them all slaves to fear and despair. Once he had all in his power, no one could ever again cause him the terror, disgrace, and guilt that wracked him during the Last Battle.

"Two of the remaining Wizards, by the by, disappeared centuries ago. One other, Frackett, was so weakened by his ordeals that his role was reduced to being a hermit in Landsend wilderness. When asked by Flarman and me, he did agree to keep a trained and suspicious eye on Frigeon's activities nearby."

Douglas looked again at Flarman, this time in surprise. *Frackett, a Wizard?* Flarman nodded confirmation without opening his eyes.

Augurian went on, "I'm close to the end now. Bear with me, friends. After years of searching, Flarman found the Pearl. Learning of this, Frigeon decided to proceed immediately with his first attack before its secret could be discovered.

"Frigeon raised Eunicet over Dukedom, believing that Flarman would become absorbed in helping his neighbors against the usurper's misrule and cruelties. This, Frigeon believed, would divert his enemies' attention, allowing him to conquer Sea while we were without Flarman's help."

He paused again. The listeners moved restlessly.

"Fortunately, Flarman found a capable assistant, his Apprentice, Douglas Brightglade. With Douglas's help, he was able both to counter much of the effect of Dead Winter and continue to work with me on the solution to the Gray Pearl. While Flarman did his own distraction by visiting Eternal Ice, the seemingly lowly Apprentice carried the Pearl across Sea to Waterand, undetected.

"Not knowing this, Frigeon gathered allies, followers, and slaves for this great Sea engagement. He has both Mortal and Near Immortal forces at his command. From the brutalized warrior septs of Landsend he drew trained mercenaries, the Dreads, to whom life is simply an excuse to snuff out anyone else's life, friend or enemy.

"Others were drawn, attracted, forced, or bribed to Frigeon's service—outlaws, pirates, evil-minded men and women—fully a quarter of his Ice Forces are fearsome, female warriors—drawn by promises of spoil, rapine, untrammeled looting and killing, and, of course, intense excitement and total debauchery. Frigeon keeps them well. They obey—or they freeze.

"His hybrid, icy magic also has brought him the allegiance, if not the loyalty, of dozens of ghastly subcreatures, singly and in packs, troops, and armies. Some are Werewolves, tearers of flesh. Icy Whirlwinds with minds seeking to inflict revenge on Men of Kingdom, their archenemies of old. They were the servants of the Devilmen.

"Trolls have come in platoons, lugging huge, spiked clubs taller than they are, with which they take delight in knocking off their enemies'—and in lieu of that, their friends'—heads.

"Banshees are Frigeon's gourmets of death. Unable to inflict death themselves, they can inspire mind-shattering horror if one is unwary. The Landsenders fear almost nothing, yet the appearance of Banshees can turn even their knees to water and their minds to gibbering mush.

"There are Afancs—dark, muddy half men born in magic

whirlpools that suck whole ships into their depths and spit out their bones.

"From the barren mountains of the Far West no man has ever climbed and lived, came Goblins and Trolls. Although manlike, they are frightfully deformed and twisted in mind as in body. They are almost fearless in battle and they live in deadly hatred of anyone not a Goblin.

"Frigeon depends upon such as these to defeat our confederation. Our defense against them is simple: bravery, intelligence, sacrifice when necessary, the certainty that our cause is just, and a unity of purpose."

He took a moment to look all about the hall.

"As to numbers, if they mean anything, Frigeon can field an army about equal to ours in strength. His roster is seventy percent inhuman. Ours is about sixty percent human, forty percent not."

"And it is well known and admitted even among the Fairies," said Queen Marget aloud, "that Men are the best warriors of all. In battle or long war, one trained Man is worth ten of Frigeon's monsters."

Augurian nodded his thanks on behalf of all Men, and now began the discussion of technical details of the coming battle.

"The Asrai will be on our side, even if it is only useful at night," said Marget, Queen of Faerie, during lunch. "They can be terrible opponents, I hear."

"Asrai?" asked Douglas. "That's one I haven't yet met."

"Oh, but I thought you knew it," said the Faerie Queen, fork poised halfway to her lovely mouth. "It saved you from drowning, I heard."

"Oh, you must mean Sea Fire! I thought its name was Phosphorescence."

"Yes, but we wee folk call it Asrai, which means the same thing and is less effort to say," the Queen said, laughing.

Among the Highlandormers Douglas saw an old, familiar face. He excused himself and rushed over to greet Crimeye, the former spy.

"My good, good friend!" said Crimeye. "It's so very fine to see you again and safe, too! I hear you captured old Eunicet alive and that nasty Bladder, too. Congratulations!"

"Are you still spying?" asked Myrn, who had a way of asking rather direct questions.

"No, no! Although there are times when I wish I was the same, simple, old Crimeye, again! Now I have *responsibilities*," he sighed. "Then, I was as free and carefree as the Sea Gulls. Come and go as I pleased. Chief Tet took a liking to me and I to him and, well . . . we got on so famously that he's made me his heir!"

"Not really!" cried Douglas, astonished but delighted.

"Truly, truly, younger Wizard. At first I hesitated. Oh, I love the old warrior like a father, you know, but I was afraid that his Highlandormers wouldn't take to me."

"And have they?"

"Uncommonly well, I think," said the other, blushing in modesty and obviously filled with pride. "They've adopted me, also. I'm their Young Tet. I am most flattered! They are a wonderful people, my people, and very good soldiers while remaining very humane and loving at the same time.

"I've discovered," he said, "when people depend on you, you tend to try to live up to their expectations. Officially I am Young Tet, but my friends and even my new father still call me Crimeye."

A tall, uncommonly handsome Fairy in full golden plate armor entered and went directly to the head table, where Augurian, Flarman, and Marget sat, talking earnestly.

" 'Tis her Prince Consort, Aedh of Faerie," Crimeye told them. He had lost none of the inquisitiveness that had made him a spy in the first place.

"How handsome he is!" breathed the pearl fisher's daughter. Despite himself, Douglas had to agree.

Marget, Flarman, and Augurian listened carefully to what Prince Aedh had to say. Then the Water-Adept stood and rapped the table three times. Silence fell, even among the gaily chatting Faerie youths in the back of the hall.

"Prince Aedh has detected the advance units of Frigeon's fleet," he announced. "He has been hidden by the Lasting Mists southeast of Highlandorm, but he is now out and sailing as swiftly as he can in this direction. Swift, of course, relative to how fast his slowest ship is. He will be within our waters tomorrow or the next day. The north wind is fair for his course.

"We will not await Frigeon here. We'll go out to meet

him. We have picked a battle water, where hidden reefs and
rocks awash are many and menacing. We doubt Frigeon has
useful charts, but we do, thanks to the creatures of Sea,
especially the Porpoises.

"I ask all commanders to meet with me at once for last
words on dispositions."

There was the beginning of a great stir but Augurian
rapped for silence again.

"I have an announcement to make. I have for some years
been seeking someone appropriate and capable to learn the
art, craft, and science of Aquamancy, as my Apprentice.
Flarman's success in doing the same I mentioned this morning. His Apprentice, now Journeyman, has shown his ability
to all. He has carried out a most important assignment and
was solely responsible for capturing one of our most dangerous enemies."

"Hardly 'solely' at all," protested Douglas, but no one
paid any attention.

"Now I, too, have selected an Apprentice. If this person
is as hardworking, as intelligent, as gifted as I believe, she
will make one day a splendid Wizard, the first of her sex."

" 'She?' " gasped a dozen voices, including that of Flarman's former Apprentice. He turned and looked directly into
the eyes of the young lady seated beside him.

"Her name," Augurian went on, "is Myrn Manstar of the
Isle of Flowring."

The crowd in the dining hall broke into loud cheers and
enthusiastic applause and stood to signal their approval,
while Douglas threw his arms about the new Apprentice
Wizard and gave her a very heartfelt buss on the cheek.

"I'll help you all I can," he promised her. "I couldn't
have made a better choice myself."

That evening the Journeyman Wizard was sent to the top
of the tallest peak on Waterand, where lookouts reported
a fearsome band had landed—twelve full-grown Great
Golden Dragons, green scaled and with fifty-foot wing-
spreads.

No one had known whether the Great Dragons would join
them. They were a snobbish, standoffish species, who had
never been known to war with anyone. Their kin, the smaller
Sea Dragons, were firm allies of Augurian, but these fiercer,

larger cousins usually took no interest in the doings of Men, Fairies, or Dwarfs.

When Douglas arrived, accompanied by Bryarmote and Caspar Marlin, the Grand Dragon at first haughtily refused to speak to them. When told that Douglas was accompanied by the Dwarf Prince, however, he became the soul of friendliness and hospitality.

"Why, of all the good reasons put forward by that Water Person (meaning Augurian, of course), the one that convinced us at last to come was that Smoke Ring Blower would be here. He is the inventor of our sport! We sit by the year, blowing round rings, square rings, oval rings, even smoke chains!"

He demonstrated his own prowess, blowing three differently colored smoke rings, one each about the heads and shoulders of his visitors.

"If I survive this confrontation, I intend to spend several decades working on spirals."

"Why should you not survive?" asked Caspar, awed by the creature's size, hauteur, golden color, and talent for smoke rings. "What could harm you, sir?"

"Despite rumor to the contrary, we are Mortal and live short lives, no more than a few dozen centuries, at best. Secondly, we are easily killed, as you could learn by listening to the old histories of knights in armor and captive virgins—most of whom, if you want the truth, were voluntary guests who knew dragons would not threaten their chastity or sanity, whereas most knights—well, knights are often deplorably blind to anything except their own glory and honor.

"Also," he added, ticking it off on the third of five fearfully long, razor-sharp, emerald claws, "we will be fighting our own kind."

"Your own kind?"

"Unfortunately. Just short of half the available Dragonage in World are beholden to Frigeon for some silly reason I don't understand, and will begin, at least, on *his* side. I hope our involvement will persuade them to drop out."

"You will cancel out the Dragon opposition, at least," said Bryarmote, thoughtfully. "Just as the Dwarfs . . ."

"Will cancel out the Trolls, which are Dwarfish, if not

true Dwarfs," finished Douglas. "Too bad, really. Too bad!"

"Cancel 'em with an iron mace!" agreed the Dwarf, ferociously. "That feud has gone too far and too long and been too bloody simply to be forgotten and forgiven."

"Still, forgiveness is a goal we must reach, come the end of hostilities," said Grand Dragon. "Some of Frigeon's allies are misguided, misled, forced to follow him by magic or fear. I believe the last is the case of the Other Dragons."

"Well, perhaps, but the enmity between Dwarfs and Trolls goes back to before Frigeon. Before Kingdom and the Last Battle; almost to the beginning of time."

"Flarman has said the end of battle will not be the end of war, and the end of war will not be the end of troubles," said Douglas. "I guess we'll have to take it one step at a time."

Chapter Twenty

"WE have our own work to do," Flarman said to Douglas. Then he grinned excitedly. "We may not wield a sword with Thornwood nor draw a bow with the Brownies, but we have a weapon more powerful than all of theirs and we must now use it."

"The Pearl?" Douglas guessed, running to keep up.

"Come on!" was all Flarman would say. He led the young Wizard down to *Icicle Princess*, which Douglas was surprised to discover had been renamed *Flame Daughter* since he had last seen her.

"Later! Later," Flarman called to Douglas's unspoken questions. "We sail at once, Fribby. Get under way!"

The Ice Fleet moved slowly over the uneasy waters, its speed that of the slowest ammunition scow. The sounds of the fleet were terrifying: moans, groans, wails, curses, clanks, thumps, shrieks of pain, roars of anger, and cruel, maniacal laughter. Evil makes a tremendous amount of noise.

Frigeon needed some peace and quiet to think and plan. He'd had a sanctum built next to *Snowstorm*'s keel. It had thick walls and heavy oaken doors both to keep the noise out and the cold within. It was chilled by fifty-pound blocks of the super-cold metallic ice of his home glacier. They would not warm enough to melt in months.

Frigeon was seldom seen on deck. Few of his multitudes ever clapped eye on him. For his commanders he held council in his cabinet but councils were apt to be brief. Chattering teeth, in those species with teeth, tended to drown out the sound of their dire Master's voice. Those of saurian aspects tended to go torpid very quickly in the cold cabinet.

When moist Sea air met the cold that seeped from *Snow-storm*, she trailed a vast plume of chill mist. In high latitudes, the other ships scurried to keep free, but as the air warmed with their southing, ship's captains were vying for places in the cool mist as protection from heat and sunlight.

Among the fleet were dozens of galleys, driven not by the wind, but by pitiable slaves pulling long, heavy sweeps. A galley's strength was in her ability to move against the wind. Her weakness was that the rowers were often whipped without sense or mercy and were always underfed.

The stench of the never-bathed, often-sick galley slaves was overpowering. Not even the most hardened sailor could stand downwind for long. The galleys were, therefore, relegated to the aftermost rank in the fleet and as time went on they fell farther and farther behind, despite the cracking of angry whips and shouted counting of the row masters.

Tempers, never good, flared constantly, not just between the different species but within the ranks of each host. Troll fought Troll in bloody free-for-alls below, where the light was dim and the air foul and close. It was worth a Goblin's life to be caught in a part of a ship claimed by another Goblin tribe. Each night, the watch heard the splash and screams of victims being tossed over the side. Edible bodies were quickly torn to pieces by carnivore fish who had come along uninvited.

Thought the Ice King to himself, They all will soon be busy enough with battling to bother each other too much. The most important groups, such as the Banshees and the Dreads, would remain disciplined and loyal, being bound to him by dire oaths and deathless spells they could not break if they wanted to.

These breeds would see that many of his allies would never survive the aftermath. Frigeon saw no need to pay warriors when there was no longer war. He didn't plan to share his new power with any of them.

Such thoughts were interrupted by a scraping on his ice chamber door.

"Come in and it had better be good," snarled Frigeon. "Oh, 'tis only you, Clangeon. What news?"

His Chief Steward crept into the cold room, bobbing his head and cringing fearfully. To come into Frigeon's presence at the best of times was fearsome. You took your life and your sanity in your hands to come with bad news.

"O Great King, soon-to-be Ruler of World, the Moray Eels have brought word."

"Oh?" said the Ice King softly. "And what do they say?"

"Porpoises in Augurian's service have seen us and run now southward to apprise Waterand of our presence."

He shivered and cowered, expecting blows at best to follow this news, but Frigeon's icy wrath was stilled, to his surprise.

The King merely stared at his servant and finally nodded.

"I expected it. You can't sail a huge fleet like mine in open Sea without being discovered sooner or later. It makes no difference. Tell my Captains all to get themselves over here this evening when the moon sets for a final meeting."

He turned back to his charts and scribbled notes. The Chief Steward slithered out, patting his bald head to make sure it was still firmly attached, and went to signal the council.

Below the oil-smooth surface of Sea the first squirmishes were fought in total blackness and deepest silence. The forward line of Augurian's Porpoises attacked the outpost lines of nearly invisible Medusa jellyfish. They tore great, soft, poison-spurting chunks of the jelly away, letting the dead sink into the depths.

In a few minutes the Porpoises reduced the Medusae to less than half their strength and scattered the rest. The Moray Eels of the second line, the messengers of the fleet, fled before the Porpoises' attack, hiding among the ships' bottoms.

While the brief fight raged, Skimmer threaded his way among the ships and found the largest bottom, *Snowstorm*. He swiftly moved amidships and laid his starboard ear hole against the coppered hull, listening.

By dawn Augurian had a report of the decisions taken and orders given at Frigeon's briefing.

The weather to the south, east, and west was beautiful, warm, and dry, but the entire northern horizon was a mass of black, roiling, clouds, towering up almost halfway to the zenith.

"Yonder comes Frigeon!" said Augurian to Thornwood, his Fleet Commander. They paced the quarterdeck of fast *Donation,* the flagship.

"We'll fight this afternoon, then," said the Duke, feeling for his sword's hilt at his shoulder.

"According to Skimmer, Frigeon plans to hit us with two or three hours of daylight left, sending in his conventional units against our center."

"His Men are better fighters by day, of course. If he can't see 'em he won't trust 'em," observed Thornwood. "But the Banshees are a different matter."

"Our task is to break Frigeon's first line, his Men. We must do what we can to resist the mind-wrenching attacks of the nighttime things."

"I wonder what Douglas and the old Fire-eater are doing right now," said Bryarmote, whetting the edge of his battle-ax. But the Water-Adept had turned to speak to one of his officers.

Flarman and Douglas were seated at a small table on the quarterdeck of *Flame Daughter,* eating a hearty breakfast and watching the black clouds move away to the southeast. North winds off Eternal Ice were ramming headlong into a strong, warm south wind above Battle Shoals and throwing each other high in the air, where the moisture in them condensed into thick, boiling black clouds heavy with rain. Lightning and thunder shattered the sky continuously. Whirlwinds sought to tear masts from ships and drive the smaller ones under the waves.

"Sea Fire should have no trouble bringing the Pearl to us, despite the weather over there?" asked Douglas.

"Storms don't bother Asrai," said Flarman, comfortably. "I'm rather glad I'm not over there under that cloud cover myself."

Sea's surface was stormy. Lines of breakers charged each other and leaped high as if trying to join the updraft winds.

The ships of both Fleets, now just in sight of each other, were leaping themselves, rolling and pitching as crosswinds and crosscurrents tore at their timbers and caused them to groan and shudder like living things in pain.

Frigeon, up from his ice-cold sanctum, leaned precariously over the taffrail as flunkies waved fans and wet cloths at him to keep him cool in the hot, humid air. Beside him stood a sweating Clangeon, who had come below to tell the Ice King that the Morays wished to speak to him in person.

In the heaving waters below, Frigeon spotted long, thigh-thick coils and dull black scales, whipping and squirming, then a flat, ugly snout adorned with a mouthful of razor-sharp, inward-pointing teeth. Head Moray grinned insolently at his Master.

"What is it you are saying? What is it?" ground out Frigeon in a terrible voice, fighting the queasiness of his stomach as the ship took a headlong dip. "Tell me quickly. We are about to launch our attack."

"And you're lucky," sneered the Eel. "We below have been fighting for our lives since early yesterday evening. Fully forty of my strongest, longest mates are already dead!"

"Sniveling fish-snake! Did you expect to fight our enemies without casualties? What have you to say, aside from spineless complaints?"

Head Moray ground his teeth in exasperation but said, "You ought to know your fleet is heading into shallows, shifting sandbanks, rocks, and reefs barely awash. You will need to proceed with extreme caution."

"Guiding us among hazards is your duty," shouted Frigeon over the sound of the wind and waves. "Not one ship must strike reef or go aground, do you hear?"

"We'll do all we can. We hate the enemy as much as anyone. However, we cannot watch and guide them all, all the time. We can take care of the great ships but the small boats must shift for themselves. Besides, many are too fast. We are not fast swimmers. The dhows and the frigates are way beyond our powers to pace."

Frigeon hurled profanities and obscenities at the toothy fish-snake but at last he nodded. There was nothing he could now do about the Eels' reduced numbers.

"What of the Medusae?" he asked.

"We're trying to round them up. Perhaps they can watch over the smaller vessels. Perhaps not. We'll try. At best we can put them in a screen before your advance."

"When battle is joined you can expect most movement to slow," Frigeon said thoughtfully. "Keep all your slime-crawlers on best behavior. No malingering!"

"Hard to promise when there's bound to be fresh meat around," said the Eel, doubtfully.

"Pustuled ingrates! Why should I suffer you to exist at all? If they shirk their duties, kill them! The frigates and the dhows will just have to look out for themselves. They are, after all, Sea's best sailors, or so they have told me dozens of times. We'll see."

He studied Augurian's approaching line, his officers identifying Thornwood's flagship, *Donation,* and several other of the Confederation's ships of the line. His plan remained, he barked at them. Hit the center, divide the Confederation fleet in twain, and defeat each half separately.

Grunting with sour satisfaction, he handed his spyglass to Clangeon.

"Call me when we are within bow shot. Stay topside, Clangeon. No poltroon, pusillanimous snuffling about below the waterline! Send me word every half hour. Get me something cold to drink."

And he stomped below to the cold comfort of his iced room.

In a line in front of Thornwood's tall ships, three hundred Porpoises clicked and squeaked to each other nervously. Skimmer surveyed them a moment and then turned to a third-degree youngster beneath him.

"Swim fast to *Donation,*" he ordered, "and tell them we are ready."

"Yes, sir!" squeaked the youngster, and he was off like a streak. Skimmer watched him go with a fond smile, then turned to order his line into motion. "Brave and steady, good friends! Do you expect to live forever?"

Aboard *Donation* all was ready, too. Dwarfs checked their short swords, spiked maces, and keen axes. Brownies strung their recurved bows and stuck sharp arrows into the yards upon which they perched, close to hand. The wild toss and pitch of the mastheads didn't bother them. They were used to shooting from wind-tossed grass blades or boughs of quaking aspen.

Men, Fairies, and Dwarfs, Brownies, Nixies, and Pixies, separately and together talked about their homes, families, and past battles. They all tried not to watch the approaching fleet.

At the same time, on the ships, galleys, barges, schooners, sloops, brigantines, barges, and yachts of Frigeon's line the uproar was horrendous. Sergeants bellowed curses and orders, intermixed, at the tops of their gravelly voices. They were already hoarse from insulting, threatening, castigating.

Their troopers responded with sullen resignation and then fierce glowers when the sergeants' backs were turned. Tempers roared into flame and blows were driven home by fist, whip, or flat of scimitar. In some cases, by sharp point of knife or edge of sword.

Tension was high. Everyone pretended it wasn't, especially in the high ranks of Trolls, Goblins, Werewolves and all other frightening tribes, sects, and species. The commonality merely rolled their bloodshot eyes, silently promised revenge someday, and allowed themselves to be pushed and driven into position to fight, perhaps to die. They lifted their weapons to the inspecting eyes of their superiors and, as often as not, secretly swore to use their weapons on the leaders if chance arose in the confusion of the fight.

Below the chop and wrack, Skimmer's line hit the outranks of the Medusae, which were milling lacklusterly in the demi-gloom four fathoms down. The confusion of the wind and waves at this depth, which they usually avoided at all costs, addled their lightweight brains.

Now a slashing attack by the feared Porpoises came from below, ignoring the stinging tentacles, tearing with sharp teeth, and smashing with strong flippers. The attack at once destroyed what discipline Morays had labored to instill in the Jellies. Those who survived the first three minutes of attack fled downward. In their haste they tangled their long, thin tentacles with those of their fellows and became helpless as the Porpoises launched a second attack.

"Down, down, down," the Medusae leaders keened, and the Jelly mass sank into the black depths beside Battle Shoals. There they hid until long after the battle was over.

■ ■ ■

Fairies, Men, and Brownie archers and Dwarf crossbow-men looked somewhat out of place aboard ship in their forest-colored tunics. They could see gray, dark brown, and black figures perched in the rigging of the Ice King's ships of the line as the two columns of square-riggers drew closer and closer on converging courses.

Bright flashes from drawn knifes and swords were like pinpoints of fire. Hoarse cries and bellowed orders flew faintly across the intervening, heaving Sea.

Snowstorm's Captain ordered more sail, and she began to move ahead of *Donation,* leading the Confederation Fleet line. In doing so, she pulled ahead of her sister ships. These were sluggish to follow, putting over their helms to make the angle of attack sharper. All ships wallowed heavily in the sharp chop stirred by opposing winds.

Aboard Confederation ships, arrows were nocked to strings and drawn to pointed fairy ears, aimed high to carry across the closing distance. Eyes strained for targets, ears for the command to fire.

From *Snowstorm*'s foretop came a ragged, black cloud of screaming, purple arrows tipped with steel and deadly poisons.

The first shots of the battle had been fired.

But fell short, disappearing unseen in the furious waves. Aboard *Donation* Thornwood heard the whiz and whine of the arrows and marked their shortfall.

"Next volley will strike," he said to Bryarmote. "Tell all to shoot once and take cover. No heroics, now."

The order was passed, Bryarmote saying, "Don't shoot until you are sure of reaching your mark."

A cloud of brown and sky blue shafts left two thousand bows as one, shrieking into the rigging and upper works of the five tall, black Ice ships opposite.

Trolls and Goblins screamed hopelessly and, clutching at arrows protruding from thighs, arms, chests, bellies, or necks, plunged head over heels into the water or onto decks. Even many not seriously wounded fell, unable to keep their balance on the wildly bucking yardarms.

Those who lived to hit the water pleaded for rescue. The ships plunged swiftly by without a glance. A fallen comrade was so much garbage, and to slow long enough to throw a screaming swimmer a line invited a thousand more arrows.

To *Donation* and the other ships of the line of Confederation Fleet the first deadly blows came from a flight launched by the tough, dour Dreads. A few Men aboard failed to duck down fast enough and felt the shock of steel tips armed with poison.

Fairies and Dwarfs were hit, but not fatally. The poisons used by the Dread bowmen could not harm them. They plucked the arrows out of their arms or legs and jumped up to shoot again and again, carefully aiming each shot.

Doctors and hastily trained aides, including many from the Valley of Dukedom, rushed on deck amid fresh storms of arrows to retrieve the fallen Men and carry them below.

The lines sheared off slightly from one another on first encounter. They ran parallel, archers of both sides pouring sheets of arrows and bolts into each other. Confederation Fleet archers took the greater toll, as Frigeon's archers were trained to launch great broadsides rather than to make each arrow count.

Details of third-degree Porpoises dashed about rescuing those who had fallen overboard and brought them to smaller schooners and sloops in the rear. The least lucky of both sides were victims of the voracious Morays, hiding now in the walls of reefs on either side of the course of the fight.

The eels' protective darkness was shattered by the arrival of Sea Fire, called Asrai by the Fairies. Brilliantly illuminating the black foot of the reef, safe from the sunlight above, it showed the way for a swirling storm of small, bright-colored fishes who schooled about living and dead to hide them from the flesh-eating eels. Drowning Men were nudged quickly up to the surface until they could be rescued by the Porpoises and Great Sea Tortoises brought by Oval.

A fierce secondary battle followed Sea Fire's appearance. The Tortoises, angered at last, attacked the Eels in their lairs, ripping apart the coral bastions and dragging them forth with inexorable strength to snip off their heads. The Tortoises' hard shells were proof against the Eels' terrible teeth.

Ice Fleet ships of the line were within a stone's throw and less, surging forward, hoping to cut across Confederation

Fleet's bows to engage quarter to quarter on an opposite course. Waiting foot soldiers girded themselves to carry the attack onto enemy decks when the ships collided.

With shattering force and terrible uproar, Dwarf mangonels and catapults fired their loads into the Ice Fleet's hulls, masts, and rigging, followed by balls of unquenchable fire that hit decks and at once spread to rigging and the clothing of soldiers and sailors nearby.

Crewmen had to be called from fighting and sailing duties to pump water on the fires and throw the burning balls of pitch and tinder-dry Seaweed over the side. Frigeon's ships dropped slowly aback, losing their chance to cross in front of Thornwood's line.

Shouts and cries died away suddenly; silence fell for the first time since the fight had begun. As the Ice ships slowed and veered out of line, Thornwood sent up red and white signal flags. His big ships suddenly altered course, sailing directly away from the enemy—"showing them our heels," said Bryarmote.

Another signal and another lightning change of course. *Donation* led her sisters abreast back into the enemy line, slicing between *Snowstorm* and the ship immediately behind her. Arbolasts at *Donation*'s waist sent hundreds of sharp, feathered darts screaming down the length of both enemies' decks.

The other tall Confederation ships followed suit. Almost every Ice ship veered out of line again as the Dwarfs' catapults threw more balls of red-and-yellow fire.

Augurian shouted a spell of wind words and waved his arms in a wide, magic gesture. The southerly wind died and Thornwood's ships changed course at once to take advantage of Frigeon's own northerly blasts to run up along the less heavily defended starboard sides of the enemy men-of-war. More clouds of brown and blue arrows flew as the Goblin, Troll, and Men warriors dashed wildly from the port to the starboard side to find new stations.

Struggling to avoid striking their fellow ships, Frigeon's men-of-war swung about in a badly coordinated maneuver. Three of the five had serious fires burning and their firepower was sharply cut. Fire arrows from their best archers repeatedly hit Thornwood's ships, to no avail. Flarman had fireproofed almost every inch of rigging and decking before they sailed from Waterand.

"It is time to start our planned withdrawal to the Shoals," Thornwood suggested to Augurian.

"Carry on, Lord Duke. Night is about to fall. It will be the time I fear most for our people."

Thornwood ordered new signal flags hoisted to the flagship's maintop and the new maneuver began. Frigeon's ships milled about, uncertain what to do next.

Frigeon had dinner served on his quarterdeck during the lull. It was still a bloody mess but he thought that a war leader must be seen by his officers and men. He was approached by an ugly toad of a young man who touched his hat respectfully.

"Sir, the enemy is changing course again. . . ."

"Who are *you*?" interrupted the Ice King. "I don't know you. Why are you daring to speak to me?"

"Draggle, formerly Third Officer of *Snowstorm*, sire."

"Dash and blast! Why are you addressing me, your exalted King, and not your cowardly coast hugger of a Captain?"

The young man opened his large mouth to speak but Frigeon shouted him down. Baiting underlings was his favorite sport.

"Speak up, snotnose! Is your tongue shot away? Why can't I get a simple answer out of you, son of a scrofulous galley slave?"

Draggle gave his sovereign a totally disgusted look and shouted back in a voice trained on a dozen quarterdecks amid storm and battle, "Sire! I *was* Third Officer but your blithering idiot of a Captain had the unmitigated stupidity to step in the path of a Brownie dart and died with it sticking out his left ear. That made me Second Officer for twelve and a half minutes. Then the new Captain, formerly the First Officer, went into the drink rather than burn to death when a fireball hit at his feet. Then *I* became Captain myself, which I have been for an hour now."

Frigeon gasped in surprise and before he could speak, Draggle went on at the top of his voice.

"As your new Captain, I report to you that Augurian's lackeys, who to this moment have conducted this battle with imagination, daring, and, above all, success, are turning away westward in line, and those dunderheads you put in command of your other ships are letting them get away! I suppose they are awaiting your orders. I, for one, don't plan to float idly around waiting for you to finish your dinner."

He paused, out of breath. Frigeon looked at him with some wonder and new respect.

"Ah, well . . . well," he managed at last. "What do you suggest, What's-your-name?"

"Draggle, sire. *Captain* Draggle."

"Yes, well, *Captain* Draggle, why don't you just . . . carry on? Carry on, won't you? You seem to be in the best position to decide what to do next. Personally, I'm a strategist, not a tactician. He was, as you say, an idiot—whatever his name was, the one with the silly arrow stuck in his left ear."

Draggle, finally at a loss for words, merely stepped back, saluted raggedly, and turned on his heel to address the ship in a loud, high voice.

"Listen up, you scum! I am now Captain of this scurvy ship and Admiral of this fleet. You *will* immediately stop that gaggling, caterwauling, and other noise making. In other words, fall silent or fall overboard!"

A sudden and very surprised silence did begin to fall.

"Listen to my orders, damn your tongues, rotting teeth, and bleary eyes! Clear the dead from this deck. Bo'sun, start rerigging. Helmsman, course is due west after the enemy. Sailing Master, clap on all possible sail. Signalman, send the same orders to all the other ships. Above all I want silence. *Silence!*"

After a few of the noisier Trolls had been spitted and tossed to the Morays, everything became very quiet indeed. Crewmen hastily set about repairing the damage to the flagship. In an hour they were under way again, following Augurian's Fleet.

"Bright boy," Frigeon commented to Clangeon, who had reappeared on deck now that the uproar had ceased. "I like him. I'm glad I picked him to Captain this ship and Admiral the Fleet."

"My goodness!" cried his Chief Steward in awe. "Look at 'em scurry!"

"Watch your language," snapped the Ice King, "and bring me some cold duff with hard sauce."

Draggle reported the ship once more ready to fight.

"The thing we must do is divide them and take on a half at a time," suggested Frigeon, not as sure of his strategy as he once had been.

"Easier to devise than do," said the Captain, gruffly, reaching for a dish of plum duff. He hadn't had a bite to eat in twelve hours, and command gave him an enormous appetite.

"Come about, come about!" Draggle shouted a few minutes later, and sailors scurried to ratlines and halyards, driven by the captain's urgent tone.

"What? What are you doing? Belay that! We were gaining on them. Don't turn away now!"

"King you may be and know how to wear a crown well, but you are a crippled novice at handling ships," yelled back the new Captain. "Put her hard down," he added at the top of his voice to the helmsman. *Snowstorm* swung drunkenly off course and a few moments later the rest of the line followed suit. They were now speeding southward before the North Wind.

"But! But! But!" sputtered Frigeon, beside himself.

"Coolly, King," advised Draggle. "It is best if you don't speak and prove yourself a fool before the men."

"Me? A fool? Me!"

But something in the Captain's confidence made him pause to regain his composure. If the ugly runt proved wrong, time enough to spit him, freeze him, or maroon him later, he thought.

When all his Fleet was trailing away southward, moving more and more slowly as the northerly winds died down and the warm southerlies gained strength, once more Frigeon called the Captain to him.

"Now, what was the reason for your change of course?" he asked calmly.

"Easily explained if one uses one's head instead of one's mouth," said the Captain, more than a shade sarcastically. "We were going aground on a reef. I saw signs of shallows ahead, and one of your nearly useless Eels signaled to warn us. There was no time to consult anyone, if we wished to remain afloat."

"What will we do, then? Sail on to Waterand and despoil Augurian's treasures?"

"Treasure will do us no good if we don't settle with the Water-Adept first, Sire. He'd just attack us in port or on our return to Eternal Ice, although I must say I can't see any sensible reason why we should return to that sun-forsaken place, ever."

"Hmmph!" replied the Ice King. He needed Draggle too much just then to turn him into an icicle.

"We must draw Thornwood out of his Shoals, which he evidently knows well, and resume the fight. In the meantime, we can use a few hours for sleep, food, and repairs. The supply ships can come up with ammunition and replacement troops."

Frigeon agreed that was the wisest course, although he was at a loss as to how they would tempt Thornwood and Augurian out of the Shoals before they were ready, also.

"Time to think of that, later," he said to Clangeon.

"I wish to speak of something that has bothered me all day," said the Chief Steward, timidly.

"Later, scurvy rat. Is my bed prepared? This heat is killing me. I have to give the Banshees their orders for the night. They'll teach Thornwood's sailors about terror! Ha!"

And he tramped almost happily down to his ice cabinet to begin the spell to call the undead night spirits. They were the next phase of his grand strategy.

"Ah!" exclaimed Thornwood. "Someone with a grain of sense and a daub of Seamanship seems to have taken charge over there! See? Got themselves about and into line. They were wallowing in ineptitude an hour since and close to running on the reef."

"Frigeon is always dangerous, especially when he seems to be floundering. What will you do?" asked Augurian.

Donation, safe for the moment within a surrounding coral reef and in calm waters, stood down for supper. Many fighters took advantage of the lull to lie down to sleep where they stood.

Bryarmote, who had gone over the side to confer with Skimmer's Porpoises, came up to report.

"They say the rascally Moray Eels have been guiding Frigeon's ships, which explains why they were able to pull up before going aground."

"Do they know who is the new commander over there?" asked Thornwood. "I am certain he is a Man."

"They will try to discover that after dark," replied the Dwarf. "They will also drive the Eels from under the ships and keep them too deep to be of use to Frigeon's new Captain."

"Night," murmured Augurian. "We had better warn everyone again of what will come when darkness falls."

"Every man to have at least one companion; no one to be alone. Take a Fairy or a Dwarf as watch mate, if possible," Bryarmote recited the orders. "Mortals are the prime prey of the Banshees. Only they dread death so much."

As night deepened Frigeon's Banshees began their invasions—not of Men's persons but of their hearts and minds. Stalwart bowmen and pikemen whispered when they told of that night to their children, decades later.

A Man, walking alone from the forepeak of one of the tall ships threw up his hands, clutched his ears and then covered his eyes, and screamed in utter fear. An eerie, grating, mournful wail filled the ears of all aboard, and the lone man suddenly rushed to the side. He would have thrown himself into the clear, warm waters of the Shoals, had not two Nereid warriors tackled him and dragged him off to the forecastle, where his crew mates were resting from the fray.

"It told me of my own death," wept the victim in both terror and relief. "I saw my grave! I heard my family mourning for me. Such terrible grief!"

" 'Tis gone now?" his sergeant asked, softly.

"Gone," agreed the other. "But never forgotten . . ."

"Ye are with friends now," said another. "We can all see and hear the dreadful dreams, but if we stick close together, they won't drive us mad, or worse."

"No one goes on deck, or anywhere, alone," ordered the bo'sun, sternly. "Now you have some idea of what these Banshees will do, as Duke Thornwood said."

One of the Fairy soldiers said, "Listen, I've heard singing is the best way to keep them at bay. I'll teach you a Faerie ballad, and then you teach us one of yours."

He began to hum and shortly the circle of companions grew to half a hundred singers and listeners. The wails of the Banshees were ignored and faded away at last.

■ ■ ■

The Fairstrand fishermen in their tidy little smacks deep within the Shoals, found themselves and their patients gathered close about Maryam Beckett, who was telling them ghost stories.

"Familiar ghosts are a specific against evil outsiders like these Banshees," she explained. " 'Twas ever thus, which is why our forefathers began to tell ghost stories at night at Sea in the first place."

Bronze Owl, who hardly sensed the presence of the Banshees, went on to tell Fairstrand's solution on dozens of other ships, and in many of them the ghost stories worked until almost dawn, when at last the undead creatures would flit away, unable to stand the light and warmth of the new day.

Despite their countermeasures, not a few Confederation Seamen and soldiers disappeared during the night, overboard, or destroyed by their own hands. And none who heard the wailing were ever quite the same.

What turned the tide of battle underwater was the arrival of Asrai. While the Porpoises were creatures of the surface and bright sunlight, the Eels were happier and more comfortable in deep gloom or even full darkness. Fathoms below, Sea Fire lit the arena like day.

Giving up, the Eels beat a final retreat to the darkest and deepest places of the foot of the reef. So narrow was the undersea canyon here that a few guard Porpoises and a myriad of the tiny school fishes could keep watch on them and ensure that there would no longer be underwater guides to tell Frigeon's Fleet how to avoid the rocks and reefs.

Leaper, leaving the scene when it was certain that the Eels would no longer be of use to Frigeon, skimmed along at twenty fathoms and came up under *Snowstorm* well after midnight, where he took the position of Skimmer before him, left ear hole pressed hard against the bottom copper, listening to what was said in Frigeon's cold chamber.

At midnight, Draggle fell into his bunk and slept a fitful, dream-filled sleep of exhaustion. Everywhere in the ship living men and beasts slept where they stood, ignoring the coming and going of the Banshees as best they could. Madness and unreasoning fear was all too common among them to pay special attention to a slight overlap of the Banshees' terror.

A soldier lying on the deck of a ship of Westongue, uneasy from dreams of having his hands frozen by unutterable cold, held his hands up to check them as he awoke. Through his fingers he saw the first gray and pink streaks of the coming sun and sighed mightily.

"The Light!" he cried aloud in a strong, carrying voice. " 'Tis dawn and a new day, mates!"

Pure golden sunlight sprang over the horizon and suddenly the sounds and fears of night were gone.

Frigeon rose from his ice-cold bed and called his chief steward to get him breakfast. Clangeon, asleep at the foot of his master's cot on the hard deck, rose shivering and went about his work.

"Clang," said the King, "leave that food here and go wake up that lazy boy of a captain. Tell him I say it is time to renew the attack, now that the enemy is half-crazed with Banshee terror and drugged by lack of sleep. How I wish I could have been there!"

Clangeon found the captain already on his quarterdeck, inspecting the repairs to the rigging and burnt timbers. A ragged crew of sailors was hard at work before breakfast, holystoning bloodstains from the deck.

"We're already under way," the captain told the Steward. "It's going to be a beautiful day for continuing a battle."

Frigeon came on deck and looked about in sour satisfaction. Sails were set, booms were being hauled about, and the pale blue flag of the Eternal Ice kingdom was flapping listlessly at the maintop. The Fleet was up and about, also, regarding the resumption of the battle with renewed interest, if not exactly enthusiasm. Even at long distance Draggle made things happen.

"Sire," began Clangeon. "Sire, could I have a short word with you?"

"I suppose so, old stinkpot," said Frigeon good-naturedly, at least for him. "What is it you have been trying to tell me for twelve hours past? Are we short of butter? Is the supply of cold turkey gone? No matter. I'd even eat hot cakes this morning, I feel that certain of victory."

"Sire, I have had a feeling . . . this has been bothering me as I watched the fighting yesterday. There was no fire. . . ."

"What do you mean, stupid servant? Look at the charring on this boom, and that burned sail, over there. There *was* fire."

"I know, Sire," said the Steward, becoming a bit exasperated, "but it was not the fire that would have come from Flarman. It was not *magic* fire!"

At the sound of his archenemy's name, Frigeon stopped pacing and stood stock still.

"Go on, Clang."

"Flarman could have bathed all of our ships in fire and driven half our men to jump in Sea. You know of his powers, better'n I do. I just wonder . . ."

"Ah," said Frigeon, finally understanding. "What you are suggesting in your roundabout way is that Flarman *isn't here*?"

"That he is somewhere else, doing something he considers more important."

Clangeon sank down on a coil of rope, suddenly exhausted and weary, despite a few hours' sleep.

"Where, if not here?"

"Eternal Ice," murmured the Steward, and he fell in a dead faint right there.

"Eternal Ice! With the Pearl!" swore Frigeon, leaping to his feet. "Captain, go about! Set course for Eternal Ice!"

"Now?"

"Don't argue with me! We have a far more important thing to do than play water games with Augurian. Order the rest to stay put and fight to the death, but take me to my Palace, at once. *Now!*"

Draggle threw up his hands in disgust but began to issue orders and signals that countermanded those given only minutes before.

In twenty minutes *Snowstorm* plunged forward, heeling steeply away with the south wind that still blew over Battle Shoals, running before it toward Frigeon's glacial palace.

Across the boiling water of the reef now almost awash with the low tide, Augurian, Thornwood, and Bryarmote trained telescopes on the fleeing square-rigger.

"That's *Snowstorm*, Frigeon's flagship! Think it's a trick?" asked Thornwood of them all.

"Hardly," said Bryarmote. "Frigeon wouldn't trust his commanders enough to leave them unattended for several hours, let alone a day."

"No, it isn't a trick," said Augurian, softly, "Frigeon has at last tumbled to our ruse."

"Ruse?" exclaimed the Dwarf, flaring. "A ruse for what?"

"You know of the Gray Pearl," Augurian said calmly, "and the importance of using it to defeat Frigeon is clear."

"So, we here were giving Flarman a chance to slip around the end of the Ice Fleet and get to Eternal Ice before Frigeon realized that he was gone?"

"Exactly," said the Water-Adept. "I thought you suspected that."

"I-I guess I really did when Flarman didn't show up, but I forgot it in the heat of battle."

"No one fought or died in vain here," Augurian assured him. "The only way to defeat Frigeon ultimately is to destroy the Pearl and break Frigeon's harshest spells. We discovered only recently this must be done in Eternal Ice. *If* Flarman gets there, and *if* he and Douglas manage to destroy the Pearl before Frigeon gets there, we have won the battle!"

Frigeon stood in *Snowstorm's* prow, trying in vain to pierce the warm mist ahead with all his powers. He could see naught of Flarman nor his Journeyman, although he knew they were ahead somewhere.

"Flarman carries the Pearl to Eternal Ice!" he shouted, a sound of agony, defiance, and uncertainty. "I thought no one could ever guess the Pearl had to return to its home to be dispelled!"

He raised both fists and shook them at the clearing sky.

"Flarman! I will catch you this time and put you deep in Ice forever!"

Chapter Twenty-one

SO high they were almost invisible against the slate-colored sky, three Sea Gulls swept around in lazy spirals. Douglas wished he could be a bird for an hour, to escape the depressing grayness of this coast. He was just exploring the possibility of a transformation spell when the Gulls dropped like stones to the deck, forsaking their normal grace in the air.

"Ice is in sight!" screamed Cerfew. "At last! Tell the Wizard!"

Flarman had been napping in the cabin but awakened to the excited Gull voices and came on deck.

"The Ice!" Trotta repeated, flying over his head.

"How far off, best Gullfriend?"

"Twenty miles, dead ahead, Wizard! We saw whiteness and ice pinnacles. And felt a breath of the chill, even this far away. Hark!"

There was a sudden sharp report followed by a rumbling roar in the distance, like thunder.

"Ah, the Ice!" exclaimed the Fire-Adept, nodding. "I recognize it now."

"What was that?" asked Douglas, climbing upon the rail to get a better vantage.

"Floes breaking off into Sea from the edge of the glacier," explained Flarman. "Now, m'boy, we don't want to go much closer. 'Tis impossible to find safe anchorage nearer, except at Frigeon's port, and he will have soldiers and probably worse there. I'll ask Captain Fribby to find us someplace along about here to put us ashore. Cerfew, can you see . . . ?"

"Done!" cried the Gull, and he and his companions threw themselves into the air once more.

Fribby brought the ship about to skim the coast more closely—and slowly. There were unmarked rocks and shoals here, too. The Gulls signaled the way to a rift in the cliffs just wide enough for *Flame Daughter* to squeeze into a narrow, deep, steep-sided fjord.

"It'll take hours to climb these cliffs!" Douglas protested.

"More than that, Journeyman," Fribby said, and nodded. "Take a goat to scramble to the top and once ye are there it is all crumbled and jumbled rock. Very slow going, I'm afraid, sir Wizard."

"We won't be going that way," said Flarman. *Flame Daughter*'s anchor rattled loudly through the hawse, disturbing a cloud of shorebirds nesting on the cliffs. The Gulls screamed back at them.

Although it was early afternoon, so narrow and high was this inlet that, looking up, Douglas was surprised to see stars shining in a black sky.

"Augurian wishes to know how you are and where," said a voice at his elbow. Deka the Wraith had arrived.

The Wizard carefully described their position: "About twelve miles east of Eternal Ice in a tiny, nameless ria, as you can see. Things are going well but we chance being seen by Frigeon's Home Guards, and will be cautious on our approach."

"Augurian says," recited the messenger, " 'Yesterday, Frigeon in *Snowstorm* fled suddenly north from Battle Shoals. His Fleet then lost heart and scattered to all points of the compass. We in *Donation* follow Frigeon. We are yet a day or more away to the south.' "

"Our timing is becoming closer than I had hoped, then," mused Flarman. "But we should be able to reach our destination and do our work before Frigeon arrives. Augurian will do what he can to provide adverse winds."

"Adverse winds will slow Thornwood, too," Douglas pointed out.

"All the more reason to send for the Grand Dragon and his cohorts. Deka, will you do this for us? Tell the Dragons they are to act to delay Frigeon's ship, if possible."

"Of course, and return at once."

"Excellent, lady spirit!"

Deka was gone in a blink.

"Now, Douglas, you have the Gray Pearl safe?"

"Here," said the journeyman, tapping the toe of his left boot.

"No need to wait until full dark so we can call the Phosphorescence to carry us," Flarman said, pacing the deck as he spoke. "It is already deep night here in this cleft. A good, hot dinner will be essential, and some warm, waterproof clothing."

Looking after him, Douglas called, "You won't tell us what you have in mind, will you?"

Flarman paused in the doorway to his cabin and turned to look at him, quizzically.

"It was so little a time ago that you were but a lad as short as me," he said, apropos of absolutely nothing. "I'll answer shortly, Journeyman."

Douglas Brightglade went to his own cabin to pack. Seems like packing is one thing I have really mastered this past half year, he thought.

He finished his task quickly and went forward to *Daughter*'s main cabin. Bigbelly was just lighting the oil lamps over the center table against the increasing gloom of the northern evening.

"Are you ready to go?" Flarman asked as he entered.

"Ready as ever I will be, sir, not knowing where we are headed," Douglas said, but with a smile to soften the barb.

"You must have figured out most of this," said Flarman, seating himself at the table.

"Oh, yes, I suppose so—some of it. I know we carry the Gray Pearl and that it is a talisman to defeat Frigeon. I know we are on the edge of his enchanted glacier. I suspect we are about to cross the Ice and that's as far as I get. What will we do with the Pearl when we get there?"

"Well, I'll answer you in a moment, Douglas, m'boy. First, I must give Captain Fribby instructions. Then dinner and it'll be dark enough to call Sea Fire to take us on our last journey."

This sounded ominous enough to silence the Journeyman as the Wizard sent for the Captain.

"No, you will not go with us onto the Ice, Fribby," he said, nodding at the old Seaman's worried look.

"I don't mind going anywhere with you, sir. I'd even cross the Ice to that damned Palace if you said I should follow you . . . or the young Wizard here. No, sir, I am afraid only because I know we will *not* be going with you to help.''

Flarman reached over and slapped the sailor affectionately on the shoulder. ''My good, good friend! If I could lead a direct assault on Frigeon's Palace, I would want no better men than you and Bigbelly, believe me. Unfortunately for us all, there is no place here for direct, honest action. To defeat Frigeon we must be devious, tricky. After all, some say that is what Wizardry is all about and what Wizards are for.''

''Not at all!'' cried Fribby, stoutly. ''I have never been more straightly dealt with than I have been by you and young Douglas here.''

''Thank you, Fribby! That is a supreme compliment to a Wizard.''

They sat down to eat.

''Now you are right, Douglas. I must tell what we are to try to do, hope to do, must do. Augurian knows; like you, Thornwood and Bryarmote know some but understand less.

''First, the Gray Pearl. You know that it contains, magically, the whole of Frigeon's humanity: love, respect, humility, appreciation for the arts, faithfulness, and responsibility. Integrity. Sportsmanship. Pity, grace, charity, a sense of humor—a vast, vast number of qualities intertwined in a person's heart, mind, and soul, no matter how evil he seems.

''During the terror of Last Battle something, I'm not sure what, happened to deeply embitter and transform Frigeon. He began to believe that all pain, evil, and wrong came from being Human. He created the Pearl to rid himself of his better self. He then could be totally cold and impervious to everything that might ever hurt him again, as Augurian said some days ago.''

''Protective camouflage, in a twisted sort of way,'' Douglas mused. ''I see.''

''*But* what he didn't realize was that there are other qualities, just as Human, that, if he had put them into the Pearl, would truly have made him *totally* invincible. He forgot that the best of us are at times stupid, vain, uncaring, reckless, prideful, greedy, selfish . . . and blind to our own faults. He left these qualities within himself. They'll be his downfall. Or rather, his return to sanity and humanity, if we do this correctly.''

"And of course, the Pearl *was* found. You bought it from Caspar Marlin."

"In these last weeks we at last found the simple answer to the puzzle. As our part in Battle of Sea you and I are hastening to undo the spell by physically destroying the Pearl. This can only be done *under* Eternal Ice. Only there! Frigeon believed, not only would no man ever want to destroy the precious, beautiful gem, but, if he did, he couldn't get into the Ice to do it."

Flarman waited for Douglas to comment, and when he did not, he went on: "Once the Pearl is destroyed, Frigeon should be a complete Human again. His good qualities will, we hope, balance his bad. We will wait to judge him finally until we see how close this balance is."

"He'd be just like anyone else? But that means . . . anyone could be a Frigeon!"

"Correct . . . or almost! Certainly any *Wizard* could make himself like Frigeon, if he decided to stuff his own Pearl."

"Now I understand a lot of things," said Douglas with a sigh. "Go on!"

"Once he is emancipated Frigeon becomes manageable. If he is defeated, he will either regret and repent—or he will retreat and seek revenge—but, once whole, he can never *believe* himself invincible or totally evil ever again. That in itself is a glorious outcome for us.

"Now," Flarman went on after a pause, "we'll leave here in a few minutes. Our course is very dangerous. I would gladly go alone but I need a trained and trusted assistant. Augurian might have served, but his role was to provide a convincing diversion, to draw the Ice King's attention away from his Palace so we could get under it and find the very spot the Pearl was created.

"We will enter beneath the Ice, from open Sea. After we finish with the Pearl, we will escape as best we can."

The four sat around the table in a circle of warm, yellow light, silent and thoughtful for a long while before Douglas said, "I will call Sea Fire, then."

"Please do that," said Flarman, rousing himself. "Deka, we will need you. You will go with us?"

"Of course, Firemaster. Wraiths fear no being nor any danger."

Fribby, that portly old captain, drew himself up and said,

"I would far rather go with you into that frozen hell than to stand off and on here for days. But we will wait until there is no longer hope and a few days more. Or until you tell us you have escaped otherwise."

"Good man!" cried Flarman, his good humor restored by the other's simple stoutheartedness. "Well, let's be about it!"

Just as they were preparing to step over the side there was an awful clatter and metallic banging as Bronze Owl arrived to join the quest. Before Flarman could object, Owl said he had word from Wizard's High and all was well there. Black Flame had returned on the Wizard's business before battle—a Wizard always tried to put his familiar out of danger if possible—and "the ladies are doing very well. Pert and Party have both littered four kittens each, and that keeps them busy and happy."

"Oh, I wish we could be at the High right now!" exclaimed Douglas, suddenly homesick.

"I do, too," admitted Flarman. "Shortly, m'boy, if all goes according to plan, and even if it doesn't. When we get back, we'll have a party better than all the others, and longer, and we'll invite just about everybody."

Fribby and Bigbelly, his mate and friend, watched them go.

"This place has no name," Bigbelly said. "I misdoubt Frigeon has a name for it, but we could add it to our charts with a name of our own devising, Captain."

"What do you suggest? How about 'Wizard's Inlet'?"

"No, no, I favor something more descriptive. Oh, say . . . 'Hiddenaway'? No, too long! Here, how about 'Hidden Wait'? It tells the story."

"Suits me," nodded his captain. "Drink on it?"

And they did, until it was time to roll off to bed.

Flarman could not resist the temptation to instruct.

"The glacier is a river of ice, you know."

"Yes."

"Over the millennia it has scoured a deep, flat-bottomed, steep-sided valley that goes considerably below Sea level off the coast. The ice itself extends several miles out to Sea, and it is here that Frigeon built his Palace, on the floating ice. We are going to pass under it until we are under the Ice Palace, itself. Then we'll find a way in, from below.''

"I see," said Douglas, somewhat sleepily. "Let me know when we get there."

Flarman gave up and settled himself more comfortably within Sea Fire and watched the scenery pass swiftly by. Overhead, ice was at first as smooth as the Sea bottom, but shortly they entered an area of ice stalactites depending from the roof above, some reaching all the way down as columns, fifty or more feet, to the floor of the sunken valley.

"Here is the true shore," flashed Sea Light. Not far ahead of them the bottom rose to meet the underside of the glacier, forming a sharp, clear horizon.

"Find an air pocket where we can work above the water. We will melt out a ledge to stand upon and a stairway up under the foundations of the Palace. There's the Palace!"

Through the translucent ice, Douglas, now awake, could see a vast oval of darkness, the underside of the Palace. It seemed to float in frozen clouds.

"How far up do you figure it is?" asked Bronze Owl.

"About a hundred feet to the stonework," judged Flarman, "but the workshop is in the ice itself under the foundations. I think we can just about see it from here. There, see?"

"I think I see," said Owl. "Only thing to do is dig."

Hot, blue flames made work easy and fast as they carved out a stairway leading upward. The meltwater was a problem. A separate channel for the runoff prevented the water from refreezing after them. Here, within the ice itself, the air temperature was much warmer than Douglas had expected.

"Ice is a pretty good insulator," explained Flarman. "The glacier has a very cold, tough surface, but inside it has a warm heart."

"Relatively speaking," said Bronze Owl, who was fanning his wings to keep the working Wizards cool—strange as that seems—adding considerably to the din on the work site.

Deka hung in the background, unable to assist except to flit back and forth between the tunnel stair and the workshop, guiding their efforts.

"Now," said Flarman, wiping his brow with his handkerchief. "First, Owl, stop that racket and get below to the bottom of the steps and wait for us there. It is your job to keep the stair open, at all costs.''

The Bronze Owl nodded twice and spread his metal wings to glide down the stairway.

Deka faded upward but returned a few seconds later to report that the stair was within ten feet of the passageway from the dungeons to the workshop. All was quiet in the Ice Palace.

''I took a quick look around,'' she said. ''It is strange, but almost everyone seems sound asleep, though it is mid-morning.''

Said Flarman, ''Frigeon just doesn't trust anybody, and he has sleep-enchanted his people while he is gone to keep them from getting into trouble—or out of it.''

Douglas could make out the passage, and to one side, a regular, opaque oblong area that must be the Ice King's own workshop.

They broke through into the passageway. There was a rush of frigid air that almost at once froze the meltwater solid. Douglas glanced up the passage toward the dungeon. It was quite bright here as light seeped down from above through the Ice.

''Keep warm,'' warned Flarman. ''You could freeze fast, wet as you are.''

Douglas spent some magic warming the fabric of his clothing, wringing out his socks, and drying his boots.

''Come on,'' said Flarman. He started down the corridor in the other direction. There was no sound around them. ''Ah, here we are, already!''

Ahead was a solid oak door bound with broad, black iron straps up and down and across. Flarman considered blasting it away with concentrated power, but settled, for the sake of quietness, with melting the ice around the lock and hinges. In less than a minute the door creaked and fell to the floor with a loud *wham*.

''Think that woke 'em up?'' asked Douglas, glancing over his shoulder.

''Deka can check. Let's see what we've got here.''

The two Wizards entered the Ice King's laboratory and Flarman gestured to turn on hidden lights. What they saw changed their plans immediately and drastically.

■ ■ ■

Along two long walls of the huge room were deep niches, and in each stood the frozen form of a man, or in a few cases a woman, covered with white rime and staring blankly out at the newcomers.

Some were dressed in garb out of fashion centuries ago. Some were evidently kings or princes in richly jeweled cloaks and brightly colored, fine fabrics. Many seemed merchants or professional people.

Walking along the display in horrified awe, Douglas stopped at the seventh on the right and cried out.

"Father! He's frozen to death, Master! My father!"

He rushed forward and attempted to touch a tall man in a leather apron and heavy gloves.

"Here, 'tis my own, dear father we thought lost at Sea! The wicked Ice King, that Frigeon, has killed him!"

"On the contrary," soothed Flarman, pulling the young man back from the frozen figure. "He is enchanted, not dead. This workshop is a prison for these people who were a nuisance or danger to Frigeon. I imagine the empty niches down at that end were reserved for you and me, m'boy. And one for Augurian, too."

He waited until Douglas recovered his aplomb.

"Now with this we must begin to work quickly, very quickly. The Pearl must come second, for we must rescue these unfortunates, first and foremost."

"Of course!" cried Douglas. "Papa, we'll get you out of here and warm again. I promise you."

The Wizards conferred at the vast central worktable.

"I can handle the prisoners," declared Douglas, grimly. "You must find the means of destroying the Pearl, now that we are here."

"The actual destruction must wait until the last possible moment, because to destroy the Gray Pearl will mean destruction of the Palace and a large part of Eternal Ice, which is supported by the same spell. Do you know what to do?"

"I had plenty of experience thawing frozen people during Dead Winter," said Douglas, his shaken confidence returning rapidly. "I imagine the same spells would work here."

"Good man! Go to work."

Flarman turned back and began searching in a systematic manner the top of the table and the shelves, cupboards, and drawers, rapidly rejecting hundreds of chemicals, medicines, specifics, elements, compounds, and talismans as he went.

Douglas started at the niche nearest the door. Within was a tastefully and richly dressed woman of middle years, still quite comely. She looked vaguely familiar.

In less than a minute the lady stepped forward timidly, glancing rapidly about in confusion and fear. She shivered uncontrollably until Douglas stepped up her spell of warming.

"Oh, oh, I feel I am going to faint!"

"Now, now, my Lady," said Deka, strongly, " 'tis no time to do any such thing. You must bear up and follow me below to our means of escape. Quickly!"

But the lady had turned to Douglas, who had already begun the spell on the next victim.

"Are you my rescuer, young sir? I am eternally grateful . . ."

"Lady, I am certainly one of your rescuers but right now I have nineteen others to save and little time. You must go with this lovely Wraith down the stair to the . . . the Phosphorescence, who will take care of you and get you out of here."

"Of course, of course," said the lady, still bewildered by her rescue. But when Deka took her elbow to guide her to the door, she shook the Wraith off without seeming to notice her.

Flarman Flowerstalk came over, saying, "I've not yet found what I am looking for . . . My Lady! What a pleasant surprise! You are Duchess Marigold, are you not?"

"Yes, now that I think of it," said the Duchess, brightening. "It is coming back, my memory. And you are Flarman, the Wizard?"

"Correct, my Lady. This is Douglas Brightglade of Perthside, my Journeyman assistant. Lady, may we ask you to help us rescue these others? Many are your subjects, such as this man. I don't remember his name but I recall meeting him once in Capital."

"Tell me what to do, then," said Duchess Marigold, suddenly all business, as her sense of duty was invoked. Leading others was something she understood, instinctively.

Flarman gestured toward the still-frozen and said, "We must hurry, if you please, ma'am."

Duchess Marigold and Douglas worked as a team, with Deka helping the Duchess. Douglas pulled the victims from their niches as soon as they could move, warmed them, and turned them over to the Duchess, who started them moving toward the stair.

"Master Gallisher!" Thornwood's mother would say, graciously. "So nice to see you again! Eunicet never did like you, as I recall, and you were betrayed by the wicked usurper, as I was. Fortunately my son, Thornwood, escaped, I am told, and is even now fighting the evil Frigeon."

"I remember when he brought me here," said Gallisher. "When I saw you there, frozen in the ice, I lost all hope of ever seeing my home and wife and children again."

"Can you walk now? Come this way and we will help all these nice people escape."

Douglas began the spell to release his father and had to start it again as tears choked his voice, spoiling his cadence. The leather-clad shipwright staggered forward and Douglas caught him in a tight embrace. Douglas of Perthside looked at his young rescuer without recognition, bewildered.

"Thank you, young sir. I will be fine in a moment."

"Father, I am your son, Douglas," cried the young Wizard.

"My son? No, my boy is but a child, this high," he answered, gesturing with his hand. "I cannot . . ."

"You have been here eight years!" explained Duchess Marigold, gently. "Sons have a way of growing, especially when you don't see them for a while."

"I have always heard it to be so," the shipwright said, still bemused. "Yes, I can see your mother's smile and hair in you, s-s-son. Eight years! What is your age now, may I ask?"

"I am seventeen, almost eighteen," said Douglas. "I was ten when you disappeared, captured by Frigeon and imprisoned in this Ice."

"You poor man!" the Duchess cried. "Come with me. We must rush to avoid recapture. We'll both have to wait to talk to our sons, I am afraid. Come along!"

"I'll come," said the older Douglas. "My son, Douglas, please excuse me. I . . . I . . . still feel a bit dizzy."

"We'll have plenty of time to talk later, Father."

"My goodness," said Marigold, leading him to the door.

"I recognize your costume as that of a Perthside shipwright. I am Marigold, Duchess—or rather, Duchess Mother, now—as I will certainly abdicate in favor of my son, Thornwood. Have you ever met him? A wonderful lad, now a grown man like your own boy, I understand."

And they went off together toward the stair, chatting like old friends.

Douglas dashed tears from his eyes, whether of sadness or happiness, he couldn't tell, and went back to work on the remaining victims without missing another phrase.

At last they were all on their way. Deka came to say, "We must be making too much noise. I slipped above and some guards are awake."

"Better see if you can do something to distract them," said Douglas. He went over to Flarman, standing in the midst of a great pile of bottles, boxes, casks, crates, and jugs, shaking his head.

"There has to be something here to destroy the Pearl. I've tried everything I can think of. We either do it now and here or . . ."

"Have you tried stamping on it?"

"Yes. It is hard as a diamond. Didn't even scratch it!"

"And no spells affect it?

"None I have tried yet. Have you any ideas?"

"The Horniads told me that pearls are manufactured by the oyster from the same secretions that make up their shells." Douglas said, reviewing everything he ever learned about the gems. "When they 'plant' seed pearls, they actually place a tiny bit of sand in the shell, next to the oyster. The oyster covers the sand with layers of smooth material until it doesn't irritate the oyster any more . . . and you end up with a pearl."

"Very interesting. I didn't realize pearls are grown," said Flarman. "If a pearl is made of natural matter, then, perhaps something would dissolve it."

"Maybe some sort of acid? Most organic material will dissolve in acid," asked Douglas.

"But there's no acid here. Frigeon was wise enough to get rid of it."

Suddenly the older wizard snapped his fingers and began to examine the walls of the workshop with a magnifying glass he drew from his wide left sleeve. Douglas watched, mystified.

"Where there are glaciers," said Flarman, moving along the wall, inch by inch, "there should, must be . . ."

"Glacial acetic acid!" crowed Douglas, and in a few moments they had found tiny white crystals on the ceiling in a far corner. Even in that cold place, acid-bearing water seeped from the ice and evaporated, leaving the crystal.

It took but a moment to scrape some into a small glass beaker. Flarman added a tablespoon of water, warming the whole with his cupped hands.

"Now, the Pearl," said Flarman, excited as Douglas had ever seen him. Douglas hopped on one foot to whip off his left boot. He fumbled for the tissue-wrapped Pearl, almost dropping it as he handed it to the wizard.

Flarman held the Pearl over the beaker.

"Deka, ask Sea Fire to take the former prisoners out to *Flame Daughter,* swiftly," he said, calm again. "Things are about to happen, and fast, once I pop this Pearl in the acid."

Deka disappeared with a *whoosh*. Douglas could smell the sharp, vinegary tang of the acid.

"Now for it!" exclaimed the Wizard, and he dropped the Gray Pearl in the beaker.

It plunked . . . and fizzed instantly.

A soundless cry filled their heads, but it was a cry of joy. A heady, fresh-air aroma of sunlit meadows and wildflowers filled the room, like a spring morning along Crooked Brook.

The Pearl hopped about, spinning over and over in the liquid. It seemed to expand, and changed from shiny gray to dull pewter, from gray to dark green; the outer layers began to crack and slough away in layers.

Then the big Pearl, humming almost happily, split in two. There was a tremendous bang, and a great cloud of hot, pungent steam shot in the air, filling the entire room.

Looking up, Douglas saw the ceiling wrinkle and snap as it began to melt and drip down to the floor.

"Look at that!" cried Flarman. The heart of the Pearl was uncovered at last. It shone like a firefly in the misty gloom around them. After a long, breath-held moment, it sighed aloud and winked out.

The floor quivered and they heard a muted rumbling, rising quickly to an earsplitting roar. They heard shouts and cries.

The Fire Wizard dropped the beaker, smashing it on the tabletop. The acid spilled out. The table collapsed.

"Well, we've done it!" shouted Flarman over the uproar, dusting his hands together. "Now to get out of here."

They rushed for the door. Three heavily armored men in Frigeon's livery approached from the dungeon stair, running and shouting.

" 'Tis the Fire Wizard!" one of them called. They hesitated as if wondering how best to slay Flarman. There was an even louder roar and the ceiling of the passageway collapsed, hurtling them through the hole in the floor and down fifty feet into the water. Falling chunks of ice filled the hole at once.

"Come now, Master," shouted Douglas, pulling the Wizard along past the cave-in. "This way is clear."

Flarman looked once more at the rubble in the hole that had been a stair, and said, "Oh, dear me!" before turning to follow his Journeyman into Frigeon's deepest dungeon.

Chapter Twenty-two

"LOOK out!" shouted Douglas, skidding to a halt on the brink of a five-foot-wide crack in the floor of the ice corridor. A tremendous convulsion a moment before had wrenched the palace foundation away from the surrounding ice.

Looking up, they could see a streak of brilliant sun above.

"The Palace is breaking away from the Ice," shouted Flarman over the din all about them. "We'd be better off not going into the building."

"But there are people in the Palace," objected Douglas, forgetting these people were his enemies.

"We'd risk our own lives! They're almost not worth it . . . but, of course, you're right, m'boy. We can't just let them die. Let's go!" yelled the Wizard, and with a wide sweep of his right arm he sheared a two-ton slab of ice-stone from the wall and jammed it into the crack.

The two dashed across this slippery, makeshift bridge and into the dungeon beyond, just before the whole palace shuddered again and the bridge cracked in twain, tumbling end over end into the abyss.

Douglas followed Flarman as the Wizard plunged into a labyrinth of narrow ice-stone corridors and dank, cold rooms at the base of the Ice Palace. The whole structure shook like a gelatin mold, making terrible cracking and creaking noises that curled the tips of Douglas's ears.

Chunks of ice as large as a man's head fell from the arched ceiling, and partition walls collapsed like blown-upon cards. A thick, acrid, chill cloud of gray ice dust filled the air, blinding them. They found the up stairway by feel, falling to their knees when they tripped on the bottom step.

"This way up! Up!" Deka's voice came from ahead.

Falling masonry didn't faze her. As they started up the buck-
ling, swaying steps, Douglas saw a huge mass of ice plunge
right through the Wraith, obliterating the landing they had
just left. Deka gestured for them to hurry and led the way
through the thickening clouds of dust.

Two flights, then a third, then a long fourth. Looking
back, concerned about the old Wizard's wind, Douglas, who
was himself coughing and gasping for breath, caught a
glimpse of his Master, levitating an inch above the floor, his
head in a sphere of fresh air, gazing about himself with
concern but little consternation.

And I thought *I* thought like a Wizard! thought the Journeyman to himself. Floating through all this to save his legs
and filtering out the dust to save his lungs!

He spelled furiously as he ran and a few seconds later
managed to levitate as well. He overshot and struck his head
sharply on the low ceiling before he adjusted his altitude. He
created an excluding globe about his head that allowed air,
but nothing larger, to pass. For the first time since the ice-
quake began he breathed without choking.

The going became smoother and faster. They reached the
top of the last stair and a burst-open door led them into an
enormous room in which dozens of half-dressed, madly
screaming people, Frigeon's courtiers and servants, were
running around in fear-crazed circles.

"This is the Great Hall," said Flarman as they paused to
look around. "I've been here. The door out is over that way,
but it's blocked! We must herd these people out that way."

He pointed to the great window behind the rock crystal
throne. The plain of Ice and snow outside was rippling like
the surface of a pond in a breeze.

Flarman cupped his hands and spoke. His words were
amplified a hundredfold and blasted at the panic-stricken
Palace dwellers, shocking them into listening. Obeying was
second nature to them when orders were bellowed in a loud,
clear voice. That fact saved many of them from death.

"Listen to me now," Flarman said. "The Palace is about
to break loose from the Ice and sink to the bottom of Sea.
Your only hope is to leave at once by the great window
behind the throne and run across the Ice to the left."

Shouted Douglas, "The window is stopping them."

"Blow it out, then," yelled Flarman, forgetting his words were amplified. "Blow out the window!"

The Journeyman Wizard hurled a tremendous bolt of fire with all his might at the window. It burst with a sound like a million crystal goblets shattering.

Flarman cupped his hands again. "Out the window! Rush! The ceiling is about to collapse!"

The crowd clambered and clawed over the sill. The Wizards stepped out on the Ice after them. The whole palace roof fell in, blasting sharp shards of ice, pieces of tile, splinters of smashed furniture, and a great deal of dust and filth after them. A number of escapees were cut and thrown to the ground by the blast of air.

Douglas and Flarman, unhurt, began herding the dazed retainers toward spines of rock sticking through the snow a distance away. None seemed to feel the biting cold in their fright, but many had to be turned about and headed in the right direction. Women wailed and wept, men cursed and sobbed, but the voice of the Pyromancer filled their ears and forced them to their senses.

"Are they all out of harm's way?" shouted Douglas. Flarman stood still for a moment, holding his hand over his eyes to shade them from the brilliant midday sun on stark, glaring ice.

He said sadly, "The palace is about to plunge through the ice and even you and I could not survive that, let alone save the few still left behind. If it's any consolation, if they'd found us, they wouldn't have hesitated to skewer us."

Earth-shaking things happened in a split-second sequence that left all watching breathless.

Eternal Ice cracked completely in two, down its middle from north to south. The edges on either side of the rift sprang fifty feet apart, with the most nerve-scraping sound anyone could ever have imagined, like the ripping of a piece of canvas as large as the sky.

There was a sudden cry and a rush of armed men from around the Palace's crumbling outer wall, swords raised but fear distorting every face.

Then there came the sudden and complete plunge of Frigeon's entire Ice Palace in an instant, through the glacier to the submerged valley floor, two hundred feet below.

Waters of Sea, displaced by the palace's mass, geysered
up in a great, gray-white fountain of slush and Seawater,
fully a hundred feet in the air. Those soldiers who escaped
being tumbled into the chasm to their instant deaths fell to
their faces and covered their heads.

Then came a fiery blast of very hot air. The rising waters
turned instantly into roiling steam, puffed into a vast, lofty,
mushroom-shaped cloud, which hung over the ice for long
seconds before it began slowly to disperse in the south wind.

When the ice split, Flarman and Douglas, at the very edge,
were staggered by the violent eruption. Before they could
fall, however, they were snatched bodily into the air by two
sets of saber-sharp emerald talons and borne swiftly aside
and aloft.

Meanwhile, the cowering soldiery were caught by rising
waters, which rushed about them and almost at once froze
about their bodies, imprisoning them as securely as irons.

The man who led the charge had been snatched up by the
fountaining waters and tossed high in the air, screaming in
insane fear—Frigeon!

His sword and helmet were torn loose as he shot upwards,
reached a zenith, and began plunging, cartwheeling slowly,
around and around, toward the great open cauldron of Sea
that had replaced the palace.

But from the cloud covering the site there came a Golden
Dragon, shouting in triumph. He plucked the Ice King neatly
out of thin air, just before he was about to plummet into
seething Sea.

"Whew!" shouted the Journeyman Firemaster. "Nice
catch!"

"Thank you," said the Grand Dragon who clutched them.
"My brother did a very workmanlike job. You two made
that great water spout? That blast of hot air was ours. It got
rid of a lot of our frustrations, believe me!"

"Well, well, and well again," gasped Flarman from the
Dragon's left claw. "Maybe you'd better put us down somewhere. There are a number of people who should be helped
off Eternal Ice before it breaks up completely."

"Frigeon's people?" snorted the Grand Dragon, cocking
his head toward the fleeing crowd. "Why not just let them
drown or freeze?"

"Not my style," said Flarman. "No one deserves to die like that! If we can help it."

"Oh, well, put it that way," sighed the Grand Dragon. "My people will take care of them. A little fear of death won't hurt them, though. I will put you on *Donation*. She's only a few miles out to Sea. And the former Ice King, too, I guess, although the boys would love to play catch with him for a few hours or days or years."

"Bring him along. Even Frigeon deserves to be confronted by his accusers and tried by a court of his peers. Hmm! Yes, I think we can now call him 'former' Ice King. His fleet is scattered, his Palace is sunk to the bottom of Sea, and he is a Captive of his foes. Plus, I think we'll see a change in him, now that the Pearl is dissolved."

"A mouthful for a gentleman who is hanging by his coattails from a Dragon's claw," the Grand Dragon said with a chuckle, banking away to the south. "Quite a sight, isn't it?"

Douglas was absorbed in the scene from a hundred feet up.

Ice had indeed split, and the two halves were quickly breaking into smaller and smaller pieces, already beginning to float out to Sea. Puffs of the Dragon's hot breath kept the floes from re-fusing and a warm south wind was beginning to blow strongly. The survivors from the Ice Palace were huddled together for warmth on a rocky crag off to one side, circled by the flying Dragons.

"Frigeon's spells evidently included the subfreezing temperatures on the glacier," observed Flarman as they crossed the coastline. "Eternal Ice will not re-form, now that his spell is broken. I think the climate here will soon be much like that of Highlandorm. They are on the same latitude."

"My father is somewhere down there, and Myrn, too. And I'd like a hot meal. I think, spells and all, it will take me a month to feel completely warm and cozy again."

"Nonsense," sputtered the Fire Master. "I'm as warm as toast. Put us down on the quarterdeck, Grandy. There, where Augurian is looking at us with his glass. There is an uncommonly pretty lass with him, in Apprentice's robes. She looks familiar."

Douglas hit the deck running and swept Myrn into his

arms shouting with joy and relief. Flarman did the same with Augurian, and then Duke Thornwood.

The second Dragon deposited a fainting, weeping Frigeon amidships. A squad of Dwarfs seized him and bound him to the mainmast.

"I found my father!" Douglas babbled to Myrn. "And we cut a stair in the underside of Eternal Ice right up to Frigeon's workshop, and Flarman found acid in the ceiling to melt the Gray Pearl! And Thornwood's mother was there, too."

"Slowly, slowly," advised Augurian, coming over to shake Douglas by the shoulder. "Unhand my Apprentice, please. She is supposed to be learning primary incantations at this hour."

"I'll come along and help," offered Douglas, taking Myrn by the hand.

"No, no," said Augurian, quickly. "We want to hear your story right away and then we must decide what to do next."

"Later," Myrn promised Douglas with a rueful smile. "I am sure I will never master the most basic spells."

"Oh, if I can do it, you surely can," Douglas assured her.

Thornwood called for chairs and, sitting on the sun-warmed quarterdeck, watching the continuing spectacle of the breakup of Eternal Ice, the whole story was told and retold.

Chapter Twenty-three

THEY heard about the Battle of Sea for the first time, from the earliest skirmishes to the moment when the Confederation Fleet watched in shocked surprise as Frigeon's *Snowstorm* turned abruptly and sailed away.

"Where is *Snowstorm* now?" asked Flarman. "She is one of the finest examples of Farango Waters shipbuilding. In fact, Douglas's father was her designer and builder. I think Frigeon imprisoned him to keep him from building ships for his enemies."

"She was captured in Frigeon's port," said Thornwood. "I think we should keep her name. I rather like the sound of *Snowstorm*."

"She's yours to do with as you like. She was built for Dukedom in the first place," said Augurian.

Frigeon's Ice Fleet had scattered all over Sea after the Ice King was seen fleeing. A few were sunk or driven onto Battle Shoals and their crews eaten alive by the Morays and other of their former allies. Some were lucky enough to be rescued and set ashore on desert islands by the Sea Fire, Sea Tortoises, or the Porpoises.

Others had run for the coasts of Dwelmland, Highlandorm, and Parch. Tet of Highlandorm had taken his warriors home to hunt them down, to make sure they were disarmed and returned to their homes. Flarman suggested a general spell of oblivion for them all, and Queen Marget and the Water-Adept agreed.

"Too many have died already," said Flarman. "It shall be done."

Caspar Marlin sailed in *Diamondpoint* with the Dwarfs and the Highlandormers as passengers. The latter would protect Bryarmote's principality and his Mother, Lady Finesgold, from the new stragglers.

"Although I suspect," said Douglas, "that Lady Finesgold can take care of herself very well. I forgot to mention that her advice to you, Flarman, was to wear your galoshes."

"I'm happy to say that I did, or I would have had trouble negotiating all that Ice," Flarman said with a long, fond laugh.

The Faerie Hosts had agreed to patrol Dukedom until Thornwood could reorganize his sheriffs and bailiffs. Sea Sprites would keep an eye on the Warm Sea islands, where isolated units of the Ice Fleet might make trouble.

The men of Flowring asked to borrow *Pinechip* to sail back to their deserted island. Douglas, who had captured the sloop, gave her to them as a gift. Myrn said good-bye to her family and friends and promised to visit them often while she continued her apprenticeship to Augurian.

One of the first things Flarman did was to send the tireless Bronze Owl off to Wizard's High and Valley to spread the good news.

"Tell Blue Teakettle to clean house and air the bedding," said Douglas. "I think we'll be home in a short while."

Douglas was one of the commission named to deal with the surviving Dreads who had fled east by northeast to the Desert Sand Coast. He sailed with Marget and her husband, Aedh, in *Snowstorm* the very next day but one.

His father came along so they would have time to get reacquainted and to hear each other's adventures.

"We must send word to your mother that we both are alive and safe," the elder Douglas said. "I know she is safe and probably happy in her convent, but . . ."

"I have already done so, by Deka the Wraith. Mother heard the news hours ago. Deka says she was beside herself with joy and will resign from the convent and be awaiting us at our house in Brightglade."

They talked and talked, and the shipwright used his spare time, while Douglas was helping to convince the Dreads to surrender, repairing and refining *Snowstorm*'s sturdy timbers and rigging. His time in Ice, he said, had given him leisure to think a great deal about ship construction and hull design.

■ ■ ■

Flarman went to Waterand, where Augurian called a
Great Court to try captives, especially Frigeon. Frigeon
seemed quite subdued, weeping sometimes in self-pity,
sometimes in frustration, and sometimes in deep, bitter remorse. He was treated fairly and housed in a coral cottage
near the top of Waterand's Lookout Hill. He was guarded by
the Golden Dragons who reported that he gave them no
trouble.

"But, then, who would?" thought Flarman aloud when he
heard it.

Marget, Aedh, and the two Douglases returned from the
Desert Sand coast. They had cast an oblivion spell on the
Dreads and settled them in that nearly empty land. The na-
tive tribes, nomadic Dunemen, whom Marget had absolutely
charmed, agreed to watch them for possible backsliding.

Under a Fairy ban against leaving their new country for a
hundred years, the Dreads would have a backbreaking struggle to wrest their livelihood from that barren place and little
time to make further trouble. The Dunemen suggested they
take up fishing. Dunemen would not go near Sea, but loved
seafood of all kinds.

"We are examining Frigeon's life and works—not a very
pretty picture—with a view to deciding not just what is to be
his punishment, but whether he even should be allowed to
live," Augurian announced.

"He has, then, been tried?" asked Marget.

"The trial is over. None of us were involved."

"No, the Judge was Grand Dragon, who is as unbiased as
anyone in World. The jury was made up of people from
out-of-the-way places whose lives were unaffected by Frigeon's wickedness, as yet," explained Flarman.

"They were scrupulously fair. They found him guilty as
charged. Sentencing, however, is our responsibility," the
Water-Adept said, most seriously.

They were once again sitting on the sunlit terrace outside
the Reception Hall of Augurian's Palace.

"Consider the death penalty," stated the Grand Dragon,
who filled three-fourths of the veranda while daintily eating
lime sherbet from a crystal bowl. "It seems to me he, because of all the people who died in battle and before, deserves death."

"Perhaps," said Augurian. "I am not opposed to death for deadly crimes, but there is this to consider. There are hundreds, maybe thousands, of Frigeon's spells and enchantments still in effect, unknown and unbroken. Only he can tell us where to find them all and how to dispel them."

"I see," said Douglas. "It would take us centuries to discover and unravel them without his help."

"It would be more merciful to these victims to keep the perpetrator alive and force him to repair the damage," agreed Flarman.

"The violence of death is not necessarily atoned by another death," Marget mused, thoughtfully, chin in hand. "*If* we can ensure his future good behavior. Would you hold him prisoner for eternity?"

"There will still be a lot for us to do," said Douglas, spreading a warm roll with lots of butter and strawberry jam, "even if we are just to deal with Frigeon, which I must say doesn't appeal to me all that much."

"I could take up the task of cataloging Frigeon's crime spells, with the assistance of my Apprentice. I trust I can call on you all to help break them," offered Augurian.

"That part goes without saying. I mean, breaking all those spells," said Flarman. "The real question is, what shall be done with Frigeon, afterward? I don't want him in Dukedom. He is still a source of too many unpleasant memories for all of us. And I am sure you don't really want him imprisoned on Waterand, Water-Adept."

"Men can be extremely vindictive in the aftermath of war, as we Faerie folk found out once," said Marget, softly. "He should be imprisoned or held enchanted secretly in some out-of-the-way place."

"Yet, now that he is humanly complete again," said Flarman, "his durance should not be so vile as to stifle the good qualities he has just recovered."

They agreed to think it over some more and went on to other problems.

"Some of the Dreads have returned to Landsend, their traditional homeland," said Aedh. "What of them? They are really Thornwood's problem, but his Dukedom is too small and has no wish to create another Army to watch these unpredictable and violent Men. They need a very strong and able ruler."

"I've suggested to Thornwood and to Chief Tet that the Duke ask Tet's adopted son to be Governor General of Land-send," put in Flarman.

"Who? Crimeye?" asked Douglas in surprise. "And on second thought, why not?"

"Our former spy is much more able than most people think," replied the Wizard. "Also, he is son and heir to Tet, whom all Landsendmen, and even the Dreads, highly respect and fear. Tet is a long way from retiring or dying, but Crimeye—Young Tet, as they now call him—will need practice in governing if he is to be ready to rule Highlandorm when the time does come."

"Tet can help him if they give him too much trouble," agreed Augurian. "I think that solution is a very good one. Do you all agree?"

They did.

"Back to Frigeon," said Marget, finally. "I do not think an oblivion spell is the answer just now. We need his memory. Also, I feel he deserves the punishment of remembering what he has done now that he has a conscience again."

"A terrible burden to bear, my dear," said Aedh. "But I agree, if just to serve an example to later would-be tyrants."

Each one around the luncheon table expressed an opinion on the fate of Frigeon. They came last to Douglas Bright-glade.

The Journeyman stood to speak, silent for a long moment before he began.

"Frigeon deserves of me no goodwill.

"However, I cannot find it in my heart to be vindictive or bitter, for my own misfortunes have been repaid, in large part. I wish it were so for everyone, but I know it can't be so.

"I cannot entirely forgive him, either. I cannot condemn him to death, for, as Augurian says, there has been too much of dying already, and another death won't solve any problems. Revenge seems to me very hollow. Perhaps I am wrong. I'm not that wise.

"I do recommend one of the prime ingredients of good Wizardry as taught me by Flarman Flowerstalk: common sense. I propose, first, that Frigeon be required to undo all his wicked spells and enchantments.

"Second, that when this is under way and after, he be sent to the land that is laid bare as Eternal Ice melts. There I propose he be kept under watch spell until this Court decides that he has righted all possible wrongs.

"Afterward, he should continue to be solely responsible for the New Land. He should be accountable for its management—go hungry, if it is managed badly and be given full credit for any good he accomplishes.

"New Land today is a tumbled, barren, empty, faceless wasteland. It *could* be made useful and even fruitful by years of hard, caring labor.

"The mouth of the glacial fjord will probably make a good deep-water port, something like Farango Water, where I was born. The silt ground down by glacial action over millions of years, with cultivation, can be some of the richest soil in World, I am told.

"If it is nurtured and fostered . . . if Frigeon can give it that kind of care, make it develop and be fruitful, then I say, in time, he will have earned our forgetfulness, if not our forgiveness. Maybe even our praise."

The matter was warmly discussed until at last, toward dawn, they agreed to Douglas's plan. One last change was requested from an unexpected quarter, the tiny Brownie Leader, Floot.

"Names mean more to some peoples, perhaps, than to others. After more than four hundred years of quaking and shaking when the very name Frigeon was mentioned, it would be an easement to we Little People if the convict were to change his name."

When all these things were put to the former Ice King, former Air-Adept, he accepted the decision at once, and the challenge and opportunity of New Land, also.

"I am heartily ashamed of what I have done."

"You know," said Myrn to Douglas in a whisper, "I believe he is sincere."

"I think we should wait and see to be sure," replied Douglas.

"To be enclosed, to be watched, to be expected to repay debts that I have incurred, to make amends for my wickedness, these are not the hard things to do," the former Ice King went on.

"To go hat in hand to try to help those whom I grievously

harmed by my selfishness, is. But I will overcome it and justify your small trust in me."

He paused. "My fellow Wizards have judged me fairly, and this amazes me, for they have the power to destroy me. Yet it pleases me, too, for it restores a once-firm faith in their Fellowship.

"Young Wizard," he said, looking directly at Douglas, "you of all the Fellowship I will try hardest to convince of my new self. Someday when your children come to New Land, they will be treated as honored guests, as princes. They will, I vow, be greeted by a happy, contented, hard-working people, living in stout houses, raising laughing children, well ruled by themselves, not by me. . . .

"One more thing only. At the suggestion of the little man in brown, I will indeed change my name. It was a false, vainglorious one from the beginning. I will henceforth be Serenit!"

He bowed to them all and walked down to the dock, where a longboat manned by Wateranders waited to take him out to Captain Fribby's *Flame Daughter,* which would carry him to New Land, there to await Augurian's instructions and begin the difficult tasks ahead on the barren land.

Douglas and Myrn sat on a flat rock at Seaside, watching the burnished path of the setting sun. Great, towering clouds on the distant horizon caught the colors and fire of the sun, glowing long after dusk had settled on Waterand Island. It outlined the sails of a number of ships standing away for distant parts, carrying the last of the warriors home.

Flarman came strolling down the beach, accompanied by Bronze Owl, flying creakily overhead.

Myrn greeted the Wizard with a smile and a hug, and a wave at Bronze Owl, but Douglas seemed preoccupied, staring out to Sea.

"I had a dream once, shortly after I came to Wizard's High. I was standing on a beach and I set the sky on fire."

"You never mentioned it," said his Master, taking a seat beside him on his rock. "Why?"

"Oh, no reason," said his Journeyman. "But this was the place I dreamed about, I think. It was so long ago, now. Yet it has been only five years since I first came to the High. When do lessons start again, Magister?"

"Lessons! Lessons? Don't you think you know everything there is to know about Fire Wizardry by now?"

"Don't tease me, Magister. I've got a whole lot yet to learn. I hope to earn my Master degree this century. My father and mother will expect me to, and my wife to be and our future children."

"Who? You are really quite a remarkable young man, Douglas Brightglade! You do have a lot to learn and Myrn, also . . . and me, too. We need never to stop learning. When we do, we're as good as dead, and I, personally, am a long way from that!

"Here, now, you young Adepts . . . strike me a fire! Get me a drink of water in this desert of coral sand and salt! Let me see what you can do."

An old farmer called his plump, rosy-cheeked wife to the door of their neat, freshly thatched farmhouse on the banks of Crooked Brook.

"Lilac, me cozy, your eyes are much better'n mine for distant seeing. Who do you see coming up River Road?"

"Let me see, old man," said Lilac, toeing out of her path a pair of Wizard's High kittens, a black male and a tortoiseshell female from the latest litters.

She shaded her eyes with a strong, worn hand, looked, and laughed aloud.

"Why, 'tis himself, the Wizard Flarman and a young man who looks a lot like that boy of his who used to eat sugar cookies here and run our errands to Trunkety. Only a lot bigger."

Flarman, for her eyes were very good and it *was* Flarman, waved his staff in greeting and Douglas ran ahead to pound Priceless on the back and give his good wife a hearty hug and a kiss.

"Welcome! Most welcome home!" cried Lilac. "Come in a moment and have a cup of tea to wet your whistles . . . or, better, Priceless, get a demijohn of your cider, the best you've ever pressed."

Priceless ran to do so, spry as can be for a man of his advanced age.

"The pressing this spring was remarkable, the best and sweetest," he said, pulling the corncob stopper and pouring brimming cups of the amber liquid. "Hola! Here's to old times."

"But you are better off than you were then," observed the Journeyman Wizard. "I remember this house when it hadn't had a thatching for ten years."

"Since Dead Winter and Dry Summer things have gone better than ever for us all," admitted Priceless. "Yes, it was hard at times but the weather has been perfect and everything has gone well, all over the Valley. And ye trounced old What's-His-Name, the nasty king who put that false Eunicet over us, I hear?"

"It's a long, long story," said Douglas, downing his cider and accepting a refill. "We'll be telling it all at the Party next week. You must come and meet my parents—I found my father, who was thought lost at Sea!—and a wonderful young lady I met on a Warm Sea island!"

"A Wizard's High Party!" exclaimed the farmer's wife. "They're famous! How marvelous! Perhaps I could wait tables and bring some strawberry preserves?"

"Don't be silly!" exclaimed Flarman. "You can't wait tables. You and Priceless will be among our guests of honor."

They chatted for a while, which only whetted Lilac's appetite for their news, and set out across the rickety old Brook Bridge—"Now maybe you'll have time to fix it," said Flarman, mock-seriously, "and add that other side railing you were always going to"—to the familiar path that wound up the bank past the Wizard's High gate.

"Here was the sign hung," said Douglas, remembering his arrival at the cottage five years before. "I wondered if I could find a place as Apprentice to a Fire Wizard."

"And I had my doubts you could make the grade as a dishwasher at the Duke's castle, so I felt sorry for you," retorted Flarman Flowerstalk.

"Assistant to the Cook it was, rather," insisted Douglas. "I would have made a good cook."

They passed through the open gate and came to the great double front door. In the middle, at eye's height, hung a brightly polished bronze door knocker in the shape of an owl with wings outspread.

"Content to hang about all the time and rest on your

imagined laurels, I suppose?'' Flarman said to the door knocker.

''If you'll identify yourself,'' said Bronze Owl, gruffly, ''I'll take a message for my Master when he returns from his long vacation.''

Douglas chortled until he choked, and Flarman, after pretending umbrage, laughed fit to fall down.

The doors swung wide, letting out a cloud of pleasant, poignant, and perfect memories. They were greeted by Black Flame, who rubbed against their ankles and wrapped his long black tail about their legs.

His ladies were right behind him, Pert and Party, meowing and standing on their hind feet to push at Douglas with their front paws and knead their claws in his thick corduroy trouser legs. He scooped them both up in his arms and stroked first the one, then the other, making them purr like little engines.

From deep within the cottage came the sound of a teakettle whistling cheerily, and as they went into the kitchen, the plates, pots, knives, spoons, pans and grills, spits, slicers, and strainers struck up a chorus of rattles, bangs, tings, whangs, whistles, and calls of welcome home.

Blue Teakettle rattled her top up and down, despite her dignity of years, and ordered a full meal at once—hop to it!—although it was only midmorning.

''I hope you don't mind my coming to visit just now,'' said a bright voice with a Warm Seas accent, from the kitchen-yard door. Turning, the Wizards saw the beautiful pearl fisher's daughter in a neat Sea blue pinafore with white Sea-foam ruffles and a red bandanna tied about her slim waist.

''Teakettle and I have been talking about keeping a Wizard's house,'' Myrn said. Douglas kissed her deeply, then lightly, too.

''You belong here,'' cried Flarman, delighted, and adding his own hug and kiss. ''It's not just a matter of welcome, but of belonging.''

''I missed you, although it has been less than a fortnight. Fortunately, Augurian and Flarman have kept me busy!'' said Douglas. ''I planned to write you at once.''

''I expect you to be busy at things worth doing, even after we are married,'' said the girl of the islands.

"Married, is it?" asked Bronze Owl of the Wizard as they sat down at the huge kitchen table and sipped hot, fragrant eastern tea, awaiting lunch.

"Well, the fact is," said Flarman, beckoning Sugar Caster to come closer, "it must be a long engagement. Augurian will keep Myrn very busy for two years, at least."

"But I can escape to Wizard's High when I need, my Master promised," Myrn told Bronze Owl.

"Call first," advised the bird. "If I understand it—and I do—Douglas and Flarman will be gone as much as they are at home."

"All those lost spells to trace . . . ," agreed Flarman.

"All those basic spells to learn!" cried the Apprentice Aquamancer.

"But now that Frigeon is no more," said Douglas, "there should be plenty of time to do work right, and to play and to marry, too."

"This place could use another Wizard," said the eldest Wizard, "don't you think? Blue Teakettle is the mistress of the kitchen, none better anywhere, but we will be having a lot of visitors and a hostess is proper to have when you entertain Duchesses and Dukes, Chieftains, even Kings, Queens, and various Wizards."

"No doubt you are right," said Owl, watching as Douglas led Myrn out to the courtyard to meet his Ladies of the Byre.

"Of course I'm right!" exclaimed Flarman. "Now we've got to get busy and plan a Party!"

And what a Party it was!

Everyone who was anybody at all came. The guest book, which Bronze Owl carefully kept by the front door, read like a list of every important person from anywhere.

There were, of course, Thornwood, Duke of Dukedom, and his wonderful mother, Marigold. They say she'd immediately made Capital bloom once more, as soon as Thornwood had clapped strict regulation on the dives, cribs, and low public houses that had spawned Eunicet's Army.

Priceless and Lilac came early with strawberry preserves and jugs of cider and had a joyous reunion with their old friend Crimeye, although some people, who didn't know his history, called him Young Tet, Governor General of Landsend and heir to the Chieftainship of Highlandorm.

Deka the Wraith came, too—and went and came again, busy as she was carrying messages. Blue Teakettle had a good supply of *misctywine* on hand for her. Others said it was the best lemonade they had ever tasted.

Bryarmote came with his lively, lovely mother, Lady Finesgold, and an entourage of relations and friends, including a shy young lady named Crystal. She was introduced as the future Lady Bryarmote, much to everybody's surprise—except Flarman's. As he explained, "Dwarfs tend to be a very secretive people."

There came all the good folk of Valley—the new Sheriff Possumtail and Squire Frenstil, among them, of course. Frackett, the ex-Wizard and former hermit, came and announced that he was going to retire to Valley, if they would have him, now that Frigeon was no more and Landsend was under the care of Young Tet.

Although Serenit of New Land was unable to leave his new home, he did send his assistant Clangeon, who brought along a whole wagonload of the finest, purest, coldest ice to cool the *misctywine* and freeze the ice cream at the Party.

Clang proved to be a painfully shy, self-denigrating, middle-aged man uneasy in such company. He had a severe case of cringe, cavil, and kowtow to his "betters." He also had, however, a redeeming love . . . of cooking. It kept him in almost constant consultation with Blue Teakettle. He filled several notebooks with her recipes.

Michael Wroughter arrived in a land yacht, a light wagon driven by sails and steered by a wheeled tiller, his latest invention. He reported that the iceboxes Valley made for the Wayness trade were selling very well and at a good profit.

Everyone had a ride up and down the River Road in his wind-propelled carriage—quite a thrill, they all agreed, but doubted that it would ever be very popular because "who is ever in such a hurry?"

Another guest was Caspar Marlin, home from his first trading voyage as Captain of the Wayness merchantman *Snowstorm*. He was particularly interested in Clangeon's descriptions of the new harbor facilities a-building in New Land. He had an order from the First Citizen for ten thousand white pine seedlings to deliver that fall, and was glad that he wouldn't have to lighter them ashore on that still-dangerous coast.

The Kingdom of Faerie was well represented, camped beside Coro Kehd, as they called Crooked Brook, all the way down to Trunkety Bridge. Queen Marget was a delightful guest and her handsome husband, Prince Aedh, was a favorite of all the ladies. Marget visited all over the Valley—she already knew it well from the old days, she said—and gave each new baby in Valley a Fairy kiss on the forehead. There were a great many beautiful, intelligent and well-behaved youngsters in the years ahead as a result.

Marget and Aedh announced that the queen was with child herself, and after the long pregnancy of Fairy mothers she expected to bear a future King of Faerie. The celebration of this news extended the Party for a full two days and a night.

As the Party was getting under way the second day, Douglas and Myrn, sitting on a grassy patch of soft brook bank, noticed a strange disturbance in the pool at their feet. With a sparkle of spray and a great *swoosh,* Augurian the Water-Adept shot from the brook and landed lightly on the sward in front of them.

"Greeting, greeting!" they called, and the Water-Adept, all smiles and laden with presents for the homecomers, on the spot created a fifty-foot fountain in the middle of the pool as a memorial, he said, of the men who had fallen in the Battle of Sea.

He also brought all sorts of delicious Seafood for Flarman's guests to enjoy.

"I came all the way by water, of course," he told Douglas, "and the hardest part was the last ten miles in your tortuous Crooked Brook! More curves than a Moray Eel!"

Tet of Highlandorm was late—he was still engaged in cleaning out nests of Ice Fleet stragglers starving in Parch. He and his fierce-looking, kilted warriors and their auburn-haired wives were happy to find Young Tet there before them. They added a great deal to the hearty gaiety of the occasion. They chose to camp atop Wizard's High itself, with its grandest views of the entire Valley. It reminded them of the rugged highlands of home.

Tet had stopped by to bring the Fairstrander fisherfolk to the Party. Everyone adored Maryam Beckett, and called her "Grammer." She added her special fish recipes to Clangeon's notebooks, too.

One evening as the Party rolled along, Flarman glanced up and saw a vast flock of Sea Gulls circling the High; the White Flight, led by Cerfew. They came to say hello and thank you and to harass the Trout in Crooked Brook for hours before they returned to Sea.

Myrn Manstar's mother and father came by Sea to Farango Waters, a fresh breath of salt air, ecstatic about their daughter's betrothal, now official. The thought of having a Wizard for a son-in-law didn't seem to faze them at all; nor did having a Wizard for a daughter, either.

They gave each lady guest a perfect white pearl from the store stolen by Eunicet and Bladder, recovered when Douglas took *Pinechip*. With them from Brightglade on Farango Waters came Douglas's father and mother. The future in-laws took to each other immediately. The Manstars brought personal greetings from a number of Sea creatures who chose not to leave Sea just then—Oval, the Giant Sea Tortoise, the Horniads, Sea Fire, and the three messenger Porpoises: Skimmer, Spinner, and Leaper. A certain green fish, a Schoolmaster, sent an invitation to Douglas to speak at the next commencement.

Not the least exciting by any means was the arrival of Grand Dragon with eleven companions, roaring down from the Ridges like flying volcanoes, spouting red and yellow and purple smoke as they came, a sight to remember for Valley children. Douglas and Flarman thanked them again for their rescue from the Ice.

"It was the ideal mission for us Dragons," said Grandy. "We were pitted against mere Human opponents and the elements, not our own kind. We have reconciled our differences, by the by, with the other Dragons. We have vowed never to be divided again."

There were hundreds of others, all worthy of mention if one could remember them. Even Douglas and Flarman, reviewing the guest book later, had trouble recognizing the names of them all, or even deciphering their handwriting and marks.

"I think we should make a small change in the name of this place, this wonderful, old place," said Myrn on the eve of her return to Waterand.

"No changes needed, thank you," gruffed Flarman.

"Oh, but for grammar's sake . . ."

"What does Mrs. Beckett have to do with it?" asked Bronze Owl.

" . . . we should call it 'Wizards' High,' starting right now, as there are two Wizards living here and will someday be three or more."

"Oh, in that case . . . ," Flarman agreed.

Outside, the first chill rain of fall beat on the leaded glass of the parlor windows and an autumn wind blew across the chimneys, producing a deep, organlike note.

"Augurian's work is great and complicated and is better done from there than here," Myrn said, sadly. "I really want to be his Apprentice, but I really want to be here, too."

"It will be years before there is time for a wedding," said Bronze Owl, practical as always. "I doubt it could possibly be before next winter but one. Perhaps even the following winter."

Winter solstice was the traditional time for Valley weddings. Then farmers and their wives could enjoy them at leisure.

"More than two whole years!" wailed the maiden.

"It'll fly by, believe me," said Flarman. "The secret is to keep busy, and there is a great deal to do and a whole lot to learn . . . or have I said that before?"

"Someday," Douglas said, "we'll all three live here. Does the prospect bother you, Master?"

"I don't see why you and your bride shouldn't share the High with me," said Flarman, putting down his book. "We get along pretty well, I think."

"The best!" cried Myrn, and she kissed both of her Wizards soundly and went off to bed.

It was the coldest of winter nights, dark and overcast, reminding Douglas uneasily of Dead Winter. He was looking for Flarman Flowerstalk to ask a technical question.

The Wizard was not in his study. Douglas checked the Workshop and found only Black Flame, sleeping on a sack of lamb's wool near a low fire.

In the parlor, Chair shrugged lazily when he asked it where the Wizard could be. Blue Teakettle murmured sleepily on the back of the range, saying that Flarman had not yet said good night, but Douglas peeped into the Wizard's bed-sitting room just to be sure. Flarman was not in his bed.

At the front door seeking Bronze Owl—who was not there—Douglas spied tracks in the freshly fallen snow, leading to the old well where the Fairies had once held Court. He walked down that way, wishing at once that he had thought to throw on a coat. The air, while still, was bitingly cold. The snow of early evening had stopped and stars were beginning to break through the clouds.

Nearing the well, he heard voices. Flarman, he saw, was seated on the well curb, his back to the house, speaking to someone beyond whom Douglas couldn't see.

A step or two farther, and he recognized Deka the Wraith. Flarman was listening to her lengthy message.

Then the Wraith faded out with a smile and a wave at Douglas that made Flarman turn, aware of his Journeyman for the first time.

"You'll catch yourself a cold out here," scolded Douglas, sitting down on the curb beside him.

"What? Me, a Pyromancer, catch a cold? Use your head, m'boy. 'Tis you, sitting there, shivering. I'm as warm as toast."

"Oh, yes," muttered Douglas, embarrassed. He ran his fingers over his thumbs in a prescribed way to cast a warming spell. In a moment he stopped shaking.

"I had a question for you but now I've quite forgotten what it was. That was Deka with a message?"

"A message from an old, old acquaintance. I haven't heard from him in centuries! Probably never mentioned him to you."

"Is there there anyone in World I haven't heard you mention?" chuckled Douglas.

"Oh, a few, I should imagine. Anyway, this fellow's name is Cribblon, and he was Apprentice to one of the Fellowship, back before Last Battle. He sends word to me about a suspicious turn of events in Tigers Teeth Mountains in the Far West of Old Kingdom. He believes there is a Witches' Coven there causing trouble—disappearances, confusion and disruption, at which wicked Witches are especially adept."

"There is always something, somewhere," said Douglas with a sigh.

"Yes, but Cribblon thinks he may have caught them before they have gotten very strong and bold. They'll bear close watching and he is no longer technically an Apprentice.''

"But if they haven't done anything dangerous yet, they certainly have a right to be left alone.''

"If, if, if! I wish I could read their future, but not from here, I am afraid.''

"I'll go and have a look, shall I? Until you and Augurian give me some of Frigeon's old spells to crack, it'll be something interesting to do. Speed the time until—''

"Better than moping around here. Besides, you should visit Old Kingdom. You may need to know your way around there someday. I have to go to Augurian soon. I'd like to report this to him, in detail. See what you think and tell us, will you? Send Deka to us on Waterand.''

"I'll leave tomorrow. I can get ship at Westongue, now that they are sailing from there again. They'll be glad for a paying passenger, I should think.''

The two Wizards, young and old, sat silently, watching a falling star tear across the now-clear night sky. The faint hiss of its passing reached them as it faded and disappeared over the western horizon.

"Something ends. Something begins,'' said Flarman Flowerstalk. "There is no story without its sequel, you know.''

"Let's go in and get some hot cocoa,'' suggested the Journeyman Wizard, rising.

They linked arms to keep from slipping on the frozen path and went toward the big double front door of Wizards' High.

STEVEN BRUST

__ATHYRA__ 0-441-03342-3/$4.99

Vlad Taltos has a talent for killing people. But lately, his heart just hasn't been in his work. So he retires. Unfortunately, the House of the Jhereg still has a score to settle with Vlad. So much for peaceful retirement.

__PHOENIX__ 0-441-66225-0/$4.99

Strangely, the Demon Goddess comes to assassin Vlad Taltos's rescue, answering his most heartfelt prayer. But when a patron deity saves your skin, it's always in your best interest to do whatever she wants . . .

__JHEREG__ 0-441-38554-0/$4.99

There are many ways for a young man with quick wits and a quick sword to advance in the world. Vlad Taltos chose the route of the assassin and the constant companionship of a young jhereg.

__YENDI__   0-441-94460-4/$4.99

Vlad Taltos and his jhereg companion learn how the love of a good woman can turn a cold-blooded killer into a _real_ mean S.O.B...

__TECKLA__ 0-441-79977-9/$4.99

The Teckla were revolting. Vlad Taltos always knew they were lazy, stupid, cowardly peasants...revolting. But now they were revolting against the empire. No joke.

__TALTOS__ 0-441-18200/$4.99

Journey to the land of the dead. All expenses paid! Not Vlad Taltos's idea of an ideal vacation, but this was work. Even an assassin has to earn a living.

__COWBOY FENG'S SPACE BAR AND GRILLE__
0-441-11816-X/$3.95

Cowboy Feng's is a great place to visit, but it tends to move around a bit — from Earth to the Moon to Mars to another solar system — Always just one step ahead of the mysterious conspiracy reducing whole worlds to ash.